THE VAST UNCERTAINTY OF A RAINDROP

#whenitrainsitpours

REMONA G. TANNER

authorHOUSE®

AuthorHouse™
1663 Liberty Drive
Bloomington, IN 47403
www.authorhouse.com
Phone: 833-262-8899

Published by AuthorHouse 05/06/2021

ISBN: 978-1-6655-2507-7 (sc)
ISBN: 978-1-6655-2508-4 (e)

Library of Congress Control Number: 2021909396

Print information available on the last page.

PROLOGUE

"Before it was Burn Out bridge, it was just old HWY 90. It did not become Burn Out bridge until people died for its namesake. Some say it was the work of closet devil worshippers, who torched the bridge as a satanic offering to their mighty savior Lucifer. Some folks say it was an inexorable act of God's wrath; claiming to have witnessed the angel of death flying low right before the deadly blaze sparked. Few believe it was the Mothman, a mythological omen of devastation and heinous destruction. Remember the Silver Bridge collapse of 1967? They say that was the Mothman too. So many people died…It is possible I suppose. Heaven only knows.'

'Scared people with vivid imaginations say a lot of things. There were countless theories, but not one viable explanation for the 1973 fire on old HYW 90. Local authorities and government officials were swift in their efforts to cover it all up; But we, the people, didn't heal so quickly. We'd lost friends. We'd lost family- all burned to death or drowned. All we got in return was a patch of wooden crosses near the ruins and a wall in the sheriff's office dedicated to those who were still presumed missing since that dreadful day. A cruel, tasteless display if you ask me. They weren't missing. They didn't disappear without a trace. They hadn't been kidnapped. Their bodies are still way down deep under the weight of the dark river, the rusted cars, and the charred splinter remains of the bridge. Those bones will never rest. Those bones will never know peace. Every soul deserves the right to rest in peace. What's left of their bones, after the alligators and garfish picked them clean, will forever remain in the murky deep. They had a picture of Jeremiah strung up on that wall with the others they claim they couldn't find in the river after the collapse. 'Why?' I asked them. 'Why so cruel? What have I ever done to you to deserve this? You disgrace our family.'

"Jeremiah's truck was pulled from the river. His body was never found but the last time I saw him alive, he was driving that old beat up truck. He was leaving me behind in the dust to twist in the wind. How dare they paste my husband's picture on that wall? It! Was! Cruel! I had his three children to protect. I couldn't let them believe their father was only missing. Jeremiah Beaumonte' was dead. He was never coming home. I needed my girls to understand that. He died on Burn Out bridge in June of 1973- that was that. I waltzed right into that station and I ripped my husband's picture off that wall. Crumbled it up. Tossed it on the floor. Dared them to arrest me for it too. *I will not have my family taunted by this! I will not have our hope tried until our religion slips away!'* That happens you know; people pray for something that's just impossible and they stop believing in God when their prayers never come to pass. No. I had to think of our daughters. The truth would be better for their faith than a hopeful impossibility.'

'I remember the smoke in the sky. I remember the smell of burning flesh that swept through our town and it didn't lift for days as we mourned. I remember the screams. Half our town died that day. Jeremiah Beaumonte' had died on Burn Out bridge, the bridge that burned in Louisiana. The year was 1973. My whole life, in two sad little sentences.'

CHAPTER ONE

Buzz...tick, tick. Buzz...tick, tick, tick.

'Stupid ceiling fan, such a compromising contraption. Having to choose between cool air or tranquility, that is not fair. Bellissima's face appeared calm but deep down she was annoyed to near madness.'

'Maybe it's an electrical malfunction. Maybe a loose screw. Perhaps it wasn't properly installed.' – she thought, cringing at the absurd amount of collected dust clinging to each slowing rotating blade. Whatever the cause, the insufferable clinking made Bellissima want to claw her own eyes out. One wouldn't be able to tell by looking at her, though. No, Bellissima Beaumonte' was a by all definition a lady- assiduously strong and sufferable; raised by ladies even stronger and more poised than her. And a lady maintains her composer at all times, especially when it's most uncomfortable and unpleasant. Grandma Cat wouldn't stand for anything less than ladylike decorum in public and in the company of strangers who were free to judge the family name. She'd made that particular expectation very clear early on in Bellissima's life. When Bellissima and her cousins were little, they were forced to attend church with their Grandmother at least twice a week. Catherine would discreetly slide her shoe off, wield it as a weapon whenever she noticed her grandchildren roughhousing during worship. *'You will sit still and graciously receive the Lord's word. All the while, you will remain tolerant and mind your manners or I'll take you outside and blister your backside until blue blood rises to the surface.'*

Buzz... tick, tick, tick, tick. Bellissima's headache intensified. The contemplation of silence had become a normal part of the day for Bellissima Beaumonte'. It was an innocent, reoccurring ruminant. Fathom being unable to hear. Surely facial expressions would suffice all on their own. We know what sadness looks like without having to hear it. We know anger when we see it. I don't need to hear an uncaged bird sing to know it's happy to be free. One would understand fully well, the mental, emotional and obvious physical condition of another person without the peace altering, deafening maelstrom of what it takes to be human. It's true what they say, life has a turbulent pulse and everything with a pulse makes noise.' Imagine a life unburdened by the galling hustle, bustle, and confrontational sounds of the cruel world. Imagine sharing a thought like that in a room full of people. *Ungrateful-* they'd accuse. Hearing is a sense not everyone is born with. *Lucky to hear, blessed-* they'd say. There would be rolling of the eyes and gnashing of teeth, or whatever the bible said.

Bellissima sat in the rocking chair nearest Mr. Breaux's bed, massaging her temples. She'd been sitting at his bedside all morning fixated on the fan, waiting for him to wake up. "Life prevents silence," she said aloud.

Finally, Breaux stirred uncomfortably beneath his bedsheets. "I refuse to give up," he slurred lethargically. "I refuse to just roll over and die like a cockroach on its back." The same unrelenting declaration he made almost daily.

"No one's asking you to. You keep on putting up a fight as long as you have the strength, you hear?" It was the same response Bellissima always gave. She began to hum softly. It always seemed to soothe his irritability. "Time sure does fly don't it," she said, recollecting the first time she and Breaux met.

"Who the hell are you? What do you want?"

"Hello there, my name is Bellissima Beaumonte'. I'll be your primary caregiver here at Pennycress while I'm studying to become a nurse. I was hoping to sit with you for a spell, maybe we can get to know one another. Talking helps to ease the adjustment stress."

"Adjustment stress? That's what you call what I'm feeling? That's a load of horse manure. I have been forced out of my home where I've lived for over 40 years, a home I built with my own two hands? 40 years! And all it took was a 45-minute-long distance consultation between you Nazis and my ungrateful offspring to get me hauled off here. I can't prove it was her who made the call, but I feel it in my bones. Must have been that toad-faced heifer at the social security office that found her and told her

I was sick. Next thing I know, I got white coats in my house, poking and prodding! Adjustment stress my ass!"

"You know what? You're right. We should find a better set of terms to describe what you're feeling."

"Damn right, you should. Your generation, you're a bad batch- no respect for your elders. Ingrates! You all are!" Mr. Breaux paused to wipe his nose. "What the hell you say your name was, gal?"

"Bellissima," she answered mildly.

"That's French or Italian ain't it? Any fool can tell just by looking at you, you ain't either of those. What'd you say your surname was, again?"

"It's Beaumonte'."

"You one of those mudbug mixed ones? -Creole, half-breed mutts?"

"Creole, yes. A bug or mutt? I most certainly am not!"

"Don't be ashamed, you don't look as odd as all the other multicultural accidents. Your skin is fair, very light. Your hair isn't nappy either." Mr. Breaux had insulted Bellissima with such ease and disregard that it caused Bellissima's lips to purse. She inhaled deeply and exhaled slowly, pacing her thoughts before shouting the first defensive, possibly equally offensive remark that came to mind. "What? You disgruntled already? Well, you may as well leave now. Your skin might be acceptably light but it ain't thick enough to empty my bedpan. I'm old as dirt and my ways are set; been set for longer than you been alive. No sense in trying to change now. If you plan on getting red in the face and quiet every time I say something that hurts your little feelings, you'll turn into one of those stupid, useless mutes. Now go away!" Mr. Breaux gripped his wheelchair tires as best his weathered, stiff hands could.

Bellissima watched his arthritis- knotted knuckles trembling, struggling. "Let me help you get into bed and then I'll go."

"You simple or something! I told you to go! Now get out of here!" he yelled, throwing his denture glass at Bellissima's head. She ducked, just barely escaping its aerial path.

Bellissima took another deep breath, knelt to pick up the glass fragments and dropped them in the wastebasket. "Simple? Me?" she asked. "Not last time my doctor checked. They screen us often, thoroughly. In fact, they train us well, well enough to know you're going to fall flat on your fat, racist ass if you try to get out of that chair on your own," Bellissima instigated.

3

"You want to break a hip and be confined to a bed for the rest of your days in a room this small? Or worse, break your neck or spine and paralyze yourself just because you've got more pride and ignorance than desire to make the best out of an unfair situation. In a matter of minutes, you've insulted my ethnicity, my competence, and branded deaf individuals as stupid and useless. That last part strikes a personal chord with me. You see, there used to be two of me- my twin sister Cheniere. She was mute. She never spoke a word. I never got to hear her voice because she didn't have one. She never got a chance to hear my voice or hear me tell her that I loved her. She died. I didn't get a chance to say goodbye. Even if I'd been there the moment she took her last breath, she wouldn't have heard me. She may have been mute but she damn sure wasn't stupid or useless. Now, you've been perversely rude. The amour-propre in me wants to waltz right out of here and go find someone else to be your punching bag. But I'm a good person and I'd like to give you one more shot at a first impression. Before you decide if you want to treat me like a human being, I'd like you to consider my gentleness. It's a rare shade. You got lucky, you were assigned to a person with a little compassion. Half the people in this place only do enough to get by and fly under the radar. I'm not here for the money, if I was I would have quit this line of work a long time ago. My Grandmother raised me to value those who've earned their grey hair. She used to talk to me about the sun whenever I was sad. Look out that window over there." Breaux turned and looked. "I know you can't see it right now from where you're sitting but the sun- it's out there. It's always wherever the sky is. I know it hurts, thinking about all the times you changed your kids' diapers and the minute you need them to stick around to change yours they abandon you. I'm sorry this is happening to you. I'm not your blood so I know you don't expect me to love you but I'm your best shot at empathy and understanding. I'll handle you with the sincerest of intentions, always. That's as close to love as you can get. The sun will come out again. One day, I'd like to take you outside to see that; the sunshine in all its hopeful grandeur. You're built proudly. I get that. I'm built persistently tenacious. You get that? When people push me around or push me away, I don't bend Mr. Breaux. So, go ahead, push until you break a sweat, It's just a waste of your energy. I ain't budging. It sure would make my job a lot easier if you didn't insist on being a stubborn bigot."

Breaux seemed oddly softened by Bellissima's unwillingness to give up on him. It was a thankful sadness as if he hadn't been on the receiving end of clemency in a long time.

"I guess that'd be alright," he answered- drastically nicer. "The sun. The sky. Going outside sometimes. I'd be okay with that."

Bellissima moved in slowly. "Good. Now, may I help you to bed?"

"I don't want to get into one of those lift machines. I always feel like they're gon' break and drop me. They make me nervous."

"Okay- no Hoyer lift. We'll do without it this go around."

"-Alright."

"These levers here on both sides of your chair, they're not fashion accessories or extra pieces manufacturers glued on for appeal. These are breaks," said Bellissima- demonstrating the lock and unlock mechanism. "It's important that you remember to use your breaks, these will keep you out of the infirmary and off the cold, wet bathroom floor. I'm going to position my biceps underneath your armpits. You should wrap your arms around me and hold on tight."

"Like a hug?"

"Yes, just like an embrace. On the count of three, I'm going to pull up and once you have your footing, I'll rotate you over onto the bed." Bellissima counted and completed the transfer smoothly.

Bellissima could tell by the look on Breaux's face that he was disappointed with the bed quality. "This bed feels like the rock I slept on when I served in the war," he grumped.

"I'll see what I can do about getting you a mattress pad," offered Bellissima.

"Thank you," he mumbled- barely audible.

"What was that?" poked Bellissima.

"...Not going to say it again."

"That's okay. You'll get a lot more practice expressing your gratitude. Would you like me to leave you alone for a while, gather your thoughts?"

"No," he mumbled.

Bellissima's eyebrows raised. "Are you saying you want me to stay?'

"I'm saying I don't want to watch jeopardy alone. Been a long time since I had someone to watch with. It's no fun when no one's around to hear me shout all the correct answers, show off how smart I am. If you got things to do, you can go. I've been alone so long it doesn't bother me no more."

"I have nowhere else to be. I'd love to show off how smart *I* am."

There had been rough patches, days when Mr. Beaux was more difficult to handle.

"Lissima! Lissima! Who's this white coat and why is he trying to poison me?"

"Mr. Beaux, this is your new physician. Remember, we talked about this? He introduced himself a few weeks ago."

"No, I don't know him! Don't let him anywhere near me! I'll sue!"

Bellissima tapped the doctor on the shoulder and leaned in for a discreet whisper. "Here, let me give it a try. "Breaux, this isn't poison. I promise. If you don't take this medication, you won't be well enough to go on our picnic"

"We picnic on Tuesdays," he mumbled.

"That's right. And what's tomorrow?

"Tomorrow is…"

"Monday. And what do we do on Mondays?"

"Bingo."

"That's right. If you don't keep your immune system up, you might get sick and start moving around a little slower. You might not make it down to the auditorium early to get your favorite seat up front by the caller."

"I can never hear the numbers from way in the back," he complained.

"Yes, I know. So, will you take your medications? I'd hate to go alone."

"I guess so. Are we still going to a picnic Tuesday?"

"Yes. Just like every other Tuesday. I'll bring some potato salad from Mama's restaurant."

"Good. Best damn salad in all Louisiana."

It had been a long, challenging four years, but Mr. Breaux mellowed with time. Bellissima considered him a friend. And now, he was slipping away.

"Where'd you go?" asked Breaux- languidly.

"No place. I'm right here," Bellissima replied- leaving her rocking chair to be closer.

"Why is it so cold in here?"

It wasn't cold. In fact, Bellissima found it a bit clammy. If it had been anyone else she would have laughed and reminded them that they were in the South but over the years Bellissima learned to recognize the signs of approaching demise. Sudden coldness- Breaux was near expiration, no doubt about it. "I can switch the fan off if you want," Bellissima offered.

"No, I can't nap without the background noise. Funny how you get used to pestering things. It used to frustrate me, now I rely on it. Would it be too much trouble, getting me an extra blanket? I'd sure appreciate it."

"No trouble at all. I'd be happy to." Bellissima fetched another duvet and covered Breaux.

"I'm still freezing, "he whispered.

"I know. I'm sorry. There's no rule says you can't have three blankets. I can get you as many as you want."

"No. I get the feeling nothing's going to warm me up now. Maybe just hold my hand."

"Of course."

"Lissima?"

"Yes?"

"What if I'm finally tired of fighting?"

"I'd say you deserve to rest, at last."

Shortly after; Bellissima stood, fluffed the pillow beneath Breaux's head and repositioned his neck so that it appeared he was only asleep. Before Bellissima left the room, she shut off the fan and the ticking stopped.

"Lissima! Hold the elevator! Where you headed?" asked Jan- a fellow co-worker, elbowing her way aboard.

"-Down to see John," answered Bellissima.

"John the closer?"- A nickname the staff gave to the man who managed resident death formalities. "Oh no! who passed?"

"-Breaux."

"Long time coming. Honestly, he lasted way longer than anyone expected. Was it painless?"

"Yeah, a real easy exit. We should all be so lucky. He went down fighting, that's the way he made me promise to tell everybody he went."

"An imperious man, he was. I am sorry to see him go, though. I'm sorry for your loss. The two of you became such good friends. It was sweet of you to keep visiting him after you got certified despite companionship no longer being in your job description. God knows our workload is heavy as it is. It's weird, I never saw anyone else but you on Breaux's visitation log. Any relatives to notify?"

"I have a few phone numbers. No guarantee I'll reach anyone. You know how that goes. Some folks drop their loved ones off here and never look back. They just move on feeling one less burden lighter."

"Sounds like you've got your work cut out for you," sympathized Jan- moving closer to Bellissima to clear a trail for passengers leaving the elevator.

"Yeah, I can kiss my lunch break goodbye."

"And it's peach cobbler day, tragic. Want me to save you some? You can hide in the janitor's closet and wolf it down later."

"No time to eat today. It's straight over to admissions after I square things away with John."

"Admissions? That's right! Your grandmother is checking in today! You must be so excited!"

Bellissima imitated excitement, facetiously; smiling dramatically to emulate sarcasm. "I'm overjoyed! Can't you tell? So happy, I can barely contain myself."

"Relax Lissima. Compared to other retirement facilities, Pennycress is a 5-star resort. With you here on staff cracking your whip, your grandmother will have the best care plan. She won't be lonesome. She'll be comfortable and content. Isn't that what you want?"

"It's not my Grandmother's happiness or well-being I'm worried about. It's the sanity and safety of everyone else in this facility that concerns me. My aunts and cousins are coming in. The whole family hasn't been together since my graduation when Auntie Lou Anna signed over the cottage to me. Thank Goodness everyone's staying at the big house. The cottage is far too small. The Beaumonte' women need space. There's a little bit of Catherine Beaumonte' in all of us. It's like having kerosene, gasoline, and diesel in the same room with C4, a grenade and a bouncing betty."

Jan chuckled, absent-mindedly dismissing Bellissima's grave stare. "Listen, I know it's months away but I'm in charge of the company New Year's Eve bash this upcoming year..."

New Year's. Bellissima flinched at the very mention of the annual celebration. Her eyes snapped shut. The thought of fireworks brought back the gut-wrenching memory of Cheniere's haunting death. Bellissima's stomach turned sour almost immediately. "Jan, you know I don't celebrate the new year."

"Yes, I know," hesitated Jan. "Taking that into consideration, I was wondering if you'd sign up to work a 16-hour shift New Year's Eve. I hate to come off selfish, but those of us who *do* celebrate would like to have a good time. The board requires proof of regulated patient to floor nurse ratio before they approve the party. I don't have enough overtime volunteers yet. I thought maybe you'd be fine with working New Year's Eve the same way you always work Father's Day. You know since..."

Bellissima rolled her eyes, "...Since I don't know who my father is, and I refuse to acknowledge Father's Day?" she finished. It was true, Bellissima worked overtime every Father's Day. For reasons they were unaware of, Bellissima nor her cousins knew who their fathers were.

'Little girls don't need daddies, just great big pumpkins and glass slippers... The bible says in the book of Psalms Chapter 8, God is the father of the fatherless...I'm your mother and your father- I deserve both titles since I'm the one who does all the parenting...'

Yes, their mothers were masters when it came to avoiding the origin of their DNA. Once they were old enough to scheme, Bellissima and her two cousins sat down and strategized their uprising. They planned to corner their mothers and demand answers. They never followed through. When they became adults, they just stopped asking questions altogether.

Jan suddenly felt like an insensitive idiot. "I must sound like a self-centered jerk. Please don't hate me," she begged.

"It's okay Jan. I'll think it over and let you know," agreed Bellissima emotionlessly. The elevator doors opened and Bellissima stepped out. Jan followed.

"Let me make it up to you. Will you please let me get you some cobbler?"

"No thank you. I gotta go."

"Okay, well send for me where your grandmother arrives. I'd love to stop by and meet her."

"I won't have to come to get you. You'll hear her long before you see her."

The loudspeaker crackled. *"Nurse Beaumonte', you're needed in the North wing. Nurse Beaumonte', please report to admissions right away!"*

"Is it me, or did she sound scared?" asked Jan. "There must be a bug in the intercom system. Remind me to have maintenance look at that."

Bellissima hung her head and her shoulders sank." Oh no, she's early."

"Early? What a nice surprise! You want me to come with you, help her get unpacked?"

"No, you're a stranger. You'll only spook her and make things worse."

"Spook her? Jesus Lissima, you make your grandmother sound like a wolf with rabies."

"When Catherine Beaumonte's mad, she's far worse than a rabid wolf. Do me a favor, run these papers over to John. I have to go before she gets another assault charge."

"Another?" asked Jan standing alone in the hallway watching as Bellissima disappeared around the corner.

From a distance, Bellissima heard the echoing of profane paranoia. "I said don't touch me! Let me at her! That bloated cow was giving me the voodoo hex eye! I'll kick her ass from here all the way to the Atchafalaya!"

As Bellissima grew near, she saw her mother, Kay- struggling to detain Grandma Cat alongside two orderlies. "Mom! What's happening? What set her off?"

"Bellissima! Thank Goodness you're here!" cried kay. A look of relief began to settle on her face.

"I can't control her! She's having another one of her tantrums! It's a bad one!"

"Okay, everyone step back! Give her a little space! Stop pulling on her! Grandma Cat, talk to me! Tell me, what's the matter?" Bellissima begged- taking control of the situation.

Catherine looked up and her eyes began to squint behind her glasses. "Bellissima, my precious grandbaby! You have to help me! Get these hyenas off me!"

"Grandma Cat, why are you causing all this commotion?"

"It's that witch across the hall!"

"Witch? Granny, there's no witch here."

"Oh no! She's gotten to you already! You're under a spell, that's why you can't see her evil hidden agendas! She's gotten to Kay too! Your Mama was just going to let them kidnap me! My own daughter! Working for a voodoo priestess! Lord no! Take me instead!"

"Mother, you stop lying this instant and hush all these foolish hysterics! You're embarrassing your grandchild on her job! Compose yourself!" Kay demanded.

"-Compose myself? How can I when there's a witch right outside this room! Bellissima, avenge my mortal soul, go kick her diapered ass! Defend the family name!"

Bellissima peered into the dormitory directly across the hall. There stood old Mrs. Talbert, jaw dropped with her knitting needle trembling in hand. "Grandma, that poor woman is nearly blind. She needs binoculars just to do her sewing. I highly doubt she's looking at you a certain way. She can barely see you at all. She makes blankets for the community poverty shelter. I'm pretty sure she's not a witch. I will not go into that defenseless woman's room and do her harm."

"Sheer mutiny! Get me up on my feet, I'll go knock her block off myself!"

"Catherine Beaumonte' that's enough!" yelled Kay. "You know beds at Pennycress are had to come by. The waiting list is a mile long. You should be thankful and not make waves."

"They're not doing us any favors! I have money!"

"No, you don't! You have the big house and the land, the land we built the cottage on that no longer grows a profitable crop and the little bit daddy left us all those years ago, and there's not a lot left. Now, Bellissima had to cash in a lot of favors to get you in here. Your behavior reflects on her and you will not make my child look bad. You understand? You haven't been here 15 minutes and you're already making death threats? Do you think that's proper?" Catherine began to settle down, rolling her eyes and curling her lips. "Apologize to these nice people."

"I'm sorry if I hurt any of you," said Catherine- her regret thin as paper.

"-And now you apologize to your granddaughter," ordered Kay.

Catherine looked up at Bellissima again, as if seeing her for the first time. "Is that you, love bug?"

Bellissima's smile was melancholy as she cupped her grandmother's wrinkled cheek in her palm. It was 8 months ago when Kay first noticed her mother's mind slipping away. She was inconsolable, bawling uncontrollably when she had to phone her two sisters to forward the bad news. *'Mama has Alzheimer's.'* The disease swept in like a typhoon, disrupting Catherine's cognitive abilities. It was little things in the beginning, like how to sign her name but then her thought pattern derailed in a dangerous way. A concerned neighbor called Kay while she was working at the restaurant. *'There's been an incident. Your mother somehow managed to pull herself up onto the tractor. She stripped down, stark naked, and rode into town throwing breadcrumbs into the street like she was in a damn parade or something. She eventually crashed. Fortunately, she didn't hurt herself too bad or kill anyone, but she's got a few cuts and bruises. You better come on home. There's a load of police poking around.'* When questioned, Catherine said she was tending to the chickens. *'A starved chicken won't lay a decent egg. They asked me for some of my pumpernickel.'*

Authorities were puzzled. *'Mrs., Beaumonte', are You telling me you learned to speak chicken?'*

'Well yes, I'm speaking it right now. If you can understand me, you must speak chicken too. Are you part chicken, dear? It's nothing to be ashamed of. All of us are mixed with something down here in these parts.'

'Can you tell me why you were naked, Mam'

'Goblins stole my panties right off my cooch...'

Those delusions sealed Catherine's fate. She was officially declared a high-risk elderly liability. When paramedics tried to put Catherine into the ambulance, she resisted violently- pulling a whole fistful of hair from one of their heads, roots and all. The hospital insisted she be placed in an assisted living facility.

"My sweet angel! Come and give your Grandma a hug. I have some butterscotch candy in my sweater pocket. I'll sneak you a piece when your Mama's not paying attention. I'd offer to bake you a lemon cake; but these terrorists won't let me near sharp objects, so the kitchen is off limits to me.

They're right not to trust me. I can't say I haven't thought about cutting one or two of them, but I resist 'cause I'm a good Christian woman."

"You don't have to bake me anything, Granny." Bellissima dismissed the orderlies. "You can go now. I'll take it from here. Thank you so much for your help and patience. She turned to her mother, Kay. "I wasn't expecting the two of you so early."

Kay groaned. "I went down to the hospital this morning to start the discharge paperwork- you know those documents take forever to fill out. I figured it would take all morning. I wanted to get a jump start so we'd make it here on time at noon as we planned. But when I got to the hospital this morning, they'd already packed Mama's belongings. She was waiting outside near the bus stop. They said they'd be happy to fax over everything if I promised to never bring her back. It was as if they couldn't wait to get rid of her. I can't imagine why," Kay replied sarcastically.

"Don't talk trash about me like I'm not even here, Kay!"

"Sorry, Mama."

Catherine grabbed Bellissima's wrist and pulled. "Have a seat on Grandma's lap."

Bellissima dallied. "I think I'm too big for that now. I could put a strain on your joints. Do I need to bring my osteoporosis chart in here and remind you how feeble your bones are again?"

"Never mind all that! I'm not made of glass. I'm sick and tired of you all treating me like I'm some fragile soap dish! Now come! Sit I said!" Bellissima obeyed. Catherine swept Bellissima's hair behind her ear so that she could see her face clearly. "What is that?"

"What's what?" asked Bellissima, dumbfoundedly.

"That thing in your nose. Don't pretend you don't know what I'm talking about. Play dumb again, I dare you!" threatened Catherine.

"It's just a nose stud."

"A what?"

"It's a piercing."

"A piercing? You mean to tell me, you went and let some hippie drill a hole in your face? Kay, did you know about this?"

"Yes Mama, my daughter doesn't keep secrets from me. And despite her being a grown woman, she asked my opinion <u>and</u> permission before she had it done. Lots of East Indian parents participate in this tradition. Some have it done to their daughters when they're infants and some allow their daughters to pierce their navels when they're just teenagers. I think it's culturally beautiful. She has a right to express herself however she chooses."

"You allowed this self-mutilation?"

"It's her body, Mama."

Catherine shook her head, disapproving. "You didn't hit her enough when she was younger, Kay. You let the fear of God slip right out of her. That's what's wrong with these kids today."

"I hit Lissima plenty. Not enough to traumatize her. Not too little to spoil her and look at her. She turned out perfect," professed Kay- gazing affectionately at Bellissima.

"I don't know if I'm perfect, but I'm certain my Mommy is so, I must be darn close," countered Bellissima.

"That's all fine, just fine. Your mother/daughter relationship is all butterflies and dandelions, but God gave you all the holes you need child. You put one more hole in your body and I'll tear your rear end until you're scared to sit in chairs without cushions. You hear me? You never outgrow ass whippings. I smacked your mama twice on the ride over," said Catherine. Bellissima looked over at kay with skepticism.

"Yeah, she did," confirmed Kay. "It would have been three times if I hadn't ducked."

"-And I'll do it again if I have to. Once you're a parent you never stop chastising. Now here, suck on this butterscotch while I tell you about the bridge- the Burn Out bridge that killed your grandfather and gave birth to the curse that killed your sweet twin sister, Cheniere."

"Not today, Mama." Said Kay

"It was June 1973. I remember the heat. Louisiana was hotter than the taint of the Devil's ass. I'd been cooking all day long. My satin hands were ruined from peeling crawfish. Your Grandfather, Jeremiah, he loved my etouffee..."

Kay pleaded. "Mama, I said no. Please. Not today."

Catherine ignored her daughter and continued. "Can you imagine the wait? The weight of worry when you're waiting on bad news concerning someone you love with all your heart? When you just know something bad is coming. It sits heavy like chest congestion. I was waiting for the worst, not expecting it. I already knew. I could feel it. I was waiting for the ground to fall out right from under me- no pun intended. There must have been a knock at the door. For the life of me, I can't remember hearing a knock or anyone calling my name, but I opened the front door. I saw the sheriffs at the edge of my porch. I stepped out and took a deep breath. Immediately, the stench of charred driftwood dried my voice right up. The sun was setting, but I could see the sparks rising high in the distance, about 10 miles out. The bridge was on fire. Jeremiah Beaumonte' had died with the others on Burn Out bridge. The ones who hit the water alive, I could hear them screaming as the Gators and garfish ripped their flesh apart. My wedding ring is down there in the water-logged gallows. The fight we had right before it happened, it was so bad that I took the band off my finger and I threw it right at Jeremiah. It was in his possession when he died. Now both his body and my ring are still down there. My ring, that must be what's binding the curse, the curse that killed Cheniere years later…"

"Mother!" shouted Kay- nearly in tears.

"She deserves to know everything about the past! It's a part of her, Kay! The curse is her patrimony too!"

"-Enough!" yelled Kay. "I mean it!"

Bellissima sensed the growing argumentative friction and quickly deflated the tension. "Grandma Cat, let's finish the story later." Catherine smiled and Bellissima felt the belligerence release from Catherine's core as she stared off into empty space again. It was a familiar expression. She was losing her train of thought. Honestly, the timing couldn't have been better.

There was a knock at the door. In walked Lou Anna; Catherine Beaumonte's firstborn, Kay's oldest sister and Bellissima's favorite aunt.

"Auntie Lou Anna!" gushed Bellissima- leaping from Catherine's lap and into Lou Anna's arms. It had been four years since the whole family had been together but only a year since Bellissima and Lou Anna had seen one another. Bellissima was forced to make an unplanned trip to the city for her Aunt's help with something she wanted to stay a secret. When Bellissima begged Lou Anna not to tell Kay she'd gone to the city; Lou Anna hesitantly agreed to keep quiet.

"Lissima! Oh! I've missed you! Take a step back, let me have a look at you. You're the spitting image of Kay when she was your age. Of course, you're not as flat chested as she was," joked Lou Anna.

"I still have the water bra you made me wear for homecoming my sophomore year," said Kay from the corner of the room."

Lou Anna spun around, and her eyes lit up. "Kay! Oh, my goodness, you look fantastic!"

"Black don't crack, you know that. It's so good to see you. I'm happy you're here," said Kay- dejectedly.

"Where else would I be? Like it or not, she's our mother. I went to the hospital and they told me they'd shipped her off already. I should have left my business card. Everyone there seems to need psychological counseling after putting up with her. I could have made a fortune." Lou Anna put her purse down and looked over at Catherine, who was working extra hard at ignoring Lou Anna's presence. "Mother, I know you see me standing here. How long are you going to pretend I'm invisible?"

"Hello daughter," hissed Catherine dryly.

"Well, that was hardly a greeting, but I guess I'll take what I can get. You might not get any sweeter than that. Aren't you happy to see me?"

"That depends. Are you here to talk some sense into these two or did you come to throw dirt on my coffin and dance on my grave?"

"No one's putting you in a coffin," assured Lou Anna.

"You may as well! You're already treating me like I'm dead; like I have no say so over my own life!"

"May I have a hug please?" asked Lou Anna.

"Are you going to take me home?" asked Catherine- right back.

"Mama, you viciously attacked a medic and showed the whole town your pale, shameful parts. You know I can't take you back to the big house right now."

"Then no! You may not have a hug, you disobedient first-born seed of the devil!" yelled Catherine- folding her arms.

"Catherine Beaumonte' if you don't hug me, I'll leave right now and take your gift with me when I go."

Suddenly, Lou Anna had Catherine's attention. "-Gift? What gift?"

"The very expensive trinket in this tiny blue box I have right here. I bought it in the city. If you sniff the box you can still the smell the smog," sweet-talked Lou Anna.

Catherine took a moment to mull it over. "-Alright, one quick hug."

Lou Anna wrapped her arms around her mother. "You don't look a day over 21 years old Catherine. You're as timeless as you've always been, as much as I hate to admit it. It's good to see you."

"Your flattery stinks worse than your perfume. You smell like a pay-per-hour streetwalker."

"You don't like it? You're the one who bought it for me, Mama!"

"Oh, that's right. Well, I obviously didn't get a chance to smell it first. You're supposed to spray a mist in the air and walk into it, not lather with it."

Before Catherine barked more insults, Bellissima redirected the conversation again. "So, Aunt Lou Anna, any word for Auntie Minxy?"

"I called her before my flight, but her line went straight to voicemail- didn't even ring."

"I hope she's alright," said Kay- concerned.

"Don't be, cats always land on their feet!" Their heads spun. There stood Minxy Beaumonte'; Catherine Beaumonte's youngest child, Kay and Lou Anna's younger sister and Bellissima's best friend. "I hear the party is in here? Mind if I crash?"

"Auntie Minx! You made it!" screamed Bellissima- hopping up and down.

Minxy's eyes widened. "Are you my niece or a top dollar model? Look at you Lissima, you're a vision! Get over here and give me a squeeze!"

"I've been trying to video chat with you all week. I worry when you didn't answer. I can't bring myself to watch the news. I see everything that's going on in South Africa and I get so scared for you," said Bellissima- wrapped in Minxy's long elegant arms.

"I meant to call you back, really I did. There's just so much good to do and so little time for everything else. We're a few humanitarians short; but we're still making a big difference, fighting the good fight. I told you not to worry about me, I'm always just fine."

Lou Anna rolled her eyes. "Minxy, it's selfish of you to make us worry."

"I would have checked in, but my phone died once my plane from Kenya landed. There was no place to charge it on the bus. I walked to the hospital, but they said they'd discharged Mama already."

"-Bus? Walked? Minx, I offered to buy you a plane ticket straight here with no stops. It would have been faster and safer. All sorts of sketchy scoundrels lurk around those bus stations just looking for people to mug or stab."

"You know I like to make an entrance," Minxy Joked.

"Your life isn't a laughing matter," lectured Lou Anna. It was no mystery, why their conversations were always so cumbersome. Lou Anna was a domineering control freak and Minxy, the family free spirit, bucked until every reign life forced around her neck was loosed.

"Lou, could I please hug my sisters and mother before you start your nagging and delegating?"

"Of course," Lou Anna replied. "I'm sorry. Lay one on me," she said walking over to Minxy.

"Is there room for one more?" asked Kay.

"There's always room for you," Minxy replied. "You look good, Kay."

Minxy released her sisters and rushed over to Catherine's wheelchair. "Mama? Mama, it's me, Minx."

Catherine looked up at her daughter and her eyes narrowed as she focused, reckoning Minxy's face before moving in for a hug. "Minxy, my caboose-baby!" she said- eyes watering. "I cry a prayer for you every night while you're out there doing what you're doing? Do you need money? I can send Kay or Lou to the bank right now and withdraw a little something to hold you over," whispered Catherine.

Minxy smiled at the proposal but declined. "No mother. I'm alright."

"Your twelve steps have been over for years. Why do you have to travel so far away when you can do some of God's work right here in the states."

"Stop worrying so much. I have a little money stashed away, I manage just fine." Lou Anna and Kay swapped concerned glances but said nothing.

"Well it's an open-ended offer," said Catherine leaning in. "You've got to get me out of here. Your sisters are trying to kill me."

"Stop those lies, Mama!" yelled Kay.

"I'll tell you more about it later," mumbled Catherine.

"Okay," entertained Minxy with a sly wink.

"You want me to braid your hair? Come sit with me. I'll braid your hair and tell you about the day your daddy died. It was the day the bridge burned down…"

"There she goes again," mumbled Lou Anna.

"She's a Beaumonte'. She never lets anything go," said Kay turning to Bellissima. "We're going to head up to the big house. Your Aunts need to get washed up and unpacked. Do me a favor and get your Grandmother to take her pills. Make her open her mouth and show you they aren't just lodged in her cheek or under her tongue- she can't be trusted. Also, would you please pick up some food. Your Grandmother is an exhausting individual. I have no energy to cook."

"Yes Mama," answered Bellissima- kissing her mother's cheek.

"Let's leave Bellissima to her work. We will see you later mother," said Lou Anna.

"There will be no partying in my house. It's still mine as long as I'm alive. And you better stay out of my liquor cabinet. Don't think I won't be able to tell if the bottles have been opened. And don't empty out the bottles of clear and refill them with water like you did that weekend I went to teach bible study at that camp in Baton Rouge."

Both Lou Anna and Kay looked at Minxy with a convicting glare. "One time. I did that one time!" Minxy defended -storming out. Kay followed.

Lou Anna let her sisters get a lead on her. She dallied for a moment alone with Bellissima. Once Kay and Minxy were out of hearing range, she stared at her niece affectionately. "It's so good to see you doing better. I've lost so much sleep since you left the city…worrying. Crying. Don't worry. A promise is a promise. I won't tell Kay," whispered Lou Anna. "Good luck with your Grandmother. She's two handfuls," she said turning to leave.

"Aunt Lou Anna wait! Any word from my cousins? I haven't heard from them today. Are they still coming?"

"Yes, they're just running late, I'm sure. You know how those two are. One's an insubordinate nonconformist and the other's a certified workaholic. They're not as family oriented as you are. I wish we all were a little more like you." Lou Anna was twirling Bellissima's hair, staring at her so intently that it made Bellissima feel as if her Aunt were looking right through her.

"What's wrong?"

"-Nothing dear. It's just- looking at you all grown up, I can't help but think of how there should be two of you." Lou Anna quickly looked away to keep Bellissima from seeing her emotions rise. "Don't worry, I'll keep Minxy out of the liquor. She's been clean for three whole years. I won't let her throw that away. Me and your Mama, we're responsible alcoholics. I can't promise you we'll stay out of it."

CHAPTER TWO

Nostalgia's cold reminiscent shadow crept in bringing with it a dry lump of unresolved despondency that settled comfortably, throbbing on Bellissima's chest. Her palms dampened as she rounded the first rose bush lining the dirt stretch from Grandma Cat's mailbox to the front door of the big house. Although the withered ivory paint had finally began to chip, and the stone cherubim was crumbling; the big house was still a breathtaking monument with good bones. Standing 27 feet tall smack dab in the middle of a 34-acre plot, it was the oldest house in town still standing, handed down from one generation to the next. No home in town had more history. No home in town had more memories.

Bellissima killed the engine and heard music blaring from inside. She could almost feel the bass from way in the car. She stormed in like the law, arms full of cheap Asian food. "If one of you opened Grandma Cat's moonshine, she's going to make me drive into town and buy another jar from that strange pervert who stands on the corner by the laundromat! He has wandering hands! She was clear! No partying! She's going to have a hissy fit!"

"Don't bust in here and start yelling at us! We didn't turn on the music and there's nothing but spiced cider in our cups!" yelled Lou Anna with her fingers in her ears. Bellissima entered the den where she found her mother and aunts sitting, innocently enough.

"Turn it down some more!" shouted Minxy- banging on the wall.

The volume lowered a tad and Bellissima noticed her mother, Kay, trying hard to contain her excitement. "The vandals responsible for the impromptu lip-sync contest you hear going on are hiding in the kitchen," she said. Bellissima froze, panning their faces from left to right and then back again.

"That's right! Our dysfunctional seedlings finally made it in. Go on back, they've been asking for you all evening. They made us promise not to tell you they'd made it in, wanted it to be a surprise," said Minxy.

Bellissima braced herself for a flood of emotions as she neared the kitchen door slowly, trying hard to harness composure before going in. She cracked the door an inch, poked her head inside. There they were, Dria and Sadie, dancing to zydeco, laughing and bickering over who was the bigger troublemaker growing up. Dria, the Beaumonte' family overachiever, never looked more in control of her life with her jet-black tresses pulled back tight into a long stallion-like ponytail flowing down her back, revealing her high cheekbones. For a woman who constantly whined about her firm's demanding workload, she looked moderately happy and fulfilled. Sadie, the youngest of the Beaumonte' grandchildren, appeared unbiddenly vivacious as usual with her sharp, low maintenance haircut and extra holes in her ear cartilage. Any other college girl who partied as much as Sadie would look worn out and rode hard but not Sadie. No matter how late she stayed out raving bra-less and sleepless, her eyes nor her breasts ever drooped any lower. Women who covered themselves in tattoos usually have a rough, rugged appearance; but not Sadie and Auntie Minxy. Both of them treated their bodies like canvases and still maintained a mesmeric level of non-threatening femininity.

"How can you say *I* was more trouble? I distinctly remember you putting gum in the gym teacher's dreadlocks for making you run the mile in the pouring rain," said Sadie to Dria.

"She was just pissed, being vindictive because I told her that physical fitness wasn't a real class. What about you? You're the one who stole old Mrs. Wither's kitten and held the poor thing hostage until she apologized to Bellissima for making her cry," defended Dria.

Sadie searched her memory. "What did she say to make Bellissima cry again? I can't remember?"

Bellissima crept through the kitchen door and shut the stereo off completely. Dria and Sadie spun around and discovered Bellissima standing there, eavesdropping. "That miserable old fortune teller told me that my puppy was going to get hit by a car."

"Lissima!" they hurrahed. Within seconds, they'd sandwiched Bellissima in the middle- hugging her from both sides.

- *"I've missed you!"*
- *"You look great!"*
- *"I love your hair!"*, they gushed back and forth, paying and receiving compliments. Finally, the entwine disbursed. Sadie let go first. Dria held on to Bellissima a little longer. When she finally let go, Bellissima noticed shallow tears whelming in Dria's eyes; but didn't bring it up in front of Sadie.

"It's been so long. I'm so happy we're all here, considering the circumstances..." said Dria.

"Yeah, the circumstances," agreed Sadie, helping Bellissima carry the bags to the kitchen table where the three of them took a seat.

"Mama said Grandma Cat was sitting outside alone when Auntie Kay got to the hospital. I'd draw up a case and sue if Catherine hadn't signed herself out and threatened to sue them if they didn't let her leave. That woman is so damned ornery. Was she upset when they arrived at Pennycress today?" asked Dria pouring each of them a shot of cognac.

"-Mad as a banshee on fire in hell. She blames all of us for having to be there, not the dozens of professionals who put the pressure on Mama and Aunties; and threatened to go over their heads and expedite the process by making her a senior ward of the state. We had no choice. It's not safe for her to be alone anymore. That last incident could have been a lot worse. She needs around the clock supervision. I'm always working, sometimes I do graveyards. I can barely keep my eyes open long enough to make it to the parking lot, no way I can make it here every night to keep her and this place in good standing before I make it home to the cottage and crash. When would I sleep? Mama's second restaurant, two towns over, wasn't picking up business fast enough. She spends most her time out there so she won't have to hire a manager until she can afford to have one on payroll full time. I finally convinced her to rent a cheap studio closer to the business to keep her from having to drive three hours home every afternoon just to drive another three back on little to no sleep. I worry about her on the highway as it is. Kay Beaumonte' has got to be the worse driver this side of the Mississippi River. They must've been just handing out driver's licenses in her day. Mama's only here on weekends now, she's got too much riding on the chain to let it all slip away. Even still, she offered to move back in and look after Grandma, but Grandma Cat refused. *'Kay, I'm nobody's burden. I can take care of myself. You have a life of your own to live.'* Mimicked Bellissima, tossing back her cognac shot.

"I bet Catherine flipped her lid when she realized she couldn't scream or cry her way out of this mess. Auntie Kay said she clawed an old lady at the home today. Something about her being a witch? Please tell me that's not true," pleaded Dria.

"I wish I could, Dria. Regrettably, I must confirm that <u>did</u> happen. That poor old lady is scared to leave her room. She said the psychopath who just moved in across the hall is hunting her and threatened to burn her at the stake," replied Bellissima. Dria sighed and swallowed her portion of alcohol.

"-Intimidation and inevitable domination. That's the Beaumonte' way. It's how I get most of my dates," said Sadie. "That poor old lady. Pretty soon the whole nursing home will be living in fear and Granny Cat will be their dictator. Before you know it, there will be a creepy nursery rhyme about our grandmother, wait and see. Parents will recite it to frighten their children into obedience. 'Hush little children, obey and go to bed. Or else Cat Beaumonte' will come and chop your head," sang Sadie- using her finger as a blade across her own neck for tragicomic effect.

"Hell, I'd straighten up and fly right if I thought Catherine Beaumonte' was in my closet," joked Dria.

"What happens now?" asked Sadie, with a concerned face. "Our moms aren't saying much like they don't even have a plan. Is Granny going to move into Pennycress permanently or is this a temporary deal until her wounds from the crash heal? Are we just buying time until we can get some much-needed repairs and upgrades done here in the big house? We could get some sort of monitoring device to track where she is at all times. If she starts to wander again, we'll get an alert."

"You do realize you just described house arrest?" asked Dria- shaking her head.

"Oh, right. Well, never mind that. We can buy her a big screen to keep her busy and off the tractor. What about one of those electronic chairs that climb the stairs. Maybe we could get a contractor to drill in some shower bars. Dria's really good at interviewing people, we could hire a qualified live-in caregiver to tend to Grandma Cat's every need."

Bellissima snickered. "Catherine is a territorial creature. She wouldn't allow any of her own daughters to move back in and take care of her. If we hire a stranger to live in the big house, she'll murder us slowly. She's also dead against any upgrades, claims it will mess up the manor's southern charm. I once offered to buy a central air unit to replace her box fan. Catherine cut her eyes so hard at me, I feared I'd turn into dust." They all laughed, familiar with that particular glare. "I don't know what's next. I get the feeling nothing's ever going to be the same. She's never been this sick before. The disease, it's chewing through her brain like a ravenous maggot. Some days she forgets who her own children are. She keeps forgetting where she bookmarked the bridge story. I'm left with two options: remind her where she left off and relive the horror that has become our never-ending nightmare or let her start from the beginning a thousand times more." Dria and Sadie sighed almost simultaneously.

"The bridge tragedies? She's still putting you through that? Still putting us through that?" asked Dria, both drained and woeful at the very thought.

"Yes. You'd think she'd get less theatrical in her old age, but she recites the story frame by frame. Just like when we were younger. She starts it out the same way, warning us that men are the devil."

'Loving a man will kill you! Before your Grandfather died on that bridge, he killed me softly- first with his love and then by taking it away!' The three of them yelled melodramatically in unison- impersonating their grandmother, mimicking her crackled voice and facial expressions.

"What's all that horseplay I hear?" yelled Lou Anna from the den. "You girls better be setting the table in there!"

"Take it down a few notches, Lou Anna. Just looking at how tight that business suit is, I can tell you ain't missing no meals," jabbed Minxy causing Kay to nearly choke on her cider.

Dria rolled her eyes, recognizing her mother's distinct brand of impatience. "We're getting it done! Keep your inappropriately tight pants on! The food ain't going nowhere!" Dria stood. "Bellissima, you get the utensils. Sadie, get the big silver serving platter from the shelf, you're still the only one tall enough to reach it without the step ladder. I'll get the plates and napkins." Bellissima paused and grinned. "Lissima, you alright?"

"Yeah. This just reminds me of old times. Except back then, Cheniere always got the plates. You just got the napkins." For a short moment, no one spoke. "It's nice having you back home. I've missed you two."

"Yeah, we sure had some good times," said Sadie.

"-Great times," corrected Dria. "I have a fun idea! Why don't we all bed down in the den for a sleepover tonight! We can eat cake on the good dishes and beg Auntie Kay to make us some of her French vanilla hot chocolate!"

"I can't. I have to work tomorrow morning," said Bellissima.

"Can't you just go to work from here?" asked Sadie.

"Well…I could but I don't have any clothes, just what I'm wearing now. And I have nothing to sleep in."

"That's hardly an excuse. You'll borrow some of Dria's pajamas and I'll wash your scrubs. They'll be dry by morning. All your scrubs are one color, no one will know it's the same ones- clean or not," said Sadie.

"Then it's settled! Sleepover!" shouted Dria- delightfully eager.

"Yeah, I guess it's settled," agreed Bellissima- hesitantly.

Dria noticed Sadie's shot, still full to the top, on the table. "Sadie, you saving this for later or something?"

Sadie looked down at the tumbler and dithered. "No."

Dria picked it up and held it out. "Here." Sadie was very still and didn't reach out to take it. "What's wrong with you? You rather clear? I think there's some tequila…"

"No, it's just that…I'm still hammered from all the beers I had on the way here. You can just have it." Not giving Sadie's unusual behavior another thought, Dria gulped the shot and the three Beaumonte' cousins began to set the table in silence, all smiling. It was like they were children all over again. "Bellissima?" mumbled Sadie.

"Yeah?"

"Does Granny still cry when she tells the bridge story? Does she still fall apart when she gets to the parts where Grandpa and Cheniere pass away?"

26

Dria froze and studied Bellissima's reaction. "Yeah. I hate seeing her cry like that," Bellissima replied.

"Me too," mumbled Dria.

"Did Aunt Lou Anna or Auntie Minxy ever say anything about Grampa's death that made you question Grandma Cat's version of what really happened right before Grandpa Jeremiah left for the bridge the day he died?" asked Bellissima.

"What do you mean," questioned Dria.

Bellissima paused, second-guessing her decision to say anything at all. "It's probably nothing, really."

"What's nothing?" asked Sadie.

"Back when I was still studying for my certification, Mama got really sick. I had to dope her up on an antibiotic and cough syrup cocktail. In feverish reverie, she started going on and on about Burn Out bridge."

"What exactly did she say?"

"A lot. I couldn't make out all of it, but I could have sworn she said it was all Grandma Cat's fault that Grandpa Jeremiah was dead. She said Grandma Cat was to blame for Cheniere's death too."

The Beaumonte' daughters burst into the kitchen. "We think you girls should stay here tonight. We all need family time. Our old bedrooms upstairs are full of all kinds of junk; whatever didn't fit in the shed out back. They ain't fit to sleep it. We'll share the king bed in Mama's room and you girls can rough it on the floor in the den. Bellissima, warm some milk on the stove," said Kay. "I'm going to make my famous hot chocolate, and don't you girls ask for any. You're already hyper enough. Sugar will only make it worse."

CHAPTER THREE

Lou Anna ran her fingertips along the crème' thread binding the multicolored patches of Catherine's most-prized quilt. "You know, there's a store in the city that sells the most expensive bedding. I pass it every day on my way to the office; nothing but overpriced factory produced crap. This, what Mama made with her own two hands, it's the real thing. There's nothing like this in stores, anywhere. I've yet to find anything softer. Nothing's ever consoled me quite like this or kept me warmer. I remember when she taught me to sew and stitch. My index finger looked like a pin cushion. She wouldn't let me use a thimble in the beginning. She said it would make me understand how necessary pain was. I didn't understand what she meant by that until I got older."

"Bring it over here. Let's have a look at it," said Kay- making room for Lou Anna in Catherine's bed next to her and Minxy. Lou Anna stretched the quilt to cover all three of them. "There's a patch from each of our baby blankets on this old thing. One from each of our babies' too," said Minxy feeling the different textures all weaved together into one immaculate tapestry. "Feels like a lifetime since we've all been together like this."

"Sure does," agreed Lou Anna. "Is that our children I hear still making racket downstairs. It's well after midnight. I stress to them until I'm blue in the face, sleep is essential for a healthy productive mind, but do they listen? No. They're a bunch of busybodies, especially Bellissima- sha baby. The poor child never powers down. Last year I had to pry her phone out of her stiff sleeping hands," said Lou Anna.

Kay's eye-brows burrowed. "Last year? It' s been longer than that since you've seen Lissima."

Lou Anna paused, realizing she'd inadvertently revealed that she'd seen Bellissima more recently than Kay was led to believe. She looked away quickly, hoping Kay wouldn't read more into it. "Right. Of course, it has," shrugged Lou Anna casually. "I work so much lately, I have no sense of time. It just feels like a year, that's what I meant to say."

Minxy eyed Lou Anna suspiciously. "That's a big lapse," she muttered, studying Lou Anna's reticent behavior. There was another thump downstairs, followed by loud laughter. "Don't make me come down there!" threatened Minxy.

Lou Anna and Kay sniggled. "Our daughters are probably down there laughing at you, Minx. You don't scare them, you never did. You were always the fun one."

"I was tough sometimes."

"No, you weren't," said Lou Anna. "Remember when you were supposed to punish the girls for taking the tractor on that joyride. You sent the girls to separate rooms for exactly nine minutes and made them swear to tell us you'd spanked them. You could never handle being the bad guy, not even for ten full minutes."

"They told you I never spanked them! Little Snitches," said Minxy aghast. "I know they could have gotten hurt, but I was proud of them for sticking together. No matter how much you two yelled, they wouldn't tell whose idea it was to steal the car in the first place. You two really put the heat on 'em. You gotta admit, they stood their ground. What's so bad about being the fun one? I was cool to hang out with. They still gave me the proper amount of respect even though I wasn't good at the discipline part of parenting."

"It's not entirely your fault. You were Mama's baby girl. You can count on one hand- the number of times you got punished growing up, Minx," said Kay. "We all know *I* got hit the most."

"That's because you insisted on being so smart-aleck. Minxy and I never talked back. No matter how hard it was to bite our tongues, we endured every lecture, took our stripes, and said nothing to Mama's face about her parenting. You Kay, you always had something to say. You constantly defied Mama. You were the mastermind behind every scheme that ever got us into trouble!" accused Lou Anna.

"She's right Kay," agreed Minxy- nodding her head. "It was your idea to hide Mama's wooden spoon, so she wouldn't have it to smack our knuckles. Even though it was all your idea, all three of us got a beating when she found it buried under the steps. You couldn't find a better hiding place than that? You served her our asses on a platter!"

"It seemed like a good enough hiding place at the time! Mama had a nose for my mischief, it's not my fault she sniffed it out! Mama was tough on us, but just as sweet when wanted to be. She raised us with a mightier hand because she wanted us to be stronger than everyone else and I think she achieved that. We turned out alright. Catherine Beaumonte' was a strict, but a caring mother. We had some wonderful times. I guess that's why it's so hard to see her withering away."

"Yeah. It breaks my heart. You know, I had my first drink with her," confessed Minxy.

"With who?" asked Lou Anna.

"-Mama," Minxy replied.

Lou Anna scowled, shocked. "You had your first alcoholic beverage with our Mother, Catherine Beaumonte'?"

"Yeah. After the bridge disaster, you focused on school and baby Dria. Kay, natural born nurturer, stepped up and did all the things Mama was too depressed to do. You two had things to keep your mind off missing daddy. I always felt like you two had the right to be sadder than me because you knew him longer. I was so young when he died, but he was my daddy too. I needed my two big sisters to talk to me, help me process the loss but you two emotionally checked out for a while. Mama had her nightcaps and her bible. I couldn't tell which one gave her more comfort, the alcohol or the good book. Hell, I had a bible of my own and I read it often. Maybe I wasn't reading the right scriptures because I still felt alone and miserable. So, I figured it had to be the drink. One night when you and Kay were asleep, I tip-toed downstairs with a plan to steal a few sips from Catherine's flask. I grabbed it off the mantel and just as I unscrewed the top, Mama appeared out of the darkness. She'd never gone to bed. *'What are you doing up this late young lady? And don't fix your mouth to lie either! Or you'll be swallowing your teeth!'* I was scared quiet. Mama eyed me up and down. Then she noticed the flask in my hand. *'So, you want to have a grown-up drink?'* I didn't answer. There was no point in denying it. I was caught red-handed. *'Why you want to drink?'* I still didn't answer. I was embarrassed and already dreading my punishment. *'You remember when daddy caught Kay trying to smoke and he made her swallow a spoonful of his chewing tobacco?'* Catherine pulled a secret bottle of brown liquor from behind the bookshelf and gave it to me. *'Go get a glass and fill it to the top. You 'gon sit here until you drink it all. I don't care if it takes all night long and if you throw up, I'll make you clean it up and start all over again.'* Me and mama sat by that old Franklin cast iron stove we used as a heater and drank all night. She tried but just couldn't drink me under the table. At first, we were quiet. But then Catherine drummed up a little small talk. Eventually, we were talking about the bridge and loneliness and grief. There was such sweet sorrow in Mama's voice, like a caustic lullaby soliloquized by an angel in tears. A few nights later, I crept downstairs again. Without speaking, Mama poured me a glass. From then on, it was our special thing that we told no one about."

"How old were you when this started?" asked Kay.

"I was 7."

"You were 7 years old?" gasped Lou Anna.

Kay sensed quarrelsome pressure coming to a head. "Well, Mama had special hobbies with each of us, Lou Anna," she said- in attempt to justify Catherine and Minxy's unique attempt at bonding before Lou Anna flew off the handle.

"Kay! We're not talking about some innocent pastime! Mama cooked with you and she made quilts with me! What she exposed Minxy to was something felonious! I can't believe it!"

Minxy rolled her eyes. "Typical Lou, always overreacting."

"She contributed to the delinquency of her own child! It was irresponsible! She should have sent you back to your room with a red bottom! If she had, then maybe…"

"-Maybe I wouldn't have turned out to be the sister you're embarrassed to claim as blood?" interrupted Minxy.

Minxy had accused Lou Anna of being hypercritical and careless with her feelings in the past. It suddenly occurred to Lou Anna that she'd picked a bad time to be judgmental. Kay hung her head and Lou Anna looked away from Minxy's condemning stare. It was then that she noticed the picture frame at Catherine's bedside. "Oh, my goodness, look!"

"What?" asked Kay.

"It's a picture from the Cal-Cam fair the year we all won the big obstacle course!" Lou Anna picked up the picture and all three sisters huddled close to look at it together.

"Wow! Look at us!" said Minxy, wide-eyed. "I remember it like it was yesterday. Dria and Lou climbed the big ropes and rang the bell at the top. Sadie and I mastered the high wire over the mud pit without falling. Kay and Mama won the talent round with their baton twirling and..." Minxy stopped speaking. Lou Anna grabbed Minxy's hand and rested her head on Kay's shoulder.

Kay cleared her throat. "My twins brought home the win, finishing the mile- first place, hand in hand."

"We all look so happy in our bright yellow shirts," said Lou Anna.

"It was Cheniere's idea to wear yellow. Bellissima was her most favorite person in the whole world and Bellissima loved the sun. She figured we'd dress like the sun," said Kay. "You know, I come down every weekend and stay here with Mama. I clean her room all the time and I've never seen this picture here. Do you think she hides it away where I come over? So that I won't see it and get sad?"

"Yes," answered Lou Anna.

"That's awful kind of her," Kay replied.

"Sure is..." agreed Minxy.

The Beaumonte' grandchildren sat in Indian style downstairs atop their sleeping bags in the den of the big house, laughing and carrying on. "Which one of our moms is that I hear threatening to come down here if we don't go to bed?" asked Bellissima.

"Sounds like Auntie Minx," answered Dria. All three of them laughed hysterically. "She's the least scary of them all!"

"Yeah but even the weakest of them is still pretty scary," said Bellissima. "Sadie! Quit hogging the pecans!"

Sadie reluctantly passed the nut dish. "Am I really here? It seems unreal, being back in the country after adapting to the cold bustle of the city life. I'm..."

"-You're home..." smiled Bellissima.

"Yeah, you're right," Sadie agreed, soaking it in. "So how are things at work?"

"It's going well. Most of the people I work with are selfish idiots, doing everything but their job. The janitors and housekeepers do a hell of a job making the place look like a million bucks but in the heart of it all, hardly anyone cares who lives or dies. I thought I would be making the world a safer, healthier place."

"You sound like Lou Anna," joke Dria. "What's wrong? Isn't that what you're doing? - Making the world a safer place by keeping your patients healthier than they would be if they were all alone in their homes?"

"I think I am."

"-Corporate confusion, that's why I'm not in a rush to graduate," said Sadie.

"Oh, being a professional student isn't a job?" teased Dria.

Sadie rolled her eyes. "Shut up, Dria," she replied- hitting her in the face with a pecan husk.

"I mean, I'm doing my part but sometimes I feel like I'm the only one doing my part. Pennycress is just a building full of white coats that pride themselves on cutting corners and accumulating vacation time. I feel like everything I do is undone, overshadowed by their negligence, laziness, and lack of bedside manner. I'm a small ripple in a sea of slackers."

"Lissima, you're a caring person. You've always been sensitive to the needs of others. Your good deeds aren't going unnoticed and they're definitely appreciated. I just read about a poor old man who died at home alone in his recliner. The only reason his body was found was because people in the condominium started complaining about a foul smell. He'd been in a crap filled diaper for days before his ticker stopped ticking. The family that was supposed to be looking after him skipped town with his monthly benefit check. It's a shame. That could have easily been one of your patients, Lissima. Thank God your heart's so big."

"Dria's right, Lissima. I tend to put myself first. I've always envied your kindness," said Sadie.

"Well as long as we're being honest, I've always envied your legs," confessed Bellissima. The three of them laughed.

"-But seriously, remember that scripture Granny drilled in our heads; *'Let us not be weary in well doing,'* said Sadie.

"It's like Grandma Cat is right here in the room with us," said Dria pulling her blanket tighter. "I just got chills."

"You and me both," said Bellissima. "How's school, Sadie. You never skyped me back to let me know how your exam went. You better not tell me you scored any less than a perfect 100, we studied for hours."

Dria's face sank. "Skype? You guys skype each other?" She asked.

Bellissima and Sadie exchanged glances. "Well...yeah," answered Sadie.

Dria turned to Bellissima. "How often?" she asked, clearly bothered by the fact that her two cousins, secretly, talked outside of their family email chain.

Bellissima cleared her throat. "Not much," she lied, looking down.

Dria switched her focus to Sadie, who had no problem telling the ugly truth. "-At least three, four times a week. We video chat with Mama too; and Auntie Lou and sometimes Auntie Kay when she's not tied up at the restaurant," she answered.

There was an awkward lull and since Bellissima didn't know what to say, she simply turned to Sadie and repeated the same question. "So... school? How's it going?"

"School is good. I'm learning a lot about myself since I switched my major. By the time graduation comes, I'll be ready to hit the ground running. Lately, I've been getting serious about my future."

"-Future? That's the first time I've ever heard you use that word. Vodka, one-night-stand, keg- these are words I'm used to hearing you say," poked Dria.

"Actually, I've been scaling back. I haven't been partying as much lately."

"Yeah right!" doubted Dria.

"No, seriously. I've been engrossed in personal growth," defended Sadie.

"-Growth?"

Sadie appeared frustrated by Dria's cynicism. Bellissima backed Sadie's optimism. "Well, I think that's great. You're growing up and we're proud of you. In fact, pour us another shot, Dria! We'll drink to our baby cousin's coming of maturity!"

Sadie quickly excused herself from the circle. "I'll have mine later. I need to pee."

Once Sadie was out of sight, Bellissima nudged Dria's arm hard. "Ouch, what the hell!" gasped Dria.

"Stop bullying Sadie! You should be happy she's taking her life more seriously, not giving her a hard time about it!"

"I was just kidding."

"Yeah, well she's obviously bothered by it. You should be more supportive."

"You're right. I'm sorry. It's just hard to be more supportive of her life when I'm barely a part of her life. It's not like I'm ever invited to Skype with her…or you," mumbled Dria- morosely.

"Yeah. I know. About that…" started Bellissima.

Dria interrupted. "It's okay, Lissima. I know we've grown apart. But…" Dria clearly had more to say but stopped.

"-But what? But what, Dria? You always stop and leave me without answers! Why don't you ever say what you need to say? What happened that night? Why did you do that to me? After Cheniere died, you were all I had! We were so close and then you just changed! Whenever I ask you right out about it, you shut down or stumble around like you still don't know how to talk to me! You're not allowed to pretend to be hurt about us being strangers if you don't love me enough to tell me why that night ended with Grandma Cat picking bits of gravel out of my bloody feet with tweezers! The sticker bushes left cuts on my face and thorns embedded so deep that my whole body turned red from the swelling. And you! You didn't smile for months, you wouldn't even look at me! Can't you see how not talking about it has torn us apart?"

"I know I hurt you, Lissima!" Dria was suddenly breathing harder. "It happened for reasons you don't understand right now but I've had years to work on healing. I'm still a work in progress but I'm ready to unravel the past! I'm ready for us to be like we used to be!"

"Then talk! I'm waiting," demanded Bellissima.

Before Dria could explain, they heard Sadie's footsteps. Before she re-entered the den, Dria leaned in and whispered. "I promise I will. Just not now, okay?"

"Fine."

Bellissima put on a collected face. "Hey, I thought you fell in or forgot where the bathroom was," she joked to mask the uncomfortable tautness.

"No, just not feeling well," Sadie replied.

"There's some ginger in the Kitchen. I can get Mama to make you a tonic," offered Bellissima.

"You need some bismuth? I keep some in my purse. I never leave home without it," said Dria searching her bag.

"No. Thanks though. Probably just queasy from traveling. I just need some rest."

"You know the first to fall asleep gets a permanent marker to the face," said Dria with a sneaky smirk.

"I'm a light sleeper," replied Sadie with an equally sneaky grin. "Don't let the bedbugs bite ladies," she said shutting off the light.

CHAPTER FOUR

Barely awake, Sadie's stomach rumbled. *Morning already? Hungry again?* She thought- perversely annoyed by the reality of both natural realizations. She yawned big and stretched, following the sound of her mother and aunts cackling like hens in the kitchen.

"Well good morning sleepy head," greeted Kay- Kissing Sadie on the forehead and handing her an empty mug. "The coffee's fresh. You hungry?"

"Starving! I could eat a horse, hooves and all."

"We're fresh out of horse, but I got some swine I could fry up for you."

"Bacon? Yes, please. I'd love some, Auntie Kay."

"You still like it extra crispy and blackened, damn near burnt?"

Sadie smiled. It had been a long time since anyone offered to make her breakfast. Most of Sadie's dorm guest were men who left long before the sun came up after they'd borrowed her body for the night. The warm thoughtfulness reminded Sadie that being home meant being loved. "Yes mam, extra crispy."

"Coming right up," said Kay smiling back.

Sadie took a seat at the table. "Good morning Mama, Aunt Lou Anna."

"How'd you sleep?" asked Minxy, licking her finger and wiping stray mascara from Sadie's face. "-Stop squirming," she nagged.

"I slept like a rock. How is it that Grandma Cat's floor is more comfortable than my bed in the dorms? Could you pass the tea, Aunt Lou? I'm trying to cut down on my caffeine intake."

Lou Anna passed the tea and sugar. "Floor or bed, the Beaumonte' ancestors will rock you right into a coma-like trance. Being home will have you sleeping like a baby." Sadie's cup slipped out of her grasp and spilled. Lou Anna eyed her nervy behavior. "You okay, Sadie?" she asked. Minxy

37

looked up from her oatmeal, waiting for Sadie to answer Lou Anna's question.

"Yes. Like a baby…I slept," Sadie replied. "That's the best kind of sleep…the baby kind." Sadie could feel the heat of their stares. "How's that bacon coming," she asked- purposely transferring everyone's attention back to breakfast.

"Almost crunchy! Just gotta save the fat and it's all yours," replied Kay.

"I can't believe you still collect fat drippings," said Lou Anna disgusted; watching Kay carefully dangle the skillet over a blue glass decanter.

Sadie noticed two jars of oil on the kitchen counter. "You saved all that oil from meat?" she asked in awe.

"No child, only this half of jar. This teal mason jar is blessed olive oil. It's one of my deaconess duties- making sure to meet with the assistant pastor down in the olive oil field every month and gather pure oil for healings and blessings. That's the only way to make sure it's undiluted, find a planter with a green thumb and a healthy prayer life. I'd heard about the olives but never believe it until I saw it with my own two eyes, an olive field flourishing in Louisiana. Who'd of thought? We just don't have the right weather or soil for it to bring forth olives year-round, but the crop just keeps on giving. I just about called everyone in the whole church a liar, but it's true. You can walk right up and pick an olive yourself if your heart desires. We go out and collect them ourselves and they're turned into to oil. We use the oil when we're helping the Reverend in the prayer line."

"Kay, you didn't tell me you joined the deacon board. Mama must be tickled pink?" said Lou Anna.

"Storing blessed oil, I understand that; But why do you save meat grease?" asked Sadie, innocently curious.

"It's an old tradition that stuck with your Auntie, unfortunately. You can use it for just about anything," answered Minxy.

"Oh yes! You want good cornbread? Line the pan with bacon fat before you pop into the oven. Folks at the restaurant keep asking, What's my secret? How do I give my food that smokey kick, that keeps them coming back for more? I never tell, though. Just another one of Catherine Beaumonte's best kept kitchen secrets. Mama kept an old tin can right next to the stove. Whenever she cooked, she'd strain all the charred parts out until the oil was golden brown. She'd use that fat for everything: Greasing pans, squeaky door hinges, ashy elbows…"

"-Widening tight shoes," interrupted Minxy- smiling at Lou Anna who was frowning. Kay and Minxy laughed riotously.

"That's not funny, Minx!" barked Lou Anna.

"Widening shoes?" questioned Sadie- her face puzzled.

"I had chubby feet when I was growing up. There weren't wide shoes back when I was a kid. I'd always complain my penny loafers were too tight. Instead of buying me bigger shoes, Catherine just slicked my feet with the fat," explained Lou Anna. "Every day, my feet would sweat and kids at school made pig noises whenever I walked down the hall." Kay and Minxy laughed even harder. "THAT'S NOT FUNNY! You two didn't have to burden that ridicule! You wore my hand-me-downs! The pig smell was long gone by the time they fit you two!"

"Whose horse playing in the kitchen now?" asked Dria- shuffling in, wiping her eyes. "What's so funny?"

"Your mother's pig feet," answered Minxy.

Dria heard it all before. "Again, with the sweaty, grease feet? Mama, you've got to let that go," she said Kissing Kay and Minxy before joining them at the table.

"Good morning to you, too," hissed Lou Anna, secretly jealous that her own daughter didn't have an extra kiss to spare.

"What are you hungry for?" asked Kay.

"I'd love some fluffy, buttermilk pancakes; but I'm sure Grandma Cat doesn't buy premixed batter or microwavable waffles," answered Dria.

Kay clutched her chest. "Premixed batter? Microwavable? What's this you talking about?"

"The city ruins children," muttered Minxy- sipping her coffee.

"That would have killed Catherine for sure," said Lou Anna shaking her head disappointed.

"Dria, we have all the ingredients right here in this kitchen to make our own pancake batter from scratch."

"-Batter from scratch? Sounds like a lot of work," Dria complained.

"It's not. Come over here, stand next to your Auntie Kay. I'll show you how."

"Yes Mam," said Dria joining her favorite Aunt at the stove.

"Oh! My! God!" yelled Bellissima stomping into the kitchen- frantic. "I overslept! Why didn't anybody wake me?" Everyone stopped and stared, their eyes wide. Minxy's lips pursed to keep from laughing out loud. "It's after 9 o'clock! Didn't one of you hear my alarm go off?" The whole family stood still. No one said a word. Bellissima scanned the kitchen, surveying their blank faces. "Hello!!! Earth to family! Did anyone think to wake the nurse?"

The corners of Kay's mouth began to curl into chiseled dimples. She quickly covered her lips with her hand to hide her apparent amusement. "We're so sorry sweetheart. You were sleeping so soundly, we didn't want to wake you."

"-Soundly indeed," teased Lou Anna.

"-Sweet! Thoughtful! But now I won't be on time to make my morning rounds! I wanted to get a jump start on the day so I could find time to visit with Grandma Cat!" whined Bellissima- tripping over her pant leg as she struggled to get dressed. Still, they stared. "What's wrong with all of you!"

"-Nothing," answered Sadie- grinning.

Kay grabbed a brown paper bag off the counter. "I made your breakfast to-go; French toast with powdered sugar and blueberry syrup on the side. It's still warm."

"Thanks, Mama. I'll see you all later. We can start planning Grandma Cat's birthday dinner when I get off. Gotta go, bye. I love you all!"

"We're not going to let her leave the house with her face looking like that, are we? We should stop her, right?" asked Minxy feeling a tad guilty.

Everyone looked at Kay, thinking surely, she'd stop her own daughter from making a fool of herself. "What? Bellissima obviously fell asleep first. Beaumonte' tradition says she gets a permanent marker to the face. All is fair in sleepover war," replied Kay winking at Sadie.

"What can I say, I'm a light sleeper," bragged Sadie with a shrug. "Dria helped, she did the whiskers."

•

Bellissima strolled into Pennycress with her mouth still full of breakfast. She hadn't finished chewing before she approached the nurses' station nearest the main entrance. "Hey Jan, sorry I'm late. It's been a rough morning. You see my clipboard back there?"

"-Rough morning? Rough night, too- apparently."

"Huh?"

"Your face looks like an etch-a-sketch! Did you party like it's 1999 with a bunch of bored pre-teens?" Asked Jan- mercifully sliding a compact mirror across the counter.

Bellissima opened it and was immediately mortified. "No, just two very bored and childish adults."

"The shower room is empty, you should go get cleaned up before someone mistakes you for a homeless party clown. I'll make your rounds this morning while you pull yourself together and please go see about your grandmother. I heard she gave the graveyard shift a pretty hard time. One of our seasoned, most dedicated nurses threatened to resign after spending only twenty minutes alone with her."

Bellissima slowed as she neared Catherine's room. She could hear her Grandmother singing through a crack in the door. *"…No fame or fortune, no riches untold. I'd rather have Jesus than silver and gold,"* She sang with an opened bible and untainted white handkerchief across her lap."

Bellissima tapped lightly before entering. "Good morning, Granny."

Catherine smiled. "My sweet Lissima, is that you? What on earth are you doing in this hell hole?"

"I work here. Don't you remember?"

"Oh yes, that's right. Well, I wasn't expecting company. If I'd known you were stopping by, I would've put my face on. Where's my make-up bag? Hand me my comb."

"No, you don't need make-up. I'm no celebrity, you don't have to impress me. You're beautiful without all that manufactured mess. That's what you always tell us, right? I won't be long, I just thought I'd stop in and see how you're doing; maybe visit with you for a minute. You got time?"

"Sweetheart, my schedule is wide open," replied Catherine. "Hop on in this bed next to your Grandma. I'll play in that pretty hair of yours." Bellissima kicked off her shoes and snuggled next to Catherine. "You know, Kay knew she had something special baking in her belly when she discovered she was with child, well with children- on the count of there being two baby girls in her oven. When she said to me, *'Mama, these little ones are going to be great little people. They'll change the world,'* I believed her. I felt that same way about all three of my pregnancies. Every mother thinks their child is different, more special than the rest. But we Beaumonte' women, we don't think. We know. You'll know that joy one day, don't be in a hurry though," warned Catherine kissing Bellissima's head. "The love, it starts the very moment you feel something's stirring in your lower parts. It's just a little tickle at first, like a butterfly wing trembling right underneath your breasts. Then it's a bigger tickle, like a thousand of those butterflies swarming in the pit of your stomach. Don't get me started on your heart, you're feeling all sorts of things. It's an excitingly scary experience. You feel such hopeful things."

'With your eldest aunt, Lou Anna- I woke up one morning and all I could think about were wild strawberries. I got up on a Friday morning and left walking- didn't stop until I reached the Tripper Patch. It was a stretch of Strawberry patches back then. It's long gone now, but back then the ground had been fruitful, and they were the biggest, sweetest berries in all Louisiana. It was owned by a sweet old married couple named Mr. Louis and Mrs. Anna Tripper. I sat down smack dab in the middle of a plump patch and started eating. Imagine the look on your Grandfather's face when he came looking for me. *'Cat, have you gone mad? - Trespassing and stealing?'* I just laughed, perfectly content with my hands full of berries, nightgown stained blood red. *'You're going to be a daddy,'-* I told him. Jeremiah didn't believe me right off. *'You haven't seen a doctor yet, Cat. How can you possibly know that?'* But I didn't need some doctor to help me realize the blessing in my own body. Jeremiah offered to pay the old couple for the fruit I'd helped myself to without asking, but they didn't take any money. The old farmer looked down at me and then over at his wife and then at Jeremiah. *'My wife stole a whole pound of grapes when she found out* we were with child. Put your money away, it's no good here. Just promise you'll bring the baby by once she makes her grand entrance.' He said. They sent us away with a whole basket full of free berries. Unfortunately, they passed away before Lou Anna was born, first, the farmer and then his wife died of a broken heart shortly after. It was Jeremiah's idea to name her after them, for their kindness. I wondered how they knew I'd be having a girl."

Catherine sighed. "Lou Anna, my little girl with the healing hands. She couldn't have been more than nine years old when the mail carrier fell out on the porch at the big house. Lou Anna and I were hanging laundry on the clothes line when we heard him collapse. We didn't know it then, but he was having a seizure. Hell, the way he was flopping around, I thought he was possessed or something. I was afraid but not your Aunt Lou. One second, Lou Anna was at my side with her arm full of wet clothes and the next she was gone- weaving through the sheets bellowing off the line. I ran after her as fast I could, but I was weeks away from giving birth to Kay. I waddled but couldn't keep up. By the time I got to the front steps, Lou Anna had turned him onto his side, loosened his tie to get the pressure off his neck and propped his carrier bad underneath his head- tilting it slightly to the side to keep him from choking on his own vomit. I remember she was counting. *'Forty-one, forty-two, forty-three.'* I was out of breath and scared, but Lou Anna was very much in control of the situation. She looked me dead in the eye- *'Mama, stay back. If his arms start to flail again he could hit your tummy and hurt my baby sister. Get the phone. Call for help. Forty-nine. Fifty. Fifty-one....'*

I sat back and watched Lou Anna keep him stable. Help arrived, and the paramedics approached Lou Anna. *'Can you tell me what happened here, little lady?'*

Lou Anna looked up at me. *'It's alright, tell the nice man what you did.'* I encouraged proudly.

'He fell down and started to shake. He couldn't breathe so, I turned his head and cleared the liquid from his throat. There's a little bump on his head, in the back. It's bleeding. He must have hit it when he fell.'

'That's mighty impressive little one! You did a good thing here today, helping him. How long do you think he was shaking for?'

'Eighty-nine seconds, give or take a second or two- I counted.'

I'd never been so proud. Lou Anna told me she wanted to be a doctor when she grew up. She said she wanted to heal people's bodies. Jeremiah promised Lou Anna he'd buy her the best education we could afford without starving if she kept her grades up. Thank God, she earned herself a scholarship because we damn sure wouldn't have been able to send her to that fancy college in the city without some kind of financial assistance. And as promised, Lou Anna studied allopathic medicine. It seemed her future would be bright. Things didn't get rocky until she came home for the holidays, her first year. I sent Lou Anna out to the market to pick up a few things. She came back with more than just groceries. Some drifter came back with her, hanging on her dress hem."

"-Drifter?" asked Bellissima- suddenly more attentive.

"Yeah, some raggedy wanderer she'd met. She let him follow her back to the big house, like a dog. Jeremiah and I stood side by side on the porch. Your grandfather never said much. He was a man of action, but when he spoke it was always something wise. '*This ain't good. I can feel it*'- he mumbled that day. That vagabond, he tipped his hat and introduced himself but for the life of me, I can't remember his name. He said his folks lived up state somewhere. I remember he shook your grandfather's hand. '*Can he stay for dinner?*' Asked Lou Anna. My stomach just about turned inside out. Jeremiah's jaw tensed up the way it did whenever something made him angry. I heard his teeth grinding. This man was at least twice Lou Anna's age and I knew her daddy didn't like it one bit, but Lou was of age to make her own decisions, fancy whatever man she wanted. Even though we didn't like it, we allowed him into our home. What harm could one dinner do? Lord help us if we'd only known." Catherine stopped stroking Bellissima's hair and her voice was suddenly grave. "We were so sure he was just a phase; that Lou would go back to school and he'd drift on to another town to charm another sweet girl, leave our perfect angel alone. Lou Anna was a little more impressionable than I thought. That dirty stranger started twisting my little girl's mind. She became obsessed with sacrilegious homeopathic remedies and dark holistic healing. Lou Anna stopped reading her textbooks altogether and when she'd come home, she'd run off for hours with him collecting strange herbs and seeds. When Jeremiah and I found a book of voodoo in our home, we sat Lou down and demanded answers. Turns out that drifter was some self-proclaimed medicine man, roaming the world claiming to heal folks; but really just preying on sick people that would give all they had if it meant they'd get better. He'd been persuading Lou to drop out of school and join him on the road to help him con and swindle- all the while puffing some Haitian hallucination dust in her face. Lou claimed it sent her on spiritual journeys to the spirit realm. He promised her it would open her mind to the secrets of inner healing, make her one with the Voodoo deities who walk alongside the devil. I smacked Lou Anna silly. *'But me and my household, we shall serve the Lord! I will not have this! - Gambling with the one soul God gave you!'* Jeremiah and I preached until we were blue in the face, but she was turning into someone we didn't know anymore. Lou Anna came home from school every chance she got to be with that weirdo, dancing around fire and chanting spells. At some point, their relationship became romantic. Lou got knocked up."

"Dria…"

"Yes, our first out-of-wedlock grandchild. Lou was so scared to tell us. Hell, we were disappointed to hear it, but God doesn't make mistakes-especially when it comes to creating life. That scoundrel unloaded his juices in my child and then left her without a penny. She came crawling back to her daddy on her hands and knees. Lou Anna promised Jeremiah she'd go back to school as soon as Dria stopped breastfeeding. She promised to find a cheap apartment in the city for her and Dria to live while school was in session and she'd come home during spring break and summer time. Jeremiah made peace with it. That's when he found that small plot of land a few miles from the big house. He wanted Lou Anna to feel like she had some privacy, let her come into her own as a mother. He built the cottage before little Dria came along and made Lou Anna promise that no one specific person in this family would ever own it. It would be open for you all to dwell indefinitely if any of you ever found yourselves out on the street. *'I hate that old brown.'* That was Lou Anna's only complaint- the color of the wood. Other than that, she was overjoyed and doing well in school again. She was finally back on track. My granddaughter was born healthy, and the mysterious drifter was gone. Until he wasn't."

"-He came back?"

"Snakes always come back, Lissima. You never got to meet your Grandfather, neither did Cheniere or Sadie but if you had- he would have spoiled you rotten just like he spoiled baby Dria. Her memory of him may be vague but they were inseparable. She'd scream her little head off until Jeremiah picked her up and screamed even louder if he tried to put her down. When he died, I cleaved to Dria. Being around my granddaughter made me miss Jeremiah a little less. I was ecstatic when summer came. One summer day, I got up early and went to Mipsy's to stock up on junk food for my little grandbaby. I grabbed a few toys while I was at it- an orange teddy bear. I tied your grandfather's pocket watch to the little bear's paw. The ticking helped Dria to fall asleep. Lou Anna was dedicated to her internship at the County hospital and she'd found a daycare for Dria, one where she could learn and play with other children. I thought I'd go over to the cottage, let myself in and drop off some things while I was there. I walked in and everything changed in an awful way. The cottage was dim. I shut the door and headed for the kitchen to put the groceries away, but I stopped. I thought I heard Dria, cooing. I tried to convince myself I was hearing things. It didn't make sense, Dria was supposed to be at daycare. I heard someone stirring. It was obvious that I wasn't alone in the cottage. Someone else was there. I tip-toed, following the noise. That's when I found them, that wayward drifter and my grandchild. Dria was naked, playing with her toys. He was watching her in a way that made my blood boil and my insides churn. Then I noticed his hands in his pants, fiddling with his male parts for pleasure. I remember clutching my chest. There was a sharpness that came out of nowhere and I felt like I was about to die. I must've screamed because I remember him jumping out of his chair and I must've frightened Dria because she shrieked. I ran to my grandchild and I scooped her up in my arms. *'What are you doing to her, you devil!'* I yelled. I was trembling and Dria was so afraid, but I couldn't stop yelling. Of course, he started talking fast trying to explain what I'd walked in on. He claimed it was some bare bottom potty training method, tried to convince me that he wasn't a pervert, but I know what I saw. There was something horrible going on. I wrapped Dria in a blanket and sped back to the big house. Your mother, Kay, was pregnant with you and Cheniere. She was sitting, resting her swollen feet when I rushed in carrying Dria. She jumped up. *'Mama! What's wrong?'* I was weak, damn near falling over. *'Check her!'* I yelled. Kay looked at Minxy and then back at me. *'Check her? Mama, I don't know what you mean.'* I kept on yelling. *'Check her! I can't* bear to look myself. Look between your niece's legs and tell me if anything's torn up! Is she bleeding? Has she been touched?' Minxy knocked the books off the den table and laid little Dria down. She took a deep breath and opened Dria's legs- examined her. 'She's alright Mama. She's okay down there.' Dria was still screaming. Kay took Dria in her arms and immediately she began to settle down. Minxy helped me off the floor and once I could catch my breath, I told them what I saw.

Lou came running in a few hours later, frantic. She found us all in the den, waiting for her. Kay was still rocking Dria. 'Oh, thank goodness! I got home and couldn't find my baby!' I was worried sick!' Said Lou Anna, reaching out for Dria. Kay pulled away, hugging Dria even closer. 'What are you doing? Give me my baby, Kay.' She demanded. Kay refused. Lou Anna turned to me. 'Mama, tell Kay to give me my child!' Before I knew it, I'd jumped off the sofa and slapped Lou Anna across the face. 'Worried sick? You can't be! Not when you let what is sick into your home, near your daughter!'

'He was only babysitting, Mama. I was going to tell you, but I knew you'd overreact! He's just passing through, on his way to New Orleans! He's going to heal the sick at Bayou St. John. He wanted to apologize for leaving so abruptly, but he had to. He wanted to see his child, spend time with his daughter for a few days. That is all. We lost daddy; can't you see how important it is for Dria to have a father?"

"Only Jesus heals the sick and doctors who pray!" sassed Minxy

Lou Anna told Minxy to shut up and mind her own business and God help me, I slapped Lou Anna again. "Was he just babysitting, Lou? Or was he getting his perverted fix making your child model naked for him? Or was that just him healing her? Tell me, has he been laying his healing hands on her? You have been living dangerously in a fool's paradise. You have been laying up with the devil! Have you forgotten how much younger you are than him? You were a late bloomer, Lou! You still had chunky cheeks and feet, Lou! When he sniffed you out, you were damn near pre-pubescent! More child than woman!"

I dragged Lou Anna out onto the porch and tried to reason with her, but she snatched Dria up and left. She changed the cottage locks and filed paperwork down at the court house for complete ownership of the cottage. That's why Lou Anna had the power to sign the cottage over to you. She didn't talk to us again until Kay went into labor with you and your sister.

Thank God for that day. Our family was complete again, mended in perfect peace. Lou Anna and I talked about the episode. She begged your aunts and me for forgiveness. She was thinking more clearly, praying to the right and only God in heaven again. I made Lou promise me to never let him near Dria again. We went on with our lives the Beaumonte' way, with our heads held high, stronger by our discord. We thought we'd never be plagued by that sick bastard again. It took him over a decade to show his ugly face again"

"He came back again, even after Aunt Lou said he wouldn't?"

"What did I tell you before, Lissima? Snakes always come back."

"Aunt Lou Anna went back on her word?"

"Heaven's no! It was Dria who let him back into all of our lives to do even more damage!"

Bellissima was confused. "But…why would Dria do that?"

"Lord, Child the things you don't know are going to change you forever," Said Catherine kissing Bellissima's cheek. "The more Lou thought about it, the guiltier she felt for leaving her toddler with that monster. She needed security, a way to feel safe again. She needed something in writing. He had no home so that meant no address, but Lou Anna did track down his parents and had the Marshall serve a restraining order. Lou nearly chewed her nails off, worried he'd retaliate by fighting for his parental rights?"

"It's not like he ever lifted a finger to support Dria in any way. What rights did he have?" asked Bellissima.

"In my eyes, none. Dria was Lou Anna's child and her child only. By law, he had the right to fight for his day in court and demand to see Dria, but he never reacted legally. For years, it was quiet. I don't know how old Dria was when it started, but he must've laid in wait for Lou Anna to leave Dria home alone at the cottage one day. He knocked, told Dria who he was and that she had to keep him coming to see her a secret. Dria was just an impressionable child that wanted to know who her daddy was. She didn't tell Lou that he started coming around, but Dria started changing after a while. She was ashamed of her breasts and when her period came, she cried for days. She was cagy and didn't like people touching her. None of us knew it was him that was doing it. Then, when Dria was almost 16 and you were…"

"I was 13…" finished Bellissima.

"Yes, you were. You were supposed to be spending the night with Dria at the cottage, but you showed up back at the big house all alone. You'd walked from the cottage by yourself; through the corn fields, through the woods in the dark. Night clouds hid the moon- that's a whole different kind of darkness. You had thorns stuck in your arms, sticker buds in your legs and feet. Do you remember what you said?"

"A man showed up and Dria kicked me out. She yelled at me. She told me she hated hanging out with me and then she pushed me. She made me leave," answered Bellissima.

"Yes, those were your words. Minxy jumped on your daddy's tractor and sped to the cottage but it was too late. He was gone. The damage had been done. Dria's precious virtue became a blemish that would never escape her memory. Dria wasn't Dria anymore."

"What had been done?" asked Bellissima, slowly understanding the things Catherine wouldn't say outright.

"You need to know, Lissima. Dria was only trying to protect you."

"What does that mean? Protect me from what?"

Catherine continued, unpeeling the painful recollection, carefully so that Bellissima could grasp the severity of the ordeal. "It had been going on so long that Dria barely even flinched when I asked her if it happened. Dria barely blinked when she offered up the filthy details. It was like she checked out of life so that she'd feel less of his hands on her body. I washed Dria and she stayed at the big house that night. She wouldn't let no one besides me and Kay touch her. Minxy was too full of rage to keep from badgering the child. When she was tired of answering questions, she simply took her hands and covered both ears- poor sweet child. Lou Anna got word and rushed to her child's side but she didn't know what to say once she was there. She just kept crying and crying. Dria didn't know how to tell you what had happened to her and how sorry she was. You were far too green and confused. Maybe she didn't tell you anything to preserve what wide eyed innocence you had left. Dria waited until you and Sadie were asleep, and she curled up next to you. I'd gone upstairs to pray, but then I got up off my knees when Don came knocking."

"Who's Don?"

"You've met him dozens of times, you were just young, so your memory is vague. He's an old friend of your Auntie Lou; smart little tart he is. Don started out small and humble, keeping books at the law office down by the railroad tracks. Now, his name is the biggest name on the sign outside that firm. He grew up with my daughters. I worried about my girls hanging out with boys, but I never had to worry about Don on the count of him liking boys. He still handles all our family affairs to this very day. His own blood treated him like trash because he was different, but Jeremiah and I had more than enough room in our hearts for him. Hell, we had tried for a boy three times and ended up with all girls. It was nice having him around. Don was always over at the big house spreading androgynous joy, but that night was different. He came knocking with fury riddled all over his face. I smelled the seething anger when I came downstairs and found him huddled with my daughters, whispering. *'Are you sure it was him?'* asked Kay. *'I'm certain! I was in the office late locking up when he walked right past me- heading to the tracks. He must be waiting to jump the stagecoach out of town. We ain't got much time.'* Urged Don. *'You sure you want to come along for this, Lou? Believe me, I won't try and change your mind if you're sure,'* said Minxy. *'Get daddy's slugger,'* cried Lou. *'Where ya'll going with that?'* I asked. They all looked at each other but neither of them answered me. *'Keep an eye on the girls for us, won't you?'* asked Kay.

It was almost dawn when the four of them made it back to the big house. Kay rushed to the sink and scrubbed her hands 'til they were damn near raw. Then she started making breakfast. *'I'm going to fry some eggs up with some smoked cheddar- won't take long at all. I'll mix the girls some oatmeal. Made some mayhaw jelly, it's good on wheat bread.'* Minxy set Jeremiah's slugger back on the mantle after wiping it with an ammonia drenched rag. Then, she poured herself a drink. Lou Anna kissed Dria's head and snuggled up with you kids on the floor. I looked Don in the eye and he looked back at me with not one ounce of regret. *'We were all at the office tonight, Mrs. Catherine. We had business matters to discuss concerning your husband's land and such. If anybody were to ask you where we all were, that's where you should say.'* I nodded. *'Go on in the kitchen and get washed up. Kay's gon' feed you,'* I said. Don hugged me, and we never spoke of that night again.

"Dria's father...I could never remember his name, but he was from up state. A little town called Alexandria. Lou Anna learned to hate that town and hate the name she chose for her daughter. *'It's just Dria'*- she'd say. Catherine stared into space, catatonic again. Did I ever tell you about the day the bridge burned?"

"No," lied Bellissima- bracing herself to hear the same old sad song and dance.

"Loving a man will kill you! Before your Grandfather died on that bridge, he killed me softly- first with his love and then by taking it away! Everyone had a reason why they were on the bridge, none of them good enough to gamble their life."

"I'm curious Grandma. I've always been curious. Bridges don't spontaneously combust. What happened Grandma? What or who started the fire?"

"After it happened, people came up with all sorts of stories about what *really* happened. I've heard it all, everything from the practical and possible to the supernatural and scientifically implausible. The most inventive tall tale is the one of the woman with the broken heart. Some say if you go to the bridge ruins at sunset you can see her dark figure there crying with a box of wet matches in her hand and a barrel of gasoline at her feet. They say her spirit stands there striking wet matches, sobbing even harder after those wet matches won't strike."

"They think a woman burned down old US 90?"

"Some people do. You see, there was a low life by the name of Dougie; a fast-talking self-proclaimed entrepreneur. He was nothing but a scheming opportunist if you ask me, as dishonest and conniving as the days are hot in the South. When the bridge construction started, Dougie ran down to city hall and bought a slowly receding islet that sat smack dab in the middle of the river between the Texas and Louisiana. People thought he was crazy for working so hard to own a piece of land with so little value and potential, but that sly Dougie had himself a devious plan. He told the people in town that he planned to open a bait shop only reachable by boat. That got the peoples' attention for sure, saying how the state's promise to bring more job opportunities to Louisiana was more than likely a hollow offer. Dougie prophesied that Louisiana would give all the new jobs to

Texans once the bridge was built. That was enough to rile people up, get them to sign his petition for a ferry to load near both ends of the bridge and let him also purchase an acre at both ends of the bridge for parking. He promised that his business would help his people and his people only-fellow Louisiana natives."

"A bait shop in the middle of a river. That kind of sounds like a good plan. I mean, folks in both Louisiana and Texas do a lot of fishing in that river. People from all over come down here to noodle catfish with their bare hands and drift through our swamps to get up close and personal with the gators. Lots of restaurants in the south make a living off seafood. Mama's always complaining about how much it costs to keep the restaurant stocked with crawfish when it's crawfish season, but it pays off big. She could take steak and pork off her menu altogether and stay afloat on just seafood alone if she wanted too. Sounds like a solid business plan if you ask me," said Bellissima.

Catherine laughed. "A bait shop was never Dougie's plan. Folks here started noticing strange exotic women walking around town with Dougie and one of them had loose lips. She confessed to one of the handsome husbands in town that she was a working girl and Dougie was her pimp. Dougie was building a whore house right underneath everyone's nose. Wives were furious. They cornered Dougie and ripped that ferry petition to pieces. That wasn't enough to stall his operation. He cleared trees near the base of the bridge on each side with his own tractor and paid off the right people so that cars could park at the base of both bridges without a parking lot as long as they didn't block the permitted bridge traffic. Dougie hired men who'd work for pennies and free trim from his whores to run boats; picking up customers, rowing them to his juke joint to get their fix and dropping them off again."

"What does this have to do with the bridge burning down?" asked Bellissima.

"It's the tall tale about the lady and the matches; the ghost of the arsonist scorned wife they say haunts the ruins. They say she discovered that her husband was a regular at Dougie's spot. He had a favorite whore name Cayenne- a hot immigrant that was paid well to do all the things that his wife felt she didn't have to do after she got her husband to put a ring on her finger. The angry wife allegedly confronted Cayenne and asked her nicely to stop having sex with her husband. When the whore Cayenne refused, the wife was paddled back to shore where she took a barrel full of flammable fluid out of her car, dragged it up on the bridge and started pouring from one end to the other."

"That bridge was over a mile long. You telling me nobody noticed a woman dragging a big barrel over a mile-long bridge?"

"They say plenty people saw her, but nobody stopped her. Maybe they didn't get close enough to her to smell what it was she was soaking the bridge with. Maybe they saw her and decided whatever she was doing was none of their business. Maybe they saw all her tears and stayed away so that they wouldn't have to lend an ear to her problems; you know how insensitive people can be. They say once the entire bridge was soaked, she stood at the middle of it looking down at the whore house. She struck a match and the bridge lit up. She didn't run away. She sat down and let the flames eat her skin- killing herself along with all the others. She blamed the bridge for opening Pandora's box. Flaming wood fell on the club and the fire spread. They say everyone in Dougie's place who tried to swim back to land drowned from either exhaustion or pieces of the bridge falling on top of them, sinking them under. Imagine how stupid we all felt when that bridge came down. We were so excited about it being built. It was all the rave, all people cared to talk about. A quicker route from Louisiana to Texas! We thought our little town had arrived! We were going to be somebodies! People would know about us and see that we were more than dirt famers and culturally mixed people that made good Cajun food and threw pretty beads from colorful Mardi Gras floats. We were foolish. We didn't know the bridge would kill half our town's people."

CHAPTER FIVE

Stir-crazy, Dria roamed the big house; rediscovering mementos of her childhood as if seeing them for the first time. She ripped the curtains opened wide to let the sunshine in and then coughed uncontrollably as the dust escaped the drape's beading. Before wiping the windows clean, Dria used her finger to write- *Sadie's a bedwetter* but doubled back to wipe it away after remembering Bellissima's bullying homily.

The banister still felt loose from all the straddled sliding they'd done as children. Dria wiggled the newel back and forth before venturing upstairs, slowly, to admire the heirlooms on display in the stairwell. The room nearest the stairwell landing once belonged to Lou Anna. The door read- *Lou Anna's Lounge*, in faded periwinkle paint. Dria peeled at the decorative golden star stickers stuck to the framing. "Adhesives? I guess she wasn't always a mulish buzz kill." Inside, there were loads boxes, taped up and neatly labeled. So many that her mother's old room looked more like a storage unit than a bedroom. Dria would never admit it but she felt a tiny bit of admiration as she idolized Lou Anna's scholastic memorabilia. It was no secret; Lou Anna had been an exceptional student, but there were more awards than Dria could count. There was a small shelf set aside from Lou Anna's things, reserved for Dria. Everything from her baby teeth to her first macaroni dinosaur. A big smile stretched across Dria's face. There it was, underneath Dria's first report card, her senior yearbook. "Good 'ol adolescents…"

Dria fingered though the senior section until she reached familiar faces from her graduating class. She held the book close, staring at a photo of her former self. "My teeth! What was Lou Anna thinking, bolting those damn braces on me? -High School superficial syndrome," she whispered to herself, shaking her head at her own ignorance. Even with a mouth full of metal, Dria was still the most beautiful prom queen in E.K Cal High history.

She flipped several more pages and paused. Down in the lower left corner, was a picture with a metallic heart drawn around it. Colin Hardy. Dria could barely catch her breath. Before a tear could fall from her sorrow filled eyes, Dria slammed the yearbook shut and put it away.

The shady turf underneath Grandma Cat's prized oak tree had always been Sadie's favorite hideaway. She'd spent many evenings there as a child, soul searching. Countless conversations took place there, in its umbral solitude. Was it praying out loud to God or talking to herself? Sadie could never decide. Either way, she always left feeling better about life.

"It's nice out today, isn't it?" asked Kay.

"Yes mam, sure is," replied Sadie. "I've missed the humidity. It gets so cold in the city."

"It's past noon. I thought I'd bring you a little snack. Is fresh grapefruit ok?" asked Kay holding out a saucer with the fruit sliced straight down the middle.

"That sounds great! You read my mind. Thank you!"

Kay chuckled. "Your mind? No, I think I read your belly," she whispered with a guileful grin.

Sadie paused, unsure of what to say next. "What do you mean?" she stammered.

"I brought you a little salt. I had a feeling you might like a little salt on your fruit. Am I wrong?"

"-Salted fruit? How'd you figure that?"

"It's something your mother used to do when she was pregnant with you. Yes, Minxy salted everything, especially watermelon. History has a way of repeating itself." Sadie was still holding her breath, wondering if there was still a way to hide her secret. Kay sat on the tree root beside Sadie. "So, what's it going to be? Salt or no salt? Truth or are you going to waste your time lying to me?"

Sadie sighed and took the saltshaker from her aunt's hand. "Maybe just a sprinkle."

"Strange craving isn't it?"

"I used to love sweet things. Now sweet things aren't complete without salt or cayenne pepper. And if I eat something sweet, like ice cream or sorbet, I have to chase it with something greasy and unreasonably unhealthy. Ever since this parasite started putting its lunch order in, I have no control over my stomach or my taste buds. God forbid I eat outside its comfort zone. Then comes the nausea, constipation…"

"Me, your mother, your Auntie Lou; we've all experienced what you're going through. Women all over the world know what you're going through. I have some special recipes down at the restaurant for expecting mothers. No matter how outlandishly disgusting their cravings are, I deliver," said Kay consoling her worried niece. "How far along are you, Child?"

"-Four and a half months."

Kay gasped. "What? I would have guessed four days! You're not showing at all!"

"Thank Goodness for good Beaumonte' genes. No one can tell, yet."

"We Beaumonte' ladies carry our baby weight in all the right places," joked Kay with a playful shove. "How long are you planning to hide this? – That was going to be my first question but *Why* are you hiding this? – I think that's a more important question." Sadie hesitated, but Kay continued. "No, don't worry about answering that right now. Chances are you're not ready to give your answer yet, but you better figure it all out soon. Don't matter how good your genes are, that baby won't stay a *little* secret forever."

"Are you going to tell Mama?" asked Sadie.

"It's not my place to tell Minxy she's going to be a grandma. I'll keep quiet as long as you promise to tell her soon and stay healthy. I'm here if you need anything."

"Thank you, Auntie Kay," said Sadie Solemnly.

Kay reached out, wrapping Sadie in her arms. "Oh dear, don't look so sad. This is a good thing, you'll see. I know you're unsure about a lot of things right now, but the good book says lean not to your own understanding. Sometimes we waste so much energy panicking about problems we never even bothered to pray about and Got the nerve to expect God to fix what we haven't left on the alter. If you spend that time praying about what's troubling you- the solution, the resolution, or the lesson will be revealed, no panic required."

"It feels good to talk to someone about it. I love my mama but I'm not sure a friend is what I need right now. I need a mother, someone who can help me become a mother. Minxy Beaumonte' has been a party pal all my life. Now, she's out of the country mothering strangers in refugee camps. You've always been the easiest to talk to. Thank you for picking up her slack all these years, Auntie Kay."

"Oh sweetie, we all fall short sometimes. That's life. Minxy's your mother. I know growing up with her as your legal guardian was like a long playdate, but I think she'll surprise you if you give her a chance. Minxy has a way of stepping up to the plate when things get real. She's got a lot of wisdom to pass down. With Catherine as her mother, there's no way she didn't inherit a little of her loving care. Now you just stop worrying and enjoy your fruit. Sit out here and collect yourself before you come back inside. And if you really want to thank me, do so by finding a better name than parasite for your baby," said Kay walking away.

"One more thing, Auntie Kay. How'd you figure it out?"

Kay laughed. "I kissed your forehead this morning, my love. You're warm, but not fever warm. A women's body picks up a few degrees when she's baking something in her oven, that's what Southern folks say. It must be true. None of us were ever able to hide our pregnancies from Catherine. Also, your skin feels like silk and your breasts look filled up. That's good Beaumonte' genes."

Minxy watched Kay and Sadie from the kitchen window where she stood at the sink washing dishes. Back when the girls were younger, Lou Anna was the one they turned to whenever they needed help with homework or studying for a test. Minxy, of course, was the one they went to whenever they needed an alibi to skip school, stay up late or boy advice. Kay, she was they only one they talked to about the things that truly mattered: their feelings and their fears. Minxy covertly envied Kay for that reason.

"Look at those two out there, thick as thieves," said Lou Anna joining Minxy near the sink. "Isn't it nice having the family here all at once?"

"It sure is, considering," answered Minxy.

"Yes, considering the circumstances," finished Lou Anna. "I'm not surprised to see Sadie out back. She and Lissima- they loved being outdoors. Dria, on the other hand, I had to force her to put the books away."

"Undying dedication to her work- a trait she inherited from you no doubt."

"I hate it when you're right, Minxy."

"I know it," replied Minxy with a grin.

"How long they been out there?" asked Lou Anna, watching Kay and Sadie talk.

"-Not sure, a half hour maybe."

"I wonder what they're talking about. Don't you?" asked Lou Anna studying Minxy's reaction out of the corner of her eye.

"No, I don't wonder. Kay is Sadie's Aunt. Kay's family. Whatever they discuss, it's still under the confidentiality of the family. She's not seeking guidance from anyone who'll steer her wrong. What's there to wonder?"

"Nothing, just thought maybe you should join them. I mean, you and Sadie have been apart for some time now, with you hopping from one Third World country to the next. Sadie's your kid. She should be talking to you, confiding in you, coming to you for solitude."

It suddenly occurred to Minxy that Lou Anna shared the same jealousy; Kay being closer to the girls. "Even with all your fancy clothes and jewels, you're so transparent," muttered Minxy.

"Me? Transparent? - How so?"

Minxy snatched the rubber gloves off and slammed them on the kitchen counter. "Lou Anna, Sadie and I talk. And not just about fun and partying. We talk about real things too, sometimes. Even if we talked once a month, we'd still have a better relationship than you and Dria. Keeping in touch with your daughter via email is sterile affection, Lou Anna. Yes, Sadie and I laugh and joke around our issues. Yes, we used to get high and drunk together but at least I don't treat my daughter like she's a business correspondent just because…"

"-Just because what?" asked Lou Anna defensively.

Minxy stopped. "I'm sorry. I shouldn't have taken it there." Minxy turned to leave the kitchen but turned back. "You know, glass houses Lou Anna. Glass houses…"

"What's that supposed to mean?"

"Back when Sadie was little, and she got in trouble at school for fighting and feared she would get expelled; she went to Kay. She knew she could trust Kay to stay calm, figure out how to make things right. Kay promised Sadie that she wouldn't tell me about it, because that's what Sadie needed to hear but Kay came to me and told me all about it because Kay understood that I was still Sadie's mother. I never told Sadie that Kay told me. There was no need. The problem was fixed, I was in the know and Sadie continued to trust her Aunt. At least Kay didn't keep me in the dark like you're doing her."

"I don't know what you're talking about," lied Lou Anna.

"The last time we were all together was 4 years ago, but you saw Bellissima last year, didn't you?" Lou Anna looked away. "You slipped up, Lou. If you insist on keeping that away from Kay, you're going to have to be more careful. When it all falls apart, she's going to want to know why you two worked so hard to keep that away from her. And then, Kay will wonder why you didn't respect her enough to tell her what's going on with her kid. She's still Bellissima's mother and you're hiding something serious. I can feel it in my bones. Now..... that's something to wonder about."

CHAPTER SIX

"Drawing on my face! What are you, a kindergartner?" yelled Bellissima storming into the big house. The entire family was out back, all except for Dria who burst into laughter at the very sight of Bellissima entering the kitchen.

"You know you still have a little marker residue on your nose?"

"What? I could have sworn I got it all off! You mean to tell me I've been walking around like this all afternoon?"

"Yes, and that makes it even funnier!" said Dria, laughing even harder, so hard she had to catch her breath.

"Which one of you did it? Tell me right now and my revenge will be sorted accordingly! Don't tell me and you both will feel my wrath!"

"You know I can't tell you that, Beaumonte' rules. Not our fault you fell asleep first," said Dria wetting a paper towel, scrubbing at the remaining marker above Bellissima's upper lip.

"Yeah, yeah, yeah- Beaumonte' rules."

Dria stopped rubbing. "I give up. It's going to take a few washes to get that off or maybe some nail polish remover. Come, help me with the marshmallows and gram crackers. Everyone's waiting outside. We lit the fire pit."

"The pit hasn't been lit in years. I'm surprised it still holds a flame."

"We weren't sure if it would, but I'm glad it does. I haven't had a s'more in years."

"Yeah, me neither. I stopped doing a lot of things when you and Sadie went away," said Bellissima turning away.

"You okay?" asked Dria.

"No, I mean yes," answered Bellissima.

Dria was confused. "Well, which is it? Are you okay, or aren't you?"

Bellissima leaned in. "I sat with Granny for a while today. She was quite the chatterbox. She started talking about our moms and the bridge, again."

"-That's nothing new," shrugged Dria.

"It's odd; the things she said. Catherine was rather specific and more in detail about things we've wondered about our whole lives. I don't know how; but she's recollecting things from our past that I never knew happened, truths that we were never granted."

"-But how? She has a medical condition that makes that impossible."

"I know but it's happening." Bellissima paused. "I think if I let her talk long enough, Granny Cat might even accidentally tell us who our fathers are." The tray fell from Dria's hands and she quickly knelt to pick it up. Bellissima eyed Dria's sudden nervous disposition. "Are *you* alright?"

"Yes. I'm fine," she answered casually dismissing Bellissima's concern. "I think it's great, having all our dark places lit up. It would be nice to fill in all the holes our mothers left, But *I* don't need to know anything about *my* father. I gave up on that. I hope you and Sadie get the answers you need, but I'm just fine living with my question marks. So, there's really no need to ask her about my father."

"You're not even a little curious anymore?"

"No. I know enough. He was a man from Alexandria. That's enough for me," lied Dria, reloading the tray. "Let's go make smores!"

"Lissima! How great to see your face!" teased Kay.

"Very funny mother! I can't believe you'd let your own daughter walk out into the world looking like an idiot!" Bellissima reproached

"I tried to get them to turn you around, baby doll. Come, sit by your Auntie Minx," coaxed Minxy.

"Gladly!" pouted Bellissima- sticking her tongue out at the others before joining the circle around the fire. "Pass me a roasting stick."

"Did Grandma Cat have any pretzels?" asked Sadie.

"Yep, pass this bag down to Sadie," said Dria.

"What about the jalapenos?" asked Sadie, causing everyone to scrunch their noses.

"Yeah, I brought some out- even though I have no idea what place they have on a s'more," answered Dria.

Everyone stared at Sadie. Kay could tell that Sadie was getting a bit uncomfortable with so many eyes on her; as if they could see straight through to the secret growing in her womb. Sadie had no response to explain the peculiar pregnancy craving. "I've heard of that. It's a West Coast city thing- jalapeno honey smores on pretzels. I read about it in…. a new cuisine magazine I subscribed to. You know, I'm always looking for the latest food trend. Bellissima's always telling me to think outside Southern dining," said Kay

"Pretzel jalapeno honey butter smores is a new thing?" asked Lou Anna.

"Yes. In fact, we should all taste it."

"You want us all to eat our marshmallows on salty pretzels instead of sweet gram crackers- the way the good Lord intended?" Asked Bellissima.

"Yeah. I was thinking about featuring it at the restaurant. Sadie thought it would be a great idea to get you guys' opinion on it first. Right Sadie?" asked Kay.

"Yeah, that's the grand plan," stuttered Sadie.

"I'm always open to trying new things…" hesitated Dria. "Why not?"

Everyone hovered their sticks over the blaze. "So, did you old ladies decide on any birthday plans for Grandma Cat's dinner?" teased Bellissima.

"Old is a state of mind and today my mind feels about 25. My body still feels young enough to kick your butt. -And No, we can't agree on anything. Lou wants a double-decker pecan pie instead of a traditional birthday cake," complained Kay. "Whoever heard of blowing out a birthday pie candle?"

"Well, Minxy wants barbecue and hot wings," said Lou Anna sucking her teeth.

"-And what's wrong with hot wings?" asked Minxy appalled.

"It's our Mother's 100th birthday celebration, not a frat party," said Lou Anna. "But that's still better than Kay's fondue idea."

"Yeah, fondue is fon-stupid," agreed Minxy. "There would be hot cheese and chocolate all over the place! We'd never get the big house clean again! Ant's will march in and carry the whole house off while we're sleeping!"

"At least I'm thinking outside the box!" yelled Kay.

"Hey! No hitting below the belt ladies! This is your Mama's birthday we're talking about! There are no bad ideas as long as you're all planning it together," said Sadie.

"I don't care what we have as long as we decide on something!" said Bellissima.

"Yeah," agreed Dria.

"Well, I'm glad you girls feel that way," said Minxy. "Because we <u>did</u> agree on one thing?"

"What's that?" asked Sadie- her mouth full of raw peppers.

"We decided that you girls would take on full responsibility for the entire dinner."

"What?" gasped Dria.

"That's right! Every time we get together, your Auntie Kay busts her hump making the menu and then she drags me and Lou in the kitchen where we're trapped for hours, slaving! The only pressure you girls endure is the tightening of your waistbands after you're all stuffed! This time, we're going to be the ungrateful little pigs!"

"That's not fair!" shouted Dria.

"Is too fair!" replied Lou Anna. "Your Auntie Minx is right. It wouldn't hurt for you three to get back to your roots; learn how a proper household is kept. I may not have stressed the importance of homemaking when you were growing up, but it's never too late to learn how to make rice and gravy."

Bellissima began to pout. "Mama, is this for real? I've been looking forward to your cooking," complained Bellissima.

"Don't you start with all that pouting, Bellissima Marie Beaumonte'. Now, you know my recipes like the back of your hand. If you do it right, you <u>will</u> be eating my food- right down to the very last ingredient. A hot kitchen will bring a family closer. You will burn a hand or both. You'll slice your fingers to the bone, wrap it in a dish towel and keep on pushing. At least one of your dishes will burn and you will have to start it all over. Cooking will humble you, oh yes. When everyone's sitting down; stuffing their faces with your hard work- you will know what honest fulfillment feels like and it will be worth it. I want you girls to sit down tonight and write up a menu. Each of you should have an opinion and each opinion should be heard, no matter how ridiculous it is. There are three of you. You'll vote on what dish makes the cut and which ones don't."

"-But Mama, tomorrow's my day off! I'd like to sleep in and plus, I have no clothes here!" argued Bellissima, recycling last night's excuse.

"Me and Sadie planned to go see Grandma Cat tomorrow!" said Dria

"Don't worry Lissima, I went over to the cottage today and grabbed you some pajamas and a dress. You can thank me later. Your aunts and I are going to visit with Catherine tomorrow after church, we're hoping to butter her up with news of all her grandchildren cooking for her. That way she'll be more compliant and willing to talk seriously about her future. You girls can see her day after tomorrow. I want you girls to get up bright and early and head to Mipsy's grocery. Pick up everything you need for the dinner, early, before you miss out on all the fresh produce."

"-But the dinner is days away! Can't we just get the stuff we need the day before?" demurred Sadie.

"Mipsy's gets a fresh shipment tonight, that means all the best ingredients will be out tomorrow morning. They won't get another fresh delivery before Catherine's birthday. You want to eat what folks have already touched, picked over and put their germs on? Buy what's not yet ripe and set it in the window seal. The sun will have it ready by the time you're ready to cook it. Get the meats home, season 'em with a dry rub and then freeze 'em. You won't need to defrost and marinate until 18-16 hours before you cook. Lissima, you know how it's done. You'll show your cousins."

"Okay fine, but who's cooking for us tonight?" asked Sadie.

"Not us, we have plans," said Lou Anna.

"Plans?" asked Dria in disbelief.

"Yes, we're going out to the casino. You girls can feed yourselves," confirmed Kay. "We want you all asleep at a decent time tonight. After you return from the market tomorrow, we have church."

"You're making us go to church too?" asked Dria. "Well that's just great!" she whined sarcastically.

Bellissima turned to Minxy as if to say- *help me get out of this.* "Don't you go giving me puppy dog eyes. That won't work this time. You heard what your Aunt and Mama said. Missing church for work is one thing but you said it yourself- you're off tomorrow," said Minxy.

"Feels good calling shots, don't it Minx?" asked Lou Anna with a smirk.

"Sure does. We have spoken! Now let's try these s'mores, we gotta go get dolled up and hit the town Beaumonte' style!"

Everyone took a bite of their inventive smores and their faces went sour.

"Um...Kay?"

"Yeah, Lou?"

"Please don't make these for your restaurant."

Kay spat into her paper towel. "Okay. I won't."

Everyone stared at Sadie as she wolfed down her ill-flavored treat. "I think they're amazing. You don't like it? Pass it over here!"

CHAPTER SEVEN

"How's your peanut butter sandwich?" asked Dria, with her chest poked put proudly- as if making a sandwich was hard work.

"You mean the stale bread you smeared with a smidge of past expiration peanut-like spread? It sucked," Bellissima insulted.

"I have to agree with Bellissima," said Sadie- sucking her fingers clean.

"-But you finished your whole sandwich, Sadie." Snapped Dria- offended.

"Yeah, because there are too many kids out in the world starving to death for me to waste food, but it wasn't very good."

"Well Bellissima's the only one of us with real stovetop experience and she refused to cook! At least I stepped up and kept us from starving to death. You're welcome!"

"I can't do much with frozen meats. Mama didn't take out anything to thaw. There's nothing microwave friendly in there to heat up. You know Kay Beaumonte' doesn't allow any of that processed junk food in the house. I told you, we should have ordered out before everything closed, but no- you wanted to save the day. Had I known this sad sack of sandwich was your master plan, I would have just ordered a pizza behind your back."

"I can't believe they left us to fend for ourselves."

"Don't be so dramatic, Dria. You make it sound like they drenched us in pig's blood and left us out in the woods."

"-Same difference," mumbled Dria.

"Stop complaining, they deserve to step out and cut loose for a night. Neither of them has a social life. They never have fun. Even *my* mom is boring now; has been ever since she joined that addiction amends cult-like group of do-gooders," said Sadie.

"I can't believe Auntie Minx managed to stay clean this long. Not going to lie, I didn't think she could do it. How long have *you* been off cocaine?" asked Dria, bluntly- causing Sadie to look down, ashamed.

"Dria. Really?" said Bellissima; glaring at Dria with extreme consternation.

Sadie pretended that Dria's impassive approach to such a sensitive subject didn't bother her. "It's okay Lissima, You guys can ask all the questions you want. We are family. We can talk about it."

Still, Dria felt the need to apologize. "I'm sorry, Sadie. Sometimes I don't think before I speak. I'm so used to dealing with people on a professional level that I subtract emotion without trying. People are pieces of paper to me, but you *are* family and you don't deserve to have your feelings handled that way."

"It's okay." Sadie took a deep breath. "I suppose I owe *you* an explanation most of all, Dria. If it wasn't for that call you made to the dean on my behalf, I probably would've been kicked out after my second academic probation letter came. Auntie Lou Anna didn't have to pitch in after I lost my financial aid, but she did and I'm thankful. Court ordered substance abuse might be the best thing that happened to me. The counselors encourage us to talk about it, you know? No one starts off using a drug that powerful. Back when me and Mama used to prowl, all we needed was liquor, a little weed and maybe an ecstasy pill or two. Things changed when I got to college. No one tells you how dangerous leaving home can be; being around so many different people with so many different habits. I picked up a bad one. I was turned on to cocaine and he was my boyfriend. You know how it is when you first start dating someone, you want to spend every minute of every day with them. All I wanted to do was lay up in bed with cocaine up my nose. I wish I could blame it all on being a freshman but we all know I had problems long before that. I'm truly my mother's daughter.'

'It was my first year at the university. The city was so big and I was all alone on the West Coast. Bellissima, you were still doing your studies down here. Dria, you and Auntie Lou were on the East Coast flourishing. I was too proud to admit I was lonely. I felt like a small-town girl who wasn't going to make it on her own. I was happy when Mama got kicked out of her apartment again. I knew she'd rather die than run back to the South with her tail between her legs. To keep her from hopping to one homeless shelter to the next, I let her crash with me and my dorm mate. Her name was Lena, but everyone called her Lighter on the count of her always being high. I don't think I ever saw Lighter when she wasn't lit. She was a seasoned user, but I don't judge. Hell, I spend most my days hoping people don't judge me. I'd never met anyone like Lighter. She was the bold artistic type. Her unwillingness to conform was so sexy and beguiling. I'm not ashamed to say that on occasion I let her explore my body. Her biggest pet peeve was someone forcing their morals, concerning the body, on others. She did not like being told what to do. She would pull her breasts out for no reason at all. I mean, I'm sure there are some candid photos of my boobs online from a night out; but when I pull mine out, it's for a free drink or to defuse a brawl. Lighter would flash her knockers just because she was happy to have what she called- miraculous feeders, perfectly sculpted by mother nature. She was still a good person though. She welcomed Mama with opened arms. In return, Mama did Lighter's homework for her every night. Thanks to Mama, Lighter finally had passing grades. It was so much fun having her with us. She'd even cook gumbo on the hot plate I snuck in. We had the whole campus lined up for a bowl. After Aunt Lou Anna got wind of my first academic probation threat, she put the pressure on me to get good test scores. I was studying all day but still partying all night with Mama and Lighter. I tried to talk to Lighter about it- tell her that I should slow down. That's when Lighter turned us on to cocaine. *'Your problem isn't drugs, it's your choice of drug. You think marijuana's gon' keep you up and focused? You need energy drinks and Adderall and a few bumps, that way you can party all you want and still have the zeal you need during the day to function like a dedicated student.'* It was true, the old hooch and paper joint wasn't doing it for me anymore. Lighter gave me and Mama a small tiny plastic bag with a little powder in it. Before I took my first hit, I looked over at Mama, who looked more like one of my peers than a parent- wearing one my university sweaters and tight jeans. She looked nervous or anxious, like maybe she didn't want me to try it, but she didn't stop me. Even though she was apprehensive, Mama stuffed her nostril full of cocaine too. I'd never felt anything like it before. I wanted to marry it. I wanted to have sex with it. I wanted to get naked and rub it all over my body. It was like finding a new religion. We embarked on the journey together as mother and daughter, chasing the high. Me and Mama, we didn't use often. But when we did, we used hard. Trouble found us a few times, of course- but nothing too serious. Mostly we were just having fun. Men hit on both of us, saying there was no way Minxy the minx was old enough to be a mother and we'd drain their wallets at the bar buying bottles. We belonged to the night. Nothing mattered. No place mattered. People didn't matter; not even you guys- our own family. You never crossed our minds when we were high, not once.'

'This one time, we got in from a long night of revelry. The sun was just about to come up. Somehow, we'd all gotten separated at the club the night before. Only me and Mama made it back to the campus. Lighter and I had class, but she was absent all day. I got back to the dorm and asked Mama if she'd seen Lighter, but she said no. Me and Mama didn't use that night, we didn't drink either. We just stayed up playing cards for jelly beans. When I finally fell asleep, Mama stayed up and typed Lighter's midterm paper. She printed it out and laid a copy on Lighter's pillow before curling up next to me in my twin sized bed.'

'Lighter wasn't in any of her classes the next day either. She wasn't in the library. None of her stoner friends had seen her. Then I saw the post. It was all over social media. Lighter had mixed way too many drugs and started bleeding on the brain. She fainted and never woke up. Years of drug use had finally caught with her. When I found out she'd died, I went wild. I partied for days in her honor. I quit going to my classes. Hell, I stopped going back to my dorm. I just slept wherever I passed out.'

'A few days later, the sorority hosted a big bash. I was the drunken main attraction, giving free lap dances; taking sips out of stranger's cups and smoking whatever I could find. Mama came out of nowhere. I hadn't invited her; I don't even know how she knew where to find me. Partygoers parted like the red sea as Minxy Beaumonte' made her way to the table I was twerking on. '*Sadie! Get down from there!*' Minxy yelled. 'It's cool guys, she's my mom but she's cool. Somebody get my hot mom a Moscow Mule! She loves those!' The crowd went wilder. They thought that was so cool, my mom being my wing woman and all. I kept on dancing, even sluttier. '*Sadie, I said get down!*' I could tell from her tone she was serious. Minxy Beaumonte' pulled me off that table, covered me in a jacket and dragged me outside. '*No more. That's enough. I want you to be alive, to live. You are my child. I've been failing you, but I'm awake now. It could have been you! Sweet Jesus! It could have easily been you!'* She wasn't making any sense or maybe she was making perfect sense, I couldn't tell because I was hammered. Mama took care of me. She took me back to my dorm, cleaned me up and tucked me in. For days I fought off withdrawal, throwing up and shaking. I begged for it. I begged for the drugs on my knees, but Minxy stayed strong for us both. She spoke very few words while I was coming down from the bender. Mama emailed my teachers, told them I was under the weather, that I was having a hard time coping with Lena's death and she kept up with all my classes online for me. When I was better, Mama left me. She didn't say goodbye, just left me letter scribbled on the back of an old party flier. Minxy Beaumonte' disappeared. I didn't hear from her for about two weeks, which was unusual; because she always called- even when she was on a bender. She made sure she called so we could say our prayers over the phone together before bed like when I was a kid and she left me here with Grandma or Auntie Kay. Two weeks flew by. By then, she was in Africa. She'd joined some group that goes on dangerous excursions, volunteering to help sick and enslaved people to have a better life. It's the way they made things right with God for wasting their gifts- whatever that meant. It's a horrible thing to admit but I was hoping Mama had safely relapsed and she'd be coming back to me, so we could still party and she could still be my best friend. *Safely relapsed-* I hear myself saying it and I realize how out of my mind I was. Mama made me promise to join a program and I did. It took me a little longer than expected but I finally kicked the cocaine and pills. I still drink but hell I had to pick a battle I could win. It's going to take years to undo a childhood of alcohol dependency, but I definitely slowed down on the drinking. Mama probably exposed me to alcohol when I was still in the womb. My amniotic fluid was probably 90% vodka. At least I can handle the liquor. I know I've had enough when my stomach starts to burn. The other stuff we were using, that's the stuff that keeps you from knowing when you've had enough because enough is never enough. Addictions are very needy habits. That's the fine print."

"I know you still party and drink, but you're off the hard stuff, right? How long have you been clean, truly? We won't judge you?" questioned Dria.

"Only two months. I listened to addicts tell their horror stories in the group and I was going through the motions, but I honestly didn't even *try* to quit until four months ago. I slipped up two months in and went wild for 24 hours, but I haven't used since then. That's the truth! I swear! Sometimes I sit back and wonder, what would Minxy's followers think if they knew her only daughter became an irresponsible drunk and junkie just to bond with her?"

"So, what happened four months ago that made you want to try?" asked Bellissima. "Addicts always talk about experiencing a wake-up call or some sort of epiphany or rock bottom."

Sadie squirmed. "I just felt the sudden urge to be a better person. I wanted to treat my body better. I stumbled only two months in, what does that say about me? Ain't I a weakling?"

"Don't feel bad because you colored out of the lines a little bit. A late start is better than no finish at all."

"-But what about all those other months, all the days I continued to pump poison into my body, not thinking twice about how I don't have extra organs on standby for when these give up on me? I lay awake and cry thinking about how rotted my insides must be."

"You're talking crazy. You're young. You'll heal. Our bodies are built to survive puerile stupidity. We were all baptized too, our Mama's gave us back to Jesus- just like all Southern mothers do. The Bible promises that we'll always find our way back to the throne no matter how lost we get," said Bellissima optimistically supportive.

"Yeah, I'll heal," Said Sadie. *But it's just not my health I'm worried about. What about my little baby's life?"* she thought to herself.

"Hey, let's play cards like we used to, "suggested Dria to lighten the mood.

Bellissima beamed. "I'll get the candy cigarettes and sunglasses. Beware of my poker face! My palms are itching!"

"What's the buy-in tonight ladies? Twenty gummy bears or twenty sour licorice sticks?" asked Dria, smiling at Sadie.

Sadie smiled back, "Licorice sticks- of course. And I'm dealing. Lissima starts cheating when she starts losing," she answered.

•

Kay Beaumonte' was a lady, from her voluminous perfectly pinned hair down to her perfectly pedicured feet. She was a selfless mother who loved unconditionally. She was an encouraging sister who was always ready to give support and a sturdy shoulder to lean on when times were tough. She was a devout Christian, slow to anger but quick to forgive. She was a moderately obedient daughter, a famed cook, and a beloved Aunt. Kay always smelled of vanilla extract, even when she was sweaty. Her ringlets never frizzed, no matter the weather and her lips had a natural cerise tint even without lipstick. If she was ever bloated or a few pounds overweight, no one could ever tell. Most of the time people were too busy being mesmerized by her fierce strut. Heads turned whenever Kay Beaumonte' and her sisters walked by men. Jealous eyes rolled whenever they strolled pass women. Neither distract a Beaumonte' woman- no they just keep walking without recognizing any obsequiousness or acrimonious shade.

Minxy peeked in on Kay as she dressed. "You look gorgeous," she complimented.

"Thank you, Minx. I should say the same, what a lovely sundress. Where did you buy it?" asked Kay with a smirk- knowing full well Minxy had borrowed it without asking.

"This old thing? Just something I picked up from the Kay collection," Joked Minxy. "I should have asked you first…"

"Don't be silly, we're sisters. You're the youngest. My hand-me-downs are your birthright, it's an unwritten rule. Besides, it's fitting you in a way it's never fit me before. It was obviously made for you. In sports, they retire a jersey after someone makes their mark wearing a certain number. Looking at you in that dress, fashion should retire the color red in your honor. That neckline requires something shiny; it'll draw attention to your collarbone and cleavage. Come over here and let me string a necklace on you." Minxy walked over and stood between Kay and Catherine's mahogany gaper. Kay rummaged through their mother's jewelry chest until she found the perfect piece. "Close your eyes." Minxy smiled and did so. "Okay, now open."

Minxy gasped, running her fingers along her bosom, in complete awe of Catherine's rose gold encrusted locket. The pyrite embellished crucifix at the center of the encasement sparkled. "It's so pretty! I've never seen anything like it! I've never seen Mama where this before!"

"Catherine wore it every day, just tucked under her blouse where no one could see it."

"Whose picture does she have locked inside?"

"Open it and see," urged Kay.

Minxy's eyes widened. "Is that daddy and Cheniere?"

"Yep, daddy couldn't have been more than 25 years old when this picture was taken. And that's Cheniere when she was in preschool, her very first day of big girl school."

"She looks just like…"

"-Like Bellissima? Well yeah, identical twins tend to favor," teased Kay sarcastically.

"No, I was going to say like you. Most times Bellissima and Cheniere were hard to tell apart but, in this picture, - Cheniere doesn't look like anyone but you. Her beautiful mother, Kay…my favorite sister."

Lou Anna barged in. "I put some coffee on to brew!" Minxy quickly clasped the locket shut. "I hope I'm not interrupting anything," said Lou Anna, smiling curiously at both her sisters.

"Not at all. I was just helping our baby sister get ready."

Lou Anna scanned Minxy from head to toe. "Wow! Look at you!" Lou Anna joined the two of them in the mirror. "What a beautiful necklace."

"This old thing?" jested Minxy with a sideways wink at Kay.

"Old? Maybe, but still amazing none-the-less. And that dress, you look fantastic. An amazing dress for an amazing woman."

Minxy wasn't used to getting compliments from Lou Anna. It was difficult to respond without a surprised expression. "Um…thanks."

"You still need earrings. Here, take mine," said Lou Anna pulling at her earlobes.

"Oh, no Lou. You don't have to do that," said Minxy, attempting to gracefully decline Lou Anna's generous offer.

"I insist, Minx. Please, I want you to have them. Besides, my hair looks better when I let it down. With no earrings, I'll need to cover my naked ears." Lou Anna kept one earring in her hand and gave the other to Kay. Kay clipped Minxy's left ear and Lou Anna clipped the right. All three sisters smiled and moved their faces closer together for a better look at their reflections. "See, picture perfect."

"The dress off my back…" said Kay.

"The bling off my ears…" added Lou Anna.

"Makes for the perfect picture…" finished Minxy.

"We should leave soon. I don't want us walking in late. Are the girls back from the market yet?" asked Kay.

Lou Anna snickered. "-Back from the market? Honey, they're not *back* from anywhere because they never got up yet."

"What?" squealed Kay.

"They're still sleeping down there, snoring like hogs. All three of 'em. Guess they're not taking, what could be their grandmother's last birthday, seriously."

"Oh, hell no, they're asses are mine!" declared Kay- storming downstairs.

"Don't say hell or ass, Kay! We're on our way to church!" shouted Minxy.

Kay marched into the den ranting. "Up! Get up! Get your lazy butts up right this instant!"

Dria, Bellissima, and Sadie stumbled to their feet- shaken by the hysterical yelling.

"We're up!"

"What's happening!"

"It wasn't me!" Bellissima screamed, out of habit- shaking the sleeping bag loose from around her ankle.

"Didn't I tell you girls last night to get up early and make a grocery run this morning?" Kay stood tapping her foot impatiently with her hands firmly on her hips. No one answered. "Well! Don't all speak up at once!" she shouted.

"Yes, mam. You told us to go to the market," answered Dria-ashamed.

"Then explain to me why the three of you are standing here with sweet dream slobber and sticky candy residue all over your faces?" Dria looked over at Bellissima and Sadie who were staring at the floor. "I'm waiting!"

Dria nudged Bellissima's arm. "Ouch! Jesus Dria! You trying to bruise me?"

"If your Grandmother was here and heard you taking the Lord's name in vain on a Sunday, she'd bruise your behind! I'm ten seconds from bruising all three of you! I told you to decide what we were serving for the birthday dinner!"

"We did, I swear!" lied Sadie. Dria and Bellissima's faces hardened, staring at Sadie.

"Shut up," mumbled Bellissima.

"Oh, you did?" asked Kay, pessimistically unconvinced. "Well hand it over. I'd like to take a look at it."

"Huh?" replied Sadie.

"You claim you decided on the spread. I can't wait to see the list. Hand it over."

Bellissima cleared her throat to fib some more. "We did. We just didn't get a chance to write it all down yet."

Kay could always tell when the girls weren't telling the truth. Dria sucked her bottom lip whenever she was being dishonest. Sadie nodded her head excessively when she wasn't telling the whole truth. Bellissima purposely avoided Kay's eyes whenever she was lying. Bellissima looked everywhere in the room except at her mother. Kay began to grin. "Okay, then tell it to me, right now! And don't you dare start whispering to each other, trying to get your story straight."

"What did we miss?" asked Minxy as she and Lou Anna as they joined the heated discussion taking place in the den.

"Our little liars were just about to tell me what's on the menu for Mama's dinner since they *didn't* just clown around all night long and sleep in all morning."

"Looks like we came down just in time. We'd like to hear that too," provoked Lou Anna- facetiously.

"Go on girls, we don't have all day," said kay- folding her arms impatiently.

"Cake or pie?" asked Lou Anna.

"And if cake, what kind of frosting, whipped or buttercream?" asked Minxy.

"Will we be serving dinner inside or outside? If outside, did you bother to inspect the big dinner table out in the shed to make sure termites haven't chewed it dust? Front yard or back? The backyard has the nicer shade tree, but the front yard makes for a shorter walk for our guests that don't get around to well without a cane, walker or wheelchair. Which of you is going to rake up all the leaves and twigs? We can't serve an outside dinner with a yard full of leaves," interrogated Minxy.

"What meat did you decide on? Beef? Turkey? Pork? Duck?" questioned Kay- frustrated.

"It wasn't my idea to play cards all night!" confessed Bellissima – tilting her head in Dria's direction.

"I hope you're not trying to be inconspicuous- tattle tell!" yelled Dria.

"Narc!" said Sadie- her insult disguised with a fake cough. "Sorry, the was some betrayal stuck in my throat."

"Alright just hush it! All of you!" screamed Lou Anna, with her finger pointed at them. "Kay was very clear, you girls had important matters to tend to, things to discuss and plan! We wouldn't tell you to make a plan if it wasn't important!"

"Look at you, standing here looking like three blind mice who got washed, wrung out, hung out to dry and then dragged back in by a filthy alley cat. Just a mess!" yelled Kay.

"The whole family is expected to attend the service today. Kay's leading the prayer line this Sunday. We've got to get there before everyone and press the choir robes. They're singing your Grandmother's favorite church hymn in honor of her upcoming birthday. You three will not make us late. We're heading to the church," said Minxy.

"Okay Good, we'll just stay here and rest up some more," suggested Sadie.

"You most certainly will not!" said Lou Anna. "Grab your purses and go the market like your Auntie Kay told you to! Now! Folks are gon' start showing up for service in about an hour and a half, so I expect to see you girls there in an hour and a half! No excuses!"

"Fine! We're going! I'll go change clothes," said Dria with an exhausted sigh, heading for the staircase.

"Change clothes? You don't have time to change clothes. If you'd gotten up on time, you would have time to gussy up. Grab your purses and go just how you are, in your pajamas," Said Minxy.

Dria stopped and studied Minxy's face as if she were waiting to detect humor but Minxy didn't crack a smile. Dria looked at her mother and then at Kay. "Auntie Minxy, you can't be serious. I'm wearing pajama pants with yellow rubber duckies on them. Bellissima has a bonnet on her head and Sadie's the worst! She's wearing her old Barbie doll nightgown from when she was eleven!"

"You're just mad cause it still fits," said Sadie with a satisfied sneer.

"Enough with the bickering! You heard your Auntie, now march!" demanded Kay.

"But mommy...my hair," Bellissima pouted.

"Don't even try it! You're not getting any sympathy from me," Kay replied.

Dria, Bellissima, and Sadie headed for the front door- huffing and puffing and rolling their eyes. "And don't roll your eyes!" shouted Kay smacking Bellissima's butt as she stomped out.

"No hitting!" Bellissima yelled back.

"You're my child! I'll hit you as much as I need to! One hour and 30 minutes! You better not be late! We want you on the front pew where we can see you!"

CHAPTER EIGHT

"Slow down! Wait up for me! Why are you walking so fast?" squawked Sadie trying to keep up with Dria and Bellissima as they power walked through the parking lot of Mipsy's grocery with their heads down.

"I don't know Sadie, maybe because we don't want people to know you're with us," mumbled Dria.

"-And why not?" asked Sadie- offended.

"Maybe because you're dressed like an elementary school stripper and people are rubbernecking," teased Bellissima- pulling at the hem of Sadie's Barbie nightgown as if that would somehow make it cover more of Sadie's thigh.

"Oh, am *I* the embarrassment? Maybe they're gawking at Dria's hideous pajamas or those nappy neck hairs hanging out of your bonnet!"

"Shut up Sadie!" barked Bellissima, pulling down the back of her satin hair cap.

Trying hard to hide their faces, the Beaumonte' granddaughters shuffled to the market entrance where Bellissima noticed an unattended child she recognized. "Gabby, sweetie what are you doing here all alone?"

It was little Gabriella Withers, great grandchild of the town clairvoyant turned psychopath. The child spun around and smiled at first but then quickly frowned. "Ms. Lissima, what's wrong with your hair? You sick or something?" she asked innocently.

Bellissima parted her lips to respond but stopped, cutting her eyes at Dria who'd burst into laughter. "Sick hair? This kid is hilarious and she's not even trying!"

Bellissima cleared her throat. "No, my hair isn't sick. It's just...ill-prepared for the day is all. Why are you standing out here by yourself?"

"I came to tape up these fliers I made. Captain Crisp hasn't been home in days. He's missing," said Gabby- showing Bellissima the stack of fliers.

"Who's Captain Crisp?" asked Sadie.

"It's her rabbit," answered Bellissima. "I'm so sorry to hear that. I'm sure he just lost his way home."

Sadie sucked her teeth and grunted. "Don't go telling this child lies, Lissima." Sadie knelt, grabbed little Gabby's shoulders and looked deep into her eyes. "Listen to me little one. This is the South, where critters eat critters. Captain Crisp is long gone by now, dead. But don't be sad. His little bunny body has been chewed up and eaten by some bigger, hungrier animal and now that animal is stronger from all the protein *your* plump pet provided. Your little guy gave his life so that another animal could live. That's what you call the circle of life. It's all in that documentary, The Lion King. It's the circle of life!"

Dria smacked Sadie on the back of the head. "You idiot! That wasn't a documentary it was a beautiful PG-13 classic about jealousy, revenge, hierarchy, and an orphaned exiled lion cub! How dare you!"

"Both of you! Shut it!" yelled Bellissima. "Sadie, you should never talk to kids. About anything. I can only imagine how creatively you'd describe the birds and the bees!" she scolded.

"Yeah, you're probably right," Sadie replied, stepping away.

Bellissima turned her attention back to Gabby. "Don't listen to them. We're going to church today. I'll ask Mama to say a special prayer for Captain Crisp. Now, I think you've taped enough fliers for now." Bellissima rummaged through her purse for loose change. "I want you to go on home. Take this dollar and stop at Mrs. Creasie's, it's on your route. Get a scoop of ice cream but then go straight home after that! No talking to strangers. If someone offers you a ride you pedal your bike faster and don't stop until you're at your front steps."

"Okay Ms. Lissima," she replied courteously but still sad.

"When you get home, you tell your mama Katina to stop letting you roam around town without a grown up to look after you! You're not molester bait!"

"What's molester bait?"

"Just say it to your Mama just the way I just said it to you. She'll know what it means. Now go on," ushered Bellissima.

The three of them watched as Gabby rode away on her bike with rainbow streamers. "Old Mrs. Creasie's still passing out treats to the neighborhood kids?" asked Sadie.

"Yeah. Poor old lady doesn't even leave the house anymore. She's a complete shut it. She barely opens her front door anymore. She serves the kids from her kitchen window. You know the saddest part? Before she gave up on the outside world, she started getting dressed for all the town events, but wouldn't physically attend them. She just sat on the porch all dressed up. Alone."

"I can't believe a mother would let a kid *that* cute out alone into the world *this* dangerous," said Dria shaking her head.

"I know. That's how kids end up on milk cartons," agreed Sadie. "Did you see how cute her little dress was?"

"Quit eyeing it Sadie, that's one you *can't* fit," joked Bellissima.

"We only have an hour and ten minutes left now. Mama says the meat anchors the entire meal, so I think we should start there," said Bellissima, taking charge.

Dria dug through the frozen meats, disappointed with the selection. "These pork chops are too small. They're mostly fat. We'd have to buy at least 50 packs to feed everyone."

"So, I guess Cornish hens are out of the question," Bellissima mumbled. "Look at the turkey selection. Why do they all look discolored? I've never seen meat turn this shade of grey. If our cooking made everyone sick, we'd never live it down."

"What about venison?" suggested Sadie, shivering.

Dria looked at Bellissima as if to rate her approval. "Venison? Deer? Lissima, what do you think? Should we feast on Bambi?"

Bellissima shrugged. "I've seen Mama prepare venison a hundred times and her recipes are bank. I'm sure we could pull it off as long as we follow the recipe step by step."

"It tastes great and it sounds fancy! Just put it in the basket! I'm freezing!" whined Sadie.

"Okay, we're eating the most majestic woodland creature in the forest. What's next?" rushed Dria, stacking cuts of deer in the cart.

"We still need an appetizer, a bread, a palette cleanser, side dishes, a birthday cake and an alternative dessert for those who don't want cake."

Dria sighed heavily. "Now I understand why Auntie Kay wanted us to do the stupid menu last night."

"I need a jacket!" yelled Sadie- causing even more people to glare.

"Pipe down! As if we're not already attracting enough unwanted attention! Go grab an arm caddy from the front by the register and load up on rice and seasonings!" ordered Bellissima.

"Is it warmer on the dry goods aisle?" asked Sadie with defiant attitude.

Bellissima massaged the base of her nose, frustrated. She huffed. "Yes! It's warmer there, Sadie!"

"Good!" Sadie replied, storming off.

"I bet you five bucks we find her on the candy aisle," said Dria to Bellissima.

"No thanks. I only make bets I know I'm going to win," Bellissima replied, calculating in the cost of the venison. "Let's focus. We're down to 59 minutes. Bread should be easy to decide on. Any suggestions?"

Dria thought hard. "What's the name of that bread we ate when I won the science fair trophy in middle school? Auntie Kay served it with a pancetta spread."

"Any excuse to bring up your awards, huh?"

Dria rolled her eyes. "Focus Lissima!"

"Okay. I remember it started with the letter *K*," replied Bellissima.

"Kifli!" shouted Dria. "It was toasted Kifli!"

"Yes! You're right!" Bellissima paused, "-But Mama made that bread from scratch."

"So, what? We'll buy the ingredients and make it from scratch too. You can do it. You can do anything," encouraged Dria with a soft smile. "Now think hard, when Auntie Kay prepares her venison dish, what does she serve with it?"

"Um… a hearty red wine gravy with fresh onions and a hint of blueberry. She'd lay it over a heap of pureed sweet potatoes. She tops it all off with some habanero mustard greens!" replied Bellissima excited.

"Okay! You go grab what we need to complete the main course and I'll go put in the order for Grandma Cat's cake," said Dria, headed for Mipsy's bakery counter.

"Wait! Get back here! We didn't decide on a cake flavor!" Bellissima shouted.

"I'll wing it!" Dria yelled back.

Bellissima stomped her feet. "That's not fair! You're just going to pick whatever flavor *you* want! It better not be marble!"

"I can't hear you, Lissima! 47 minutes left! You better get moving!"

Bellissima had a peculiar habit. She'd talk to herself, ask herself questions and turn right around and answer herself, whenever she felt overwhelmed or stressed. It was more of a nervous tick than a habit. Either way, onlookers eyed her funny whenever she did it. The only person who could ever understand Bellissima's muffled murmuring was Cheniere but only because she'd learned to read lips. *"Limes...peppermint- lime punch- Auntie Minxy's favorite. That's what we'll drink. We can serve it out of the big crystal punch bowl. I wonder if pecan crusted macaroni and cheese is too simple to serve as the appetizer? We can bake them in those little soufflé cups, serve 'em fresh out of the oven. But if they're too hot, someone could get burned."*

"-Lissima?"

Bellissima grabbed her bonnet and ducked. *"Damn it all to hell..."* she mumbled. *"If I don't turn around maybe they'll just walk away."*

"Bellissima Beaumonte', is that you?"

"Shit." Bellissima heaved and turned around slowly. "It was Colin, a local friend of the family. His family had been like family to the Beaumonte' clan, for decades. In fact, Colin's mother and Lou Anna were pregnant at the same time. Their due dates were so close that Dria and Colin were born only days apart. Naturally, they were each other's first love. *'They were written in the stars, destined to fall in love'*- Auntie Lou would say.

"Colin...Hey, how you are doing?" asked Bellissima, still partially hunched over.

"I'm doing alright," Colin replied, ogling at the repugnant bonnet on Bellissima's head. "You look...well." There was an obvious pause in the response just before the compliment. Clearly, she looked ridiculous; but Colin was raised right, well enough to always compliment a lady no matter how terrible she looked.

"Well thank you, Colin. I wouldn't normally leave the house looking like this...but we have Grandma Cat's dinner to prepare for. My cousins and I are doing all the cooking ourselves with no help from Mama..." explained Bellissima.

Colin was suddenly very anxious. "-Your cousins? Did you say, cousins? Dria? She's in town?"

"Yeah, Grandma Cat's getting worse. Sad to say, we may not get another birthday with her here on earth. We figured the whole family should be together before she goes. It's nice having everyone at the big house, under one roof again. Considering the circumstances…"

"Circumstances, right," nodded Colin. "-But Dria, she's really returned?" He asked again.

Bellissima's eyebrows raised as she answered. "Yes, Colin. Dria's returned. She's also in this store. All three of us came together this morning."

"What? Where?" He asked, looking to the left and right.

Bellissima grinned, "Right behind you, looking somehow delightfully surprised and scared shitless at the same time."

Colin spun around and found Dria standing there, frozen with the cake ticket shaking in her trembling hand. And even though Dria was severely underdressed in her unsightly nightwear, Colin melted at the very sight of his first love. "Dria…"

"Colin…" Dria's voice was suddenly weak as if saying Colin's name out loud exasperated all her energy at once.

CHAPTER NINE

"In every one of my prayers, I've begged to see your face again," whispered Colin, who secretly fought back tears he hid behind a mask of masculinity. Dria and Colin once wore matching promise rings, swearing they'd always belong to one another. She was his and he was hers. It had been that way until the night before Dria left for college. She never said why, but her and Colin stopped wearing their rings. Dria cried until her eyes just flat out refused to replenish tears. Lou Anna joked that she'd turned in to an emotionless zombie after Colin and even though the comparison was farfetched, Dria seemed to come to life seeing Colin again. *They were written in the stars, destined to be.'* But then something went terribly wrong. Something she refused to talk about.

The two of them froze, searching past one another's eyes and right into their souls. Both tried to speak but couldn't find the right words. "Alexandria Beaumonte' has returned to the South! Well, tie a ribbon around the old oak tree!" interrupted a voice coming from the canned goods.

Dria recognized the voice immediately, the face too. It was Emily Fuller- Dria's designated high school nemesis, now all grown up. Dria's nostrils flared red. Her top lip curled as Emily moved in closer. "It's just Dria..." Dria replied.

Emily laughed. "Oh, you're still doing that? I thought you would have outgrown that silly name thing by now," she teased. "It's so good to see you! We just stopped in to buy more grape juice for church communion."

"We?" questioned Dria.

Bellissima could almost hear Dria growling inside. She quickly dropped the onions in the cart and joined Dria's side, defensively. "You're name's Emily, right? Emily Fuller. I think I remember you. Weren't you that cheerleader who dressed up as a Ku Klux Klan leader that one Halloween and pissed of the whole state of Louisiana? You got suspended for that, didn't you? Your daddy used to run that clinic over on the other side of town before it got shut down on the cause of that big malpractice suit?"

Emily scowled, locking her eyes on Bellissima. "The costume? Yeah, that was me. This town has no sense of humor. Thank goodness my folks had friends in high places, am I right! And as far as my daddy's practice; it's still flourishing despite nasty, inaccurate town gossip. And by the way, It's Emily Hardy now." Colin looked away as Emily moved closer to his side, rubbing his arm and torso purposely over-affectionately.

Dria crumbled the ticket in her fist and the rims of her eyes began to fill. "You're a Hardy, now? That means…"

"Yes, Colin and I are married. Can you believe it!" bragged Emily flashing her wedding ring.

Dria stepped closer to Colin. "You married *her*?" she asked, aggressively. Colin lifted his head to answer but was lost in Dria's hurt-filled glower.

Annoyed by Emily's apparent ploy to rub the union in Dria's face, Bellissima moved in even closer to Emily. "So, let me get this straight. The blonde-haired, blue-eyed white girl who made a mockery of slavery married a black man?"

"-Love is blind?" answered Emily arrogantly.

"-Or is it ignorant?" asked Dria, with a brashness.

Bellissima looked down and noticed Dria's fist bawled tighter. "We'd love to stay and chat but we need to finish shopping for Grandma Cat's birthday dinner and get to church," said Bellissima- tugging Dria's arm. "Nice to see you, Colin."

Emily stopped them. "Was our invitation lost?" she asked.

"Excuse me?" Dria responded.

"Your grandmother Catherine was a great friend to the Hardy family. Just seems right that Colin and I would make the guest list."

"The Beaumonte' and Hardy families were good people to one another but you're not *really* a Hardy. Hardy by paper doesn't qualify," hissed Dria.

"I'd have to agree with my cousin on that one," finished Bellissima, turning to walk away again.

Emily continued. "Well, blood or paper- I'm Colin's permanent plus-one. What would your Granny think, you being so discourteous? Besides,

Ms. Kay hasn't replied to any of my emails. I'm beginning to think doesn't like money. The dinner would be a great time for us to talk face to face."

"What emails? What could you possibly have to talk to my mother about?" asked Bellissima.

"I've been emailing her about the property and the big house. I want to buy it."

"Like hell you will," said Dria- seething.

Colin tugged Emily's arm. "It's not proper to talk about land that belongs to a good woman who hasn't even passed away yet. Show some respect."

"Colin, can't you see I'm speaking?" Emily replied. "If *her* mother would've been kind enough to reply, I wouldn't have to bring it up in such an inconsiderate, taboo fashion. Each year your family sells an acre or two from the back of your property, so people can't tell your property lines are slowing depreciating. In a few years, you will have sold so much of your land you'll have no backyard. Isn't your family's private mausoleum a few miles behind the manor, deep in the brush? It'd be a shame if you were forced to sell to someone who wouldn't let you visit your fallen loved ones from time to time. You may as well sell the entire portion to one person, a person like me with a heart. I'll let you come on the property for mourning long after the sale is complete. It's the right thing to do."

Sadie emerged from the candy aisle with a mouth full of malted milk balls. "Hey, I got everything you told me to get. You two did your part?" She looked at Colin and Emily, clearly not impressed. "Who are these people?"

"That's Colin," answered Bellissima.

"And that's his Emily," answered Dria.

"You mean his wife," corrected Emily.

"Sounds better the other way if you ask me," said Bellissima. "She's also the woman trying to put a price on our childhood."

"Huh?" asked Sadie, popping more candy in her mouth.

"She's been trolling around, trying to get Mama to sell the big house, hounding her with emails," Bellissima explained.

Sadie's eyes widened, and she stared Emily down from head to toe. "She ain't dark enough to live on Beaumonte' land. We ain't selling you nothing. I'm sure Auntie Kay deletes them without even opening them-straight to the trash bin with trash." Sadie turned her attention to Colin, "We don't sell out as easy as most folks."

"We got church. We should go," said Dria, pulling Sadie.

"I hope you girls plan on changing first," yelled Emily with a pretentious, fake smirk. Sadie stuck her the middle finger without even turning back.

Bellissima started putting the groceries on the conveyor belt at the register. Dria leaned in. "Thank you for..." Dria struggled to find the words.

"Don't mention it. No one's a bitch to my big cousin, but me," smiled Bellissima.

Sadie's phone rang. She struggled to answer it, juggling her snacks. *"Hello. Yes, Mam. Yes, Mam. Yes, Mam. Okay! Yes, we're headed that way now!"* Sadie hung up and turned to her cousins. "Auntie Lou Anna said we better not be late and she asked us to grab the teal canteen with the blessed oil in it from the kitchen before we come, not the blue one. It must've slipped Auntie Kay's mind when she had to reprimand us this morning. And we should probably hurry. I lied and told her we were already dressed and walking out the door."

"Sadie!" gasped Bellissima.

"I'm sorry, I panic when one of them starts yelling!"

CHAPTER TEN

Bellissima barreled up the driveway, back to the big house. Dria hopped out before the car was parked. "You're not going to help us unload?" yelled Sadie, grabbing an arm full of grocery bags before jumping out of the passenger seat.

"No time! I have to look good!" shouted Dria dashing upstairs, two stairs at a time.

The girls rushed inside and frantically scattered in different directions; stuffing the food in the fridge then ransacking their luggage for something church- appropriate to wear. "If we're late, Mama will crucify us right next to Jesus on the cross they keep over the alter! Sadie, leave the shower running!" yelled Bellissima.

"No point! There's no more hot water!"

"Fine! I'll take a lukewarm whore bath in the sink; towel off my lowers and just shave from the knee down!" Bellissima huffed.

"We have 14 minutes!" Shouted Dria.

"What about my hair?" shrieked Bellissima.

"What about it?" asked Sadie, hoping out of the shower to share the sink where Bellissima was bathing to brush her teeth.

"What do mean? It's a mess! It looks like a heap of swamp moss!"

"It does not," assured Sadie, insouciantly.

"Are we looking at the same head of hair?"

Sadie sighed and slammed the toilet seat shut. "Sit down. I'll fix it."

"We don't have time to use the flat iron!"

"Who said anything about straightening? You don't need all that irreversible heat damage to look good," said Sadie- pulling a small label-less bottle from her toiletry bag. She squeezed a dab of crème' in her palm and fingered the sweet-smelling concoction through Bellissima's scalp.

Sadie used a wide-toothed comb to separate Bellissima's hair into smaller portions- twirling the strands around her knuckles a little at a time. "See, you look like you just left the salon."

Bellissima stood and looked in the mirror, speechless. "Wow! I don't think my natural hair has ever looked so good! What's in that bottle?"

"It's just a little something I mixed up in my dorm to help tame my roots. A spur of the moment quick fix that worked wonders for my edges and split ends. I needed something to do while I was detoxing. After experimenting with a few prototypes, I finally achieved the perfect blend, my very own conditioner."

"Where'd you learn how to do that?"

"It just came to me," shrugged Sadie.

"Well, I think it's amazing! People would kill for this product!"

Sadie hesitated. "That's what *I* was thinking. I was also thinking... why stay in school taking classes I know I'm never going to use when I could just stop going and pursue something I love. Like, making women feel beautiful."

Bellissima's face stiffened. "You want to quit college?"

"Yeah. I mean, you and Dria love what you do for a living. You feel real fulfillment. I bet you get all warm and fuzzy when you're helping to heal somebody. I get all warm and fuzzy inside when I think about making people feel good about themselves. I'd never encourage conceitedness, but we all have the right to feel confident. I don't want some mind-numbing career where I'm stuck just counting the days until retirement. I want the warm and fuzzy feeling, the feeling you feel when you stay with those people until they pass away, so they don't feel alone." Bellissima was quiet. Sadie looked down, discouraged. "You think it's stupid, huh?"

"You want to know what I think? Honestly?" asked Bellissima.

"Yes."

"I think you and I should talk; get a business plan together. I have some seed money stashed away. If you're serious about this, you're going to need an investor."

Sadie smiled and hugged her cousin tight. "Thank you, Bellissima. Are you going to rat me out?"

"No. It's *your* education. It's *your* life plan."

"- Had to double check...You were always such a tattle- tell."

Dria rushed in. "We don't have time for hugging and small talk! Sadie, why do you have on heels and a towel? Go put some clothes on! Bellissima, blot your lipstick! It's on too thick! Auntie Kay will send you straight to the bathroom to wash it off! Let's go! Move it! What are you sitting around staring at me for?"

"Damn Dria, you going to church or happy hour?" asked Sadie, snapping her fingers.

Bellissima blinked a few times as if to make certain she wasn't seeing a mirage. "You look runway ready. How the hell did you pull this look off in 8 minutes!"

"Do you usually get this fancy for Jesus?" asked Sadie with a sly glare.

"Stop asking stupid questions! If we're late, I'm blaming the two of you! I'll be in the car! Hurry up!" pressured Dria.

"Hold your horses! I won't be but just a minute!" huffed Bellissima pushing pass Dria with a hard shoulder bump.

"More pep in your step!" barked Dria.

"On your way down, could you please grab the blessed oil from the kitchen for Auntie Kay?" asked Sadie.

Dria rushed to the kitchen and went to the counter. "There are two bottles? Which one did she say to grab?" she yelled.

"…The blue one!" answered Sadie.

CHAPTER ELEVEN

Sunday service was about to commence. The Beaumonte' daughters stood outside the sanctuary doors, shaking hands and welcoming church attendees.

Kay looked down at her watch and then over at Minxy and Lou Anna whose faces were frowning. "Where the hell are they?" mumbled Kay, her lips barely moving like a ventriloquist to appear calm.

"Don't. Say. Hell," corrected Minxy again, crossing her heart.

"I hope Jesus doesn't mind scooting over a bit cause I'm going to kill them! And then hang them right up there next to him!" said Kay.

"Not if I get a hold of them first," Vowed Lou Anna.

No sooner than Lou Anna could finish her threat, Bellissima's car came speeding into the church parking lot. The three granddaughters stumbled out of the car and staggered up the stone steps, out of breath. "We're here! We made it!" wheezed Dria.

"Calm yourself! Steady your breathing before you have an asthma attack, today isn't about you! And don't expect a pat on the back, you're still late!" fussed Lou Anna.

"Yes! Late!" mumbled Kay, still waving. "Now get your butts inside! Front Pew! Before the preacher's welcome hymn is over, go and refill the prayer vial with the blessed oil. It's nearly empty. It's the gold canteen near his podium. Once you're seated, no bathroom breaks, no giggling and you girls keep your hands to yourself. Absolutely no shenanigans. When the choir sings, you better stand the whole time no matter how longwinded the lead singer gets. Go on! Git!" ushered Kay.

If there was one thing Dria hated, it was being late to an organized seated gathering. People tend to turn and stare at the entrance with socially shaming glares. Those stares always felt hot and judgmental. "Is the whole town in attendance?" mumbled Sadie grabbing Dria's left hand and Bellissima's right.

"It's a Baptist church in the South, so yes. Almost everyone in town is in this one building. No one makes plans on Sundays that don't include going to God's house," whispered Bellissima. Some churchgoers whispered. Most just smiled but they all gawked, especially Colin. He couldn't take his eyes off Dria. Emily's eyes narrowed as the Beaumonte' grandchildren strolled by. "-Mission accomplished," said Bellissima as they sat.

"What are you talking about?" asked Dria, trying to pretend that Emily's envy was never part of the plan.

"Like you don't see Colin back there drooling and his cunt wife boiling right beside him," said Sadie.

"Is *Colin* Staring at *me*? I hadn't noticed," said Dria with a pleased sneer.

"Like I said, mission accomplished," said Bellissima, laughing as she turned back to give Emily a petty nod.

"Hey, don't forget to replenish the blessed oil," reminded Sadie.

"Oh right! Dria pass me the decanter," said Bellissima. Dria rifled through her bag and pulled out the glass canteen. Bellissima looked down at it and immediately panicked. "NO!"

"No what?" asked Dria, curious about the cause of Bellissima's sudden dread.

"Dria! You grabbed the wrong one!"

"What do you mean? Auntie Kay told Sadie to grab the blue one, right Sadie?" asked Dria.

Sadie was hesitant. "Yeah... wait. Maybe she said _not_ to grab the blue one..."

Bellissima's face reddened. "You idiots!" She uncorked the container and sniffed its rim. "This is Mama's meat fat!"

Dria's armpits started sweating. "Oh no!" she cried ashamed and nervous. "What do we do?"

"What do we do?! There's nothing we can do!" said Bellissima, turning back to find her Mother still preoccupied with Sunday greeting. "She's not looking. I'll fill the preacher's vial and hide the bottle. Maybe no one will smell the difference. We'll figure out a lie to cover our asses later!"

Bellissima slipped behind the podium and poured the drippings into the vial and rushed back to her seat.

The preacher stood and addressed the congregation. "Let the church say Amen!" The crowd shouted in unison. *'Amen!'* "Can I get another Amen from God's people?" *'Amen!'* They yelled even louder the second time. "Before today's sermon, I'd like us all to join hands. Link arms if your hands are full. One of our most devoted members, one of our closest friends, has fallen ill. She's not with us here on this Sunday. Only God knows how many Sunday mornings she has left here before she's called on home." Bellissima watched as her mother and aunts grew emotional. At that moment, Bellissima realized how scared they were to lose their mother. She couldn't imagine losing her mother or either of her aunts or cousins. Then she remembered what it felt like losing Cheniere. "I'll be reading from the book of Romans. Chapter 8, verses 17 and 18. *And if children, then heirs of Christ, if indeed we suffer with him, that we may also be glorified.* The last time I saw Sister Beaumonte', I asked her; Are you in pain my dear? She looked up at me and answered my question with a question. *'What is pain when you have grown numb to the afflictions of this world? What is pain compared to what's waiting for me in the sky? May his will be done?'* And then, she told me to bow my head and *she* prayed for *me.* I thought I was the one who was going to be doing the praying!" the crowd laughed. "That just goes to show, we are all here to sharpen the countenance of one another and we are all responsible for keeping one another covered in prayer. Catherine may not be in this building today but she's here in spirit and we have her beautiful family here. Her daughters tell me that Sister Catherine put in a special birthday request, all the way from Pennycress. That sounds like her, doesn't it? Putting her order in from miles away?" Everyone laughed again, familiar with Catherine Beaumonte's unique panache of damsel self-entitlement. "I'd like the choir to stand now. My songbirds, would you be so kind as to sing her favorite song? Sing it with your whole body, loud enough so that she might hear it clear across town. So loud Jesus can hear it way up on the throne."

The pianist started a slow melody. "And as they worship in song, I'd like you all to come forward for prayer if you need it. Deaconess Kay Beaumonte' is going to anoint you all and we will pray with you. All of you who have pain, come up here. Rather it's physical, something we can lay our hands on or emotional, something we have to put our hearts on-come. If you're afraid of something, the Bible says fear not, I am with you. Come up here. Don't worry about what person may judge you for coming forward. At least you got sense enough to know you need fixing, let them talk! God forbid Jesus comes back right after the gossip rolls of their lips! God forbid they get caught in their sin while judging you for coming forth to lay yours at his feet! Your neighbor doesn't need to know what's hurting you. That's between you and God- come up. Claim your chains broken."

Bellissima looked over at Sadie who looked like she really wanted to go up. "Sadie, you alright?"

"Yeah, I'm good." She quickly replied.

"Sadie, Mama says it's not good to sit idle if God's calling. You should go up there," urged Bellissima.

Bellissima felt Sadie's grip tighten but she didn't step forward. "I said I'm good, Lissima."

Dria, Bellissima and Sadie watched as everyone gathered up front. Kay grabbed the oil canteen and dabbed her palms. "She's got the oil! Just look down, don't make eye contact!" warned Bellissima.

The first local in need of prayer positioned herself in front of Kay. Kay pressed her palms together and rubbed them briskly. Her upper lip curled as she sniffed. Kay paused, looked down at her greasy, slick hands and then cut her eyes at the girls. The prayer line was long that Sunday morning. There were people in need of anointing. Kay used what she had and blessed them all with meat grease.

CHAPTER TWELVE

"Baptist church in the South never really ends, does it" complained Sadie. "We're standing outside and they're still praising and why do they all keep hugging us? When can we leave?"

"What's the rush? There's nothing wrong with a little attention," said Dria grinning.

"Is it appropriate? Having Colin eye- hump you on holy ground? You're having way too much fun making his wife eat her heart out," mumbled Bellissima between hugs.

"I haven't had fun in a long time. It's high time I enjoyed myself a little,' replied Dria, rubbing it in with a friendly wave to Emily.

Minxy approached. "Cutting it close today, aren't we girls?"

"It was really all Dria's fault, she got way too chatty at Mipsy's and then she hopped in the shower first leaving me and Sadie with little-to-no hot water!" sniveled Bellissima.

"No hot shower! You poor thing! You looking for some sympathy?" joked Minxy.

"Yes, a little clemency would be nice. Ya'll been riding us hard all morning," she pouted.

"Okay. Lean in and I'll coddle you for just a minute. Hurry before your Mama sees," said Minxy grabbing Bellissima tight.

"Great! More hugs!" said Sadie.

"Why are *you* so crabby?" asked Minxy, observing her daughter's attitude warily.

"My feet hurt! And I'm starving!"

"Are you sure that's all," asked Minxy, suspicious.

Sadie squirmed uncomfortably," Yes, now stop looking at me like that! All day! We've been gawked at! We've had enough! Well, Lissima and I've had enough. I'm sure Dria doesn't mind the admiration."

"What do you mean?" asked Minxy.

Bellissima patted Minxy's shoulder, "It's a long story. Don't pull at that thread, not while we're still on the holy ground."

The Preacher walked over, eager to shake their hands. "It's truly a blessing, having all of you in attendance today! Sister Catherine would be so pleased. Just look at all of you! You've grown into benevolent angels!"

"It was a wonderful sermon, Pastor. Thank you for having us. We can't begin to express our gratitude for everything the church has done for our family and this community. Work has had me tied up lately but if there's anything we can do for the congregation, please don' hesitate to ask," offered Bellissima.

"Actually, there is something you could do. Our youth administrator is battling a gout flare up. It's unexpected and unfortunate news but inconvenient news for the kids. They don't have anyone to chaperone them at the Cal-Cam fair."

"The Fair's in town?" asked Dria, excited.

"Oh yes, it's that time of year again for fall festivities. The carnival crew just set up a little after daybreak this morning."

Dria grabbed Bellissima's sleeve, ecstatic. "It's been so long! We used to have so much fun there!" she exclaimed, hopping up and down.

"I bet you did. The kids love all the rides and games, just as much as you three did growing up. Everyone knows the opening day is the best day. The first day and the last day when they stage the big obstacle course. They'd be heartbroken if we had to cancel or reschedule. Would you girls mind looking after them for a few hours?" Bellissima's face went pale and she was very still. Minxy, Dria, and Sadie exchanged glances. Pastor cleared his throat, "If you girls have plans, I'm sure I can convince Sister and Brother Hardy to step in…"

"You mean Emily and Colin? No need, we'd be happy to do it!" agreed Dria. Bellissima looked away and crossed her arms.

"Are you sure? I wouldn't want to trouble you," said the Pastor.

"Will the usual treats be available? -The cotton candy? Funnel cakes? Shrimp on a stick? Caramel apples?" asked Sadie anxiously.

The Pastor laughed, amused by Sadie's enthusiasm concerning food. "Yes, all the usual booths. In fact, our older youth members are vending their hemp flip flops this year. They've decided to use the proceeds to enrich the community."

"-Food and flip flops! Sounds good to me!" said Sadie, turning to Bellissima for confirmation.

Bellissima was hesitant but agreed only because she felt like she had to. "Sure, we'd love to look after your flock."

"God bless you Beaumonte' women. The church bus is all fueled up and ready to go! I'll go tell the children that the plans stay the same!"

Once Preacher was out of hearing range, Minxy turned to Bellissima, worried. "What was that all about, tin man? You just froze up! You alright?"

"Yes, Mam. It's just…"

"Just what? You can tell us, we're family."

"We haven't been to the fair together as a family since the year we won first place in the Cal-Cam obstacle course," answered Bellissima.

The revelation hit Dria and suddenly Bellissima's apprehension made perfect sense. "You mean, we haven't all been to the fair as a family since Cheniere died," said Dria.

"Yeah, Dria! That's what I mean! But I guess all that really matters is that you look like a superstar in front of Colin's wife. Congrats! Emily saw you save the day!" yelled Bellissima, storming off.

"Maybe we shouldn't go," said Sadie.

"You could always stay here and explain to your Auntie Kay why the entire prayer line smells like pork grease," said Minxy.

"On second thought, it might help her heal," said Sadie. "We should get going." Sadie moved to the center of the church lot. "Attention future ministers! Form a single file line behind me! It's time to go to the fair!"

CHAPTER THIRTEEN

"You look nice all dressed up, together- modestly decent, dare I say presentable," complimented Catherine. Her voice was shallow, and every other vowel slurred. "If only your daddy could see his girls looking so pretty, rest his soul. Rest his bones in the river."

"That's so nice of you to say. Thank you, Mama," said Kay. She, Lou Anna and Minxy took turns hugging Catherine.

"We thought it would be nice to come and see you today. You feel like company?" asked Lou Anna.

"You're already here, might as well stay. It's not like I can tell anyone *not* to come in. The damn door doesn't even have a lock on it. Do I really have a choice over who trespasses or comes without invitation? How foolish of me, thinking I'd earned the right to have some privacy or shut people out," Catherine replied bitterly.

"You seem a little frustrated today, Mama. Is there anything we can do to make you more comfortable?" offered Minxy.

"Frustrated? Is that what I am? Hell, I'm allowed to be a little frustrated. Don't you think? You'd be frustrated too if you'd been forced out of your own home and left to rot."

Minxy moved in closer and began to brush Catherine's hair. "Mama, I wish you wouldn't talk like that- so grimly. There's a steam room here, a mandatory daily tea tree oil soak for your arthritis and I hear you get to vote on a movie to watch in the theater. Honesty is it really *that* bad here?"

"She's just being overly dramatic as usual, Minxy. Don't encourage her. Don't feed into her pity trap," Lou Anna interjected. Minxy's head spun, glaring at Lou Anna with her eyes wider and her lips pursed. Kay also turned her attention to Lou Anna, eyes narrowed as if to say- *don't poke the bear.* Lou Anna shrugged, rolled her eyes and looked away from them both.

Kay cleared her throat. "I'm sure you'll be excited to hear the good news. Your grandchildren went out this morning and picked up all the birthday dinner fixings."

"-And guess what? They offered to cook the entire meal themselves with no help from us!" added Minxy.

Catherine grunted, "Did they offer or were they forced?"

"-Same difference. They're our children. They will do as they're told. Either way, it's a thoughtful gift. You should be grateful," muttered Lou Anna under her breath.

Catherine laughed. "What do you know about children and gifts? Just because you have lots of money to buy things for people doesn't mean you know how to give. Just because you have a red canal between your legs that brought forth a child doesn't mean you've mastered the art of parenting and how to be a good mother. What about the gift of honesty? Before any of you start talking about gifts, you ought to give your children the gift they've been wanting years for. Do you ever plan on telling them who their fathers are? I didn't have a lot to give when I was a young mother but at least I gave a name and face to the man who helped create you. Jeremiah was my husband, not a fling, or a one-night stand or reoccurring bad decision I let crawl in and out of my bed to hump me with no intentions to ever love me. Hell, I'm surprised your daughters don't hate you. How they manage to respect you? I'll never know."

"Don't say hell Mama. It's God's day," whispered Minxy stroking Catherine's hair.

Catherine snatched the brush from Minxy's grip and threw it on the floor. "Every day is God's day child! It's like you want me to hit you!"

Kay walked up to Catherine and concentrated on her eyes. "Just as I suspected, her pupils are abnormal. The doctors have been planning to up her dosages. Sometimes the medications make her irritable."

"And disrespectful? Is that also a side effect?" asked Lou Anna, galled.

"When are you going to talk to the girls? When will they finally know their full selves? Bad enough one of my granddaughters died before she knew her papa!"

"Mama, you've gone too far now," said Minxy. "Now I'm sorry you're uncomfortable here but that's no reason to be cruel. It's not the time or place..."

"Place? Of course not! Time? It's long overdue! It's an injustice, what you're doing to them and you know it!" The room was quiet for a moment. "Lou Anna, my little mind shrinker, the entire year you were two years old; I couldn't get you off my hip. I had a crop to tend and a house to keep. I had to do it all with you clinging to me like glue. You idolized me, your mother. I'd put you down, but it never lasted. You'd stare up at me with those big hazel puddles, begging me to carry you around. Knowing full well you could walk on your own, I indulged you. That was before I believed in self-soothing. One day, I was busy with my cleaning. You were playing marbles on the floor and somehow got underfoot. I accidentally stepped on your hand. I heard your little bone snap like a twig. You didn't cry right off, you just looked up at me so devastated that I couldn't move. Finally, your shock sprang all at once. You shrieked and ran upstairs, crying. When I reached your bedroom, I found you underneath the bed. I tried everything I could to coax you out so that I could see about your hand; get you to a doctor. You refused to come out. The way you looked at me... like I was a monster. At that moment, I was so scared for my little girl. I felt so bad for not being more careful. I'd started to cry too. I'd forgotten that I wasn't alone. I'd forgotten that you were conceived out of love, a love that God had sealed with a promise of forever. You had a father to be there for you when I wasn't your most favorite person. Finally, Jeremiah came home. He heard you screaming and ran up. He was able to get you to come out. You curled up in Jeremiah's arms and he was able to get you the medical attention you needed. You wouldn't let me touch you or hug you for weeks. Did it hurt my feelings? Yes, of course, but I had your father to fill in for me. All the love you needed, you got it from someone who loved you just as much as I did. It was safe love, not the kind of love you left your daughters ill-prepared to defend themselves against. How many times has love exploited them, abandoned them or made them beg like dogs? What if Jeremiah hadn't been there? What if you'd never known him? You probably would have ruined your life earlier on or got knocked down and stayed down, in life. You see, when kids are confused or unsure of who they or afraid of something- they run. If they don't have the right people to run to, you risk letting them run into dark places to the wrong people or straight to the devil to get comfort and confirmation. All that bravery and independent woman strength- it's beautiful, it's wonderful but this generation has made a mockery of fatherhood. Even if you're ashamed of who's seed you let swim on inside you, even if he regrets you just as much as you regret him, even if you choose a monster to mate with…those girls deserve to know! Or do you think there's honor in breaking little girls? Now they've grown into beautiful little women with missing parts."

Lou Anna stood and grabbed her purse. "You say you're surprised our daughters don't hate us?" You should be more surprised that we don't hate you, Catherine." Lou Anna slammed the door behind her.

"Mama, I think I speak for all of us when I say that was painfully unnecessary force," said Minxy running after Lou Anna.

Kay took a deep breath and closed the door behind Minxy. "I'm going to lay out a gown for the nurse to put on you tonight before bedtime. Is that okay with you Mama? Mama?" Kay sat down next to Catherine and took hold of her hand. There was that look again, the lostness.

Catherine smiled big. "Kay! What a nice surprise! When did you get here! Where are your sisters? Are you and Lou Anna keeping an eye on Minxy? Please don't let my baby fall off the wagon, again. She's been doing so good. I hope the good Lord sees all her good deeds on the ledger when he calls her home. You know, I've never told anyone this, but it's my fault Minxy was ever on the wagon, to begin with. I have so many regrets. Did you girls ever make it to Old Mrs. Fontenot's farm to see about her leg? That gash is gon' lead to gangrene, you wait and see. She could lose her leg and then what will happen to that poor stuttering son of hers? He already has no friends, it's so sad. He's a sweet kid. You girls go down there and do right by her, you hear? When you see a chance to do God's work, you don't sit on the bench. He's watching. Did I ever tell you about the day your daddy died? He died on Burn Out bridge."

Minxy wandered around Pennycress until she spotted Lou Anna sitting all alone on a bench outside of the facility in the courtyard. "Don't get so upset, Lou. She's not herself, you know that. She hasn't been for a long time. Catherine lost a bit of herself when daddy died and now the illness is taking over. She'd never talk to you that way if she was still normal," said Minxy approaching.

Lou Anna shook her head. "It's either the alcohol or depression or the illness, now- either way! She's *never* to blame for treating me like a shit covered stick, huh? You know what kills me with you and Kay? You never stand up for me. No, Kay just stands there pretending not to hear Mama cutting me down. Typical ambivalent Kay. You Minx, it's like you're scared Mama will love you less if you act like you love me. Sisters are supposed to stand up for each other, protect each other. Our daughters have their tiffs but neither of them would dare let someone treat the other like garbage right in front of them. I'm not surprised you're making excuses for Catherine. That must be nice, having someone in your corner no matter what. I wouldn't know what that feels like. You were her live-in bartender, her drinking buddy," snapped Lou Anna. Minxy looked away and Lou Anna realized her tone and choice of words. "I'm sorry. I don't mean to take it out on you."

"It's okay. I know Mama gets under your skin sometimes."

Lou Anna fished a pack of cigarettes from her purse. "That sober group you're in, they still let you smoke cigarettes?"

"It's the only thing I'm still allowed to smoke," Minxy replied.

"Come. Sit. Have a few puffs with me before Kay catches us," said Lou Anna- scooting to make room on the bench.

The two sisters sat, puffing casually. "I don't know why I let her push my buttons. I'm not saying she's wrong. That whole father situation is a loose end I always meant to tie up, but I just didn't know how," said Lou Anna- Calmer.

"All three of us have our reasons. Sadie stopped asking me about her daddy when she was about 10 years old. I guess she got tired of me lying to her. She knew damn well he wasn't Batman or Superman or the president," said Minxy, laughing.

"Yeah but we're wrong. We were thinking of ourselves by not telling them what they needed to know. We were only thinking about how uncomfortable it would be for us to have that conversation with them. Their wholeness is worth a little discomfort. Our stupid decisions led us every-which-way but right. I can't tell you how many times Dria asked me to allow her father to be in her life. I always talked my way out of that corner quick or pull rank on her- told her that I was the mother and I didn't have to explain myself. It gave me an ulcer, keeping that big of a secret. I hate keeping secrets."

"Speaking of secrets, I've noticed you've been avoiding alone time with Kay."

"You ever tried to keep something from Kay? She's a walking lie detector. I'm scared to look her in the eye. The very second I do, she'll know Lissima and I are hiding something."

"You remember that time when Dria let Bellissima sit on the handlebars of her bike and Lissima's foot accidentally got caught in the spokes?"

"Do I remember? Dria and Sadie carried Lissima in the house screaming bloody murder! You'd think she'd lost the whole foot, the way they were carrying on! I saw all that blood and half expected to see a bloody stump just below her ankle!"

"Thank goodness it was only her toenail that got ripped off. We decided we wouldn't tell Kay about it," said Minxy- exhaling, passing the cigarette back to Lou Anna.

"Yeah, Cheniere hadn't been gone that long. Kay turned into the kind of mother that worried all the time, so much that she barely gave Lissima any room to grow up. We patched up her foot and made her wear sneakers for the rest of the summer so Kay wouldn't find out," said Lou Anna.

"Once the pain was gone, Sadie slapped a coat of nail polish on all ten of her toes- even the toe without a nail on it. She painted the skin so good, you couldn't even tell there wasn't a nail."

"I was so glad when it grew back. We didn't have to tell Kay what had happened. You remember when Sadie was having those nightmares about the Mothman? Some little snotty nosed brat at the school told Sadie that the Mothman ate her grandpa and her cousin. Sadie was convinced that the Mothman slept on our roof, waiting to eat her next. Lissima went up on the roof to prove to Sadie there was no nest on our roof, remember that?"

"Yeah, I remember," laughed Minxy. "Lissima came tumbling down right on top of Dria. Bless Dria's soul, sweet girl was only trying to catch

Lissima right out of the sky so she wouldn't crack her skull. Dria was the lucky one. She only got a small bump on the forehead. Lissima's sweater got caught on the shutters halfway down and her shoulder got dislocated. Thank Goodness you were able to pop it right back in place, Lou. The strength in our little Lissima, she barely made a peep when you jerked that bone back. We didn't tell Kay about that one either." Minxy turned on the bench to face her sister. "You know Lou, I get the feeling this secret you're keeping from Kay isn't like the toenail or the arm. Bellissima's my niece too. If there's cause to worry, I deserve to know. Now I can't make you tell Kay. But if you don't tell me what's going on, I'll ask Bellissima myself."

Lou Anna inhaled the nicotine deep and exhaled. "Brace yourself, Minx. Prepare for your skin to start crawling. It's not easy to explain. I'm not even sure it's worldly enough for either of us to understand. It ain't one of our pretty little toenail stories."

"I've seen enough unpretty things. I'm sure I can take it," said Minxy.

"Don't be so sure of yourself. The hairs on the back of my neck still haven't relaxed since it happened," said Lou Anna.

"You're scaring me, Lou."

"Good. I'm a little scared myself, just getting ready to tell you about it." Lou Anna closed her eyes. "It was last year when that big shot corporate rep came down here to Louisiana to tour Pennycress, in hopes to build a similar facility up North. Bellissima's department head nominated her to show him around the building, brief him on company procedures. He was so pleased with Lissima's passion and professionalism that he offered her a job. He wanted Bellissima to relocate; said the company would cover the cost of relocation and that she'd run the entire nursing division from a desk in a huge private office. Her salary would've been tripled, fewer hours and more authority. *'You'd be crazy not to take it,'* I told her when she called me about it. She sounded strange over the phone, but I thought maybe she was just tired or something. I should have called her back."

"What happened?"

"Later on, that night, Bellissima called me again. It was a little after 1 AM. I answered the phone in a panic, thinking something had to be wrong for her to call so late. When I answered, Bellissima didn't say anything, but I could hear her breathing. *'Bellissima? Sweetheart, what's wrong? Lissima, you there?'* I must have said her name a dozen times but still, nothing. The line went dead. I tried to call back, but it went straight to voicemail. I sent texts, but no reply. I messaged her on social media, no reply. I started to pace, thinking maybe I should call Kay; but Kay was three hours away handling restaurant business. Besides, something in my gut told me not to call Kay. She'd break her neck jumping to the worst conclusions and try to make it back home to Bellissima as fast as she could. I didn't want to upset Kay and cause her to drive home recklessly emotional in the dark. Especially when I wasn't sure what was the matter. But deep down I *did* know, something wasn't right. I paced away the early morning hours. I called my receptionist and told her to clear my day. I sat and stared at the phone, fighting my sleep. Eventually, I nodded off on the couch. Frantic knocking woke me. I ran to the door and there she was, Bellissima, standing in the rain. I was so relieved to see her face. I grabbed my niece tight and I started asking questions. *'You had me worried sick! Why weren't you answering my calls! Are you hurt? What are you doing here, 8 hours away from home?'* She wasn't answering any of my questions. She just stood there, crying. *'Bellissima, say something, please.'* I begged. *'Is something wrong with Kay? Have you gotten into trouble? Please love bug, say something, you're scaring me!'* Bellissima lifted her arms slowly and she held her hands out in front of her body, where I could see them. Then, she started signing."

"Signing? You mean, using sign language?" asked Minxy, confused.

' "Yes. Minxy, I had to catch my breath. My heart started racing. For a second, I could have sworn It was Cheniere, our dead niece, standing at my door instead of the living one. And even though I knew it was impossible, I almost called her by Cheniere's name. It was impossible, I knew it; but still. We'd buried that one, so how was she standing in front of me? I got chills all over my body. A gust of wind swept through the threshold and I felt ice all around me."

"What did Lissima say, I mean, what did she use her hands to tell you?"

"I put my knowledge of sign language on the shelf when Cheniere died. It had been a while and I was rusty, but I understood exactly what Lissima signed. *'I'm not answering because I can't-'* that's what our little Lissima used her hands to tell me."

"I- don't understand," Minxy replied.

"Before Bellissima went home to the cottage to sleep, she was fine. When she woke up, she was completely deaf and unable to speak."

"What!" asked Minxy, her face suddenly grave.

"You heard me right. Bellissima went to bed hearing and speaking but woke up incapable of either. She looked like she'd seen a ghost and she was shivering so profusely that her teeth were chattering. I pulled her inside and dried her off. Soon as she was calm enough, I found a pen and pad for her to use so nothing was lost in translation. I didn't want to misinterpret anything she needed to tell me. The minute I gave her that pen, she began to scribble. What she wrote froze my bones cold."

"What did she write Lou?"

"Two sentences I'll never forget. - *Nightmare took my speech. Nightmare took my hearing.*"

"What did she mean by that?"

"I still don't know. She was scared to death. In all, Bellissima stayed with me in the city for three days and she didn't mumble a single word the whole time. Bellissima had written, -*please tell no one* on the pad and I promised I wouldn't. How would I have explained it anyway? Dria stopped by unannounced while Bellissima was asleep. I had to get rid of her quick. One look at the rings under Lissima's bloodshot eyes and Dria would have known something was amiss. I had to be short with Dria, told my daughter that she should have called first. I knew it would piss her off enough to make her leave right away. Once Dria was gone, I went to tuck Bellissima in. On her wrists, there were cuts- deep ones. It was then that I realized how serious her condition was."

"Cuts?" asked Minxy, trembling.

"Yes."

"She'd never do that, Lou. Bellissima would never harm herself. No, someone must've done that do her."

"I flat out asked Bellissima if she tried to kill herself, Minxy. She couldn't account for what happened. She swears no one broke in. She was all alone. I have no choice but to believe she self-mutilated. I know it's hard to believe. Our little Lissima was so afraid, so alone, that she tried to take her own life. I felt weak all over. Our Lissima, she's the strongest of all our babies. Most would think Dria's the strongest, the way she struts with her chin so high; but no. Dria's confident, there's a difference. Sadie's never cared about rules or what anyone thinks, and with that mindset- it's impossible for her to think she's incapable of doing anything. Lissima's the strongest, the way she's kept going despite all the tragedy our family has seen. While Lissima slept, I researched and made calls to some of my fellow psychiatrists. The best explanation: extreme stressed induced temporary deafness. It's not uncommon for people to suffer visual <u>and</u> auditory hallucinations when stressed, so that could explain the nightmare. All the books said her hearing would return, eventually. Before I went to bed on the third day, I wrote a prescription for Bellissima and gave it to her, a drug I thought could give her a better grip on reality. When I woke up on the morning of the fourth day, Lissima was gone. All I could think about was my beautiful newly deaf niece roaming the dangerous city by herself. I ran outside, and down the sidewalk yelling her name and then felt stupid. *She can't hear you, Lou.* I ran back inside ready to call a search party but then my phone rang. I answered, and it was Bellissima. She said my name; *'Auntie Lou'* and I broke down in tears. She could speak again. She could hear again. She told me she was stopping to gas up and that she was almost home. She didn't want to wake me but wanted to make it back home before Kay. Before Bellissima hung up, she asked me again not to tell Kay about the whole ordeal, and I stupidly agreed."

"Why wouldn't Lissima go to Kay?"

Lou Anna took another long puff. "She never said, but if I had to guess, I'd say Bellissima believed that whatever was happening to her was a mental or supernatural thing. Bellissima's a smart girl, she didn't just wake up and come running. I'm willing to bet she thought like a nurse. She researched and prayed and failed to find a plausible medical explanation first. Kay would have given her love. Bellissima didn't think love would bring back her senses. Love wasn't going to fix her. She came to me afraid, thinking something in her head was broken. Maybe she thought she'd gone crazy." Lou Anna tossed the cigarette butt and turned to lock eyes with Minxy. "But whatever her mind's eye saw in that nightmare, it was real to her. And it scared Lissima to deaf."

CHAPTER FOURTEEN

"No one gets a sweet treat or gets in line for a ride until your vendor booth is set up! It takes at least two people to man the sails: one to collect money and give change and one to bag your merchandise! You'll alternate every thirty minutes so that everyone gets equal work and play time! You will not get personal with strangers! You will not step out of the fairground perimeter! If someone tries to take you outside of the perimeter, I want you to scream as loud as you can!" said Dria as she helped the older youth members unload their vender materials. She picked up a pair of the hemp slippers. "How much are you guys selling these for, anyway?"

"Two bucks a pair, a dollar for each foot. We're going to use the money to build a wall."

"-A wall?"

"Yes, Mam. We decided to build a tall fence out by Burn Out bridge. We want to put it right where the road ends and the water begins to separate the town from the ruins. Maybe then, people will start to forget. Heal."

Dria smiled. "I think that's a beautiful, noble idea. Your parents must be so proud. Your hearts are truly in the right place." Dria reached into her bra. "It'd be an honor to be your first customer. I'll take three pairs, one for me and a pair for each of my cousins. Here's a hundred-dollar bill. Keep the change and keep being the change this world so desperately needs."

Dria walked over to Sadie. "Here, your ankles are so swollen they look like water balloons. Might be time to lay off the salt or see a doctor about a diuretic. Put these on, they're way more comfortable than they look. I can understand why Jesus wore them," said Dria giving Sadie a set of the flip-flops.

"You're a lifesaver," said Sadie- kicking off her heels. "I'm finished with the headcount and I've got an emergency number for each kid. How's the vendor booth coming along?"

"It's almost open for business. Where's Bellissima?"

"She's over at the ticket booth buying wrist bands for the group. She didn't say a word the whole ride over here."

"You think she's still mad at me?" asked Dria- genuinely concerned.

"Probably but understandably so. You *did* get a little self-centered. What's the deal with you and that Colin guy anyway? It had to be something serious to get you acting like a bitch in heat."

"You know, I still get shivers every time I hear or speak his name," said Dria- fanning herself.

"Was he your first love?"

"Yes, my first love and my greatest defeat. He was the only thing that made perfect sense in a world that was nothing but one big question. He and I took place back when we were too young to be held responsible for our feelings but too old to pretend they didn't exist. He was easily the best thing that ever happened to me, defeat included. I was barely here for a full 24 hours when we all came down to celebrate Bellissima's graduation, four years ago. I was on a plane ride home before the ink on the cottage paperwork was dry. I was here and gone before I had a chance to run into him. It's funny, I was almost sad that I didn't get a chance to see him. Now that I have, I don't know what to feel."

"What ended it?"

"-Bad things. I keep thinking that I should have made it harder for the devil to rip us apart."

"Maybe you should've."

"Maybe you're right," agreed Dria. "I must admit. It does feel weird being here without Cheniere. I can't imagine what's going through Lissima's head. I'm going to apologize."

Dria tapped Bellissima's shoulder. "I come bearing gifts, sweet blister, and bunion relief." Dria dangled the hemp slippers in Bellissima's face.

"I'm not a horse and that's not an apple," snapped Bellissima, turning her back to Dria.

"I know. It's a peace offering. I know your feet are killing you." Bellissima continued to count the bands. - ignoring Dria.

"Okay! I'm sorry. I got swept up in the gravity of my ancient bad romance. I was insensitive. Please don't let my behavior ruin what could still turn out to be a great day. I know you're dealing with a lot of bittersweet memories, but this is the first time we've all been here in a very long time. Who knows when we'll get another chance? It would be great if I could just enjoy these festivities with my most favorite person."

Bellissima turned back to Dria and took a deep breath. "Okay. We're here, may as well make the best of it."

"So, we're good?"

"I forgive you for volunteering me for the sake of revenge, but you know we still have some things to talk about."

"I know."

Two children from the church group rushed over, dragging Sadie behind. "Let's go Ms. Bellissima! We want fried ice cream!"

Bellissima's lip twisted. "Do you want fried ice cream or does Ms. Sadie want it?"

"Usually we ride all the rides first and then we rack up on snacks. That way your tummy doesn't get upset," strategized Dria.

"Yeah some of these roller coasters, they spin and loop really fast, with lots of twists and turns. If you're stuffed to the limit, you could throw up," agreed Bellissima.

Sadie threw her head back, "Laisser le Bon temps rouler! So what if we throw up? We don't have to clean it up!" cheered Sadie. "We're going to binge until we throw up! We're going to ride until we throw up! Either way! We're going home covering in throw up! Let's go!" she screamed, running through the entrance gate full speed ahead.

Bellissima shook her head. "Okay, hand over those hemp floppers. No way I'm going to keep up with them in these shoes." She kicked off her high heels and released a sigh of relief. "Please! Let's all stay together!" Of course, Bellissima's attempt to maintain order was unsuccessful. Everyone scattered in separate directions.

"We will regroup at the Ferris wheel, 6 PM! You all have cell phones or watches! If you're not there by 6, It better be because you've been kidnapped!" yelled Dria. "No one rides the ring of fire until the end! It's Beaumonte' tradition!"

A third of the group followed Sadie to indulge. A handful joined Dria at the ring toss. All the rest trailed Bellissima who went straight for the skee ball machines. *'Step right up! Try your luck!* "I don't know how lucky I'll be. My twin sister was better at Carnie games than me," professed Bellissima, sadly. *'The fair is a magical place! You never know, you just might win!'*

At 5:55 PM, Bellissima and her small cluster of followers approached the Ferris wheel where she found Dria sharing a blooming onion with the kids. "You're eating junk food before the ring of fire? You grow a cast iron lining in your stomach since you moved to the city?" asked Bellissima.

"I think I can manage to keep one snack down. Our baby cousin is the one you should be worried about," replied Dria- pointing at Sadie, who emerged from the crowd with a hoagie in each hand. She appeared sluggish and gorged.

Bellissima gasped. "Sadie Lynn Beaumonte'! For goodness sake! Did you do anything in the last four hours other than eat?"

Sadie burped and uncouthly wiped her mouth on her sleeve. "Yes, I won a goldfish. I think I'll name it Goldie. It's a unisex name. I can't tell if it's a girl or boy."

"Goldie? How creative," teased Dria.

"Ya'll are just jealous cause you two never win anything!"

"I'll have you know, I won this all on my own," bragged Bellissima- shoving a tiny stuffed unicorn in Sadie's face.

"Is that it? A 2-inch constellation prize?" mocked Sadie- with a sarcastically commiserated expression.

"Constellation prize? I earned this the old-fashioned way, with skill!" huffed Bellissima.

"Did you? Or did the game attendant dig this out of the loser box for you?" asked Sadie, trying hard not to laugh.

"-Loser box?" questioned Bellissima.

Dria gave Bellissima a pat on the back. "It's okay, Lissima. I'm sure you tried your very best. It's…a cute little loser prize, though." Sadie high-fived Dria. "Look they're loading the next round of passengers on the wheel. Let's get on!"

The Beaumonte' grandchildren boarded the Ferris wheel, piling in the same passenger car. Once they were fastened, Dria grabbed the wheel attendant's arm. "Would you mind stopping the rotation when our pod reaches the very top? It's kind of our thing," she whispered hopefully.

Higher and higher they climbed, laughing all together. Sadie rocked the cart just to make Dria squeal the way she did when they were little. Dria tossed kernels of popcorn at the kids in the pod beneath them, just like old times. Bellissima stuck a wad of chewed bubblegum on the roof and scribbled *the Beaumonte' beauties were here* with four stick figures on the seat the way she did in the years past. One stick figure for all in attendance and one with a halo on its head for Cheniere. "We're almost at the top! Countdown time!"

"3-2-1!"- they hailed.

As requested, the Ferris wheel came to a screeching halt with Dria, Bellissima and Sadie at the very top. "Look how pretty the sky is! Dria, you timed it just right! We caught dusk red-handed, sneaking up on the sun. Have you ever seen a more beautiful shade of orange?" asked Sadie.

"Never," answered Dria, equally awed. "I don't even think there's a name for this color. Just like there are no words to describe what it feels like to be this close to God. Seems like yesterday we were all here, happy just being kids. Happy, just being alive and having one another to grow up with. We didn't give two shits about tomorrow or the what the future held. Good old-fashioned reckless bliss."

"Why'd she have to die?" asked Bellissima. "I miss her so much. Whatever God needed to prove to our family, couldn't he have done it without killing Cheniere? Every day, I miss her. I miss her until it hurts."

"We miss her too," said Sadie.

Their moment in the sky was over. The wheel began to spin again. The rambunctious group waited at the bottom of the wheel for Dria, Bellissima and Sadie's Ferris cart to unload. *"It's time for the ring of fire!"*

Dria looked up at the roller coaster and suddenly her throat felt narrower. Bellissima noticed Dria's deliberation and giggled. "What's wrong, Dria? Getting a case of the old cold feet?"

Dria tried hard to mask her fear. "Don't be silly. It's just, the ring. It looks a lot bigger, a lot higher than I remember." Wind from the track tousled Dria's hair. "It seems to be moving a hell of a lot faster than I remember too." Meanwhile, Sadie was busy reading the cardboard list of warnings near the height requirement chart. NO ALCOHOLIC BEVERAGES. NO CAMERAS OR PERSONAL BELONGINGS. NO PREGNANT WOMEN…

Bellissima laughed harder. "That's because it *is* bigger and faster. The ring of fire underwent a few upgrades since the last time we rode it. I read all about it in the local paper. I guess our little town's news doesn't make it to the big city. Folks around here wanted a little more thrill."

Dria's eyes narrowed. "-And you just kept that information to yourself?"

"Yep!" Bellissima replied with a devilish grin stretching from ear to ear. "If you're scared, you better get over it quick! It was your bright idea to come here! We're not leaving until we ride!"

Dria shrugged nonchalantly. "I'm not afraid of anything!"

"You never were," said a voice from the back of the line. They all turned to find Colin approaching. "You were always the bravest in any crowd."

"That was a long time ago, Colin. A lot has changed," Dria replied.

"Not everything. You still take my breath away," confessed Colin staring into Dria's eyes for an uncomfortable length of time. Sadie and Bellissima swapped glances.

Dria stared back into Colin's eyes and parted her lips to respond but was interrupted by Emily's crude ranting. "-Move it! -Coming through! -Watch my shoes!" she fussed pushing through the pandemonium. Emily approached Colin's side, her stare fixed on Dria and her entourage. "Colin, I turn my head for one second and you go off wandering. Isn't that just like a man?" Emily joked, confrontationally. "What do we have here? The same old ghost. You know, I go over a decade without seeing your face and Now it's all I've seen all day! Hello again, Alexandria."

Bellissima corrected Emily with a prominently aggressive tone. "It's just Dria. She reminded you earlier."

"Right. It must have slipped my mind," replied Emily behind one of her famous fake smiles. "What are you all talking about?" she asked-clinging to Colin.

Sadie grinned mischievously. "Colin was just saying something about his breath. Please, Colin, continue."

Bellissima interrupted. "We were talking about the ring of fire. Me and my cousins are going to ride with the kids. They're boarding now, so bye!" shooed Bellissima.

"Still Beaumonte' traditionists, I see. I'm in, that's if you don't mind me crashing the party. I haven't ridden in years," said Colin- rubbing his hands together, anxiously.

Emily squeezed his arm. "Darling, we should let them do their little tradition thingy alone. I'm sure the ride will be overcrowded…"

"No, it won't. He can have my seat," offered Sadie.

Both Dria and Bellissima's smiles turned upside down. "You're not riding with us?" asked Bellissima- disappointed. "Why not?" Sadie's stomach rumbled. She clutched the bottom of her abdomen where the baby settled comfortably, causing pressure. It suddenly occurred to Sadie that her secret unborn child wasn't too happy with the overeating. Everyone stared, waiting for Sadie to answer but she just stood there rubbing her belly. Bellissima snapped her fingers in Sadie's face. "Earth to Sadie!"

"Huh?" mumbled Sadie.

"I asked why you're not riding with us. And why are you fondling yourself in public?" she asked pointing to Sadie's hand caressing her midsection, causing everyone's attention to shift to the barely visible bump she'd been hiding.

Sadie quickly stopped rubbing and began to stutter. "Um…I…"

"I think I know what's going on here," said Dria.

"You do?" asked Sadie nervous.

"Yeah." Dria rummaged through her bag until she found a tiny bottle of bismuth. "We warned you not to eat so much. You always overdo it. Now you have a sour stomach."

"We warned you," agreed Bellissima- shaking her head.

Sadie chuckled, relieved. "Yeah, you sure did warn me. Now I'm sick. That's why I can't get on the ride! I'll take that bismuth, thank you."

"Okay kids, the ride's about to start seating! Give all your belongings to Ms. Sadie! She has to sit this one out!"

Dria and Bellissima lined up with the youth group and Colin got in line right behind them. Emily's face reddened. "You're not really getting on this death trap with *her*?"

"Yes, Emily. I am. Unlike you, I still like to have fun. I used to like being happy and I gave that up without a good enough fight. I'm not missing this," replied Colin.

Emily looked at the Beaumonte' cousins who were all grinning, eavesdropping. "Well then, I guess I'm coming with you."

Dria laughed. "Are you sure you want to do that, princess? Doesn't really seem like your style. Wouldn't want one of your expensive earrings to fly off and injure someone."

"I'll just have to take them off!" Emily replied.

Colin grabbed his wife's arm and leaned in. "Emily, this ride goes almost 130 miles per hour and it flips upside down. Just stop. You don't need to be so extreme."

"Obviously I do, Colin!"

All aboard! The ring of fire! Who's brave enough to ride the flame!

"Alright then! Let's do this!" said Bellissima showing the ride conductor her wrist band. He quickly recognized her from Pennycress.

"Lissima! Mon Cher! How you doing?" he asked. It was big Oscar. He'd moved his mother into Pennycress months before and checked in on her often. When asked who her favorite nurse was, she quickly answered- 'Bellissima the little creole beauty.' She'd learned to trust to Bellissima and loved her like family.

"Oscar! I didn't know you were working the fair this year!" Bellissima gushed, giving him a hug.

"Oh yes, anything to keep Mama's Pennycress tab paid up. You know it ain't cheap!" said Oscar with a playful nudge. "Mama brags about you nonstop. She says you go out of your way to make her smile. I appreciate that, Mon Cher. You're the daughter she never had."

"I'm just doing my job," replied Bellissima- humbly.

"I beg to differ. The rest of your staff, they do just enough to not get fired. What you do, you do out of love. If there's anything you ever need, you let me know. You hear?"

A clever smirk stretched across Bellissima's face. "Actually, there is one little thing you could do for me."

"Anything! You just name it!"

"You see that prissy little thang taking off all her jewelry? Could you make sure that she sits all the way to the back, alone? Seat her as far away from my cousin, the pretty woman with the perfect face wearing the burgundy, and that tall handsome man wearing the black. I'd like for them two to sit as close as possible."

Oscar smiled and nodded. "Consider it done!" he smiled- kissing Bellissima's cheek. Bellissima sat and strapped herself in. Colin and Dria boarded the ride and went for the vacant seats up front. Emily, her vengeful glare locked on the two of them like a heat-seeking missile, attempted to follow. Oscar stopped her. "Mam, I'm going to need you to sit in a vacant seat towards the rear of the ride." Bellissima quickly covered her mouth to keep from laughing uncontrollably.

Emily's face twisted. "Excuse me! My husband is sitting up in front! I need to be sitting with him!" argued Emily. "Now step aside old man!"

"I will not step aside little lady. This is a matter of safety, weight distribution and all. Now you can either sit in the back or get off my ride. Make up your mind. You're delaying everyone's good time."

"Yeah! Hurry up!" yelled the Kids.

"Fine! Just run this ride as quick as you can, get this over with!" fussed Emily, with her finger pointed in Oscar's face.

Oscar looked over at Bellissima, "You hear that, Mon Cher? I think I heard her ask me to make it last as long as I can. What you think?"

"Sounds good to me," Bellissima replied.

"Here we go, folks! Hands in the air!" Everyone lifted their hands, except Bellissima. Her focus drifted away with the memories of Cheniere and the last time they'd rode together- side by side. Oscar noticed Bellissima's spirit saddened. "This here is the ring of fire! And it ain't moving until everyone's hands are way up high!"

The little boy next to Bellissima smiled big. "You have to put your hands up Ms. Lissima."

Bellissima looked over at him. "You're awfully tiny. Is this your first time?"

"Yes mam," he answered flashing what was left of his baby teeth. "I'm finally tall enough!"

Bellissima remembered not being tall enough. Cheniere hit a growth spurt and made height requirement before Bellissima, but Cheniere refused to ride without her twin. "Looks like she might need a little encouragement Ya'll," Said Oscar on the blow horn. "Everybody say it with me: hands in the air little Lissima!" *Hand's in the air little Lissima! Hands in the air little Lissima. Hand's in the air little Lissima!'* – They chanted. Bellissima cracked a sideways smile and put one arm up. "Ladies and gentlemen, we got one arm! One more to go!" *Hands in the air little Lissima, you can You can do it!'* Up went her other arm.

"There you have it, folks! It's time to feel the burn!"

The ride slowly built momentum but quickly spun faster and faster. Sadie cheered, while snapping photos, secretly happy she didn't get on. The children were having the time of their lives, but the adults were horrified, holding on for dear life and screaming until their voices cracked.

When the ride finally stopped; Dria, Bellissima and Colin staggered off. "I feel so alive!" yelled Dria.

Sadie squeezed between her cousins and snapped a group selfie. "Hashtag, wild for the night! Hashtag, forever young!" she said posting it to social media.

"I can't believe you did it! The look on your face before, I thought for sure you'd chicken out!" said Bellissima.

"I want to thank you guys for letting me a part of that. It brought back a lot of memories," said Colin. "And Dria, thank you for riding with me. It's embarrassing to admit but, back when we were in school, that's all I ever wanted- to sit next to you. Once I knew how amazing it was to sit next to you, no other spot in the classroom compared," he said- grabbing Dria's hand.

"You're welcome Colin," said Bellissima, since Dria was frozen still.

"It was fun," said Dria- finally pulling her hand back.

"I don't know how long you're going to be in town but…I'm glad you're back. It's going to hurt me something serious to see you leave again," said Colin.

"Colin! What are you doing?" yelled Emily, stumbling off the ride platform.

"He was just saying goodbye," answered Dria.

"I wasn't talking to you! Colin, we're leaving right now! Let's go!" demanded Emily.

"Do you always talk to him like that? Belittle him that way? You should be thankful he's a gentleman. Any other man would have told you to shut your trap by now!" said Dria. "You ever consider talking to him like he's your equal instead of your subordinate? You ever try respecting your husband? I know a lot of good women who'd be happy to stand by a good man like Colin."

Appalled, Emily stepped into Dria's face. "I will not take marital advice from a woman who's love story ended in grade school! This is between me and Colin, it's a marriage! It does not concern you, Alexandria!"

Dria didn't back down. In fact, she stepped closer to Emily. "Bitch, it's Dria. Not Alexandria!"

Fight! Fight! Fight! Fight! Chanted the children, instigating more discord.

"Okay settle down guys! There's not going to be any fighting! This preppy skank ain't crazy enough to take a swing at my cousin and get her ass kicked in front of the whole town!" said Bellissima.

"Damn right there's not going to be a fight! But there might be a beat down if little miss teen racist doesn't get the hell out of my cousin's face!" hissed Sadie- taking a physically threatening stance between Emily and Dria.

"Emily, step off!" demanded Colin. "Dria hasn't done anything wrong. You're embarrassing yourself and me."

"What? You're protecting her now!" yelled Emily, shoving Colin.

"You're the one who's going to need protecting if you think for one second..." Sadie stopped ranting in mid-sentence and tried to cover her mouth, but it was too late. Vomit sprayed from Sadie's mouth and spewed all over Emily.

The crowd gasped and then all at once, everyone burst into uncontrollable laughter- including Colin. "You're a disgusting creature!" Emily screamed, shaking clumps of regurgitated nachos from her bangs. She grabbed Colin by the collar and disappeared in the mass. People continued to laugh long after they disappeared into the parking lot.

Bellissima turned to Dria. "How's that for a good time?" she asked.

CHAPTER FIFTEEN

The Beaumonte' sisters stood outside the cottage; arms linked. Kay turned to Lou Anna, "Do you remember when daddy broke his arm bricking that chimney?" she asked.

"Wasn't the chimney's fault. It was gravity and the ground that did it. It didn't keep him from finishing it though; no way, no how. Jeremiah Beaumonte' was a determined man, especially when it came to giving his family the best life he could," said Lou Anna envisioning their father's face.

Minxy laughed. "I remember him letting me draw little hearts on his sling. I'm glad he was secure in his masculinity. It couldn't have been easy wearing it around town."

"When did daddy ever care what people thought? Our opinions, the opinions of his family, were the only ones that mattered."

"I'm so glad Bellissima painted. I always hated that old dull brown," said Lou Anna.

Once inside, Kay went upstairs to get more clean clothes for Bellissima. Minxy curled up on the couch with a box of old photos while Lou Anna polished Bellissima's credentials.

"Are you cleaning?" asked Minxy.

"I'm still reeling from our visit with Mama. Cleaning is a nervous habit I have yet to break."

"More like a boring habit."

"I'm so proud of Bellissima. She's accomplished so much," said Lou Anna- polishing one of her plaques.

"Yeah, she sure has. You know Dria's accomplished a lot too," said Minxy.

"Of course she has. Dria's always had a healthy appetite for education and a strong work ethic. She graduated three semesters early. She left my GPA in the dust. Yes, my child has done well for herself," agreed Lou Anna.

"*Well?* Dria did *well?*" asked Minxy, shocked by Lou Anna's downplaying. "She did better than *well*, Lou. Dria did great, she's doing great! Why do you always do that?"

"Do what Minxy?"

"Diminish your daughter's accomplishments. It's a wonder how she grew up to be so great; with your incessant criticism. I've watched you cut Dria down her entire life. I was almost sure she'd grow up thinking she'd never be good enough for anyone or any dream."

Lou Anna sighed. "I don't mean to."

"Really? Because you do it so often that it seems intentional. You're her mother, not her bully."

"Dria and I have a complicated relationship. I give her focus and drive through tough love. She appreciates that."

"No Lou Anna, you drive her away."

"The distance between me and my daughter isn't all my doing! Dria's not the kind of child that responds to gentleness. I've tried to get closer to Dria."

"No, you haven't tried. You know what's worse than talking in circles? Talking in straight lines. You two avoid anything that might lead back to your deep seeded issues."

"Minxy, don't analyze me. I'm trained to do all the analyzing." Lou Anna stopped polishing and sat down beside Minxy. "Where did I go wrong?"

Minxy put the pictures down and moved closer to her sister. "You remember when Kay burned her hand trying to make her famous stuffed bell peppers that one Easter?"

"Yeah."

"Do you remember what happened after that?"

"Yes." Lou Anna nodded and took a deep breath. "It was a bad burn. I was running around the house looking for the first aid kit. When I found it, I rushed back to see about Kay but Dria was already helping her. '*I made it all better mommy!*' When I got closer, I saw that Dria had gotten a stick of butter out of the fridge. She was rubbing Kay's burn with it. 'What are you doing?' I asked her. *'This will keep her from getting a blister.'* I dropped the kit and the back of my neck felt hot. 'Where did you learn that?' I asked. *'It's a home remedy, Mama'*. I lost it. I grabbed Dria's arm so hard my grip bruised a finger pattern. 'No! I will not have you talking all that holistic nonsense!' I shook her. 'Do you hear me Alexandria?' I felt myself losing control, but I couldn't stop myself. For the first time since I'd given birth to Dria, she looked like her father. Hearing her talk like that, she sounded just like him. Dria shook loose and ran off and things were never the same. She didn't want anything to do with medicine after that. My child wanted nothing to do with all the wisdom I had to pass down. In Bellissima's eyes, I was still brilliant."

"You've made great strides in mental health but if you had stayed on course studying physical wellness, you would have become the greatest physician that ever lived. Dria's father used his gifts to lead you astray. Then, he used his gifts and mystery to harm Dria. When Dria refused to practice medicine, you resented her for it because you'd learned so much, you needed to pass it on or else all the pain would have been for nothing. Maybe Dria turned away from medicine because of him the same way you did. Did you ever think about that? Lou Anna, Dria had to choose her own path."

"Minxy. I failed Dria and when she rejected my wisdom, she rejected me with it. I had the nerve to make her feel like she failed me when she didn't want to become a doctor. It's crazy how we think we have the right to dream for our children. I should have let her come into her own gifts no matter how they drummed up the past. It's funny how we let things go on so long that they become normal behaviors. It's gone on so long that our relationship's unfixable."

"Nothing's unfixable. Nothing's impossible with God and a little prayer. Look at me, I was a junkie and an alcoholic. I turned my daughter into a user and then I abandoned her so that I could get clean. I was with her when she got so far gone. Then I couldn't bear to look at the monster that I created. I got it set in my mind that I had to get better first and then I'd come back to Sadie- make things right. Truth is, I couldn't stomach any more of my child's suffering. What if Sadie and I have nothing to talk about now that I'm clean? What if I find being her drinking buddy more fun than being her mother and we both relapse? God's working on me. I'm not saying Catherine getting sick is His way of answering my prayers for change to come, but I did beg him to put me in a position where I have no choice but to face my child, face my demons and rise to the challenge- be a good mother for once in my life. You know Lou, what happened to Dria wasn't entirely your fault."

"You say it, but I feel fully responsible. My little girl was violated. It almost ruined her and Lissima's bond. Lissima still doesn't know and if she doesn't know, how can she understand? What if they're never close again, Minxy?"

"You're underestimating how amazing our girls are. They're more forgiving than we can ever hope to be. They forgave God for letting them be born to women like us."

For Kay Beaumonte' having twins was the greatest gift. She'd laugh whenever strangers struggled to tell which one was Cheniere, and which one was Bellissima. They never guessed correctly the first time, but Kay always knew. There were little things that made them separate little people. Her babies looked the same, but they smelled different. Cheniere, who was nine minutes older, always smiled whenever she saw the color green and her newborn scalp smelled like coconuts. Bellissima's favorite color was yellow and the few strands of hair she had smelled like fresh satsumas. Upstairs, Kay made Bellissima's bed and gave her pillow a big sniff. *"Sweet Satsumas,"* she whispered.

Kay pulled a few outfits from Bellissima's closet and some undergarments from the dresser.

"Kay! What's the hold-up! I wanna get out of these clothes and climb into something with an elastic waistband!" Minxy shouted.

"I'm coming! Just looking for her overnight bag!" Kay dug through Bellissima's purses and luggage. "Found it!" When Kay grabbed Bellissima's bag, a folded piece of paper fell out. Kay picked it up, unfolded it and sat down on the bed- shocked. It was a discarded prescription slip with Bellissima's name on it. The prescribing doctor was Lou Anna Beaumonte'. The prescription was a year old.

CHAPTER SIXTEEN

The bus ride home from the fair was noisy. The children sang spirituals at the top of their lungs, still hyperactive from their adventurous evening. Sadie, still delightfully satisfied with her vomitus victory, smiled between sips of bismuth. Bellissima, stuck between two kids fight over a nearly finished churro, smiled through her discomfort as she contemplated the idea of silence, again. Dria sat way in the back alone. She gazed out the window; first out into the night and then up towards the stars. *'Those are our stars, Colin'* - she whispered with her hand pressed against the glass as if to reach out and touch the stars far away.

Back when they were younger, there was a secret hideaway in town where all the teenagers went to misbehave. Behind the church, over the draw bridge, through the graveyard where old slave Jubilee was buried- the youngsters gathered. It was a rivulet they called dynamite hole. It was a place of equanimity. Most of the town's offspring escaped there to smoke or listen to explicit music but it was also a place where lovebirds hid to canoodle. Colin and Dria met there often when they were younger. While their peers participated in adolescent debauchery, the two of them strayed from the bunch to cuddle and decipher the stars. Before Dria left for college, she and Colin met there. They were there together when it ended.

Dria waited for Colin by the rope swing, looking up at the sky. She hadn't heard him approaching. "No one wears the moonlight quiet like you, Dria Beaumonte'."

Dria turned to find Colin leaning against the old lover oak tree where all those who were courting carved their initials. "How long you been standing there watching me, Colin Hardy?"

"If I answered that question, you'd swear I was a stalker."

"No, never. A man in love, maybe, but never a stalker," Colin smiled but it quickly faded as he thought about Dria leaving. "Come. I want to show you something." Colin joined Dria beside the creek and the two of them walked in, ankle deep. "Do you see those two stars, the ones close to the dipper?"

"Yes," answered Colin, wrapping his arms around Dria's waist.

"We've been watching these stars together since we were old enough to sneak out and back in without getting caught. We've looked at them a thousand times, but I've never truly seen them until now. Those two stars have always been brighter than all the rest. They've been watching us right back. Do you think they can see us shining brighter than all the rest of the people around us just like we recognize their uniqueness.?"

"I don't know, Dria. I do know all the stars in the sky combined could never shine as bright as you."

"I wonder, what would happen if that star was left all alone. Would it still hold the same fire for its counterpart? keep on shining or start to dim, let themselves burns out?"

"Is that your way of asking me if my love will change once you leave tomorrow?" asked Colin.

"Maybe."

Colin gently kissed Dria's forehead. "It won't change. It can't. It never will because I won't let it. You and I are written in the stars, ain't that what our Mama's say?"

"Yeah."

"Well, I believe 'em."

A bright flashlight beamed, separating their lips. Colin and Dria, blinded, shielded their faces. "Alexandria? Alexandria Beaumonte' is that you?" It was Emily and her sadistic posse' of privileged cohorts. They neared the creek, snickering amongst themselves. "Who's that with you? Colin Hardy, the football phenom? Look at the two of you, cheek to cheek. It's like homecoming night all over again." Emily, clearly smitten, stared at Colin as if she were hungry for him. "Hey there quarterback," she said with a wink. "I hope I'm not interrupting anything."

"Actually, you are. I'm leaving tomorrow. We kind of want to be alone as much as possible," said Dria.

Emily sneered, "That's right! You're the talk all over town! The perfect little Valedictorian is heading to the big city. You're right, the two of you should be alone. Break-ups are difficult. We should go so you guys can cry it out," said Emily, unwrapping a cherry blow pop. She licked it inappropriately while staring at Colin.

"Break-up? Who' breaking up? Dria's going away but we're not breaking up. With a brain like hers, she'll graduate in no time and then we'll be together again. We've pledged our hearts and our bodies to one another, forever," said Colin.

Emily and her group of friends began to laugh so hard that Emily had to stop and catch her breath. "Your hearts and your bodies?" She turned to her friends, "Y'all hear that? Alexandria has pledged her body to Colin Hardy! What a load of bullshit!"

"It's not bullshit," defended Colin.

"Oh yes, it is, Colin. Did you know your little Alexandria had an appointment scheduled at my daddy's clinic a few months ago? Silly daddy, sometimes he forgets to lock his office. I love it when he gets forgetful. I get access to all sorts of things: pills, his prescription pad, his doctor's excuse pad so that I can skip school whenever I feel like it. Most importantly, I get full access to all his patient files. That's really fun. I got a chance to go over Alexandria's file, every page of it. Colin, you may have saved yourself for her, but she's already pawned her cherry. Sorry to be the one to tell you."

Dria felt weak and Colin stepped back, confused. "What's Emily talking about, Dria?"

"It's not what you think Colin. I didn't pawn off anything, that's not what happened! It was…"

"Just stop! The proof's here in writing!" Emily turned to Colin. "I'd be happy to show you. I made copies, lots of copies!" laughed Emily.

"No!" yelled Dria- ripping the documents from Emily's hands, causing them to fly everywhere.

Emily, remorseless, laughed even harder. She slid the candy out of her mouth and offered it to Dria. "Here, you want my cherry pop? Take it, it's used but like new…just like the cherry between your legs, child."

Dria ran away, leaving Colin alone in the creek. Colin called out for Dria, but she never looked back.

CHAPTER SEVENTEEN

Bellissima and her cousins crept in the big house, trying hard not to make noise. The three of them poked their head in the den. "Relax, Kay's already in upstairs, in bed with a headache," said Lou Anna- comfortable on the couch reading with Minxy right beside her.

"You bacon fat thieves are safe for now. She was so preoccupied with her head pain that she didn't bother investigating just yet," said Minxy.

"Thank God," said Bellissima, relieved- collapsing on the den floor. Dria and Sadie flopped down beside her.

Minxy found their exhaustion humorous. "You three look awfully beat."

"We are! How can they be so little and have so much energy?" complained Sadie.

"Now you know how we felt taking you girls to that fair year after year, right Lou?"

"Yeah, I remember having to come back here and soak my legs from having to keep up with you girls."

"A soak sounds wonderful. I feel like my entire body is one big blue throbbing contusion," said Sadie.

"That sounds bad. You alright?" asked Minxy- placing her hand on Sadie's forehead.

"She ate too much," said Dria. "Lissima and I warned her. She was a non-stop eating machine the whole time we were there. I'm surprised that ugly fish made it home alive. If she had any stomach room left for sushi, she would have eaten that too. Then, she showed everyone what digested carnie food looks like."

"Well, that's no good. You still feeling nauseous?" asked Minxy.

"-A little," answered Sadie.

"Come on. Follow me upstairs. I'll draw you a bath with some Buchu botanicals. It's a little something I smuggled into the states from South Africa. They don't make you bend over and cough if you don't give them a reason too. You'll soak in it for a while, it'll make you feel brand new," said Minxy- helping Sadie off the floor. Sadie, still woozy, followed her mother.

Lou Anna closed her book and removed her glasses. "Aside from being exhausted and having to see Sadie's insides, did you girls have a good time?"

"We had a blast!" answered Bellissima, enthused.

"Yeah, so much fun I almost forgot we were the adults. It was just like old times," agreed Dria.

"Yeah, until it nearly turned into a full-on royal wrestling smackdown."

"Smackdown? Oh Lord, please tell me you girls didn't hurt anyone?" begged Lou Anna.

"No. Luckily, things didn't get that out of hand, but Sadie almost peeled the plastic off that discount Malibu Barbie, Emily."

"Emily? You mean Colin's matrimonial mistake?" asked Lou Anna.

"So, you've heard?" asked Dria rolling her eyes.

"Yeah, Kay filled me in when I saw the two of them waltz in church together. It's so disappointing. Colin's mother, rest her soul, was a good friend of mine. She would've wanted better for her boy. She'd roll over in her grave if she knew Colin had that girl living in the house her daddy's daddy left behind to be passed down."

"I cannot believe he asked for that phony bigot's hand in marriage. I guess Colin cares more about money and appearances than I thought. He went and married himself some old Louisiana money," Said Dria, shaking her head.

"-Old Louisiana money? What makes you think Emily's old Louisiana money?" laughed Lou Anna. "She didn't come from a prominent family, a proud one neither. Their wealth came from shit."

"-You mean like manure or fertilizer? Did they yield dung compost for crops or something?" asked Dria.

"No, I mean shit. The kind that comes out of people's asses!"

Dria and Bellissima looked at one another, both amused and intrigued. "-Human feces?" asked Bellissima.

127

Lou Anna's head tilted to the side. "Yes, human feces- shit! How many times you want me to say it?" Dria and Bellissima laughed until their faces were red. "Let me tell you about it. You see, back when Dria and Colin were babies; state workers used this road as a shortcut to the site where they were building Old US 90. Of course, you know it as Burn Out bridge. It was a highly inconvenient set up for us and all the other Louisiana families that owned land down this way. It made it extremely difficult to drive in and out with all the heavy utility truck traffic, so most of the local's walked or rode bikes if their destination wasn't too far. That's how Colin's mother and I met. We crossed paths one summer when Dria and I came down to stay in the cottage. I had Dria in a stroller and Colin's mother walked by with baby Colin in his stroller. We were just gon' walk on past one another, but Dria and Colin started smiling and waving at one another. Before we knew it, Colin's mother and I were walking together every day. It was a nice workout routine, but a bad route. The stench was almost unbearable. Having a walking buddy made the smell almost tolerable. -Almost"

"-Smell?" interrupted Dria.

"Yes- an awful redolence. The state lined the roadside with portable toilets to keep the workers from doing their business out in the open or in our river where boaters tossed their nets to fish. A lot of those workers were lonely men, traveling from Mississippi and Texas to find work. They'd left their wives at home. It wasn't unusual for the women of this town to bring over sandwiches and covered baskets of food for the workers from time to time. It was innocent gratitude. We were grateful for all their hard work, but one floozy was extra friendly- Emily's mother. Colin's mother and I would see her out there all the time, fawning over the laborers with her shirt buttons undone so that they'd get an eyeful of breast. It would take a truly desperate woman to flaunt her feminine wiles on a hot dirt road that smelled like ass, but she wasn't your ordinary whore. No, she was an experienced adulterer. In fact, that's how Emily was made- the sperm and sweat of a married doctor who used to do backdoor abortions. She started sleeping with him after he got rid of her third or fourth bastard child. Eventually, the doctor's wife left him and before the poor woman could get all her clothes out of the closet, Emily's mother had moved on in and shacked up with her husband. It was all fun and games until she got pregnant for the six or seventh time. The doctor refused to perform another procedure on her. He thought a baby would keep her from going astray. Later that year, Emily was born, and the doctor put a ring on the whore's finger. That didn't slow her down, though. I guess she got bored with the doctor after the thrill of sneaking around was over. Emily's mother didn't want to be a housewife or a mother. She wanted to be a cheap whore who had random tree sex in the woods with road workers. A wild animal can never truly be domesticated, and you can't turn a whore into a housewife, not if she makes no effort at all to become even moderately submissive to morality. One hot afternoon, Colin's mother and I strolled past the workers and saw little Emily sitting all alone near one of the bulldozers. We assumed her mother was enjoying a casual hump in the brush as usual and would be back for Emily soon, so we just kept on walking- minding our business. Evidently, little Emily got tired of being left unattended. Children don't like sitting still when they're that young. You must watch them. Take your eyes off a toddler for two seconds, they're liable to get into anything. Little Emily unbuckled her stroller seat belt and started fiddling with tools and climbing all over the machinery. Staring up at those big blue lavatories, curiosity got the best of her. Emily accidentally got herself locked inside and started yelling. *'You hear that?'* asked Colin's mother. We stopped on the road and I listened. *'-Sounds like a child, crying.'* We stopped in the road and turned back. That's when we saw it- a bigger truck that came along every few days. They'd hook the potty to the bigger truck and take the lavatories off somewhere to dump all the blue dye and sewage. They came that day as scheduled and hooked up, not knowing little Emily had wandered inside. The potty lifted from the ground and Emily started beating on the door. *'Stop! Wait!'* we yelled hauling ass back. We waved our arms and screamed as loud as we could until we got the driver's attention. *'There's a child in there!'* The driver panicked and accidentally hit the release button before lowering the potty back to the ground. The potty fell off the lift and spilled shit all over the road. Everyone came running. We pushed through the workers and found the child in one piece- thank goodness. We tried our best but couldn't keep from laughing. There sat little Emily, right in the center of a diarrhea puddle, a giant brown turd right on her head between her pigtails. Her mother heard all the commotion and ran out of the woods with her panties around her ankles. When the doctor heard about what happened to his daughter he threatened to sue the state.

To keep from having a big legal mess, the state of Louisiana paid him a handsome lump sum and he used a wad of it to divorce Emily's mother. With the rest, he paid off all his debt, swore off abortions and opened a new women's clinic where he handled mammograms, natural births, and basic procedural women's health. Emily's mother eventually developed serious health complications from all those untreated sexually transmitted diseases and came on home after slowly touring the world- one penis at a time. I bet her coot wasn't nothing but a black hole full of man-fluid by the time she killed over. She was bedridden from most of little Emily life. When she passed, Emily was left with her daddy- best thing to ever happen to that child. I mean, the poor thing was covered in shit and it was all her mother's fault. I'm not surprised she became what she is today. If Emily had turned into a nicer young lady, we would all feel sorry for her. Her daddy must've bathed her a million times, she still smelled like biodegradable waste until she hit puberty."

"Little brat Emily only has money because she was shittier than a wad of ass paper? That. Is. So. Good to know." Said Bellissima with a smirk.

"Glad I could help," said Lou Anna.

"I'm going to head up and say goodnight to Mama, see if there's anything I can do about that achy head of hers. If I start screaming, one of ya'll come up and make sure she doesn't kill me for making her lather the whole town in pig fat," Said Bellissima leaving Dria and her mother downstairs alone.

Lou Anna noticed Dria's unfocused gaze into empty space. "What's with this sudden concern over this Emily girl and her net worth? You still have a soft spot for Colin?"

Dria's lips pinched, "No. Why would I?"

"I don't know, maybe because he was your first love. Does anyone ever get over their first love?"

"Even if I wasn't over Colin, would it matter? He's moved on. I just thought if I added up Emily's worth, I'd somehow start understanding why God thinks *she* deserves someone as great as Colin. Maybe she deserves love and I don't."

"You don't think you deserve love?"

"Me? No. I was made for pain. I was built to endure abuse, not deserve love. There's an old proverb. It says we accept the kind of love we think we deserve. Does Colin think *that's* the kind of love he deserves?"

"No, that's crazy talk. I know Colin knows he deserves better. He'd be crazy not to see it. Just like you're crazy if you think God designed you with pain in mind. You weren't put on this earth just to feel pain and unhappiness. You think he's moved on?

Dria's mouth gaped. "He's married, Mama! It goes without saying!"

"-Wouldn't be able to tell by the way he was looking at you today," said Lou Anna standing, crossing her arms. "It's a waste of time, Dria- calculating that girl's worth and comparing her to you. You're so great, you can't be measured or added. *She's* the type of person that can be easily defined by numbers. You're a Beaumonte'. And to top that off, you're *my* daughter. And when I think of you, numbers never come to mind."

Tears welled in Dria's eyes. Her mother had never said anything that kind to her. Ever.

•

Minxy and Sadie looked at the fish together. "You going to let this little guy swim around with you in the tub?" asked Minxy

"I wish he could. He's the cutest fishy that ever lived," Gushed Sadie.

"It's so weird hearing you talk like that. When you were little you didn't like animals- dolls neither. Dria, Cheniere and Bellissima had their sock puppets until they were at least 3 years old. You weren't interested in anything that required love or caring for," said Minxy, patting her daughter on the back playfully. Minxy swirled the suds with her fingertips. "This will make you feel better. When the children fall ill at the refugee camp, we bathe them in this. I'm so glad you had a fun day. Was it nice being with the youth group?"

"It really was."

"Good. Being around children is good." Minxy pulled at Sadie's jacket but Sadie recoiled. "What's wrong?" Minxy asked.

Sadie hadn't realized how cagy she was acting until she saw her mother's reaction. "Nothing. I'm just feeling another wave of sickness like I might throw up. You should go, it's not going to be pretty."

Minxy's face was blank. "It's just a little vomit. I raised you. I've had your vomit on me more times than I can count, and I've seen much worse in Africa." She replied- lifting the toilet seat as if to call Sadie's bluff. Sadie looked into the empty toilet and then back at her mother. "There, go ahead...let it out," urged Minxy; but Sadie just stood there. "What's wrong?"

"The wave...it passed," lied Sadie.

"Okay. Good. Then let's get you out of those clothes and into the tub," said Minxy- pulling at Sadie's jacket again.

Sadie pulled away hard. "Mama! I can do it by myself!" She'd accidentally yelled.

"Sadie, you're my child! I've seen it all long before you grew anything to see! You've got the same plumbing I got down there! I saw your bikini picture on that online page you got! It looked like you were wearing dental floss! Since when are you shy?"

"I just want a little privacy, that's all!"

Minxy grinned. Something wasn't right. It seemed as if Sadie was almost ready to break and spill her confessions, but instead of pushing- Minxy stopped. She wanted the truth but didn't want it by means of pressure. "Privacy? Of Course, my child." Minxy reached into the tub and shut off the valve. "I'll take your fishy downstairs and find him a bowl. Enjoy your bath," she said eerily.

Once the bathroom door was shut, Sadie quickly locked it. She took a deep breath and undressed. Turning sideways in the mirror, she frowned. She starting to show.

Kay sat in Catherine's bed with her lab top opened on her lap. She held the prescription up to her glasses, trying to pronounce it correctly. *"Chlorpromazine. What the hell, Lou Anna?"* - she mumbled, wondering out loud why her own sister would prescribe a controlled substance to Bellissima without telling her. Anxiety set in when Kay began to wonder why Bellissima would need a controlled substance to begin with. What was she hiding? There was a tap at the bedroom door.

"Mama, you still awake?" asked Bellissima

Kay quickly slammed the lab top shut and pushed it under her pillow along with the prescription slip. "Lissima sweetheart? Come on in!"

Bellissima entered. "Hey, mommy."

"How was the fair, baby?"

"It was so much fun, Mama! I'll admit I didn't want to go at first but I'm glad we went. I forgot how magical it could be. Auntie Lou said you had another one of your headaches. Are you feeling any better?"

"Yes, I'm just fine now."

"Are you sure, I can get my med bag and…"

"No need. It's just a little migraine, it too shall pass. I think I just need a little rest, is all. You should rest too, you have work tomorrow. I went to the cottage and got you some more clothes."

"Okay, well- I'll be downstairs if you need anything."

Kay watched until Bellissima reached the door. "Lissima?"

"Yes, Mama?"

"I'm so happy to hear you had a good time with your cousins. I worry about you sometimes. I worry that you're not living, stopping to smell the roses and all that. You're the most important thing in my life. I just want you to be happy," said Kay.

"I am happy, Mama."

"Are you, baby? Are you really happy? Are things really okay with you? If they weren't, you know you could tell me, right?"

"Of course, I know I can. Everyone goes to you to talk about everything."

"Not everyone. Not everything," mumbled Kay. "Did you win anything tonight?"

"Yep! This unicorn!" gushed Bellissima, showing Kay the plush toy.

"How about one for your sister?" asked Kay.

Bellissima dug deep into her jacket pocket and pulled out a matching toy, "Wouldn't leave without one for Cheniere too. That's what twins do."

CHAPTER EIGHTEEN

Daylight broke. The moon was long gone, making room for the sun shining brightly throughout the big house. Pulsating phone vibration woke Bellissima; a virtually noiseless alarm she'd set on purpose so that she'd stay one step ahead of her deviant cousins. Bellissima shimmied out of her sleeping bag and quickly dressed for work. Once her shoelaces were tied, she crept into the kitchen, swiped the teal canteen of blessed oil and stuffed it in her work bag. Before leaving, Bellissima crept back into the den and carefully slid her hand underneath Sadie's pillow. She felt around until she found the marker Sadie had been hiding. Bellissima wiggled it free- *'light sleeper my ass.'* She uncapped the marker, grinning furtively. For Sadie: big black circles around both eyes so she looked like a raccoon. For Dria: two big devil horns and a curly mustache.

"You're looking surprisingly giddy today," said Jan, who'd been standing at the main entrance with coffee waiting for Bellissima to arrive. "I've got a hot cup of go-brew and your clipboard for you."

"Wow! You must really need those holiday volunteers!" said Bellissima- taking the coffee to her lips. "Sweet revenge, a free cup of joe and my patient chart printed and ready to go! It's going to be a great day!"

Jan's face sank. "I wouldn't start bragging just yet. We're short a floor nurse today; some guy's been calling for you non-stop claiming he's Mr. Breaux's long-lost grandson and we found a pile of meds under your grandmother's pillow. There were so many there's no way to tell how long she's been going unmedicated."

"What? A no-show?" asked Bellissima- crushed.

"Yeah."

"-Calls from some low life trying to make a quick buck off a dead man?"

"Yeah."

"Catherine's been spitting up pills again?"

"Yeah, that pretty much sums it up."

"You were right to stop me from bragging."

•

Kay stared at the empty space near the stove where she kept her meat grease collection and blessed oil, confused. She was almost certain the girls brought the wrong container to church. She planned to prove it by confronting them with the correct bottle, still at the big house right near the stove where she'd left it. She even searched the cabinets, but it was nowhere to be found. Eventually, Kay gave up searching, grabbed some eggs to start breakfast but found it difficult to focus on food. All she could think about was the prescription she'd found.

"You're up early," said Minxy strolling into the kitchen, pulling her robe tight to shut out the chill. "I thought for once, I'd beat you to the coffee pot."

"Good morning, Minx. How'd you sleep?"

"Not good, actually. Mama always said it was pointless to try and sleep with a congested mind, a longing heart, or a heavy spirit. Catherine was such a garrulous philosopher, but when she's right she's right." Minxy noticed Kay's peculiar withdrawnness. "I'm guessing you didn't get a lot of rest either."

Kay sighed. "Not a wink."

"Anything the matter?" asked Minxy- sitting down next to Kay.

"Nothing I'd like to talk about. What about you? You ready to talk about what's eating you?"

"Nope, not yet."

"Well, what do you say we just sit here and drink our coffee together like two people trying to ignore their problems?"

Minxy smiled. "Yeah, that'll do for now."

Lou Anna entered the kitchen wiping her eyes. "I woke up this morning in bed alone."

"Neither of us had a good rest. I just gave up and waited on dawn, so I'd have an excuse to get up," said Kay.

"Same here," agreed Minxy.

Lou Anna brought her full cup to the table and joined her sisters. "Well, I guess I'm the only one who earned a good night of sleep," she gloated.

"Yeah, it's like you're the only one whose stress-free, carefree. The only one of us without a guilty conscious" snarked Kay.

"What do you mean by that?" Lou Anna asked.

"Nothing. A turkey omelet sound good to you, Minx? How about fig crepes for you Lou?" They both agreed, eagerly.

Dria and Sadie burst into the kitchen, bickering at one another. "Shut up!" yelled Dria.

"No, you shut up!" yelled Sadie.

Kay took one look at their faces began to laugh uncontrollably. "What the heck are you two fussing about this early?" asked Minxy.

"Dria let Lissima get the drop on us!"

"It's not my fault we woke up looking like idiots! You were supposed to be guarding the marker! You just laid there snoring while she got us!"

"You two look ridiculous, but you had it coming!"

Dria picked up the toaster for a better look at her face. "This means war! I'm going to shave off one of her eyebrows!"

"I'm going to put her hand in a warm water tonight." Said Sadie.

"You will do no such thing!" yelled Lou Anna. "You girls are exhibiting poor sportsmanship! I'm getting a box and I'm collecting all the markers today, pens too! If you girls need to write something, you can check out a writing utensil and check it back in like a library book! There will be no more hazing until you learn how to gracefully take a loss!"

"I think that's a great idea," said Kay. "You girls head upstairs, mix some baby oil and soap. That'll get your faces back to normal. I'll make you a hearty breakfast, you'll need your strength today."

"For what? "asked Dria.

"-To ready the feast table for Mama's dinner. It's been buried out back in the shed for God knows how long."

"Why do we have to?" asked Sadie.

"I heard a few people talking about your grandma's party after church. There might be a few more guests than expected. There's no way we'll be able to fit everyone in here. The big table has got to come out. You need to assess the damage, make sure that wobbly leg gets tightened," said Minxy.

"It might need a fresh coat of primer too," said Lou Anna.

"Bellissima's not here to help us! That's not fair! We're *all* responsible for this dinner! She should be suffering every burdening task too!" argued Dria.

"Bellissima's stuck at her job with your grandmother! Trust me, she's suffering plenty!" argued Lou Anna.

Dria and Sadie stood at the edge of the shed ramp. "It looks like a crypt," said Dria. "Hey, you remember when you were scared of vampires?" she teased.

"Shut it Dria! You lead, I'll follow," pushed Sadie.

"Why do I have to go in first"

"You're older, that's why!"

"You're the one with the flashlight, Sadie!"

"Fine Dria! We'll both go in first,"

Dria sighed. "Your stupidity is exhausting. *Together*, you mean we'll go in *together*. First implies that one of us will take the lead. *Together* implies that no one leads and we both move forward at the same time."

"We're wasting time! Let's get this over with!" Dria and Sadie pried open the shed doors, releasing a giant veil of dust that caused them both to cough.

"I bet there's a Dracula-sized bat hanging out in here just waiting to suck us dry," taunted Dria. "Maybe spiders too. Yeah, spiders by the dozen."

"-Spiders?" whispered Sadie- clicking on the flashlight.

"Yep! Big, creepy, hairy, venomous ones. They're probably hungry too." Dria saw a large web and gasped.

"What?"

"I was trying to scare you and accidentally scared myself in the process. Quick, look for the table so we can seal this tomb back up."

"Look at all this junk. It's piled up to the ceiling. I didn't know granny was a hoarder." Sadie found the light chord and pulled it, illuminating the shed's clutter.

"Hoarders tend to collect useless crap for no rational reason. These things, they're not crap," corrected Dria. "No, these are Beaumonte' treasures." She pulled a box from the shelf. "These are all your pageant tiaras and sashes."

"Is that my tricycle? I broke the wheel and had to stop riding it. I thought it got hauled off to the sinkhole!" said Sadie. She noticed a line of old book sacks, three of them in a row. "Look at those, I bet the pink one is Mama's"

"You can't know that just by looking at them and besides, they all have a little pink on them."

"Yeah, but *that* pink one on the end has the peace symbol on it. That's definitely Minxy Beaumonte's backpack."

Not convinced, Dria grabbed it and pulled it down. She unzipped it and pulled out a tiny wooden coffer. Inside she found some potent marijuana and what looked like long forgotten Quaaludes wrapped in foil. "Okay maybe you're right," she laughed.

"I should have made you bet me a few dollars," said Sadie.

"Yeah, you should have. It would have been a win. Always go with your Gut kiddo," said Dria pulling down a few more boxes. "Look! It's the Beaumonte' crib. Each of our Mamas slept in this as a child, then we did. Isn't that amazing? We were all once babies in this very crib," said Dria.

Mentioning babies made Sadie very eager to get out of the shed. "Do you see the table yet?" she asked, anxious.

"I think that's it, way in the back, all covered up." They walked to the back of the shed and brushed the stray pigeon feathers away. Dria stepped back and eyed the mahogany slab. "Has it always been this big?" She grabbed the table top and attempted to lift it on her own. It barely budged an inch. "Was it always this damn heavy? Sadie, grab the other side. You'll lift and push. I'll lift and pull." Tentative, Sadie agreed. The two pushed and pulled and pushed and pulled until the table was near the shed ramp. Dria, out of breath from unknowingly making the most effort, stopped and looked down. "We're going to have to lift a little higher, there's a hump here when the shed door and the ramp meet."

Sadie let go of the table. "No. I can't do any more lifting."

"What do you mean you can't? Now's not the time to get lazy, Sadie. We're almost done, now just lift on the count of three and help me walk it down the ramp, slow."

Reluctantly, Sadie placed her hands back on the table. *One…two….* On three, Dria lifted her end and pulled hard. Sadie let go and the heavy table slid down the ramp, out of Dria's control causing her to fall flat on her back. The table slid down the shed ramp right along with Dria.

"Oh my God! Dria!" yelled Sadie- running to her aid.

Dria climbed out from under the table, dusting the dirt from her clothes. "Sadie! What the hell?"

"I'm so sorry!" yelled Sadie.

"Sorry? Tell that to my elbow!" yelled Dria- lifting her arm so Sadie could see the bleeding slash caused by the fall.

"Well, I told you I couldn't lift!"

"You're so lazy! You're such a slacker! You're always trying to talk your way out of hard work! That's your problem! That's why you keep prolonging graduation!"

"I'm not lazy!"

"Then what? What's your excuse? Your back hurts? A fresh manicure you don't wanna ruin? You're pregnant?"

Sadie paused and Dria studied her sudden loss for words. "Oh! My!."

"Shut up! Shut up! Stop talking! Don't say another word!" warned Sadie.

"You're pregnant? Sadie!"

"Dria, I will slap you senseless if you don't pipe down! I swear I will! Lower your voice before they hear you inside!"

"I'm sorry," whispered Dria. "I'm just so shocked! It all makes sense now: You've been turning down alcohol and eating like you're on death row. Your nose is even wider. How pregnant are you?"

"-Four months."

"-Four months!" Dria screamed.

"Shut your big fat mouth!" demanded Sadie, dragging her under the shade tree. "I really don't want everyone to know yet."

"Does Lissima know?"

"No, and you're not going to tell her either!"

"Why not, Sadie? This is exciting news!"

"It will be exciting news when I find out if the baby's healthy. I don't want anyone to know I'm pregnant until I find out if the fetus has any major health concerns."

"Health concerns? You're in great shape! You drink a lot of water, you get a lot of exercise when you're dancing at all those parties in your panties and I see you with fresh fruit at least three times a day. When Bellissima starts bitching about vitamins, I tune her out; but you actually take yours. Why are you so worried?"

"Because I was a selfish junkie for the first two months!" yelled Sadie- nearly in tears.

Dria recalled their previous discussion. "Finding out you were knocked up, that was your wake up call?"

"Yeah. The kid's not even here yet and I've put its life in danger."

"Sadie, you were an addict. No one's ever gotten clean without stumbling."

"Mama did. She left me and got clean. Maybe being around me, being a mother is what made her addictions get so bad. What if *I* need drugs to be around my kid?"

"No one's perfect, Sadie. Auntie Minx is still a great mom. Why can't you remember any of the good times? The ones that didn't require drugs or alcohol? She had her moments. She was still a positive role model. You will be too. When are you going to see a doctor about the baby?"

"I don't know. I've called a few places to make an appointment while I'm down here but every time I say my last name, they ask if I'm related to Bellissima and I hang up. This town's too small. I'll just have to wait until I make it back to the city for an appointment, some place where no one knows my name."

"I feel like such an asshole for giving you a hard time these last few days. You must be so conflicted and scared dealing with Grandma Cat's drama and suffering the heat on top of that," said Dria.

"It's okay. Just promise you won't tell anyone."

"I won't. Bellissima's the one you should be worried about, she's the tattle tell."

•

Bellissima entered Catherine's room and caught her grandmother in mid-escape, with one leg over the bed railing.

"Grandma Cat! What do you think you're doing?" she yelled, grabbing Catherine's leg and repositioning her back in bed.

"What the hell does it look like, I'm going fishing."

"Fishing? No, you're not! You should be in bed resting not trying to make a break for it!"

Catherine's lower lip poked out. "I'm getting good and tired of being told what to do."

"I know and I'm sorry Grandma, but this is how things are now."

"For now, or forever?" asked Catherine, the same question that everyone seemed to keep avoiding. Bellissima didn't answer. "What's that you got in your bag?" asked Catherine.

"It's evidence."

"Evidence?"

"Yeah, It's also Mama's blessed oil. If I know her as well as I think I do, she'll be looking for this back at the big house. I have no doubt me and my cousins are going to be in big trouble when the whole church breaks out with grease acne, but I'm not going to make it easy for her to catch us. I need to hide it here until she's off our scent." Bellissima felt around in her coat pocket and pulled out a handful of pill capsules. "Grandma Cat, the staff tells me you're refusing to take your medicine. Now, don't bother lying, they found the proof. You have to take your medicine, Granny."

"No, I don't, Lissima!" shouted Catherine stubbornly.

"Yes! Yes, you do! Today's a full day! I've got a lot of work to catch up on. I need you to cooperate today. I have your prescriptions here. I want you to take them and stop giving the other nurses a hard time," said Bellissima handing Catherine a glass of water.

"I don't like the way they make me feel, all loose and loopy like I'm high on grass. I don't like where they take my mind. I feel so far from the truth. Every single time I get close to my memories again, those damn pills snatch me up and take me away."

"Is that a bad thing? Not all your memories are happy ones."

"Good or bad, they're mine and I want to keep them as long as I can. All your life you've been in the dark. Your mother, your aunts- they don't want you girls knowing the truth. I haven't been taking those sedatives so that I can tell you as much as possible before it's all erased for good. You think I don't know I'm sick? I know my head ain't right. They say to pack light when you're headed to heaven. What if I can't haul these memories with me? What if I gotta unload 'em soon? Then who will give you and your cousins the answers? Don't you want answers, child?" *Answers.* Bellissima contemplated. Catherine continued to intrigue. "I guess it's really up to you. If you don't want to know, I won't force you to listen. Hell, maybe it's best you don't know, then you can die an old lady warm in your bed with some innocent ears on you. But *I* think you deserve the truth and *I* think you know that you'll never be whole with all the pieces missing the way they are. You are your Grandfather's grandchild. You know what's right and what's not fair. I want to right my daughters' wrongs. If giving me those tranquilizers is easier for you than hearing about the dark times, then I'll take them. I'll understand." Bellissima put the glass of water down and slid the pills back into her pocket. "Hop on in, I'll pick up where I left off."

"You remember where you left off?"

"I do."

Bellissima snuggled close to her granny. Catherine cleared her throat. "Your mother Kay was the second blessing my womb brought forth, my passive child. The peaceful one. She was born in the big house, right on the kitchen floor. Her becoming a master chef came as no surprise to me. By the time Kay was five years old, she could serve a whole meal all by herself with no help from me. I taught her the basics: like how to measure water for cooking rice and how to make gumbo roux, but that's all. Kay was a natural. Her daddy loved her food, maybe even more than mine. *'She's going to be a great God-fearing wife and mother'.* Those were Jeremiah's words precisely. Kay never did walk down the aisle, but he was right when he predicted her becoming a great mother. So much joy, when Kay found out she was growing two babies. Your grandfather didn't live long enough to meet you and Cheniere, though." Bellissima burrowed even closer to her Grandmother.

"Kay took her father's death so hard. Her depression went on and on for years, well into adulthood. Being pregnant and not having her daddy around seemed to make her depression worse. I feared for you girls' safety. She wasn't eating nearly enough. She wasn't sleeping enough. She wasn't taking care of herself the way you should when you're with child. You and Cheniere came early, and she blamed herself for that. She blamed herself, even more, when the doctors discovered your sister was a mute."

"Mama blamed herself for that?"

"Yes Child. She thought her mourning was the reason Cheniere wasn't right. She cried for months. It wasn't like your ordinary post-partum depression, Kay was downright unglued. I thank God for my other two children, your aunts. Lou Anna and Minxy helped a lot in the beginning. That's what sisters are for, helping you pull yourself together when you don't have the strength to do it yourself. Kay's greatest fear? - That her twins would grow apart. She feared that Cheniere's inability to hear and speak meant she'd always be lonely and left out; but then Minxy noticed something spectacular about you and twin sister. One day, out of the blue, you and Cheniere started communicating. It wasn't with words, it was almost telepathic. You were barely walking but was the only one who knew exactly what Cheniere needed. When she cried, you knew exactly what toy she wanted. Whenever she was wet, you crawled up to Kay with a diaper. Kay fed you girls side by side and whenever there was something on Cheniere's plate that she didn't like, you'd separate it from the portion of the meal she did like. I bragged on my genius grandbabies. Seeing the two of you act like twins despite Cheniere's disability was the only thing that brought Kay back to life. After that, she hit the ground running, devouring every book on raising disabled children. It was a nice distraction from her broken heart."

"Mama had a broken heart?"

"Yes. Your father…"

"My father? You knew my dad!" asked Bellissima- both excited and relieved to the point of tears.

"Oh yes. He was nothing like that trash Lou Anna brought home. You and Cheniere's father, he was much like Jeremiah in the beginning. He chased Kay and at first Kay wouldn't give him the time of day. She was focused on becoming a successful restaurateur. He was persistent, though. Eventually, Kay fell for his Savior Faire."

"Grandma, please tell me who he was."

"His name was Israel. The son of a shade tree mechanic and a dignified maid. They didn't have much but what they lacked in wealth, they made up for in grandeur. Funny how you find the most character in people who don't have the world on a string. He'd traveled here to work on the bridge just like many others did. Kay would bring him a basket of lunch every day. Lots of women did, but those men would fight over whatever your Mama had in her basket. *'You should really open your own place and sell this food. One day, I'm going to marry you and give you everything to make your dreams come true.'* You find the best character in those who barely have a string at all. Israel worked his fingers to the bone until he had enough to help Kay buy the old roller rink. She finally had a location for her restaurant. When Kay found out she was knocked up, your father fell at my feet, begging for forgiveness. *'Please forgive our past premarital promiscuity and give me your blessing. I'd like to marry your Kay, but I won't propose unless you tell me I can have her. Just know Mam, I don't want Kay. I need her.'*

"Mama was married to my daddy?"

"No such luck dear. He got on one knee and gave Kay the most expensive ring he could afford but she wanted to postpone their nuptials until after she had you two. She didn't want people thinking the only reason she was getting hitched was because she was ashamed of being an unwed mother, plus Kay wanted a big wedding. They wouldn't be able to splurge until after she'd given birth. Not long after you two came, Kay and Israel went their separate ways."

"He left us?"

"I'm afraid so. Don't be so quick to hate him for not being there. I'm not saying his absence is excusable but little children do that when they get so angry. They get so mad at their daddy's for not staying. Sometimes mother's make it hard to stay. Maybe he stopped loving Kay, or she stopped loving him. Maybe one of them started loving someone else. I don't know. All I do know is that I had another daughter without a husband. Two soiled and one to go." Bellissima and Catherine were quiet for a moment as if Catherine was giving her granddaughter a minute to let the information download. "You know, a few days before the bridge burned, the weather changed here in town. There were big grey clouds dampening the sunshine. The wind picked up in a way it never had before. The atmosphere seemed thicker, more troubled. It looked like rain for days, but just wouldn't pour. It just stayed gloomy for no reason at all. I heard Jeremiah outside the big house, putting some things in the truck. *Jeremiah wait! It looks like a storm might be coming any minute. Where are you going in a hurry? Can't it wait until the weather passes?'* I wouldn't let up. I was nagging, and I knew it but I couldn't stop.

'I have to work, Cat. I got a house full of kids to feed.' Said Jeremiah.

'You going to the mill?' I asked. It was a test. You see, I knew they'd all been laid off and none of the other wives mentioned their husbands going back to work. But he answered yes.

'Yes Cat, I'm going to work at the mill'. Why was he lying to me? People only lie when they have something to hide. I should have let it go but I'm no good at that- letting things go. *'I know you're still laid off, Jeremiah. So, you wanna try again and try the truth this time?'*

'Okay, Cat. I'm going to work but just not at the mill.'

'Where then?' I badgered. Jeremiah didn't answer me. He just kissed my face.

"You leave now, you may as well not come back Jeremiah Beaumonte', I mean it." I took my wedding ring off, to let him know I was serious.

"I love you Cat." He wrapped his arms around me tight and for a minute I thought he might stay. *"I'll still be loving you when I come back, no matter how mad you are,"* he said.

He turned to walk away, and I yelled his name. *"Jeremiah!"* When he turned back to me, I threw my wedding ring at him. It hit him square in the chest, bounced off and fell in the grass. Jeremiah bent down, picked it up, put it in his pocket and sped off without saying another word to me. I didn't like arguing in from of the kids, but I guess Minxy heard all the fussing. I turned around and there she was on the front porch, staring at me.

"Is daddy coming back"? She asked.

"Well of course he is. What a silly thing to ask."

She walked out into the yard to meet me. *"Mama, what do you call it when you're scared about something, but you don't know what? It's kind of like being nervous about what might happen or might go wrong?"*

"That's called a bad feeling, Minxy."

"Okay, Mama. I think I have one of those."

"One of what?"

"One of those bad feelings".

Jan rushed in. "I'm sorry to interrupt, but that guy won't let up. He's called again, he's on line 2."

Jan followed Bellissima as she marched to the phone. – "This is Beaumonte'."

The gentleman on the other end of the line cleared his throat. *"Hello, my name is Lincoln Breaux-Jude. I called the office and asked for a form to get my grandfather's ashes released to me and I'm told you spent the most time with him. I was wondering if there was anything you could do to convince the coroner to at least take my phone call…"*

"You make me sick!" yelled Bellissima.

"-Excuse me?"

"You heard me! Have you no shame? Who raised you like this? Do you have a real job, or do you just skim the obituaries looking for last names to borrow so you can inherit what good people worked hard to leave behind? Breaux had no one and he never said so, but I know it broke his heart to die with only a nurse here to see him go! You dare make a mockery of his loneliness? Whatever is lower than scum, that's what you are. Now goodbye! You call here again, I'll see to it you go to jail for attempting fraud!"

Bellissima slammed the phone down.

Jan grabbed her shoulder. "Woah! You okay?"

"Yeah, I'm just feeling heated. I'm going to take a walk, blow off some steam."

"Yeah, I think that's a good idea. I'll come and get you if we need you. Oh, before you go, did you get your grandmother to take her medication? You didn't mark her chart yet."

"Yeah," lied Bellissima.

CHAPTER NINETEEN

The smell of fresh basil overwhelmed Bellissima as she entered the front door. The aroma served as a much-needed comfort after a long, problematic day with Catherine at Pennycress. She followed the delicious scent all the way to the kitchen where she found her mother at the stove and Sadie at the table churning cornbread batter. "Is that shrimp and sausage jambalaya I smell?"

"It sure is! I decided to make your favorite tonight," answered Kay- greeting her daughter with a soft kiss on the cheek. "How was work? How's Catherine?"

"She's…settling in. Nothing to report," lied Bellissima again, plopping down in a chair next to her cousin. "Good afternoon Sadie, you're looking rather radiant today," complimented Bellissima with a snide smirk.

"Radiant? Yeah, I'm freshly exfoliated. I had no choice but to scrub until that mediocre example of vengeance washed off my face," snapped Sadie.

"-Mediocre? Sounds like you need another dose of your own medicine and who better to give it to you than the family nurse? You better sleep with one eye opened," threatened Bellissima.

"There will be no more hazing in this house, Bellissima! Your auntie Lou has confiscated all the markers, paints and pens- even the crayons! Count your blessings, you still have mascara and eye liner! You girls don't respect the game, you don't get to play!"

"That's not fair!" yelled Bellissima.

"You think *that's* unfair, wait until you see what task awaits you in the back yard," teased Dria, storming in- snatching Bellissima's keys off the kitchen table.

"You're bleeding what happened!" said Bellissima, noticing Dria's seeping bandage. "And where are you going in my car?"

"It's just a scratch, don't go trying to doctor on me, we don't have time. I'm going to Caraway's to buy a window unit and then me and Sadie are going to visit grandma Cat, finally."

Kay threw her head back, laughing. "A window unit? Catherine would blow a gasket if she found out," she warned.

"I'm willing to suffer one of her tongue lashings. Some of us have sensitive bodies that are changing. We need conditioned air up in here."

"Sensitive bodies? Whose body is sensitive? What changes?" asked Bellissima.

Kay looked at Sadie and then Sadie looked at Dria who realized she'd put her foot in her mouth. She stammered, trying to make up an excuse quick. "Um…. It's Mama. She's getting hot flashes," lied Dria.

"Menopause? I had no idea?" sympathized Bellissima.

"Yeah, she's pretty insecure about it though. It'd be best not to bring it up," said Dria. "Come on Sadie, let's go."

"Dria wait, what task awaits me?"

"That big hunk of wood that me and Sadie hauled out of the shed. It's officially your problem!" Dria and Sadie high-fived each other before turning to leave.

Bellissima turned to Kay. "Mama, what are they talking about?"

"-More dinner guests, we had the girls get the table out but it's looking a bit worn. It needs a little work. I put some tools by the back door for you and one of daddy's old furniture books. I'm sure you'll be able to get it done in time for the dinner."

"You expect me to restore the table all by myself!"

"Of course not, Sadie and Dria will help but they have some things they need to tend to and they did have to drag it out while you were at work. It's just fair that you put a little work in," said Kay.

"I *did* just put work in! A whole shift's worth!"

"I'm sorry Sweetheart. I know you're tired, but the sooner you get started the sooner you'll finish. All that huffing and puffing and complaining ain't gon get it done. Hop to it and you'll be finished before you know it. A little grub-work every now and then is good for you. I put my old overalls out for you upstairs. Go change so you don't ruin your good clothes."

•

"You don't have to buy an air conditioner just for me?" said Sadie to Dria. "I'm sure the baby can't even tell it's hot as Hades down here.

"That's not true. I read somewhere that babies feel a lot more than we think. The baby can feel its mother's discomfort. It's too hot in the big house, a blaring direct heat in the day and a stuffy, dry heat at night. It's the least I could do for being such a tyrant. You know, I've been harboring a little jealousy ever since I found out that you and Lissima talk more. I understood Lissima's distance, but I couldn't see my own faults with you until recently. I'm too hard on you. I'm not supportive enough. I constantly make you feel like you must earn my approval. That's the same thing Mama does to me and Auntie Minx. I feel awful about that and I'm sorry Sadie. I guess I'm more like my mother than I thought."

"You're forgiven. It's not that I don't want to be close to you, talk to you about things. It's just, Bellissima's easier to talk to. She's never made me feel that way, like I had to earn approval."

"Maybe you and I can work on being closer."

"...you going to work on being closer to Lissima again too?" asked Sadie.

"Yeah. That's at the top of my list."

"I always felt like I wasn't allowed to ask but, what happened with you two. I was the one who used to be jealous of how close you two were."

"-Painful things," answered Dria.

"Painful things are thieves. They just keep on taking if you don't take their power."

"Take their power?"

"Yeah. People don't talk about painful things because they get scared of opening those wounds because we remember how much they hurt when they first happened. Don't be scared to open those wounds. Chances are they didn't heal right the first time. Rip off the band-aid, cut it open and expose your weak parts. The dread will go away then. You know Lissima. If there's anyone who can help heal things, it's her. She gets it from Auntie Kay, her gentleness." Sadie's nose scrunched. "Frito pie! Today's lunch special at Mipsy's deli must be Frito-pie! I can smell the homemade chili from out here! Go ahead in, I'll be back."

"Auntie Kay made food back at the big house!"

"Don't worry, I'll definitely be hungry again by the time we make it back. I'm eating for two now, remember," whispered Sadie with a wink.

Dria walked into Caraway's and rung the bell at the counter. A surly old man emerged from the very back, his shirt read *Otis*. "Hi there, I was hoping to buy one of these air conditioners. I see you have a lot of used ones on the floor, but I'd like one of those new ones off the top shelf," said Dria pointing to a unit near the ceiling.

"Little Alexandria is that you, Beaumonte' gal?" asked Otis.

"Yes, well- I go by Dria now. Just Dria. Do I know you?"

Otis laughed and gazed at Dria adoringly. "Yes and no my dear. You wouldn't remember an old rascal like me. I knew your grandfather, Jeremiah. I used to bounce you off my knee when you were still in diapers. I helped Jeremiah build the cottage for you and your mother, Lou. Little Lissima lives there now, I'm so glad you all kept the cottage in the family. That's what Jeremiah would have wanted."

"You knew my grandfather?"

"Yes indeed! He was my best friend. I wasn't his best friend though. Not because he didn't love me like a brother; he just had so many friends. He'd never claim to care for one more than the next. We were all his best. I was with him when he purchased the plot for the cottage. It looked like a jungle from the property line, nothing but trees and vines. We worked on it every chance we got, even at night sometimes. Jeremiah wanted a roof ready to go over your little head, a place to call home. He loved you so much, he couldn't stop bragging about his first grandchild. Some say a man ain't supposed to cry but I shed more than my share of tears when I got word he'd died on the bridge. Jeremiah was family. He shouldn't have been there in the first place, you know."

Dria's eyebrows raised. "No Sir, I don't know. What do you mean he wasn't supposed to be there?"

Otis had said too much, and he realized that quickly reverting the discussion instead. "You say you want to beat the heat, huh? Well, that brand-new unit you pointed out will definitely cool down the big house. A big home like that really should have two units, one for the top floor and one for the bottom but if you pull the shades and turn on a few fans to help circulate the breeze, you should be a few degrees more comfortable. It's cheaper than getting vents drilled in the walls and having someone haul in an industrial unit. I'll get a ladder and have one of the shop boys get it down for you. We'll load it up."

"-Thank you," Dria replied. To pass the time, she strolled around Caraways, exploring antiques while she waited to pay.

"There goes my breath again, taken away from me just as soon as I see your face." Dria spun around and discovered Colin, admiring from near the register.

"I'm beginning to think you're following me," said Dria, accidentally smiling.

"-Following you? No, I'm just lucky is all. In a way, you sort of owe me these opportunities to see your pretty face."

"*I* owe *you*?" gasped Dria, slack-jawed.

"Yeah, for all the nights I closed my eyes tight, relying on the memory of what you used to look like since I could no longer see your smile in person."

"-And where's your wife, when you're closing your eyes and thinking of me all night long?"

Colin shrugged, impassively. "Who knows, probably busy contemplating how to make people's lives miserable. Lord knows she's succeeded in making mines that way. Maybe she's having another trashy affair."

Dria rolled her eyes theatrically with a guttural hiss. "Oh no! Don't tell me the evil princess turned into an evil queen! None of us saw that coming!"

"I know what you're thinking, Dria. I knew she was a cold bitch before I married her. I deserve all the misery."

"Damn! That's *exactly* what I was thinking," said Dria- her sarcasm replaced with real disappointment and palpable contempt. She turned her back to Colin and walked away.

Colin followed.

"If you never left my life; it would be you by my side; not my biggest regret. If only I could turn back the hands of time. I would have never let you walk out of my life."

"Listen to you complaining about time. Tell it to a horologist, for all I care. You got regrets about time, you best go tell it on the mountain or talk to the Good Lord. He won't let you go back in time though. Prayer doesn't work like that."

Colin smiled.

"-Something I said funny to you?"

"No, not at all. It's just, you sounded like Mrs. Catherine when you said that- sassy and certain," Colin replied.

Dria thought for a moment and grinned, "I supposed I did." As quickly as the grin curled, it washed away and Dria walked away from Colin again.

Colin followed. "I didn't plan on settling with Emily, Dria."

"Settling? You let Emily tell it, you two are as happy as can be- the perfect couple, meant-to-be, a match made in heaven…"

"More like a match made in hell!" yelled Colin. He looked around and lowered his voice. "If I tell you how I really feel, would it distort your image of me? If the truth should make me sound like a bad husband, would you think less of me as a man?"

"I can't respect you any less than I do right now, Colin. - Trust me."

Colin took a deep breath. "When you left, I was lost. We had plans, Dria. You were going to go on ahead, bust your ass at the university and get established. I was going to enlist, bust my ass for my country then come and meet you once you were done with school. The way you left things, I was confused. I'm a man, and I know I'm not supposed to talk about my heart, but it was broken. I went to war, thinking surely the pain and suffering I'd witness would somehow help me forget about my own suffering. I set my mind on saving the world. Ain't no place for heroes in the army. I had to find that out the hard way. When I came back, everyone was gone. They all had lives and wives and children. I thought of you and how coming back from the service was supposed to be the beginning of our lives together. Emily was still here. She made me feel like I had done something admirable by not getting shot. She never asked me how many I shot. Typical Emily, she has a one-track mind when it comes to being on top. Step on whoever gets in the way."

"What, you went for the first woman to stroke your ego?"

"Yes," answered Colin, bluntly. "My first month back home, I went to the fair. You remember the first time I told you I loved you? It was there.

The dirt arena where the fairgrounds house the horses, they'd decorated it all pretty and let the band set up. Keith Frank was playing *Pieces to my heart*. I was holding your waist real close. They played it again that night and I just about fell apart in the stands watching all the old couples bachata the way we used to. Emily came along and pressured me into dancing with her. I didn't really want to, but I did. A few months later she decided we were a couple. A few months after that she decided it was time for me to buy her a ring. I never offered. I knew it wasn't love but if there was no you, did it matter who I ended up with. It wasn't you, what did it matter? A man should feel bad for saying horrible things about his wife; but if I married the wrong woman, won't God forgive me for not loving the one I'm with? Lying about the love I don't feel for Emily would be pointless, God knows my heart. He made it."

"Colin, your marriage is between you, your wife and God. Leave me, our memories, your regret and our childhood plan out of it. Married men who look at women the way you're looking at me; they make their marriage other's people's problems. I have enough of those already. You and Emily could have a litter of ugly babies and die side-by-side on the porch for all I care."

"I'd rather spill my seed on the ground like Onan did in the bible than to deposit it inside that shrew of a woman. Better my seed dry up there than spout a life that's part her."

Dria shushed. "Nothing from the bible could ever be too brazen but anything involving Emily's baby shoot is a bit too much for me to hear. You got what you settled for, Colin. Be happy with that."

"-And what did you get, Dria."

"What's that supposed to mean?"

"Are you happy?"

"What the hell kind of question is that?"

"I don't think I could have asked it any plainer, Dria."

Dria sighed and rolled her eyes. "My work is fulfilling."

"That's not what I asked you."

"You mean am I seeing anyone? -Well, the answer is no. Not that it's any of *your* business."

"Hearing that pains me. A woman like you deserves to be held every night."

"If you must know, corporate men don't really do it for me; nothing but truly shallow men trying hard to hide their flaws behind big tall stacks of money. That don't impress me much. Maybe they'd have a chance if they wore their flaws on their sleeve and keep their wallets in their pockets."

"If I said I was happy that you're alone, I'd sound selfish," Said Colin with a flirtatious gaze.

Dria's face began to twist. "Stop looking at me like that Colin! Just stop!" she yelled, stomping through the aisles of the store.

Colin quickened his pace behind her. "When you saw me back at the grocery store, did you still feel it? Did you feel nothing, or did you look for me in the stars after the fair?" Dria was quiet. Colin grabbed her hand. "I looked at them too, Dria. I replay the night before you left. There's something you didn't tell me before you went away, I know it. What happened, so horrible, that you just ran out of my life like that? Why didn't you trust me enough to love you right straight through whatever happened? Have you no faith in understanding and forgiveness and true love?"

Old man Otis cleared his throat. "I've got your unit all loaded up," he said smirking at the two of them.

Dria jerked her hand back from Colin and turned to Otis. "Thank you. Sir. How much do I owe you?"

"-No charge," Otis declared.

"Oh, you don't have to do that. Please, I'd like to pay."

"No, your money's no good here. As I said, Jeremiah was family. That man once helped me plant my whole crop and he did it with a broken arm. He was a good man. Before he passed, I told him to talk Cat into getting a unit. He never got the chance. You take this one. It'll make me sleep better tonight knowing no one in his family will die of a heat stroke," he laughed.

"Well, then you must come to Granny Cat's birthday dinner this Friday."

"I wouldn't want to intrude. I'm sure you all want to be alone with Cat," said Otis- blushing.

"-Don't be silly, your family. You just said so yourself."

Dria looked across the street and saw Sadie sitting outside of Mipsy's stuffing her face with Frito pie. "I have to go; Sadie and I are going to visit Granny now. We haven't had a chance to see her since we've been in town.

We're all gon' eat around 5 PM on Friday." Dria hugged Otis. "Thank you for all your help, Mr. Otis. I'll see you on Friday. I don't want to have to drive down here and stuff you in the trunk," she said, climbing behind the wheel.

"What about me?" Asked Colin.

"What about you?" asked Dria with her nose in the air.

"I'd like to come Friday and eat with you and your family, honor an amazing woman. You know, Cat was like my grandmother, too."

Dria thought it over. "I suppose it's okay. Bring a muzzle for your permanent plus-one, Emily. If at all possible, leave her at home."

"…Save me a seat next to you?" asked Colin, hopeful.

"-Fat chance," laughed Dria.

•

"This place looks like something out of a travel brochure. If Granny Cat doesn't want her bed here, I'll gladly take it," said Sadie admiring Pennycress' swanky décor.

"I don't know why she's complaining. This place looks a palace," Whispered Dria approaching the nearest pennycress resident, a feeble little woman who paced with a walker. "Hello, I'm looking for Catherine Beaumonte's room, would you be so kind as to point me in the right direction?"

The little woman heard Catherine's name and shrieked, causing Sadie to grab hold of Dria. "Chasseur de sorcieres!" She scooted away quick, screaming more imperceptible obscenities in French.

Jan rushed to the old woman's side. "Mrs. Talbert! It's okay, Mrs. Catherine is in her room and she's been sedated! She can't hurt you now!" The little woman whispered something to Jan, causing her to look in Dria and Sadie's direction. Jan walked over. "Hi there. I hear you ladies are looking for Catherine Beaumonte'?"

"Yes. We are. I only asked that poor scared lady if she knew which room our grandmother was in and she flipped out! What did she say?"

"-Witch hunter. Your grandmother has made quite the impression in the short time she's been here. Follow me, I'll take you to her," said Jan. Shaken, Dria, and Sadie followed close. "You two must be Lissima's cousins. It's very nice to meet you. I've heard such great things about you and the rest of your family. Did Bellissima say if she had plans for New Year's?" small-talked Jan in route.

Catherine sat in bed with a mirror inches from her face. Her hand was unsteady, but she traced her lips with lipstick as best she could. Jan stepped in, "Mrs. Beaumonte', you have visitors."

Dria and Sadie walked in side by side and Catherine beamed. "There they are! My little cupcakes! I was beginning to think you'd forgotten all about your old granny!"

Dria embraced Catherine and held on tight. "Forget about you, how could I? I've missed you Grandma Cat."

Sadie moved in, "Please don't think I'm sad. I'm crying just cause I'm so happy to see you, is all," she said- sitting at Catherine's bedside, inhaling her grandmother's naturally sweet-smelling skin as they hugged.

"What took you girls so long?"

"You know your daughters, everything has a specific order. Their plans postponed our visit. That, and to be honest, I wasn't sure how I felt about you being locked up in here," confessed Dria.

"I could tell you how I feel about being locked up in here but that would take all day and I just said my prayers. I don't want to start cursing again so soon or I'll have to start praying for the same forgiveness all over again. I'd rather hear about how you girls have been. Tell me everything! What's new!" gushed Catherine.

"Sadie's got some rather new news," poked Dria.

Sadie cut her eyes at Dria and quickly diverted Catherine's attention. "Dria went meat shopping at Mipsy's and then went meat shopping at church," said Sadie with attitude. Dria's eyes widened and she pursed her lips. "Why don't you tell her all about it, Dria- you meat-seeking missile." Sadie teased.

Catherine grabbed the edges of Sadie's hair. "What did you do, my dear? Where's the rest of your hair?"

"I decided to cut it, Granny. It's trendy. It's all the rave in glamour magazine!"

"But your hair is your glory, why would you clip your glory? Its déjà vu. You remember how much trouble a little old hair got you all in last time?" asked Catherine. She ran her fingers through Dria's hair. "Your hair used to have a natural wave. It was like that since you were born. Why you started ironing it straight, I'll never know. Don't you girls know that God got it right the first time? You don't need to do anything extra. All my grandbabies were wonderfully made. Bellissima and Cheniere were both born with a hazel tint in their roots, it was so unique. When they got older Bellissima's tint stayed, turned into a hazel streak right out in front of her curly mane that just wouldn't stop growing. Cheniere's tint moved to her ends and her roots got dark. Still curly, though. I miss braiding her hair, seeing the colors twist and twine."

Dria reached out for Sadie's hand. "We miss her too. Sometimes when I look at Bellissima, I have to look away. I don't want her to see me sad, to think she's nothing but a reminder of who we lost," Said Dria.

Catherine's smile melted into a frightened frown. "They made you girls look away when they fetched Cheniere's body out of the water. Kay screamed, and it just went on and on like she never broke for a breath. She was so loud, you three had to cover your ears. It was surreal. I'd been standing in that very same spot years before when they fished your Grandfather's truck up out of the deep and there I was again for the second time. That damn bridge had taken another one of my loved ones. Cheniere's body was limp and discolored. Kay had fallen to her knees. When the diver walked over with Cheniere dead in his arms, Kay held out her baby's blanket. He placed her in the blanket and Kay wrapped her up like she was cold. She rocked Cheniere, back and forth. I would have been on that ground with her, but I was too busy looking down in that water. I had to stop myself from jumping in. I knew my ring was down there somewhere with your grandfather's bones. I was angry at them bones. I should have brought them to the surface long before. I should have said more to stop Cheniere."

Sadie's forehead creased. "What do you mean, Granny?"

"Do you remember when you girls got in trouble for cutting Cheniere's hair? Minxy didn't punish you right the first time. Kay and Lou had to punish you girls a second time to make sure you learned your lesson. Three days, that was your sentence. Do you remember that third night?" asked Catherine.

"Yes, Mam I remember the third night. New Year's Day. Two days before, they did everything they could to get us to rat out the plan originator: made us kneel in rice, made us scrub the big house spotless, threatened to give us the rod; eventually, they gave up and sent us to separate rooms to think about what we had done. They thought one of us would roll over on the other, but we waited out our sentences like champs. Told us we'd be in our rooms alone for three days with no games or interaction with one another. The third day of our punishment would have been New Year's Day," said Dria.

"Yes. There were sure one of you would confess but neither of you would. They'd wasted the whole day trying to get you girls to talk. They asked me to babysit that third night. Lou Anna had a dinner meeting with some big shot who flew in from the city. Kay needed affordable restaurant furniture and needed to drive out to an auction. Minxy had a date. I was supposed to be tough as nails with you girls, play the warden. I was instructed to give you food and water but certainly not playtime or candy. They reminded me that you all were being punished and that meant I wasn't allowed to have any fun with you. I couldn't help myself, though. Didn't seem fair, you kids being locked up with no human contact. Before bedtime, I sat with each of you for a while."

"-Each of us? I thought *I* was the only one you visited that night," said Sadie.

"I thought *I* was," said Dria.

"No, I visited all four of you and told you that I hadn't visited anyone else. It's kind of like the way I tell you all you're my favorite when you have me all to yourself. I have no favorites. I love you all the same, unconditionally. Telling little white lies and making you feel special is just how grandparents love. I sat with each of you that night."

'I went to you first, Dria. I brought you warm fudge cookies and chocolate milk. We talked about the stars. You always loved the stars. After you, I went to Bellissima. She loved those green tomatoes soaked in apple cider vinegar with salt and pepper. We talked about the sun. Next was Sadie…"

"We had crackers and jam. We talked about the moon," interrupted Sadie, remembering.

'Yep. I saved Cheniere for last, just because conversations with her took a little longer- on the count of us having to talk with our hands. I brought her some of Kay's leftover Dutch apple pie. She wouldn't eat it though. Cheniere was sad. *'Punishments don't last forever,'*- I said to her.

'That's not why I'm sad.'- she signed.

'I asked Cheniere why she was crying. She said she was tired of being different. I tried, so hard, to convince her that she wasn't but it was true. Cheniere was different, and she begged me to stop pretending she wasn't. I tried to cheer her up by talking about the rain. She loved the rain. Did you know Cheniere could hear the rain?" asked Catherine.

"What?" asked Dria, shocked. "That can't be!"

'It's true. She didn't share that with anyone other than Lissima and myself. Cheniere could hear the rain and only the rain. She even described it to me once, with her beautiful little hands.'

'It's like hearing God, Granny. It sounds brave.'- she signed.

'I corrected her, thinking she meant to say beautiful but no. She meant brave. Still don't know what she meant by describing it that way. I kissed her fast signing little fingers and thought it over- *brave*. Before I left Cheniere that night, she started asking me about my wedding ring and the curse. By then, you girls had heard the story of Jeremiah's death at least a thousand times. I spoke of the curse, saying it was the reason I'd fallen on hard times after he died. The troubles with the crop and my daughters and my misery and my heartbreak and my loneliness- it'd been blaming it on the curse for years. I'd said it so many times- If only my ring was still here on my hand and not submerged with your dead grandfather, there would be no curse and no more misfortune. I planted the seed, I know it.'

'I asked Cheniere- "Why you wanna know about the ring?"

'If I get your ring out of the water, will I be fixed?'

'You see, Cheniere believed she was mute because of the curse. She told me that cutting her hair was all her idea. She was scared that God couldn't tell her and Bellissima apart and couldn't tell their prayers apart. She wanted to tell but whenever she lifted her hands to sign her confession, you girls stopped her. She couldn't use words to tell on herself and you girls would never rat her out. If she could talk, she could have taken the rap and she would be the only one getting rightfully punished. She didn't think it was fair for you all to get punished for something that was her idea.'

'I want to talk, Grandma Cat. I don't want to be different anymore. What if someone brought the ring up from the water? Would the curse go away?'

159

'I scolded Cheniere for even thinking it, going to Burn Out bridge to search for that ring. I made her promise to never think about it again.'

'Years before, I scraped up my pennies and went to see the old bag lady Withers. She was an acclaimed psychic. Who knows if she really had gifts? She was too crazy to be certain, always talking to the shadow people. *Tell me how to break the curse. I fear for my family.*'

Old lady Withers refused my money and then laughed in my face. '*This here is Louisiana, where our ancestors find no peace even in death. You know that. Their slave blood, sweat, and tears made this land what it is. When we're all dead and gone; rather you're black or white, friend or foe, loved one or hated one- all that's left is pale hollow bone. The spirits, they can't tell the difference on the other side- bones are bones. Those bones belong to them now. That ring too. We don't disturb the places where they rest or collect debt from the dead. You leave it all down there and don't try to fix it no more. Might make it worse. You or anyone from your family go there to that bridge, it will be painfully regretted. You'll pay in sorrow, even more sorrow than you already have to rain on you. This much I know is true. The shadows told me so.*'

'Cheniere wanted to break the curse. She wanted to be like her cousins and her sister. I should have never let my grief plant that possibility in her head- that she could lift the curse and be made right."

•

Tap, tap tap.... "Minx, someone's at the door!" yelled Lou Anna from the kitchen where she helped Kay finish supper. *Tap, tap, tap....* "Minx, did you hear me, I said someone's at the damn door!" *Tap, tap, tap, tap* "Damn it to hell! I'll get it myself!" Lou Anna stomped pass the den where Minxy sat wearing Sadie's earbuds, listening to music, shaking her head. Lou opened the door and there stood a handsome stranger. Lou Anna stared him up and down. "Whatever you're selling, we'll take two," she mumbled.

"Hello Mam, I'm sorry to disturb you. You wouldn't happen to be a Miss Bellissima Beaumonte's mother, would you? I was hoping to have a word with her."

"No, I'm not. I'm her Aunt. Her mother's inside. You just wait right here for one second," said Lou Anna slamming the door, giddy. She ran into the den and snatched the earbuds from Minxy's ears.

"What's wrong with you! That's my jam!" shrieked Minxy.

"There's a man at the door, a good looking one! He's looking for Bellissima!"

"A man? For Lissima?" asked Minxy, rushing to the door. She yanked it open. "Hello, how can we help you?" asked Minxy- trying hard to keep her grin under control.

He reached out for Minxy's hand and kissed it. "You must be Bellissima's mother. As I was telling your sister, I was just wondering if I could speak with your daughter, Bellissima."

"No," said Minxy, lost in his eyes.

"No?" he asked, confused.

Lou Anna bumped Minxy and she snapped back to reality. "I mean- no, I'm not her mother. I'm her other, much younger Aunt. Bellissima's mother is in the kitchen. We'll go get her. You don't move, it'll only take a second. Come on, Lou!" said Minxy- slamming the door in his face for the second time, dragging Lou Anna into the kitchen. "Kay, you better get out here!"

"I got hot pots on the stove that need watching! What's the matter?" asked Kay, removing her apron.

"Your prayers on Bellissima's behalf, they just might have been answered in a very sexy way! There's a tall drink of water at the door looking for her!" said Lou Anna.

"A man for my child?" asked Kay, in disbelief. "She never has men over here. You sure he's got the right house?"

"How many little creole girls you know named Bellissima Beaumonte? He's wearing a navy-blue button down, Kay! Navy blue! No one ever looks good wearing navy blue! Get to the door! Hurry up!" hassled Lou Anna.

Kay straightened her hair and opened the door, again. He politely tipped his hat. "How many Aunts does Ms. Bellissima have?" he asked, waiting for them to slam the door again and go get another.

"No more than these two here. I'm her mother, Kay."

"Well, it's mighty fine to meet you, Mam. My name is Lincoln Breaux-Jude. As I was telling these lovely ladies here, I'm hoping to speak with your daughter. I won't take up too much of her time."

"-Pertaining to what?" asked Kay.

"A recently deceased friend of hers from Pennycress," he replied. "I spoke to a colleague of hers who wouldn't give me Bellissima's personal number or her home address but said I might be able to find her here at her family's permanent address. I hope that's alright. I hate to stop by unannounced, it's discourteous- I know."

"It's alright! This is the South, ain't it? We'd never get a chance to practice our Southern hospitality if strangers never showed up on our doorstep without calling. Pointing folks in the right direction is just how things are done in a small town," smiled Kay.

Bellissima's car pulled up in the driveway. Dria and Sadie hopped out. "Can we help you?" pressured Dria, immediately.

"Dria, this handsome man here, is looking for Lissima," said Lou Anna- fidgety with excitement.

"-For what?" asked Dria- eyeing Lincoln untrustworthily.

"-Does it matter," whispered Sadie, giving Dria a naughty shove.

"Harness your hormones pregnant lady," whispered Dria to Sadie. She cleared her throat and neared the porch where they all stood. "Is this a legal matter? You a cop or something? If so I'm going to need to see a badge. The time to state the purpose of your visit is now. I'm her big cousin but more importantly, I'm her attorney. I'm the attorney of every Beaumonte' you see standing here."

"There's no need for any of that. This is an unexpected visit but not a hostile one at all. My name is Lincoln Breaux-Jude," he answered smoothly. "I believe Miss Bellissima looked after my late grandfather. She's quite the fireball, hung up on me before I could get a word in. I won't pester her if she asks me to go away. If you see fit, you can listen in on the whole tête-à-tête."

Dria sigh. "Well alright. I guess that would be okay. She's in the back. I'll take you around to her but grab the big box out of the trunk first and put it in the den. Since you're here you may as well do some work," said Dria.

Kay took hold of Minxy's hand and panted. "Do you feel that Minxy?" she asked. Minxy shook her head and grabbed hold of Lou Anna's hand as if to let the energy flow through her and into Lou Anna too. Lou Anna's eyes beamed. "I feel it too! Could it be? Does Lissima have his rib?"

Dria and Lincoln could hear Bellissima swearing and ranting as they neared the backyard. '*Stupid table! Why can't everyone just put their plates on their laps? Or eat standing up!*"

"Lissima, you have a guest," announced Dria.

Bellissima, covered in grime and perspiration, turned around to find Dria standing beside a man she'd never seen before. Bellissima took a rag from her pocket and wiped the grit off her cheek. "A guest?" she mumbled. "Who are you?"

Even though her overalls were two sizes too big and her hair had begun to frizz, Lincoln found himself taken aback by Bellissima's natural splendor. "Forgot about me already? Here I was thinking I'd made an impression."

"Have we met?" asked Bellissima, certain they hadn't. He was the kind of handsome a woman would have no choice but to remember.

"Not in person but we did have a short conversation earlier. My name is Lincoln. You were my grandfather's best, only, friend."

"I'll leave you be, now," said Dria- walking away with a coquettish smirk.

CHAPTER TWENTY

Lincoln Breaux-Jude stood about 6ft tall and looked to weigh about 180 pounds of pure muscle. His height casted an intimidating shadow over Bellissima. He'd been standing in front of Bellissima with his hand out for her to shake for almost a full minute. "Well, are you going to shake my hand, or should I put it away before it falls off?" he asked finally.

"Oh! I'm sorry," stuttered Bellissima- peeling her gloves off before sliding her hand in his.

"I know this is a bit invasive. I went to Pennycress to talk to you in person since you were so quick with the dial tone. I wanted to show you some identification, my mother's birth certificate and a copy of my family tree; prove to you that I am who I say I am." He handed Bellissima the paperwork and she skimmed it over. Lincoln started to laugh.

Bellissima squirmed insecurely, "What's so funny?" she asked.

"Nothing, it's just- your brash phone decorum had me thinking you 'd be a lot taller, bulkier and scarier. I'm surprised to discover you're just a pretty petite lady with a bad attitude," replied Lincoln with a teasing smirk.

Bellissima winced, embarrassed. "-About that. I'm very sorry about my rude faux pas. It's true, I was rather short with you. It's just, every time a patient dies, we get folks calling us with all sorts of lies. They pump us for personal information so that their stories sound more believable when they petition the state for the decease's remaining assets, claiming blood relation means the transfer of possessions. And I'm up to my neck in family drama of my own..." explained Bellissima.

"It's alright, not the first time I've been hung up on. I can tell by the way you're stumbling through your apology that you don't often do things to people that require an apology. I bet I'm one of the few you've ever given the cold shoulder. I don't hold grudges and I understand your obligation to protect my grandfather, even in the afterlife."

"*Grandfather-* it's so weird to hear you say that word. No one ever called or sent holiday cards or came by to see Breaux. When the end was near, he mentioned a grandson, but I thought he was just talking out of his head."

"Well, he does have a grandson. He had a daughter too, past tense."

"Your mother passed?"

"No, not yet- thank God but she's disowned him long ago and he disowned her. Who knows who disowned who first. They both would rather die than admit their faults to one another or make amends for my sake at least. She's his blood but not his daughter, that what she says. He had no other children. No sisters or brothers for my mother. No other grandchildren for him besides me. They were the only blood each of them had left and still they refused to put their difference aside."

"When Breaux decided to make me his beneficiary, I urged him to track down anyone that may be better suited than me. He told me he'd reached out; tried to find you. He made calls. He sent letters from his PO box. He said he didn't trust the doctors at Pennycress; didn't want his mail going there. I guess he was afraid someone would steal his coupons; either that or he didn't want people knowing he'd moved to a home. I drove to the post office to check his mail for him every week, personally. No one ever wrote back. I tried to teach Breaux how to use a computer so that he could set up an email account and send some emails but that just ended up frustrating us both."

"Breaux tried to find me? I don't doubt it. I'm pretty sure my mother went out of her way to make sure he and I had no contact." Bellissima looked back at the house and caught her family spying through the kitchen window. They scattered just before Lincoln turned back. "That's a nice house."

"Thank you, it's my Grandmother's. When she passes it will belong to my mom and aunts. It's more of a headache than an inheritance at this point. It's ancient, needs a lot of work. Old folks get set in their ways and comfortable with how things are. She won't even entertain the thought of a remodel."

"I think it's a diamond in the rough. Some things are beautiful, perfect, just the way they are," he said smiling at Bellissima. Lincoln looked down at the table. "Is furniture restoration a hobby of yours?"

"Heck no. Five generations ate off this hunk of junk. My family won't eat my Grandmother's birthday dinner off anything else. They're big traditionalist."

"-Protective traditionalist," Lincoln corrected. "You look like you need a little help," he said rolling up his sleeves.

"Help? No, you don't have to do that," Bellissima resisted.

"I insist. It's the least I can do for dropping by like this and it's pretty clear you have no idea what you're doing," he said grabbing the sanding board.

"Okay. Thank you! Should I...go get my checkbook?"

Lincoln smirked, "No mam. I know you think I'm some leech out to make a quick buck off the dead, but I've done well for myself. I don't need Breaux's money or yours and I'm not expecting any. In exchange for my hard work; you can pull up one of those chairs, sit down, rest your feet and tell me about my grandfather- since you knew him so well."

Bellissima slowly pulled up a chair and sat. "Alright. What do you want to know?"

"Everything. I have no memory of Breaux at all, only what my bitter mother has told me over the years. All of it's negative. She didn't have one good thing to say about the man. I wouldn't even be able to tell you what his face looked like. I've never even seen his picture."

"How's that possible?"

"I guess my mother got rid of everything that reminded her of her father."

"Why?"

"I'm not sure if you knew, but my grandfather was a bit of a racist."

Bellissima shook her head and laughed sarcastically. "Really, I never picked up on that!"

"Yeah, he was, but he wasn't always that way. My mother's mother was 100% African American with flawless cocoa skin; that's the way my mother remembers her. Grandpa Breaux fell in love with her and even though Breaux knew loving her would cost him the love and respect of his parents and this community, he married her. Together they made my mother, a beautiful mixed breed baby girl with blue eyes and mulatto skin. Breaux endured being spit on and harassed by whites. He let their racist remarks but just let them roll off his back. I imagine it was hard for him, but Breaux held his head high when he walked through this town with his mutt daughter. He did so because he was not ashamed of love. After all Breaux's sacrifices, my grandmother ran off with a man whose skin was the same shade as hers. She told Breaux that their loved caused so much aching and controversy that it was no longer beautiful. She said it would just be easier to love someone more like her. No one ever spat on her, but she decided that the pressure was too much to bear. She left Breaux and my mother behind. It broke Breaux's heart. He ultimately started listening to those prejudiced remarks, letting them soak in. Then they started rotting him from the inside out. It started with small things, like him telling my mother she had to wait in the car when they went places and when he absolutely had to take her out, he bundled her in layers so heavy that she once passed out from the heat. That didn't stop him from making her cover every inch of her darker flesh. He just didn't want people to look at her skin and whisper even more than they already were. It escalated over the years. He started making mama sit in an ice-cold bleach water and peroxide mix for hours, trying to lighten her skin. He couldn't manage her ethnic hair; so, he cut it all off, scalped her completely bald."

"That's horrible," sympathized Bellissima.

"As she got older, his torture only got worse. When she got pregnant with me, my mother kept the race of my father a secret. Breaux vowed to throw his only daughter out into the streets on her ass if I came out any other color than pure white Caucasian."

"He threw your mother out of the house with a newborn?"

"No. She never took me back home to where Breaux was waiting to mentally abuse us both. She walked from the hospital straight to the bus station where she purchased her a ticket to New Orleans, 6 hours away-where we live now. My daddy was waiting there, he had a life there waiting for us. She never looked back. My mama and daddy shacked up for a few years, but they did marry. They raised me together, put me through college and helped me start my business."

"-Business?" inquired Bellissima, curiously.

"-Photography. I'm pretty good with a camera."

"So, what, you take pictures of beautiful starved models?"

"When you're starting off, you'll take on just about any gig; but I'm seasoned now. I have standards. I'm not hurting for work. I don't photograph things that aren't beautiful. I make memories and now I've done so well for myself that I hire other people to work for me, making memories. Pictures are worth a thousand words, you know?" Lincoln pulled an old photo of his parents from his wallet and gave it to Bellissima.

"Your mother, she's so lovely. And your father, well that's one handsome black man."

"Thank you. My mother thought so too. They were together until the day he died. She said he was ten times the husband and father Breaux was. I had a great man for a father. He had strong values. He believed in forgiveness and when he found one of Breaux's letters, he was furious at my mother for not telling him she'd received it. That was the only time I ever heard him yell. You see, my father loved my mother so much that a lifetime with her just wasn't enough time. He wanted to be with her in heaven too. He was worried for my mother's soul. He didn't want a silly thing like unforgiveness to keep her from waltzing through those pearly gates. I guess mama was just too scared. She refused to relieve Breaux of his guilt. With my father's dying breath, he made me promise to make things right. Breaux's dead. I know he's long gone, but a part of me just has to find what's left of him. Surely, it'll bring some peace to him in death and some freedom for my mother here on earth after all these years. Maybe then, they'll reunite in the sky. That's all my daddy wanted."

"Sounds like your parents really loved each other."

"They did."

"That must be a great feeling, knowing who your father is and respecting him."

"You don't know your father?"

"Nope."

Kay poked her head out the back door. "It's time to eat! Come on in, you too Lincoln," she yelled.

"Did your mother just invite me in for dinner?" asked Lincoln.

"Yeah, that's how she does it. Kay Beaumonte' never really asks, just makes you sit down and piles a heap of good food in front of your face. If you want, I can tell her you had to go and didn't want to be rude."

"And miss out on whatever smells so good? Not a chance."

Bellissima's cousins found the situation particularly humorous and did very little to mask their immature idiosyncrasies. Their faces remained beleaguer without pause. Their smiles were absurdly overenthusiastic and sardonic as they basked in Bellissima's discomfort. Bellissima was smitten and her family could tell. They were like gators in bloody water.

"This might be the best jambalaya I ever had, Ms. Beaumonte'," complimented Lincoln.

"Please, call me Kay," she replied- fluffing her hair again with a smile just as telling as the girls'.

"*Lincoln-* What a strong name. It's rather old-fashioned for somebody as young as you," said Lou Anna, in attempt to spark small talk.

"I agree. My mother named me Lincoln, after President Lincoln. He abolished slavery and she knew it would piss off my white grandfather," he replied.

"Your Grandfather was a white man who believed in slavery? But you're mixed. Looks like races intertwined a few times in your past, they must've for you to get the shade you are. He couldn't have always felt that way," said Minxy confused.

"He used to love black women but then he changed his mind," answered Lincoln plainly.

All the Beaumonte' women stopped, nodding slowly as if they understood but really didn't. "It's...historical. A good strong historical name," replied Minxy- trying to pass the awkward lull.

'Right!'

'Yes! Strong name!'

'Historical and honorable!'

'It's a great name!' - They all complimented at once, talking over one another to make sure Lincoln didn't feel insecure about his family's dirty laundry.

Dria's smile turned mischievous. "So, Lincoln- like the president, you have a wife at home who cooks this good for you?" she asked. Bellissima's eyes darted across the table.

Lincoln smiled, charmingly. "No mam. No wife. I'm not married, never been."

"Any illegitimate kids?" asked Sadie- her mouth still full of food. Bellissima kicked her underneath the table. "Ouch! Auntie Kay! Lissima's hitting! Geez, that hurt! It's a fair question! We don't judge around here. Hell, we're all illegitimate," she finished.

"Eat your food and shut up," mumbled Dria out of the corner of her mouth.

Lincoln chucked, uncomfortably. "No children either. It's just me and my mother."

"A bachelor who cares for his Mama! Do you hear that? Interesting and noble!" gushed Kay.

"Interesting indeed. You know Lissima's a bachelorette. No kids either and she cooks good, just like the food you're raving about right now. Tell him, Kay," said Minxy.

"She sure does cook. I taught her myself," Kay added.

Bellissima slammed her napkin on the table. "Could someone please pass the peach tea!" she said- louder so her family would sense her growing humiliation.

"That's hard to find these days, a young woman who's not afraid of the kitchen," said Lincoln.

"She's a Beaumonte', Lissima ain't scared of nothing. No matter how big or small the challenge may be," Said Sadie with an inappropriate wink. She looked down at Lincoln's plate. "You going to finish that?" she asked- sticking her fork into Lincoln's plate before he had a chance to answer.

Bellissima slapped her hand, "That's enough!" she mumbled, standing. "That was a great meal, Mama. Let's go Lincoln, I'll walk you to the door," she said fighting to hide her fury.

Lincoln stood and began to gather his utensils. "Sweetheart, you're a guest in this house. Guests don't clear the table or do dishes," said Kay.

"That's why we had children, so we'd have someone to do all the stuff we don't feel like doing," joked Lou Anna. "We'll walk you out," she said- prompting everyone to slide their chairs back from the table and stand.

"No! No! I got it! You all stay! Stay! Sit!" yelled Bellissima, like she was talking to a pack of dogs.

Dria's shoulders trembled as she watched Lincoln and Bellissima leave the table. "Woah. I just felt an unexplainable sensation all over my body. Damn near felt like the holy ghost," she said grabbing Sadie's arm.

"-You felt that too?" asked Sadie- bewildered.

"We all feel it," said Kay. "Yeah, he's the one. Neither of them knows it yet, though. We better let 'em figure it out on their own. I'll try and act surprised when he asks for her hand."

Once outside, Lincoln thanked Bellissima for her hospitality. "You're most welcome. It was nice having someone around that can look past my... colorful family."

"They're great people, lots of fun," he replied.

"I'll make some calls. It'll take a lot of signatures, but you'll get your Grandfather's ashes. I'll see to it that the paperwork is corrected. All that he had left should rightfully be yours. I never wanted anything from Breaux, and I tried to tell him that. In the end, I think he just needed a loose end to tie up, old people get like that when they think about to cross over. He mentioned some tax problems. There's a chance the bank might take the house back but after they see all your documentation, I'm sure they'll give you a chance to go in and gather a few heirlooms before they trash everything and gain possession."

"I appreciate that a lot."

"It's no problem," said Bellissima- blushing a bit. "Wait, wait, wait. Don't leave yet! I have something for you." Bellissima ran inside and returned with her bag.

"I told you, no charge," said Lincoln.

"No, it's not money. I just have this picture for you," she said digging through her wallet. Bellissima gave Lincoln the photo. "You said you didn't even know what he looked like. This is from last Halloween at Pennycress. All the nurses and patients dressed up. Breaux and I took this picture together."

Lincoln looked down at it. "Well, I'll be! Look at that! Funny how fathers and daughters can still look alike no matter the gender difference. Add softer eyes, a slimmer waist, and a wig; you'd swear it was my mother in that wheelchair next to you dressed like a pirate. You still dress up for Halloween?" he asked laughing.

"Well, everyone else was dressing up and my grandmother never let me, and my cousins dress up for Halloween. She said it was the devil's day and we wouldn't be a part of it. You can keep it. Breaux's your blood. You can put it next to the picture of your mother and father."

"This is very nice of you. Thank you, Ms. Lissima. Can I call you Lissima, or should I stick to Bellissima until you trust me?"

"Lissima is just fine and You're welcome…Mr. Lincoln Breaux- Jude." Lincoln turned to climb in his truck. Bellissima chased after him. "Lincoln! Wait! How did you find out about Breaux's passing?"

"It's the strangest thing. In the dead of night, Mama's phone rang. She answered it and stayed on the line for only a minute. She said hello but nothing else; just stood there in the parlor listening to whoever was on the other line. She hung up without saying goodbye. It upset her quite a bit. Once I calmed Mama, I called the number back and a lady told me where to find all my answers. *Find the pennycress. De'funt Grand-pe're. I am sorry for your loss.*' I traced the area code back here. I searched for a garden, a patch of pennycresses at first. Then I discovered that pennycress was a place. She meant it as a place, not a flower."

"She?" asked Bellissima.

"Yes, She. She seemed as though she was barely all there in her own mind. Does your office usually make those kinds of calls at night?"

"No, we don't," answered Bellissima.

"You know what else is strange? I called that number back over and over. At first, it just rang and rang. Then, it stopped ringing. Just a dead line, as if the line was never in service, to begin with."

Bellissima stood in the driveway and watched Lincoln drive away. "Did we overdo it?" asked Kay walking out into the yard; bracing herself for an earful about minding her own business.

"I'm sorry. I get so caught up in the hopes I have for your life that I forget it's your life to live. Go ahead and rake me over the coals- I deserve it."

Bellissima sighed. "It's alright, Mama. I don't like it but I understand why you do the over-bearing things you do. Besides, he doesn't seem like the kind of guy who's easy to run off."

"Does that mean he'll be running back this way anytime soon?" asked Kay- hopeful.

Bellissima kissed her mother's cheek as the two of them headed back inside. "Now you're overdoing it." She said with a simper.

The family navigated to the den. "What's in the box?" asked Minxy, curious.

Dria poked her chest out, proudly. "That is a brand new, top of the line window unit! That's right, I have officially declared war on the heat."

"An air conditioner! Dria Renea' Beaumonte'! Your grandmother hates those machines! She's going to start grouching about the electric bill," said Minxy.

"I know! I know! That's why I waited until I had a good enough reason to buy one, a time when I could honestly say I didn't buy it with only my own discomfort in mind."

"And what good reason is that?" asked Lou Anna.

Sadie and Kay stared at Dria; waiting for her to figure out a way to answer without bringing up the bogus menopause story. "I purchased it for you, Mama," she answered.

"Yeah for your body changes," said Sadie- speaking before thinking.

"What changes," asked Lou Anna defensively.

"The...climate changes. You've been living in the city for years now. Being back in the South, it must be tough on your skin. The humidity gets really intense this time of year. You could get a heat rash! God forbid!"

Lou Anna was moved by Dria's supposed kindness. "Dria! That's the most thoughtful gift you've given me since you were 5 years old and you made me that pinecone turkey!"

"That's so kind of you. Kay, help me get it upstairs," said Minxy.

"Upstairs?" questioned Dria- her eyebrows wrinkled.

"Well yeah silly, that's where your Mama's been sleeping. How's she going to keep cool with it down here?" asked Minxy.

Dria hadn't thought of that before she fabricated a lie that implemented her mother. "Right. Upstairs," she mumbled.

"Dria, Sadie- Let's get started on the dishes," said Bellissima, summoning her cousins to the kitchen.

They stood in a single file line, productively hustling the china. Dria washed, Bellissima rinsed, then Sadie dried and put the dishes away. Once their moms were all upstairs, they were free to gossip amongst themselves.

"Couldn't wait to get us alone so you could brag about that stallion, Lincoln?" teased Sadie.

"No! That's not why I rushed you two in here. Remember when I was saying how Grandma Cat was remembering stuff from the past?"

"Yeah,' replied Dria- frowning at the baked-on cornbread crust.

"Well today at work, she began to reveal in a whole new way." Bellissima, anxious, looked around to make sure they were still alone. "She told me about my father."

"What?" screamed Dria and Sadie simultaneously.

"Shhh!" whispered Bellissima drying her hands, pulling them closer. "At first she was just telling me about what our mothers were like before we came along. That's a can of worms I'm sure they'd be pissed to find out she's opened. Of course, she still talks about the bridge but there's so much we never knew- even about that. Today, Catherine told me about my dad. I didn't even have to beg like I've done all my life."

"What did she say about him?" asked Dria.

"His name as Israel. Granny Cat said he wanted to marry Mama."

"Marry her! How exciting! A love story!" gushed Sadie.

"Not exactly. Grandma Cat said Israel went away. She said she didn't know why, but he abandoned Mama. He just abandoned her with me and Cheniere."

"Did Grandma Cat say anything about my father?" asked Sadie.

"Not yet," answered Bellissima.

"What about mine?" asked Dria- tentative.

"No. She hasn't really said anything about yours yet either," lied Bellissima. "I'm sorry."

"Don't' be," said Dria- hugging Bellissima. "I'm just glad you got what you needed after all this time. Since we're sharing, Grandma Cat took us down the dark side of memory lane today, too."

"Really, what did she talk to you two about?" asked Bellissima.

Sadie stopped Dria from reacting. "You know, it's been such a nice day. We'll tell you all about it later. No sense in getting sad right now. It can wait."

•

Once it was time for bed, the Beaumonte' grandchildren sat awake downstairs listening to the new air unit vibrating in the window upstairs. "I bet they're sleeping good up there, all cool and conditioned in their conditioned air," mumbled Sadie, jealous.

"-Lucky them," said Dria, irritated by the temperature downstairs.

"You did a good thing for your Mama. You definitely earned some golden daughter points. You two should be happy they're comfortable," said Bellissima.

Dria and Sadie cut their eyes at Bellissima. "You're just saying that cause you're used to the heat. If we were up North and that air conditioner up there was a heater- you'd be just as resentful."

"Just deal the cards, already!" yapped Bellissima impatiently. "I'm down to my last two pieces of candy here! This is going to be my winning hand, I can feel it!" she said rubbing her palms together.

"Just give up," said Sadie chewing a wad of chocolate. "I'm on a roll tonight. Mama should have named me lady luck. I just can't lose."

"Keep talking, everybody knows that you don't start losing until you think you can't be beaten," warned Dria- divvying up the deck.

"You're too superstitious. I'm all in!" shouted Sadie- shoving a mound of assorted candy to the middle.

"Speaking of all in, what did you think about Lincoln? You ready to go <u>all in</u> with him?" asked Sadie- making kissy faces.

Bellissima refused to entertain her childish repartee. "What are we, 7 years old?" she asked instead.

"She's avoiding, Sadie," teased Dria.

"Great! Now you've got her started too," said Bellissima, huffing.

"Just admit you like him and we'll drop it," smirked Sadie.

"Admit that I like him? We're not in middle school! What's next, you want me to wait by his locker and ask him to the dance?" asked Bellissima, annoyed.

"Swear he didn't make you cream your jeans and we'll never bring him up again," baited Dria.

Bellissima lowered her cards and sighed. She stared away from their faces and didn't say anything. Sadie and Dria scrutinized her mien. "How about we just play?" Bellissima insisted instead of answering.

Sadie and Dria leaped to their feet and danced circles around Bellissima. "She didn't deny it! I knew it! Lissima's got a boy crush! Lissima's got a boy crush! Lissima's got a boy crush!"

Bellissima threw her cards on the floor and gathered the deck. "Alright! That's it! Since you two can't act your age, we're going to bed!"

"Leave my candy! I won that fair and square!" roared Sadie.

"Sore loser!" said Dria, tossing her pillow at Bellissima.

The girls bunkered down and fell asleep quickly. Despite exhaustion, Bellissima had trouble staying asleep. She was feeling guilty for withholding details of her and Grandma Cat's conversations from her cousins-, especially Dria. Suddenly the distance between her and her favorite cousin made more sense. Catherine said everything Dria never would. After all that time, the villain had been revealed; Dria's own father. The horror, it was difficult to accept but it made Dria's silence easier to understand. Bellissima crawled over to Dria and shook her.

"Lissima? What's wrong? Is it time for me and you to draw on Sadie at the same time like we got you?" asked Dria- delirious.

"No. I just couldn't sleep."

"What's wrong?"

"Earlier when we were talking about Granny Cat, I left some stuff out," confessed Bellissima.

Dria sat up and put her hand on Bellissima's shoulder. "Whatever it is, you can tell me."

Bellissima wanted to tell Dria that she'd heard all about the hobo from Alexandria. Bellissima wanted to tell Dria that Granny Cat had filled in most of the blanks and that she no longer needed Dria to explain anything. All Bellissima's anger and confusion had been replaced with compassion as she stared at Dria who was happy just being there to listen, finally being the one again. The one Lissima turned to. Suddenly Bellissima felt callous for letting one night of misunderstood strife turn into years of animosity.

But if Bellissima brought it up, it would be pressuring Dria to talk about the ordeal, maybe before she was truly ready. She decided to wait until Dria was ready all on her own. "Granny Cat's been telling me all these things because she hasn't been taking her medications. I was supposed to give them to her today, myself. I was supposed to stay with her until I was sure she'd swallowed them too deep to spit back up, but I didn't give them to her on purpose just so I could get information out of her."

"Lissima, that's unethical," said Dria, calmly and carefully so that Bellissima wouldn't feel judged.

"I know. I feel so bad about it."

"Don't beat yourself up. We all do things we're not proud of. I started seeing a therapist last year behind my mother's back. It's crazy, I know. Lou Anna Beaumonte' is the greatest shrink that ever lived. She's so respected in the world of mental health that people were turning me away just because I'm her kid. I finally tracked down a doctor from Mama's graduating class. One who was always second best to the great Lou Anna. He took me on as a patient to vex her, I'm sure. Thank goodness for patient/doctor confidentiality. He'll never be able to rub it in her face, Thank God. Me and Mama, our relationship is distorted. I see a stranger three times a week just to tarnish my own mother's character in secrecy all because I don't have the courage to tell her to her face- the way I feel about her parenting. I went to Mama last October. The weather was horrible, rain just wouldn't let up. I mustered the courage to tell her that I was unstable and troubled and withdrawn- all because of her and her selfishness and all the Beaumonte' ways. I went over to her place, and she wouldn't even let me in. She said I should have called first. My point is, we all have our crosses to bear. You have an unnatural need for factuality because you've been lied to your whole life by the people who claim to love us most. We all have. I'd like to think people lie to the ones they love to keep them as clean and pure as they know them to be or think that they are. Maybe we just don't have enough faith in them, believe that they can know all about the unclean thing's we've been through and still love us the same when it's all said and done. I don't know why we do that to our loved ones." Dria grabbed Bellissima's hand. "Talk to God about it. Tell him you had a little lapse of judgment. He'll forgive you. He's forgiven sins far worse than this one. He knows why you did it. I know you meant no harm and so does he."

"Grandma Cat used to always say that to us: talk to God more often and before you know it, all that talking will lead to a healthy prayer life. We all need a healthy prayer life, it's important."

"Yeah she did," Dria replied. She glanced over at Sadie to make sure she was still asleep. "I want you to know that I haven't forgotten about our talk. I was so mean to you that night and the way I sent you away, it was so hateful. I handled it that way for a reason, but it wasn't right, and I lost you for all these years…"

Bellissima stopped Dria. "I don't want you apologizing for anything and I don't want you to talk about that night. I know I've been like a broken record these past years; hounding you. I don't feel like I need you to explain anything to me anymore. Whatever happened, it happened, and you've said you were sorry every day since. Shame on me for making you say it so many times. In a family, no one should have to work overtime for love or acceptance or forgiveness. When you're family, all those things come no-strings-attached, no charge, no hidden fees. I don't care what happened and I shouldn't have made you work for absolution. You're here now and you love me just the same. I love you just the same, all bad memories aside."

"Thank you for that, Lissima. You have no idea what that means to me."

"Anything for you, Dria."

Bellissima turned to head back to her sleeping bag. Dria grabbed her shoulder and whispered. "You know, the old man at the shop today said something strange about Grandpa Jeremiah?"

"Strange? Like how?" asked Bellissima.

"He said something like: Grandpa wasn't supposed to be on the bridge the day he died."

"Woah. That is strange. Did he elaborate at all?"

"No, he just shut down like everyone else does in this damn town when we start asking the right questions."

"That's so weird. Maybe Grandma Cat will have more to say tomorrow; something to help make some sense of all the end pieces this puzzle seems to have. Thanks for listening, Dria."

"Anytime. You know you're my favorite cousin. Don't tell Sadie, though. She's the jealous type."

CHAPTER TWENTY-ONE

Lou Anna woke before everyone and dressed to go see the best lawyer in Southwest Louisiana. His firm handled all things Beaumonte' related and they were expecting Lou Anna. "Well smack my ass and call me donkey Eeyore! Somebody roll out the red carpet! The best psychiatrist that ever lived just strutted her fancy stuff right into my office!" said Don- an old lifelong friend of the family. He'd always been over-the-top fervent and androgynous with his mannerism and attire. "You get yourself over here and hug me right this instant!"

"It's so good to see you, Don! How are you?" asked Lou Anna.

"I'm fabulous! Just fabulous! Don't I look fabulous?" he asked spinning like a show contestant. "How are you? How is that doll of yours, Dria?"

"She's great! She took that letter of recommendation you wrote her and joined the best damn firm in the city! I can't thank you enough for doing that for her, Don."

"Every time we talk, you're always thanking me for the same things over and over again. You're welcome for convincing you to dye your hair in the springtime. You're welcome for telling you your prom date had herpes before you kissed him at midnight. You're welcome for writing a little 'ol letter of recommendation for Dria! It was nothing, honey! I can't believe she needed help from me after the academic trail you blazed through that university. You left your mark, yes you did!" Said Don, putting out his cigar in a pink leopard print ashtray. "How's Sadie?" he asked, overwrought. "Minxy's good about keeping in touch with me but stopped cashing the checks I send for Sadie. I worry."

Lou Anna grabbed hold of Don's hand, supportively. "You know Minxy. She's full of pride and independent. The little she does have, she takes pride that she got it on her own. And don't worry, Minxy thinks the money I use to keep Sadie in school comes from me. She'll never know it's really coming out of your pocket. Those two always land on their feet. Don't worry yourself. If there's ever need to worry, you know I'll call you up quick no matter what Minxy wants or don't want," she replied.

"Thank you, Lou," said Don; kissing her cheek. "I went ahead and drew up the paperwork you asked for. My associates got 'em notarized. I made copies for your sisters as well. The only thing left to do is sign." Don paused, removed his glasses and grabbed both of Lou Anna's hands. "I know it's not my place to ask, but are you and your sisters sure you all wanna do this? I mean, I've heard of heiress' turning down their birthright, but skipping it down a generation without even asking whose next in line how they feel about it? Honey, this is the south- we just don't do that! And what about the money you'd receive from the capital alone? Everyone wants what's coming to them! There's no shame in that!"

"We've discussed it enough. We even made up a bogus excuse to get out of the house a few nights ago just to weigh the pros and cons in peace. My sisters and I love the big house. We grew up there but with Mama in the home, there won't be anyone living there to look after it. Bellissima's working, constantly. Kay has her hands full with the second restaurant. Minxy's saving the world. Dria, Sadie and I have lives in separate cities. Buzzards are already hounding Kay, trying to buy with offers so low it's insulting. We'd feel just awful if we hocked a living breathing bequest like the big house. Mama would never forgive us. Hell, we'd never forgive ourselves. But we could forgive our daughters if they sold. I guess we just don't want the blood on our hands if it comes to that. It'll end up theirs in a few years anyway. It's not like we're getting any younger, or healthier," said Lou Anna- looking away as if troubled

Don rushed to shut his office door. "Lou Anna from Louisiana, what are you not telling me?" he badgered. "You spit it out, right now!"

Lou Anna groaned. "I'm in treatment," she confessed.

Don gasped climatically and collapsed, faint, in the chair next to Lou Anna. "Dear God, no! Is it Aids?"

"Heavens no! It's my breast. There's a lump in the left one. I found it doing my own at-home self-examination. I know I should have got it looked at as soon as possible but I had a lot going on with Bellissima when I first found out. She'd come into town the day I was supposed to get it checked out. Dria came by unexpectedly and I handled it poorly. I wanted her to come with me to the reschedule but she was still mad and wouldn't answer so I had to cancel again…" said Lou Anna.

"Sounds to me like you're making a lot of excuses for not taking care of yourself," said Don staring at Lou Anna with conviction.

"You're right. I had lots of opportunities to see a doctor after that, but I didn't until months later. By then, the cancerous mound was causing all kinds of problems."

"Are you going to have surgery?" asked Don- apprehensive.

"Yes, soon. First, I have to work up the courage to tell the family. I just don't feel right bringing it up with everything that's going on with Mama right now. I was hoping Dria and I would be a little closer before I went under the knife. What if I don't wake up, Don? I will have died before I really got to know my daughter or at least got a chance to say I'm sorry for how I let her life get messed up."

Don hugged Lou Anna tight. "Oh dear, God's not going to let that happen. You know he hears all our prayers. Somehow, someway- he's going to fix it. You wait and see. It's not always as fast as we want it fixed and his methods may seem a little odd but he's an on-time God. He don't sleep. How can he when the devil's working so much overtime. Did they put you on a treatment regimen?"

"Yes. I've been hiding some pills in a box of tofu in the fridge. No true blood Southerner is gon' touch that," she laughed.

"Sho! you right!" agreed Don with a chuckle.

"I haven't been taking them though. They make me so tired. It's been so long since we've all been together, and I don't want to miss a thing. What if I…"

Don threw his hands up, "No! No! No! Don't you even finish that sentence! We not gon' start talking like that! Catherine Beaumonte' raised more hell than the Lucifer and she's been hanging in there for almost 100 years! You're going to be around for 101 years just to spite her some more. But you have to take those medications, dear. If you don't, that family of yours is going to notice something's wrong. Especially that Kay, she's really good at sniffing out lies." Don pulled a Kleenex from the box on his desk and dabbed Lou Anna's cheeks. "Are you sure this is the right time to transfers heirship to your daughters? This could only further stress your health situation?"

"We've decided. When Catherine passes, our daughters will own the big house and what's left of the land. The fate of the big house and our legacy is in their hands now."

"Well, if you're sure. I support you."

"You've always been such a good friend to us, Don. I thank you for..."

Don threw up his hands, "And there you go again! Thanking me! Honey child, you thank me too much! Really!" he said hugging Lou Anna tight.

"Maybe I do, but only because you deserve to hear it. You know, I don't think I ever thanked you for that night...when we all..."

Don's stare became grave. "Don't you ever thank me for that. You know, I barely think about it all anymore. Me, you and your sisters; we did what had to be done. God saw, and I don't think he's going to hold it against us either. I believe he's thankful for what we did. We made the world a better place by ridding it of a little evil."

•

Minxy stuck her hand out to the passenger side window and rolled her fingertips over and under the current again and again like a flying dragon. Kay smashed the pedal even harder and Minxy revved just as loud as the engine. "Put the top down!" she yelled to Kay.

"I will not! I'll lose my scarf!" refused Kay.

"-Come on! Live a little!" pressured Minxy with a very convincing glare.

"-Alright fine!" yelled Kay, caving. She switched the roof back and the two of them cheered like wild teens.

Locals roared as they sped through; including the town sheriff who probably should have written them a speeding ticket but caught Kay's scarf out of the wind instead- waving it in the air and then sniffing it when no one was looking.

"It feels so good to feel loved don't it, Kay?"

"It sure does, Minx. That love will be here waiting for you if you ever decide to come on home and stop saving the world," said Kay stepping out of the car.

"I started saving the world to make up for all my selfish, dangerous adolescence. You know firsthand how lawless I used to be. I've got a lot more good to do before I can come on home. I ain't broke even yet," said Minxy.

Kay and Minxy strolled into their town's best dress store, arm in arm. The shop owner, an old friend of Catherine's, recognized them immediately. "Well if it isn't two of the three most beautiful kittens in the whole wide world!" she said, struggling to stand.

"Mrs. Ora! It's so good to see you!" said Minxy- rushing into her arms.

"Look at you! Seems like just yesterday Jeremiah was walking in here to buy your little pearl satin dress for your first communion. Kay, get on over here and hug your Aunt Ora." Ora wasn't their aunt by blood but in the South, everyone's family until you have to sort out actual blood relation to see if marriage is an option.

"It's so good to see you!" said Kay kissing her cheek.

"What are you girls looking for today?" she asked.

"We need something for Mama to wear for her birthday dinner?" answered Kay.

"Is that old bag still getting older?" teased Ora. "When we were about your age, she and I decided we were going to stop aging. I guess forever young is only for those without children. We ain't that lucky."

"I hear that!" agreed Minxy.

"Nothing's given me more grey hair than the joy of motherhood. A few of these grey strands are your mother's fault and you can tell her I said it," joked Ora. "How's she doing?" she asked, more serious.

"She's barely herself anymore," Kay replied.

"I'm so sorry to hear that," said Ora- dejectedly.

"We're sorry to have to tell you," responded Minxy.

"I hear that shit covered girl's been poking around, trying to buy the big house and the property. In my day, snakes weren't so well dressed and smug when they went about their wicked business. They were hideous and stayed on their bellies, on the ground, the way the good Lord intended.

These days, they wear knock-off heels and smile right in your face. She's been poking around here too, upsetting my daughter. I told her to never come back here! I hope you told her something similar," said Ora.

"Yes, Mam. I'd sooner burn down the big house before I sell to that devil," said Kay.

Ora shuddered. "Burn it down? Lord help us. That gave me chills, but I share your sentiment."

"You know, we looked through Mama's closet and couldn't find a suit worthy of a 100ᵗʰ-year-old celebration. We thought you might have a one-of-a-kind suit we could surprise her with. Maybe something peach or a nude pink," said Minxy.

"Well, you came to the right place!" said Ora. Ora's daughter rushed to her mother's side. Ora turned to her daughter, "I want you to go in the back and get a few pieces off the rack I keep tucked away so the tourist can't buy up all my good stuff."

"Isn't that sweet? Mother and daughter working side by side like that?" asked Kay fingering through the clearance rack."

"Yeah, it must be nice. Not everyone has a bond like that with their daughter, like the one you have with Lissima.

"The connection I have with Lissima…yes. People on the outside look in and see all the shiny parts. You know what they say about everything that glitters. Believe it or not, there are times when I had to be tough on my child. There were times when I had to accept that she was an adult and capable of making her own decisions, even if I didn't like the ones she made. No relationship is immune to rough patches. They all stand the test of time. Having a good relationship with your kid doesn't mean you have to agree on everything and it sure as hell ain't rainbows every day of the week. People look at how loving Lissima and I are towards one another and think there's no way we'd keep things from one another," replied Kay-wondering about the prescription again. "You say that like you and Sadie aren't close," she said to derail her own train of thought.

"kay, when she looks at me she sees just a friend and not a mother at all. I look back on our past and all I see are kicks and raunchy giggles. When something serious happens, I doubt she'll come to me for solace. A hangover remedy- I'm the first she'll call; but when eminent matters of life are at foot- she'd rather stew in her worry than confide in me. I thought disappearing to get clean would prove how much I loved my daughter."

"Are things okay with you and Sadie?"

"You tell me," answered Minxy.

Kay's cheeks felt hot and her neck felt clammy. Had minxy found out about Sadie's pregnancy and then found out that Kay knew all about it? "What do you mean by that?" asked Kay, on edge.

Minxy's shoulder's relaxed. "Nothing. I'm sorry to talk in riddles. I'm just feeling inadequate. I know something's going on with Sadie. I also know she's intentionally leaving me out of the loop. I can't help but think she's not talking to me about whatever's s going on because she doesn't think I'm qualified to give motherly advice."

"You think something's going on with Sadie?"

"Yes, as a matter of fact, I do," answered Minxy- irritated. "What about you? You notice anything different about her? Has she told you anything?"

Kay looked deep into Minxy's perturbed eyes. She wanted, so badly, to tell her little sister that she was going to be a grandmother, but then she thought of Sadie. Sadie was already a nervous wreck and had made it very clear- she wasn't ready for anyone to know. "No. She hasn't told me anything," lied Kay.

Ora and her daughter returned from the back of the dress shop. They brought with them, a beautiful soft rose petal pink skirt suit with gold buttons and matching hat. Minxy was in awe. "Oh! Look how beautiful! She'll love it!"

"It's one of a kind," said Ora.

Kay grabbed her checkbook, "We'll take it! How much?"

"You just put that right back in your purse! You hear?" ordered Ora.

"You don't expect us to let you give us this suit for free? The stitching on the skirt alone must have taken days!"

"When my first baby was born, I couldn't make milk. I was beside myself with worry trying to figure out how I'd keep my newborn baby alive with breasts that wouldn't work right. Catherine ate twice the protein, so she could produce twice the milk and fed my baby right alongside her oldest baby- one on each chapped, raw nipple. She did so until I could finally lactate. That's a lot to take on, two hungry babies! Even if I gave you a thousand suits, I'd never be able to repay her. As I said, it's one of a kind. Catherine's one of kind."

•

Bellissima sat all alone in the employee lounge, charting her patient progress notes. Jan tip-toed up behind her and patted her shoulder. Bellissima turned around and there stood Jan with a huge vase of blossoms. "Aren't these just beautiful!" gushed Jan.

Bellissima slammed her dossier shut. "You got me flowers? Jan, this fawning is getting out of control! Where's the extended shift signup sheet for the anti-partiers? Give it here so I can sign it!" she demanded.

"Really?" asked Jan, thrilled.

"Yeah! Hurry up before I change my mind!" Bellissima rushed.

Jan pulled the signup sheet from her pocket and unfolded it on the table. She waited for Bellissima to sign and date, then she jumped for joy. "Oh, Thank you, Bellissima! This is going to be the best New Year's party ever! I'll be sure to save you some cupcakes and a plate of those little barbecue meatballs you like. Here are your flowers. Hope you don't mind, I already read the card," said Jan- handing the flowers to Bellissima with a torn envelope.

Bellissima was confused. "Wait, you mean you didn't buy these for me?"

"No. I was going to tell you that but then you offered to sign. Don't hate me. Who's Lincoln, by the way?"

Bellissima shoved the envelope in her pocket, picked up the vase and marched away. "I don't have time for you and all your meddlesome questions. Out of my way extortionist! I have a date!"

"With this Lincoln guy?" asked Jan- stunned.

"No! With my Grandmother!"

Catherine spritzed her perfume and pinned a brooch to her gown. She'd combed her hair to the side and secured it in place with a sparkly barrette. Her preening caught Bellissima by surprise. "Excuse me movie star! I have a lunch date with my grandmother, have you seen her?" joked

Bellissima, entering Catherine's room with a small tray of vending machine tuna sandwiches and fruit punch pouches.

"Whenever I primp like this, I do feel like a movie star! Come on over here and hold this mirror so I can slide on this lip stain without getting it on my dentures."

Bellissima climbed on the bed and sat, holding the mirror steady. "It's so good seeing you all dolled up like this granny. I can remember you getting this pretty every time we went to church."

"When your grandfather was alive, I'd fix myself up every single day. Lots of married women will tell you that you're supposed to do that for your husband. That way he'll stay enticed and he won't stray. Truth is, you have to fix yourself up for yourself so that you don't forget you're a woman. It's easy to lose sight of that when you become a wife and then a mother. Hell, it takes a lot more than a painted face and a slim waist to keep your husband in tune with you. Don't you forget that." Catherine capped her lipstick and took a long look at her reflection. "Yes, perfect. I feel ready, now. You know who loved playing dress up? Your Auntie Minxy, my pin-up princess. She was easily the cutest of all my babies. I know you're not supposed to say one of your babies came out cuter than the others but it's true. They all grew up to be stone cold knockouts but Minxy had beauty all figured out from day one. She had the curliest head of hair. That explains all the heartburn she gave me when I was carrying her. Her button nose always had a little rubicund glow and she had pothole deep, baby dimples. The child never frowned, not once. Come to think of it, I don't think Minxy cried the whole first year of her life. She just showed off those dimples. Whenever I sat down to put on my make-up she'd crawl up on my lap. I'd give her a brush with no powder on it and she'd try to blush her own cheeks. Yes, Minxy had natural glamour. Even as a little girl, barely aware of her dainty wiles, she was a woman- fully aware of her power. As a toddler, she sat with her legs crossed. Minxy grew out of her flat frame before her sisters. She turned heads long before them too, even though they were older. Your grandfather took one look at her in my arms and said, *'This one's going to be trouble. I guess I'll go ahead and buy another gun.'* Getting her to buckle down on her school work was hard. She was a daydreamer. She had a hard time staying focused on the here and now. I worried about her at first when Jeremiah died. She was so young. I feared she didn't get enough discipline before he went. I was right. Your Auntie Minx was a natural born rule-breaker. The way she defied, it was almost art. She was always finding bold new ways to rebel."

"I've heard the stories," said Bellissima.

"I'm sure you've heard some stories, but you don't know the half of it! She was the first of my daughters to be arrested for no good reason. She joined every activist group that would have her and organized more protest mayhem that you can imagine. She was Malcom X, in a short skirt with a perm."

"Auntie Minx was an activist? Wait, you said the first of your daughters to get arrested? Were Mama and Auntie Lou ever arrested?"

"All of them! Hell, your mother had cuffs on her twice, all for good reason though." laughed Catherine. "But back to Minxy, wherever there was unfairness or inequality, you could find my renegade Minxy there with a sign, causing more trouble than necessary. Thank goodness she was so easy to look at, that's probably the only reason she never did any hard time. Everyone was always a little sweet on her, especially law enforcement and judges since they saw so much of her. I bet some of those lonely men took her mugshots home for some companionless nighttime comfort. Even when Minxy was big and pregnant with Sadie- she had men lining up around the corner just for a chance to lay their jackets down over a puddle for her feet. I don't think pregnancy every agreed with a woman more than it agreed with my little Minx."

"Mama and Auntie Lou said that Auntie Minx got pregnant while she was still young."

"What's young? Hell, what's old, anymore? I suppose she was a bit younger than they were when they got pregnant. Minxy was about to turn 17 years old. Can you believe she tried to hide it from me?" said Catherine shaking her head. "Mother always knows. She eventually told me. I told her that if Jeremiah was alive there's no way she'd be knocked up, but I made my fair share of mistakes with her, so I suppose it was partly my fault. Even with a baby on her hip, she got her GED and got herself into a community college."

"Did she graduate community college?" asked Bellissima, wrapping a paper towel around a sandwich for Catherine."

"Hell no! She barely finished high school, I don't know why she wanted to give college a shot. Books didn't interest Minxy. Standing up for what was right and wrong- she loved that and the nightlife, of course. The nightlife called to Minxy in a secret language that only other night lovers could speak and understand. People who love the night, they crave it because they get a chance to surround themselves with people who are looking for the same kind of pain killer they're looking for."

"What kind of pain killer is that?"

"Alcohol, drugs, dirty meaningless sex, loud music to drown their own thoughts- those are all painkillers that your Auntie Minxy thought she needed to help her deal with her life."

"Mama never talks about it. She'll never say an ill word about either of her sisters. How bad was Auntie Minxy's drug and alcohol use?" asked Bellissima- her face critical.

"Real bad. Of course, it didn't start off like that. Me and her were classy, dignified sippers. We'd have one little drink together; one little cup and we'd nurse that little bit all night. I guess when I wasn't looking, she'd have a little more and then a little more. You and your cousins ever put your heads under water and screamed for fun?"

"Yes, Mam."

"Well, that's how substances work. You get so depressed that your thoughts become deafening. You'll do anything to shut them up. After you get a little drugs or alcohol in you, the voices start to sound like they're underneath a thousand leagues of sea. Then you find comfort, impermanently. The voices always come back ten times louder, though. She was a mommy all day and then she'd beat the drum all night long, but Sadie had more than just Minxy. She had me. She had Kay and Lou. She had the best big cousins a girl could ask for. The child wasn't lacking in love. The day Sadie was born, the hospital was filled with people, all of them came to see the new Beaumonte' baby. Most of them were men. I was so scared that they were all there because they all thought they could be the father. There were over twenty men there! I prayed my daughter hadn't taken a load from them all!"

"Granny!"

"What? You're grown! I know that's not the first time you heard someone talk about a load of semen!"

"So out of those twenty men, was one of them Sadie's father?"

"Yes. Minxy refused to tell me who it was, but Lou knows. Kay knows. They said he'd been there. *'You just missed him'* they said with all that acerbity and sass that I hate."

"You don't have the slightest idea?"

"I have my suspicions, but no proof. Whoever he was, he brought a little pink stuffed animal for baby Sadie- a fox. I remember thinking, what an odd toy for a baby girl- a fox, but Sadie loved it."

"Why didn't he stay around for Auntie Minx and Sadie?"

"Because Minxy wouldn't allow it. I urged Minxy to call up this mystery man, have him help; but she said she had all the help she needed. Minxy was a good enough mother. She showed up to all Sadie's school plays and teacher conferences. She may have been sloshed and late, but she showed up, that's saying a lot. Whenever she babysat you girls, she fed you cereal all day long but at least you girls ate. Who cares what people say and trust me, people had a lot to say. Married women who think they have it all together always think they have the best advice to offer but what do they really know? Sure, a lot of them will tell you they're happy but happiness is different for everyone. Most will lie and tell you they're happy but truly, they're just comfortable or too afraid to push their luck so, they've settled for the closest thing to happiness. You can't go taking guidance from just anybody. Take me for example, I shouldn't have listened to those other wives who were quick with a plan on how to fix a problem I didn't even have. The only person I should have gone to about what was going on with Jeremiah and I was God. Remember what I told you earlier, it takes a lot more than a painted face and a slim waist?"

"Yes, mam,"

"You also need trust. I didn't have enough trust. I let acrimonious women make the void between Jeremiah and I worse and It all hit the fan the day he died. I told you about the change in the weather. I'd been wanting to get my hair blown out for days, but I was waiting on the clouds to change. They never did, so I went down to the shop where all the old hens went to rejuvenate but most importantly gossip. *'He's probably having an affair. I bet he's got another family somewhere held up in a home nicer than the one he has you and your babies in. You've got to put your foot down, a man should be at home with his wife and children every night just like they expect us home, stuck with the kids they put in us.'* They went on and on. I let them pump that negative venom in my head and I let it poison my marriage. I decided I'd cook my husband's favorite dinner and ask him nicely to stay home with me and his kids. When dinner was over, I'd make him tell me everything he'd been hiding, so we could finally get on the same page again. Forgiveness would be dessert. *'Cat, you just served our family dinner. If you like eating and being able to feed them, you have to cut out all this distrustful behavior. Those women you are listening too will never know the kind of love I give you, the kind of respect I give you. I've never given you a reason to doubt my devotion to you. Now, I told you I have to work. No matter how much I hate it, I have no choice. I give up a lot to be a good father. Putting you and I first was something I had to give up. Those kids we brought into this world, they come first. Lou's given us our first grandchild and with no daddy around- she's going to need our help more than ever. Kay has big restaurant dreams. I can tell just by looking at little Minxy that I'm going to need bail money on standby; maybe for her being a rebel hippie, maybe for me killing whatever little boy follows her home. Woman, I love you. More than anything in this world; but you got to let me be a man and a man is a provider. I don't want my daughters growing up to be just another underprivileged black family. My girls are going to be somebody in this world.'* I told him that if he didn't stay home, I was going to leave him. He took two steps towards the truck door to leave and I spun him back around. I took my wedding band off and I threw it at him. The minute I did, I regretted it, but pride is a powerful seductress. It broke his heart, I could tell. *'What kind of mother won't share her husband with her kids and his work. Here I was thinking you loved me for being the provider that I am. There's no one else. There's my children, my work and you, Catherine. All I ever wanted to do was take care of you and my little women. Everyone's so busy being excited about all the changes going on around here- the bridge. It's affected more than you can ever understand. Nothing's ever going to be the same again. Everybody smells growth. Well, the devil down there in hell smelling a fire sale for our souls. He wants to see if we'll sell or not.'* I stood outside, watched him get in his truck and he drove off. I didn't know he'd be dead hours later."

CHAPTER TWENTY-TWO

The Beaumonte' grandchildren sat downstairs with handcrafted paper fans. Dria had stripped down to her balconette and Bellissima tied her hair up with a bandana to keep her neck from beading sweat. Sadie soaked a cotton hand towel in a bowl of ice and dabbed her chest with it. "I really should have bought two air conditioners," admitted Dria, regrettably.

"You think?" asked Bellissima derisively.

"At least I took some action! Everyone else here is too scared of Granny to stand up to her and make changes around here," said Dria with her chest poked out.

"By the way, I told Catherine you put an AC unit in her house today," said Bellissima.

Dria's face sank, "Oh my God! Is She going to kill me?" she asked.

Bellissima chuckled," Ha! Not so tough now huh? Relax, I didn't tell her yet."

"How was she today? Did she let anymore juicy Beaumonte' skeletons fall out of the closet?" asked Sadie.

"Yeah. I spent my whole lunch break with her. You should have seen her, she looked like a queen today- dressed up all fancy."

"Did she say anything about my daddy?" asked Dria- guarded.

"No, but she did talk about Auntie Minxy's jaded glory years."

"She did?" asked Sadie, eager to hear the details.

"Yes. I can't wait to tell you all about it," said Bellissima trying to sit up. She collapsed back onto the floor. "-But how can I when all I can think about it this tormenting heat! That's it! Put your shoes on! We're going for a walk down to the creek."

"We are?" asked Dria, in a dither.

"Yes, we are! It's a nice night for a swim," answered Bellissima, sliding her rain boots on. "You in, Sadie?"

Sadie had already put both shoes on and was headed for the door. "Mama! Aunties! We're going out! Don't worry we got our phones and our flashlights!" she yelled. Dria and Bellissima quickly followed her out the front door.

The Beaumonte' granddaughters stretched across the whole dirt road in a straight line. "At least there's a breeze out here!" said Sadie.

"It's always so hot in the big house. Can you imagine how hot it's going to be when we're trapped in that Godforsaken kitchen, making that damn dinner?" complained Dria.

"Maybe it won't be so bad. I mean, I know ya'll hate cooking, but I think it's going to be fun. It's not like we see a lot of each other these days. I'll take whatever time I can get," said Bellissima.

"What's fun about sliced fingers and burns? You heard Auntie Kay."

"-Well at least we'll be together. Tomorrow's not promised. We could check out any day now. I'd hate to think all our good times are behind us. Surely we still have some good times coming right? Memories to make?" asked Bellissima- sadly hopeful.

"When I think of good times, I don't envision those hideous brown aprons back at the big house," mumbled Dria.

"I love those aprons! No matter how many times you wash them, they always smell sweet like Auntie Kay's pastries," said Sadie.

"-You have one of those old souls, Lissima. Things like that comfort you. You're so homey. You complain about the heat and how everyone knows everyone's business, but you love the South. Hell, you don't even travel for vacation. I don't know how you do it, I'd just claw myself right out of my own skin if I'd lived all my days in this one small town. Don't you have any big dreams at all?" asked Dria.

"Well, I do think about the snow," Bellissima replied.

"The snow? What for?" asked Sadie.

"I don't know, I've just always wanted to build a snowman; maybe get snowed in and be forced to eat soup all day by a warm fire, read some Richard Paul Evans until I fall fast asleep."

"Take it from someone who's been snowed in. It's not all it's cracked up to be," said Dria.

"If you want to see the snow so bad, why don't you just pack up and go see it before life ties you down? Wait until you have kids, you'll be stuck for sure. Suddenly you won't have time to figure out life. Life will just come crashing down like Tetris with no pause button," said Sadie.

Bellissima sighed. "I don't know."

"What do you mean you don't know? You're single. You don't have any kids. Auntie Kay has a life all her own. You work so much overtime, I'm sure you can afford to take a few weeks off for some you-time. What's stopping you?"

"-Cheniere."

Both Sadie and Dria stared at Bellissima, curious. "Lissima, Cheniere's gone. How could she possibly be keeping you from seeing the world?"

"I don't mean *her*, I mean the memory of her- I suppose. The Bridge ruins are here. She's buried here in the South. It may sound crazy, but I don't want her to be alone. Sometimes I wonder if she rests more peacefully knowing I'm still near. I go on with my life more peacefully knowing exactly where I can find what's left of her. What if she thinks I'm leaving because I'm too much of a coward to face the bridge? What if she thinks I'm leaving to forget about her?" Bellissima asked. Neither Sadie nor Dria answered. They didn't know how. Fearing she'd ruined the mood, Bellissima changed the subject. "Did you extend a formal invitation to Colin?" she asked turning to Dria.

"Are you going to invite Lincoln?" asked Dria right back.

"That's crazy!" blushed Bellissima.

"No crazier than you asking me if I *formally* invited Colin. As if I would? You know there's no way I could really keep him from coming, so don't look at me like I'm happy he's going to be there. Since you're so cool as a cucumber when it comes to flames, you should really stop pretending that Lincoln fellow ain't the love of your life," snapped Dria.

Bellissima gasped. "Love of my life? Sadie, are you hearing this foolishness?"

"Yeah, I hear you two fools talking; but it's not foolishness. He's definitely the one. We all feel it, especially Auntie Kay. It's all we've been talking about."

"We all? So what, my family waits until I'm gone to gossip about me?"

"It's not considered gossip if it's not malicious backlash, but if you're asking if we wait for you to leave to discuss your love life- then yes."

"- Are you saying he's not perfect?" asked Dria.

"Jesus is perfect, Dria. Lincoln seems…"

"-Damn close to perfect?" finished Sadie.

"-Maybe," replied Bellissima- kicking a rock in the road.

"He's the type of guy that sends flowers. I can tell," Dria responded. Bellissima stopped walking and stared at Dria. Sadie shined her light at Bellissima's face illuminating her shock.

"He already sent flowers, didn't he Lissima?" asked Sadie.

"There was a small vase…"

"I knew it!" Dria gloated. "What did the card say? You can tell a lot about a guy from what he chooses to write on the card."

"Did the card say, marry me?" joked Sadie.

"No, but it was sweet. He thanked me for the help and expressed his gratitude for letting him stay for dinner. There was some poetry. Something like: *One shade the more…*"

"*…One ray the less, had half impaired the nameless grace,*" finished Sadie.

Bellissima and Dria stopped in their tracks. "Yeah. How'd you know that?"

"It's the work Lord Byron, one of the most famous poets in the whole world. I'm impressed Sadie," said Dria.

"Why Dria? Because you think dumb stoners don't know art when they hear it?" replied Sadie.

"What does all that fanciness mean?" asked Bellissima- trying to get a better understanding as to why Lincoln borrowed that particular line of poetry.

"The title of that poem is, <u>*She Walks in Beauty*</u>," said Sadie with a soft smirk. "The title explains itself."

Dria shined her flashlight into the woods and behind them. "I heard something?" she said- inching closer to Bellissima.

Bellissima shinned her light in the same direction as Dria's beam. "I don't see anything! What? You think big foot's out here looking for a place to cool off too?" she quipped.

"-Or a hungry Chupacabra?" asked Sadie- making merry of Dria's paranoia.

"That's not funny! It'd be just my luck! Dying in these ridiculous pajamas, with one of Bellissima's ugly head wraps on!"

Bellissima gasped, insulted. "Next time I'll just let you wake up to frizzy edges then! How about that?"

"Bellissima, how much longer until we reach the creek?" asked Sadie.

"Ask Dria. She's the one who spent the most time there with Colin," replied Bellissima with a sneer.

"How much time?" asked Sadie- jeering.

Dria rolled her eyes. "Not that much time! We're almost there, we just have to cut through the graveyard now."

"I forgot about the graveyard," said Bellissima- dreading the path through.

The three of them stood at the cemetery gate, shining their flashlights over the ancient tombstones. "How many bodies you think they got buried here?" asked Sadie.

"At least a hundred," exaggerated Bellissima. "I'm so glad Grandma Cat and Grandpa Jeremiah got us a plot behind the big house for when we kill over. It must be so depressing being laid to rest here amongst all these lonely spirits. No one even comes here to visit them."

"Lissima, do you and Auntie Kay still visit Cheniere in the family plot?" asked Dria.

"Yeah, we both do. We just don't go at the same time anymore. We both cry too much, it's hard to comfort someone when you can't stop your own self from crying," answered Bellissima. "Okay, we run through on the count of three- quick so old slave jubilee's ghost don't snatch our ankles up and no stepping on graves," she stressed- looking at Sadie specifically. "No need to piss off any stiffs and start a full-blown return of the living dead type of situation."

"Fine! Geez! No grave stomping!" huffed Sadie.

One…Two…Three… They took off, running full speed through the graves- hopping over erect headstones. Dria zig-zagged through bundles of artificial bouquets. Sadie lagged behind, refusing to go anywhere near the graves with miniature stonework, afraid they were baby graves. Bellissima ran straight down the middle, not looking to the left or the right. *Forgive us, Lord, for disturbing their sleep. Please don't let them rise and eat our brains-* she mumbled.

They didn't stop sprinting until they reached the creek where they found a handful of lawless teens tailgating. "This brings back memories," said Dria.

"Yeah all that's missing is Colin with his hand up your shirt," teased Bellissima as they neared the rowdy heard.

One of the minors noticed Bellissima and quickly hid her lit joint and marijuana stash behind her back. "Ms. Lissima! It's not what it looks like, we were just…"

Bellissima put her hand up," It's cool! I ain't God or your daddy or the police. We're not here to bust you."

The kid's posture unstiffened. "Oh, thank Goodness! My folks would kill me if they knew I was down here. I saw you three and thought…"

"-Thought what? That we'd rat you out?" asked Dria- grabbing the joint from behind her back and puffing it. "Believe it or not, we used to be young." Dria exhaled and all the juveniles stared, amazed. "When I was your age we used to own this place. I'd come out here all the time and swim. There used to be a big rope swing…"

"-You mean this rope swing?" asked Sadie. Bellissima and Dria looked around but didn't see Sadie on the ground. Then they looked up and spotted Sadie in the big lover's tree with the rope swing in hand. She'd already stripped down to her sports bra and panties, causing all the young boys to stare and high five.

"Is she going to…" started Dria.

"-Jump? Yeah, I think so," finished Bellissima.

The youngsters began to encourage Sadie's reckless behavior. *"Jump! Jump! Jump! Jump!"*

Dria rushed to the bottom of the tree and shined her light up at Sadie. "Do you think this is a good idea, considering your condition?" she muttered.

"Hell yeah, I do. Any kid of mine is going to have to have a sense of adventure. May as well start teaching it now. Besides, I heard Mama roped barrels clear into her second trimester," she replied- wrapping both hands around the rope and then leaping from the tree.

Bellissima gulped and held her breath. Dria's mouth dropped as Sadie let go, soared through the air and fell feet first into the creek. She didn't emerge right away. A few of the boys took off their shirts, ready to jump in after her but then Sadie sprang from the water, cheering and shouting. "What are ya'll waiting for? It's like iced water in here and ya'll still standing around sweating to death!"

Bellissima looked at Dria and Dria looked back at Bellissima. The teens looked at them both. All at once everyone stripped down and joined in- splashing each other.

●

Back at the big house, the Beaumonte' daughters sat in their mother's room overlooking the paperwork they had Don drawn up. "Well, I guess all there's left to do is sign," said Minxy.

"Yeah, I guess so," agreed Lou Anna.

"You sound funny. You not having second thoughts, are you?" asked Kay, rubbing Lou Anna's shoulder for support.

"No. I know this is something that needs to be done. I was just thinking about the girls and what they'll decide to do once it all theirs. Do you think they still feel a connection to this place?"

"Of course they do! Our girls have been sleeping on an old hard floor for days. Dria makes enough money to buy her own hotel room. Bellissima has a perfectly good cottage a few miles away with real air circulation. Sadie can go back to school anytime she wants, she already got her chance to see Catherine and say her goodbyes. They're staying because they love us. They love each other. They love this house and everything it stands for. You said it yourself, the land and this house need a lot of attention. Attention that we can't give it anymore. We'd have no choice but to sell. It'll take all three of them to keep this place up if they decide to keep it. Either way, it's up to them now. No matter what they decide, we'll stand by them."

"I know. I just worry they'll forget where they came from. Sometimes I forget where I came from," Lou Anna admitted, humbled.

"They're Beaumonte' children. They won't forget." Assured Kay.

Lou Anna nodded and signed. "I hope you're right." Kay and Minxy signed beneath Lou Anna's signature and they sealed a complete copy in a large envelope.

"You sure you're okay Lou?" asked Minxy. "You've been a bit sluggish ever since I saw you eating that tofu junk you brought down here from the city."

"Yes, I guess I'm just full. Good eating- that tofu," laughed Lou Anna, uncomfortably. "I think I'm going to lay down for a moment, just rest my eyes a bit," she said- snoring as soon as her head hit the pillow.

"Sure, you do that," said Kay tucking her in. "Minxy and I will go downstairs and have a little snack ourselves. Come Minxy," said Kay- tugging at Minxy's arm.

"I'm not really hungry. I think I'll just go down and read a bit," said Minxy.

"No. I'd very much like you to come and sit with me in the kitchen," insisted Kay. "I want to talk to you about something."

CHAPTER TWENTY-THREE

Dria, Bellissima, and Sadie got out of the creek, wrung their hair and gathered their clothes. "That was really awesome Ms. Lissima. You ladies are pretty cool," glorified the kids.

"Thanks for letting us crash your festivities. Don't stay out here too late and make good choices with your bodies. If you mess this one up, you don't get another. Don't let an innocent enough good time turn into something you regret," said Bellissima.

The Beaumonte' grandchildren grabbed their flashlights and began their walk back to the big house. "You know, I was apprehensive at first but I'm glad we came out here tonight. My core temperature's back to normal. I got to swim alongside a few perky teens who were substantially younger than me and discovered my body is still pretty awesome in comparison and we didn't get killed by a masked murderer," said Dria. Suddenly, they heard a strange sound behind them. All three girls stopped and turned around slowly. "Did you hear that?"

"Yeah, I did. Maybe one of those kids followed us out to find their way back to the main road?" theorized Sadie. "Hello? Is someone there?" she yelled.

"Shut up! What if it's really a crazy chainsaw killer?" mumbled Dria.

"Okay, Calm down. No one's dying or getting hacked up with a saw?" said Bellissima in attempt to comfort her cousins. Just then, they heard another noise. "That sounded like someone stepping on a tree branch. Someone's definitely trailing us," she whispered.

"What do we do?" asked Dria.

"I've never died in the woods before Dria, how the hell am I supposed to know?" jabbed Bellissima.

A small briar began to rustle. Dria and Sadie grabbed a hold of Bellissima and started screaming. "*Agh*!!! Help us! Just take Dria! Let me live!"

From out of the shrubbery, appeared little Gabby with a tiny light clipped on her hat like a coal miner. Bellissima sighed. "Stop yelling! Hush! Stop! It's just Gabby!"

"Oh thank God! You almost gave me a heart attack, sneaky little runt!" said Sadie trying to catch her breath."

Bellissima pulled Gabby close and knelt. "What on earth are you doing out here in the middle of the night? Do you have any idea how dangerous this is? There are wolves, wild hogs, bears, snakes and there could be bad people who mean to do you harm!" she scolded.

Little Gabby sniffed and wiped her nose. It was clear, she'd been crying. "I'm still looking for Captain Crisp. He still hasn't come home, and I'm worried about him. I brought these carrots with me just in case I found him. He must be so hungry. He probably hasn't eaten in days," she whimpered- taking a few carrots out of her pocket to show Bellissima

"Listen, kid, I told you before. Captain Crisp ain't worried about eating because he's been eaten," said Sadie.

"Sadie, exercise a little empathy," said Bellissima.

"Does your mother know you're out here all alone in the woods?" asked Dria- shining the light behind Gabby- making sure hadn't been followed by a creep.

"No. She doesn't even know I'm not in bed. She's got the music real loud again. When the music's loud, she's having too much fun to be a mommy," said Gabby- fiddling with the carrots in her hands.

Sadie could relate. "I've been where you are little one. It sucks, I know," she said, hanging her head.

Bellissima stood, looked at Sadie and Dria who were equally saddened by Gabby's revelation. "Let's go ya'll. We're going to take Gabby home and have a little talk with her mother."

•

"How's your hot chocolate? How's your coffee cake? I've been trying out so many new deserts; experimenting with some new ingredients. What do you think? Is it menu worthy?" asked Kay- anxiously.

"It's quite tasty," answered Minxy- who'd been sitting in the kitchen with her fingers laced, watching Kay move about nervously, concentrating on the food to postpone the real reason she'd asked Minxy to come to the kitchen. "You said you wanted to talk to me about something, Kay?"

Kay dallied. "Yeah."

Minxy was on the edge of her seat. "Well…go head," she pushed.

Kay reached across the table and grabbed Minxy's hand. "Do you remember earlier in the shop, when we were talking about Sadie?"

"Yes. What about it?" asked Minxy.

Kay took a deep breath. "You asked me if I knew anything and I said no, but…"

Minxy slowly pulled her hand from Kay's. "-But you were lying?" she finished. "I knew it," said Minxy- clearly upset.

"I should have spoken up right then and there, but I was so conflicted. Sadie and I did talk. She told me some things in confidence, and I told her that I wouldn't say anything…"

Minxy stood and turned her back to Kay. "Just stop Kay!"

Kay stood, genuinely apologetic. "No, I want to talk to you about it Minxy."

"NOW? Now you want to talk about it? Today, I poured a bit of my soul out to you. I asked you and you gave me nothing but now that it's keeping you from sleeping, you want to fill me in on what's happening with *my* kid?" yelled Minxy. "Just save it! Obviously, neither you nor Sadie respects me enough to talk to me so you can keep your little secrets to yourself! Here I was feeling sorry for you for not knowing things!" she screamed, storming out of the house.

Lou Anna staggered downstairs. "What's all the yelling for?" she asked.

"It's Minxy, we were just having a loving heated discussion about secrets," replied Kay.

Secrets? Lou Anna was suddenly worried about the secret she and Bellissima were hiding. Did Minxy go and tell Kay about Bellissima being in the city? "What secret were you two talking about it?"

"Never mind that for now. Would you just please go check on her?" asked Kay.

Lou Anna stepped out onto the porch and found Minxy in tears. "What happened back there?" she asked. "Kay said something about secrets, does she know about what we talked about?"

"It's so typical of you to think about covering your own ass first, Lou. No, you and Lissima's secret is still safe."

"Good," she mumbled. "Is there anything I can do to make you feel better? You want to talk about it?"

"If you want to help me, Lou. Get the keys to your rental and take me to the bar," said Minxy.

"The bar? Minxy, what about your sobriety?"

"What about it? Are you taking me or am I walking until I can hitchhike a ride? Either way, I'm going!"

•

Bellissima's stride was swift as she waltzed into the town's poorest trailer park. Sadie's legs were beginning to cramp up. "Are we getting close or are we going to hit Egypt?"

"It's right up here on the left," replied Bellissima- leading the way with Gabby's hand in hers.

Dria tried to keep up. "Lissima, what exactly are you going to do? As your lawyer, I must advise you…"

"You can stop right there, Dria. I'm not going to punch her," said Bellissima- still contemplating. "Well, let's just play it by ear. I don't want to make any promises I can't keep."

Bellissima pounded the aluminum trailer door with her fist, hard, so that the occupants would hear over the sound system. The volume lowered. "Who the hell is that banging at my door?" yelled Gabby's mother from inside.

"It's Lissima Beaumonte'! I need to have a word with you, Katina!"

"What the hell you want?"

"- I'm here to return your baby girl!"

They could hear Katina, tripping over empty alcohol containers to reach the door. She jerked it open and saw all three Beaumonte' grandchildren standing there, soaking wet with disappointed faces. Gabby squeezed Bellissima's hand tight. Katina looked down at her daughter with clenched teeth. "Gabby? And just what are you doing out of bed again?" she slurred roughly yanking Gabby's tiny arm- dragging her inside.

"You really should be a little gentler with her, she just a little girl," insisted Dria.

Just then, one of Katina's intoxicated houseguests joined her in the doorway, a foul-smelling tattooed brute who stared at them repugnantly. "Don't tell me how to raise my child. Pop some bastards out of your own tight boujee ass and then you can raise those however you please," hissed Katina.

"You have got to be the shitiest excuse for a mother I've ever seen and trust me- I know a shitty mother when I see one," said Sadie.

The goon at Katina's side, Robbie, stepped out of the doorway and into the lot yard. "We got a problem here?" he asked.

Bellissima, clearly not intimidated, got in his face. "I don't know Robbie, Do we? What are you going to do if we did?"

"Yeah, I think we do have a problem!" answered Sadie. She looked over Robbie's shoulder and cut her eyes at Katina. "Why don't you put this inked dog away and come on out here in the yard where there's more space, Katina? We can handle it right now!"

Dria grabbed both of her cousins and pulled them back. She replaced Bellissima in Robbie's face and stared him down. "The problem we have now is you bucking up to my little cousin who was kind enough to escort that sweet little girl home. I shudder to think, what could have happened to her out here all alone. However, taking one look at you- a hot steaming heap of monkey dung, and her- a walking test tube of disease; I'm starting to think Gabby was safer being locked out in the night. Now you and I haven't met but believe me when I say- you don't want a Beaumonte' sized problem. We might be smaller than you but we're a hell of a lot stronger. I don't think the two of you have enough juice to take on the three of us. After we kick your sorry asses, cry self-defense and tell police the reason we had to come here in the first place; I'll have every agency in the state of Louisiana up in your business. When they're done turning your lives upside down- snatching welfare payments, running background checks, freezing those SSI benefits I'm sure you're using to buy your booze. I'll make a call to one of my friends down at the prison. He'll make sure your cellmate is bigger and badder than you think you are. I'll sleep like a baby at night knowing he's dressing you up like a lady and bending you over a dirty sink every night after lights out. Maybe that would humble you a bit. How's that sound big boy? You want to call my bluff and become someone's bitch, because I'm feeling really liberated tonight."

Katina walked out into the yard and grabbed her man's shoulder. "Don't let them ruin our fun, Robbie. Come on let's go to the bar and shoot some pool," she said- pulling him into a raggedy, rusted sadan.

"If you leave Gabby in that house alone so you can go catch chlamydia in a bar bathroom stall for the third time, I'll call the police on you right now for child abandonment!" threatened Bellissima.

"Step off. My Grandma is inside hooked up to her oxygen tank. She'll keep an eye on Gabby." Katina paused to pondered. "I think my grandmother knows your grandmother." Katina began to snicker. "She told me she warned your stupid granny about that bridge after it took your grandfather."

"Say one more thing about my granny!" Sadie threatened- taking her shoes off again.

Katina laughed even harder. "Your family used to come to mine for spiritual guidance all the time, just like everyone else in this ungrateful town. You've got a set of balls on you. How dare you come to my home and try and make me feel like a bad person? Do you feel bad for being greedy in your Mama's womb, little miss Lissima? It's common knowledge when one twin's born without something it's cause the other twin was selfish. My grandmother told me, she took one look at Kay's stomach and she could smell the sibling thievery. Only one of you would be born working right and only one of you would get to live a long life. I guess that one was you, lucky you. How do you feel living knowing you took your sister's ability to hear and speak? Your very existence caused an imbalance in this dimension and one of you had to go. Deep down inside you must have hated having to share your face with someone else. I suppose there could only be one, huh?"

Sadie felt a tremor in her uterus and she knew immediately that her unborn child could feel her seething fury. Katina could feel Sadie's burning eyes. "I don't know when or where, but you're going to get hit in the face for saying that. It's going to hurt a hell of a lot worse than what you just said to my cousin," she vowed.

They sped off and disappeared in the night. For a short moment, no one spoke. Bellissima collapsed, sobbing. Sadie and Dria helped her off the ground. "Come on let's get you back to the big house," said Dria.

•

Kay sat outside on the porch next to Lou Anna, who'd sparked up a cigarette. Dria, Bellissima and Sadie walked up the driveway. As the girls neared the porch light, Lou Anna noticed that Bellissima appeared to be crying. She grabbed hold of Kay's arm and squeezed. Kay stood, "Lissima? What's going on?"

Bellissima ran past her concerned Mother and Aunt, straight into the house and slammed the screened door behind her. Kay turned to Dria and Sadie. "What's wrong with my baby?"

Regretful to bring them up-to-speed, Dria told them about their venturesome night and how it took a horrible turn when Katina Withers said the things she'd said. "It really hurt her. She didn't say a word the whole walk home."

Sadie noticed Minxy was absent. "Where's Mama?"

Lou Anna sighed. "She's had a rough night too. Got mad at Kay, wouldn't say why. Then she got mad at me because I wouldn't drive her to the bar to flush her hard-earned sober years down the drain on a whim."

Sadie tried to make it seem as if it didn't bother her but couldn't hide her disappointment from her family. "My mother decided to relapse? What a surprise?" she said jocosely.

"I should go and check on Lissima," said Kay.

Dria stopped her. "Please Auntie Kay, let Sadie and I go talk to her." She insisted.

Kay wavered but agreed. "Okay. Just please make sure my baby's okay. She's the only one I have left. We're going to go get Minxy."

Sadie laughed. "Be careful, she turns into the hulk when you try to take her drugs and alcohol away," Said Sadie following Dria inside.

Minxy Beaumonte' sat at the bar all alone with an untouched lager in front of her. She'd only been there for 13 minutes and had been approached by several men offering to buy her more drinks. "Easy boys, can't you see I already have a drink here I'm not interested in? You think I need another glass to stare at? Don't be so anxious, makes you look desperate. The only thing worse than a desperate woman is a desperate man. This your first time inside an adult establishment? Desperate men don't get chosen until the end of the night when pickings are slim." she snapped. The fizzy bubbles foaming at the top of the glass caused Minxy's taste buds to water. *'Hello old friend, or is it old enemy? Either way, it's been a while. I've never seen you in this glass. It looks so good on you,'* She muttered.

The bartender, an old admirer of Minxy's who was well aware of her former addiction issues, leaned in. His voice was dog-eared and astute. "I know it seems like freedom is just a sip away but sometimes we're supposed to be a prisoner of our pain for just a little while. Teaches you how to endure things. You just keep looking at that glass for a little while longer. I get the feeling you won't feel the same way you felt when you first came in here. The ire will hush, and you'll find you're not as thirsty as you thought you were." Minxy turned her attention to the bar entrance where a rowdy couple clamored in, causing disorder. It was Katina and her loutish male companion. Boozed regulars greeted them accordingly. The two made their way to the bar to order beverages.

Katina, too eager to watch where she was going, bumped Minxy's shoulder trying to get the attention of the bartender. "Hey, old geezer! Let me get two beers!" she yelled obnoxiously. "Put it on my tab! I'll pay you when my check clears, I'm good for it!"

"Watch where you're going," said Minxy, dusting off her shoulder.

Katina started chewing her gum faster and turned to Robbie, who was inappropriately groping her for everyone to see. "What is it with everyone trying to kill our vibe tonight, baby?"

Minxy closed her eyes and took a deep breath. "If asking you to act like you have basic manners is killing your vibe than I take pride in being your personal murderer tonight. Better I kill your vibe than you."

"You a Beaumonte'?" Katina asked.

Minxy turned to her slowly, defensively. "So?"

Katina moved closer to Minxy and got in her face. "Hey baby! Don't that beat all! Those tramps we just left in the dust, this old lady here is one of them! I just had an interesting conversation with Lissima about that sister of hers who went from swimmer to floater!"

In an instant, Minxy leaped from her stool and struck Katina with a closed fist. Katina fell against the bar and then to the floor. The bartender saw the attack but turned his back without saying a word. "You call my daughter or my nieces by anything other than their names again, I'll repaint this whole bar with your blue blood. You call me old again, I'm going to sweep your teeth up off this floor and empty the dustpan in my purse. While you're picking out dentures; I'll be scamming the tooth fairy with your molars." Minxy squatted over Katina's body, "And if you ever mention my dead niece to my living niece again, I'll take you to the bridge and dangle you over the edge of the ruins and let the gators chew you from head to toe- head first, then toes. I won't stop until all I'm left holding is your crusty pinky toe." Katina's boyfriend looked around the bar, shocked by the number of people pretending not to see Minxy's actions. When no one dared intervene, Robbie picked Katina up and they scurried out. Minxy sat back down and without saying a word, the bartender handed her a towel with ice cubes wrapped in it- to soothe her combat knuckles.

CHAPTER TWENTY-FOUR

Dria and Sadie found Bellissima sitting all alone in the kitchen, crying. The two of them crept over and joined her. Neither of them knew what to say to make her feel better but luckily for them- Bellissima spoke first. "The things Katina Withers said to me; Do you think there's any truth in it?"

"Of course not. She's just a bad person, is all. She's the kind of person that gets angry and says things they know aren't true because they know where your weak spots are. They know just where to step; put all their weight on it."

"Yeah, just like the devil. You know how Granny used to say. The Devil looks deep until he finds your worst nightmare and then he uses it against you."

Bellissima wiped her tears but more fell. "Am I the reason she didn't work right?"

"No one knows the real reason why Cheniere couldn't talk or hear, Lissima. Not even doctors. They had theories, but I don't think humans have enough power to affect those kinds of things. Those are God's gifts to regulate."

"I dream about Cheniere sometimes," confessed Bellissima.

"We all dream of her every now and then. That's perfectly normal," assured Dria- putting her arm around Bellissima.

"I doubt our dreams are the same. You guys have sweet dreams. I get those nightmares you spoke of, the ones the devil uses. He handpicked a specific one just for me."

"You're having nightmares about Cheniere?" asked Sadie- worried.

"Yes." Bellissima leaned back in her chair and pulled her knees into her chest. "I had a really bad one about a year ago. As if living it as I slept wasn't scary enough, I woke and realized that nightmare stole my voice."

"What do you mean by that?" asked Dria.

"My mind was somnolent, but I could still feel my body. My toes were cold, like raw bare feet on brumal soil. There were goosebumps rising on my arms. On my forehead, I felt sleety droplets drizzling down on me. There was predatory darkness at work and I'm not ashamed to admit I was afraid. Felt like I'd been wandering, aimlessly, for eons. My leg muscles were tight and achy like I'd been walking around with shackles on my feet. Finally, I stopped walking and just stood in one spot, turning around in circles until I saw something moving. It was an obscure shadow that was darker than the darkness in contrast. At first, I didn't know what it was, and I stepped back a little; scared it was something that wanted to hurt me, but then I heard it whimpering. The shadow was a person. *Are you hurt?'* I asked, from a safe distance. I didn't hear a response, so I haltingly moved closer. As I moved in, my footsteps started to sound hollow, like they had an echo. I tapped my foot to be sure. Yeah, there was an echo for sure. I looked down and underneath my feet, there was an incandescent glowing. It was mesmerizing at first like I was getting a chance to stand right over the sun without being annihilated by its power but then it got brighter. As the light grew, it illuminated everything all around me, over me, under me, behind me and in front of me. The sky was crimson, and the drizzles weren't cold anymore. They burned like magma. It wasn't the sun at all. The flames under my feet burned the glulam wood right over the dark water and the water, it started to boil. I tried to take a deep breath, hoping I was anywhere but there. Even hell would have been a better trade; but when I exhaled, black charred smoke came rushing out of my lungs. There I stood on Burn Out bridge. Behind me, I could see the land and my footprints. Something had led me there and I'd blindly followed like I'd been charmed or something. The blaze made it easier to see the shadowy mass up ahead. The apparition's face had a face that was just like mine. It was Cheniere, my dead twin. I took off running towards her, listening to the soles of my feet sizzling, like meat in a greased skillet, louder and louder with every step I took. All around me, the bridge started falling. Wood planks crashed and splashed as they hit the boiling river. Still, I ran faster. *'Cheniere! Cheniere!'* I screamed. My sister was fading away. I could feel it. I needed her to know that I was coming for her. So, I kept screaming her name, waving my arms. As I got closer, I passed burning bodies. Not all of them were dead yet. Some of them were wailing and pulling at my legs- begging me to drag them back to land. Their abated faces were singed, and their flesh had started to peel, to melt from their bones. *'Help me!* they pleaded. Horrified, I kicked free and I kept on running. I was almost to her when I felt the bridge foundation start to shake. It sounded like one giant twig slowly snapping. It was happening. The beams were giving way. I stopped and held my breath. Cheniere tried to stand but she collapsed again. I tiptoed, trying hard to distribute my weight so I didn't fall through the planks. *Just stay still, I'm coming. I'm going to get to you off this God damned bridge! I can't lose you again!'* I yelled. She scrambled to her feet again and stood. Her face was finally fully visible through her hair. Just as Cheniere reached out to me, the bridge crumbled beneath her feet. *'No!* I screamed. I reached the collapse point and looked down into the water. I could see her disappearing beneath the fiery, swampy channel. The gators smiled- swimming circles below her sinking body, waiting. A column broke and fell on top of me, pinning me down. It crushed my ribs and blood trickled from the corners of my mouth, but I didn't even scream. I didn't try to get up either. I just laid there on my stomach with my hand reaching out for my sister until finally she was completely engulfed, and I couldn't find her in the river anymore. I begin to feel the flames climbing up my legs like spiraling snakes. Still, I refused to vocalize my agony. I wasn't going to give the devil the satisfaction. I just laid there listening to everyone dying around me, to everything crashing around me. Then it was my turn. I closed my eyes, ready to die on Burn Out Bridge right along with the others. When I opened my eyes again, I was back in my bed. I don't remember falling asleep. I know what you're thinking, *who remembers falling asleep?* I do. I always remember. I have a precise way of doing things. I walk around the cottage and make sure all the doors and windows are locked. I doublecheck all the appliances, make sure they're all off and there are no fire hazards. I get a glass from the cabinet and I fill it to the top with ice, halfway with water. The ice melts while I'm sleeping to replace the sips I take throughout the night when I stir. I set it on the right side of my bed, not the left. I sleep on the left side, but I knocked it off the bedside so many times reaching for it in the dark that I started putting it on the opposite side of the bed on the bureau nearest my bedroom window. The moonlight shines right on it and I can always find it. Then, I read until my eyes get heavy. Then, I know it's time for bed. When the nightmare released me, the glass of water was on the left side and it was full like I hadn't sipped all night. My book was across the room on the floor like I'd thrown it there. The curtains were flapping in the breeze, but I couldn't hear them bellowing. I held my hand out in front of my face and snapped my fingers. I didn't hear it. I said, 'Oh no. I know I said it because I've been able to speak and hear my whole life up until that point, so I know I mouthed the words at the very least, but I had no voice. I tried to speak and yell but when I tried all I felt was a hot burning sensation in my throat like my words had been replaced with balls of fire. On the floor, in the moonlight, I saw the wet footprints. She was there, I know it. Can't prove it but I know. I believed it then I and I believe it now. What if it's her way of telling me that she's harboring some abhorrence for me in death? What if she doesn't love me anymore? What if she never did? What if she hates me?"

"Don't ever say that again," said Dria- grabbing Bellissima's face by her cheeks. "I've never seen two sisters so close. Whatever happened in that dream was tied to some deep seeded guilt that shouldn't even be in your cataleptic mind."

Sadie leaned and put her head on Bellissima's shoulder. "I don't think it's possible for anyone to hate you, Lissima. Well- maybe Katina Withers," she said. All three of them laughed. "but she's just jealous, you have to know that. Everyone loves you. I love you, Dria loves you and if there was ever any question- your sister loved you."

"I promised myself I'd never speak of that nightmare again," said Bellissima.

"I'm glad you shared it with us," said Dria.

Sadie lifted her chin and looked at her cousins, contemplating. "I have a crazy idea."

"Does it involve a roller coaster or a rope swing?" asked Dria with a theatrically pained mien.

"No. I was thinking about the big obstacle course. The day after Granny Cat's dinner is the last day the fair will be in town before it moves on to the next parish. I think we should enter as a family and win; all of us. Mothers too," suggested Sadie.

Bellissima turned Dria. "What do you think?"

Dria smiled, both amused and intrigued. "I think you better bring home some calcium supplements for our old ass mamas. They're going to need if we're going to bring home the big Beaumonte' win."

"*The big Beaumonte' win?* - I like that. We'll do it for Cheniere," said Bellissima

Sadie was curious. "The nightmare, Lissima? The bridge being on fire, it's strange, isn't it? The bridge was already burned down when Cheniere died up there. Why would you dream of her death the way grandpa died? You've been believing all this time that it was Cheniere who sent the night terror, that it was her trying to tell you something. Did you ever consider it was Grandpa that was trying to reach you?"

"Too bad you dropped out of your dream interpretation class," teased Dria.

"You know, you're right Sadie. It has to mean something," said Bellissima, wondering too. "If we had been born into a family with less cataclysm, repletion and rotten luck- we'd know everything about the past. We'd know exactly who we are. I'm so sick of the mystery."

"What do you want to do about it?" asked Dria.

"I want the damn answers we deserve!" she replied- slamming her fist down. "I think you two should stop by Pennycress tomorrow at lunchtime, so we can all sit with Catherine," said Bellissima.

Sadie and Dria nodded. "Yeah. We'll be there," guaranteed Dria.

•

The car ride to the bar was quiet aside from Kay's occasional passenger-seat driving critiques. "Stay on your side of the road! Are they just giving driver's licenses away in the city? Do they even test you?"

Lou Anna rolled her eyes. "Would you like to drive, Kay? Because I will pull over!"

"No. I'm too worried about Minxy to get behind the wheel. I hate it when we disagree."

Lou Anna tip-toed around the matter. "What got her so upset that she would leave on foot, and for a drink? She must have really been rattled."

"It's nothing, Lou."

"Well apparently not," poked Lou Anna- trying hard to inconspicuously make certain her lies were still concealed.

Lou Anna's prying frustrated Kay. "Lou Anna it's between Minxy and I! You act as If you don't have little secrets of your own. I'm sure you have things you don't tell me," returned kay- purposely applying pressure.

Kays retort felt sharp like ice sickles. "You know I love you, right Kay?" she asked.

Kay's eyes narrowed. "Of course, I know that! Why are you choosing to remind me right now? And why the hell do you look scared?"

Lou Anna glanced over at Kay but looked away again as quickly as possible. "Here we are! The bar!" she squealed- her voice weirdly, involuntarily high pitched to mask her antsy disposition. She parked. "Listen, let me go in first. If she's hammered, she's more likely to let me walk her out than you."

"I'm not just going to wait in the car like a dog, Lou!"

"-And I'm not tying you to a pole outside, so I can run in and get a jug of milk either! I'm simply strategizing! We don't want a scene this close to Mama's dinner and we don't want Minxy getting any angrier! You ever tried to detain Minxy once she's had a few? Last time I broke up one of her brawls, I nearly herniated a disc. Damn back still hurts like the dickens when the weather changes. I don't need to watch the weather channel to know rain is coming, I just try to reach up. If there's a pain, I know there's a storm!"

"I know! But I'm the one that pushed Minx to her breaking point. I can't just sit here and do nothing, Lou," Kay replied, wringing her hands.

Lou Anna grabbed her sister's wrist. "You listen to me, Kay. Minxy is a grown woman learning how to battle her demons late in life. If a little disagreement with the sweetest of her sisters is enough to push her over the edge, she never wanted to be sober to begin with. Being broken isn't always a choice but, staying broken and breaking yourself over and over again and blaming it on other people- that's a choice, a derelict one. Self-destruction, self- mutilation, self-hatred- these things are art to an addict."

"I'll sit out here for 5 minutes. I can't promise you a minute more than that. That's our baby sister in there playing with fire. We can't lose her again," said Kay.

"We won't," promised Lou Anna getting out of the car. Once inside, she noticed Minxy sitting all alone and walked over. "You mind if I pop a squat?"

"It's a free-enough country for now," answered Minxy.

Lou Anna sat down and ordered a glass of water. She glanced down at Minxy's knuckles. "Whose blood is that on your hand? They still in the bar? Let me know now, I'm not sure if I still have my blade in my purse."

"She's long gone. I'm sure she's off licking her wounds somewhere plotting round two, probably. It was that little Wiccan cunt, Withers, who thought she could hurt my niece's feeling for free."

"Oh yes, the little fortune teller. I heard she had a brave tongue," said Lou- nodding.

"Don't worry about it. I collected what she owed and then some. I'm going to bring this towel home for our little Lissima. She can keep as a souvenir. Every time she looks at it, she'll think of how loved she is."

"All our girls are loved," said Lou Anna.

"-Ain't that the truth," agreed Minxy. She looked over at the door and saw Kay slinking in. "How long did you tell Kay to wait in the car?" she asked- patting Lou Anna on the shoulder, prompting her to turn her attention to the entrance.

"I told her to wait 5 minutes." Lou Anna looked down at her watch. "3! She stayed out there for 3 minutes!"

"I don't blame her. She's not a dog, Lou. Did you at least roll the windows down?" asked Minxy.

Kay neared the bar. "There's a table over there in the corner. I can sit there if you're not ready to forgive me," said Kay sadly, looking at the floor.

"Sit your ass down Kay. I never could stay mad at you," said Minxy.

Kay smiled and joined her sisters. She noticed the full glass in front of Minxy. "What are we drinking?" she asked- secretly hoping Minxy would say she hadn't had any alcohol.

"You were never very good at being subtle, Kay. Relax. I didn't consume," said Minxy.

"I can vouch for that!" said the Bartender without turning around.

"I'm proud of you," said Kay- leaning her head against Minxy's shoulder.

"Me too," said Lou Anna.

Minxy's eyes swelled. "You know, I'm sure glad that girl was foolish enough to disrespect me and our Lissima. If it weren't for her face hitting my fist, I think I might have swallowed the whole bar tonight," she said standing. Minxy took some cash out of her pocket. "What do I owe you for glass watching?" she asked.

The bartender stood behind the bar with his back still turned, wiping spotty tumblers clean with a vinegar dampened rag. "You remember when we were pups? You gathered a group of protestors to help boycott that pharmacy ran by the folks who spoke a different language than us? It had been a bad year in terms of natural disasters. Florida got the tsunami. Texas got the tornado. Louisiana got the flood. My Mama got that bad cut while out in the yard trying to get the cattle to higher ground. God knows my rolling stone of a daddy didn't leave us nothing else. That livestock was all we had to our name. It was rusty barbed wire and infectious wastewater that did it. Mama's leg puffed up red at first and then started turning dark olive green with a foul smell. We waited out the chaos and when the water receded enough; I scraped up all I had and went to that pharmacy to get some peroxide and iodine. Got to that register and was told I didn't have enough to save my mother's leg. I stood outside that store with a tin can begging and saw at least ten other poor people get turned away due to those foreigner's gluttonous gouging. I damn near gave up praying but then you took a stand against the man, Minxy Beaumonte'. All that marching caused people with authority to look a little closer at the crooks running the pharmacy. Just when Mama's fever got high enough to boil water, you and your sisters come walking up the road. Minxy, you bought the supplies I was told I didn't have enough for. Lou, you patched Mama's leg right on up. Kay, you cooked a tonic that tasted like Cajun soup. You served it with a loaf of bread so sweet it tasted like God had made it with his own two hands; so good Mama didn't know she was spooning medicine into her body with every bite. You three are blessed. You women are healers that came running to save a life. Your lives would have gone on just fine if you'd chosen to do nothing at all. You better put that money right back in your pocket, Minxy Beaumonte'. When angel's drink here, it's on the house," said the bartender; his back still turned.

CHAPTER TWENTY-FIVE

"Bellissima! Bellissima! Are you hiding in here?" Jan shouted- stepping into the boiler room at Pennycress. Bellissima heard Jan's annoying squawking and ducked behind a stack of cardboard boxes and listened as Jan crept around inside. "I've checked the janitor's closet and the corner table in the library…no Lissima anywhere. The only place left is…. Here!" she yelled- pouncing. "Ha! I sniffed you out! You can't hide from me!" celebrated Jan.

Frustrated Bellissima hung her head and stepped out from her hiding place. "Can't I get a little privacy?"

"What are you doing back here besides avoiding me? It's very hurtful, Lissima. Friends don't hide from friends."

"I'm not doing anything! Geez!" answered Bellissima- shoving the flower attachment envelope back in her pocket.

Jan's cheeks slowly folded into a sneer. Bellissima knew immediately that she was preparing her best sanctimonious retort, but it was too late to deny it, so she simply rolled her eyes back at Jan. "…re-reading your little love letter? That's so adorable!" said Jan- bouncing up and down, clapping.

Bellissima grabbed Jan's shoulders as if to keep her on the ground. "I don't know what you think you caught me doing but I was just looking for a place to clear my head. And even if I was, not everything requires celebratory prancing. Why are you hunting me anyway? I already gave you my new year. What? Did you get a signup sheet for liver donations now? If so, you're shit out of luck. I'm pretty sure my Auntie Minxy has dibs on mine. She beat me in a card game once and It was either my taffy or my liver. I was only 10. I wasn't giving up my candy. No way, no how."

"No, there aren't any more signup sheets," answered Jan- pressing her lips together as if she had exciting news.

Bellissima eyed her behavior curiously. "What? Did they get a new flavor of soda in the vending machine again?"

"Nope. There's someone here to see you."

"I'm expecting my cousins, but they're not supposed to come until lunch time. They must've gotten bored at the big house and escaped early."

"No, it's not them. Guess again!"

"Do I look like I'm in the mood for guessing games, Jan? Spit it out!"

"It's that Lincoln guy! He's here asking for you!" gushed Jan- dragging Bellissima out of the boiler room to the front desk where Lincoln waited.

Lincoln stood, drumming his fingers on the counter. His eyes lit up the minute he saw Jan rounding the corner with Bellissima. Bellissima turned to Jan. "How's my hair? Is there anything in my teeth?" she mumbled.

"Your hair has never looked better and your teeth are fine, but here- take this gum. I can totally smell your second cup of coffee."

Bellissima slipped the spearmint stick in her mouth and chewed a few times before speaking. "Hey! How are you?" she asked- nervously.

"I'm well Lissima, thanks for asking. How are you?" asked Lincoln in return.

Before Bellissima could reply, Jan added herself to the conversation. "You're already using nicknames? How cute! I mean, *I* call her Lissima; but I've known her for years. What does Lissima call you? *Linc- Linc* or *Coli*? Hope not, those totally sound like pet names," laughed Jan, snorting.

Jan's awkward curiosity made both Bellissima and Lincoln noticeably uncomfortable but she still, she lingered.

Lincoln cleared his throat. "I hope you don't mind me stopping by like this. I know you're on the job, but I had some good news and I couldn't wait to share it with you."

Bellissima felt butterflies and found it difficult to keep from smiling. But again, Jan beat her to the response. "She doesn't mind. I literally just found her reading your card again," Jan interjected. Bellissima lifted her leg and jammed her heel into Jan's toes causing her to yelp.

"I don't mind at all! I was actually planning to call you today and thank you for the beautiful flowers, but you're here in person to thank! This is even better! How about we take a walk?" asked Bellissima- projecting her voice to mask Jan's injured, dog-like whimpering.

Bellissima and Lincoln strolled through the courtyard garden admiring the manicured landscape. "On this side, we grow the flowers. On the other, we grow vegetables. The patients farm them, and the cafeteria staff uses them to cook. A lot of these roses were planted by Pennycress patients who are long gone. Their memory remains."

"It's beautiful out here. It's …surprising to see." Mumbled Lincoln.

"Why is it surprising?"

"These look like happy, well-tended flowers planted by happy people."

"You don't think pennycress patients are happy people?"

"I don't know what I think. I guess I just can't understand how people can let their mothers and fathers end up in a place like this to die surrounded by strangers. I'm sorry if that offends you. Without places like this, a lot of nurses like you wouldn't have jobs."

"It's okay Lincoln, really. I get it. I work here but that doesn't mean I understand that kind of abandonment. I could never put my mother in a home."

"Me neither," said Lincoln with a troubled face.

"Something on your mind?" asked Bellissima.

"When I made it back home, I sat my mother down to tell her that I'd finally found my way back to her hometown."

"How'd she take it?"

"Not good. I've never seen her that upset. She acted as if I'd betrayed her on the highest level possible. She started yelling and some things slipped out that she wished she hadn't said."

"What'd she say?"

Lincoln sat on the nearest bench. Bellissima sat down beside him. "My mother's sick."

"How sick?" asked Bellissima- saddened.

"It's bad, some rare thing I can't remember how to pronounce and that's after she sounded it out one syllable at a time at least ten times."

"Is it treatable? Can she be cured?"

"No."

"I'm so sorry, Lincoln."

"That's not even the worst part. She says she doesn't want me to take care of her; some nonsense about her being a burden on me. Says it's not proper for a son to change his mother's adult diaper. Had to accept that this is the near future- her in a diaper. She wants to be put away, can you believe that? She wants to be put in Pennycress."

Bellissima's eyebrows raised. "Here? But Breaux was here. He died here. She must know that. Wasn't she the one who sent the Calvary to bring him here those years ago?"

"No, it must've been someone else. She never cared enough to see to it that he didn't die alone. All the letters came from the PO box. My mother told me that the mysterious woman who called to tell her that Breaux passed, only said he was dead, not where to find him. Knowing my mother, she probably hung up before the caller could deliver that part of the message. Just hearing her father's name lights a fire in her. Immediately, she stops listening. I was going to tell her, but I thought it'd be best to leave that part out since she has her eye on the tennis court here. If she knew I'd tracked Breaux to this place, she'd burn it down for sure. For now, she thinks Breaux died all alone in the house she grew up in. That made her smile, thinking of him dying alone. She's barely in her 70's, she's not even that old. How can she be terminally ill?"

"What are you going to do? Fight her on this and take care of her like you want to or let her have things her way; let her have the tennis court of her dreams in the building where her sadistic father died?"

Lincoln turned to Bellissima and stared at her adoringly through his qualm. "I don't know yet."

The butterflies were back and Bellissima had to look away to keep from blushing. "You said you had good news. I think you and I have completely different ideas of what qualifies as good news," she joked.

Lincoln's face lightened a bit. "The good news? Yes, the whole reason I'm back in town. That call you made to the coroner paid off. He'll meet with me this afternoon and allow me to sign all the mandatory documents. In a few days, I'll be able to pick up a box full of my grandfather's ashes. I also talked to the bank. They didn't seem so happy about the extra paperwork, but I should be able to take a look around Breaux's house before the repossession is finalized."

"I'm so happy for you! It's like you're getting a chance to change the course of your childhood. The word family will have a whole new definition."

"It's bittersweet. Breaux's gone, and before I ever got a chance to meet him. Monster or not, he was still blood. Daddy's gone and now Mama's sick. Not much of a family left. I'll miss that warm feeling."

Bellissima thought. "Since you'll be in town for a few days waiting on the ashes and the bank, you should stop by for Granny Cat's birthday dinner," suggested Bellissima.

"You mean it?" asked Lincoln, frankly surprised by her proposal.

"Of course. I wouldn't have offered if I didn't. It's going to be a big family dinner. I know we're not your family, but you'll be surrounded by a bunch of love. You'll get that warm feeling you've been missing. Maybe you can snap a few pictures for us?"

"You don't need to check with your people first, make sure they're okay with it?"

Bellissima threw her head back, laughing. "You made quite the impression, Lincoln. I'm sure they'd be even happier than I am to have you."

Lincoln's surprise visit left Bellissima grinning from ear to ear. She stood at the scrub-up station, finding it difficult to stop smiling. Jan couldn't wait to hear the details of her walk with prince charming. "How'd it go?" she pried- eagerly.

"It was amazing!" Bellissima replied- giddy. "I mean, he had awful news about his mother but having him come all this way just to confide in me! I don't know, it kind of makes me feel…"

"Special?" finished Jan- sliding next to Bellissima at the sink.

Bellissima blushed harder. "Yeah! That's the word! How's your foot?" she asked- unremorseful.

"My big toe is swelling as we speak."

"Sorry about that, but you have a big mouth so whose fault is it that you got hurt, really?"

"Yeah, I know. Talking less and thinking before I speak- these are things on my resolution list. No hard feelings though. I owe you for conning you and I've already started working on paying you back. I restocked the gloves and bandages while you were preoccupied with your hottie- purple nitrate, not the powdered latex ones. I know the powdered ones dry your hands out. I also pushed your fruit infused water to the back of the employee fridge and labeled it so no one steals it."

"Well, that's very kind of you, Jan. Thank you," Bellissima replied, impressed.

"-And I already gave your Grandmother her meds."

"What?"

"I know you asked to oversee her medications, but Catherine can be rather difficult. I didn't want her stubbornness to ruin your day so, I crushed her pills and slipped them in her yogurt. Genius, right?" bragged Jan- unaware that she'd unknowingly derailed story time for her and her cousins and that Bellissima had been depriving Catherine of her prescriptions on purpose to ensure a revealing story time.

"Yeah. You're a genius," answered Bellissima- dryly.

"No need to thank me. That look on your face is payment enough." Jan stared down into the sink. Bellissima's nervous scrubbing has caused her hands to turn pink. "You must have the cleanest hands in this whole facility." Jan shut off the water. "Get out of here so you can get a full lunch hour with your family. They'll be here any minute. It should be a lot quieter and peaceful now that Catherine's medicated," said Jan patting Bellissima on the back before walking away.

"Yes. Quieter," mumbled Bellissima.

Catherine loved yogurt. Harvest peach was her absolute favorite. When Jan knocked on her door, Catherine was ready to dismiss her immediately and demand privacy; but Jan had come bearing deliciousness. "I was just on my way back from the dining room. The chef set out a platter of fresh yogurt and I thought you'd like some." Catherine quickly gobbled it up. About a half hour later, she started to feel a tad woozy. Her limbs were limp, but she managed to lift the spoon from her tray. Catherine pulled it close to her glasses and discovered small specs of tablet residue.

Bellissima crept in and pulled a chair next to her grandmother's bed. She grabbed Catherine's hand. "How are you feeling today, Granny?"

It took Catherine a second to formulate a response. "She dosed me, pumpkin. That preppy, overzealous nurse that still wears ribbons in her hair like a preschooler, was slick enough to dose me. She caught me slipping. I knew filling out that Pennycress survey of likes and dislikes would come back to bite me in the ass. She used that favorite snack section to do me in."

There was a knock at the door. Dria and Sadie stepped in. "We're here! Hey Grandma!"

Catherine's eyelids flickered as she fought to stay awake. "My sweet grandbabies, all four of you. That's a blessing."

Immediately, Sadie knew something was wrong. "Four? Three….you mean three. She means three, right Bellissima? Why does our Grandmother look like a concert jump-off, ready and willing to do anything for a chance to meet the band?"

"It was my co-worker, Jan. She decided to do me a favor and dupe granny. She served her some prescription strength yogurt. Granny is high as a kite."

Dria sighed- disappointed. "What? I spent all day getting myself mentally prepared for this!"

"-This blows," sniveled Sadie.

"I know. I guess story time is canceled," whispered Bellissima.

"Says who?" questioned Catherine, lethargically. "No little potion gon' shut me up!"

"Granny, you don't have the strength. Just rest. Don't fight it."

"Yeah, Grandma Cat. There will be other times for us all to talk," said Dria.

Catherine chuckled. "You're still so young. When you're young, you don't really understand how time works and how little we really have. It's adorable. How young do you think I am? Not sure if you noticed, but I got grave reservations."

"I wish you wouldn't talk like that. No one here is ready to see you go," said Sadie, sad.

"No one's ever ready to go or let go but we're going. Make no mistake," said Catherine. "Lissima, I want you to prop one of those pillows behind my back and get this hunk of metal bed to raise all the way up. Dria, Sadie; each of you grab an arm and pull me up so she can get that pillow right behind my tailbone. If I lay flat, I'll pass out for sure. Bellissima, turn that ceiling fan on. The cold air will wake me up a little."

Bellissima walked over to the switch near the door and turned the fan on high. *Tick…Tick…Tick…Tick.* The thoughts of silence returned from the depths of Bellissima's mind. The Beaumonte' grandchildren returned to their seats and leaned in. Catherine turned to Dria, "Water," she whispered, her voice cracking. Dria hopped up and slid the straw into her Grandmother's mouth. She set the glass back on the tray and they patiently waited for Catherine to begin. "The police stood on my porch with their hats off, respectfully. When I could finally speak again, I phoned Lou Anna at the cottage and asked her to come to the big house to make sure Kay and Minxy stayed put. Lou Anna arrived with baby Dria on her hip. *'Mama, why are these cops here? There's smoke in the sky, people are saying things. Where's daddy?'* I kissed her and my only grandbaby at the time. Then, I kissed my other two children and told them all to stay inside. I climbed in the back of the sheriff's car and we headed to Burn Out. They drove me as close to the catastrophe as they possibly could; about 75 feet from where the road ended. I had to walk the rest of the way. I could still feel the heat from that far back. Wood columns were still falling into the river. There were locals lining both sides of the road, mourning. The first person I passed was Ora. Her son was one of the first to float up. He had been fishing off the side of the bridge when it happened. He was probably the only person who saw who or what started the deadly blaze, but we'll never know because he didn't make it. He could have saved himself, but Ora raised him right. Instead of fleeing, he started helping people out of their cars, getting as many to safety as he could- the elderly, the crippled and the kids. He got 'em off two at a time, one under each arm. He saved 8 people that day. They say he heard an abandoned child screaming for help and he didn't think twice. He went back for the child but neither of them made it off the bridge alive. His badly burned body turned up but not the child he went back for. Some say that the last child was a mirage conjured up by the devil worshippers they claim burned the bridge- just another one of the superstitious theories no one could prove. Otis was there too, on the side of the road, crying. He didn't lose any family that dreadful day, but he was there crying for Jeremiah. He saw me walking down towards the carnage and he couldn't even look me in the eye. The sheriffs restored order as fast as they could; recruiting men who could swim well, hold their breath for a while and weren't afraid to fight off hungry swamp critters to help pull bodies out. They dove with a brightly colored nylon rope tied to their trousers. The bright ropes served as markers, easy to see in the mud water. Once they were down deep, they tied the ropes to bodies or cars- whatever they saw. Then they swam back up and dove again but this time with a chain to replace the rope. Then the tractors pulled 'em up one by one. Jeremiah's truck was one of the first to get pulled out. When I reached the bank where the truck had been pulled up, the wet volunteer was still by it- toweling off. I don't know how he knew I was the wife, but he looked me dead in the eye- full of remorse. *'Mam, I swam out for this one myself. When I first went down to flag it with my rope, I could have sworn he was still in it. When I dove again to chain it up, there was nobody. I'm awful sorry.'* He walked away to keep on searching and I was left there, alone, with Jeremiah's truck. I slowly moved closer to it and looked inside. There was a baby snake wrapped around the steering wheel, a water moccasin, black as coal. I was half hoping my husband would still be inside, dead or alive- I'd take anything long as I could see his face one last time. Ain't that crazy? Ain't that selfish? Even if he'd been burned to an unrecognizable crisp- I prayed for him to be there for my own sake!" Dria flinched. Sadie winced. Bellissima's bottom lip quivered. Catherine had found the strength to yell and that wailing came with tears. "I couldn't look at it anymore. That damn truck started to look like an old beat up coffin. I backed away and turned around. Agony was all I found unfolding around me. Agony was all this town had left."

"How many made it off the bridge alive?" asked Dria.

Catherine yawned. "Very few. The ones that survived were horribly disfigured or so traumatized that their recollections made no sense- hence the tall tales about what really happened."

"How many people died that day?" asked Sadie.

"I can't remember the specific death total, but half the town went after it happened," replied Catherine- her eyes heavier.

"Did my mother use drugs while she was pregnant with me? If so, did she care what it would do to me? Was I born with any complications? Did she ever stop to think her addictions would become mine?" asked Sadie.

"Did my mother love my father even though he was a monster? Why was I never good enough for Lou Anna? Is it because she secretly hates me because she got too old for him, to fulfill his twisted lust?" asked Dria.

"Cheniere told me she could hear the rain. I know she told you too, she trusted you. Did she tell you the real reason she went down to the bridge that night? What was she thinking, going there alone, without me? We did everything together! Why did she go there to die alone?" asked Bellissima.

It was too late. Catherine was snoring. Bellissima stood and kicked the chair. Each of them had heard one another's questions but were too embarrassed to talk about them so they all looked at the floor and pretended they didn't hear. "This is bullshit," said Bellissima. "It's like the universe is against us!"

"Calm down," urged Dria.

"I will not calm down! We never, ever get answers! Why?"

Sadie looked at Catherine's tray and got an idea. "There *is* another way."

"How?" asked Bellissima.

"Remember when you were talking about Auntie Kay being sick? You said she started talking about the bridge and *it* being Grandma Cat's fault?"

"Yeah, so?"

"You said you gave Auntie Kay lots of medicine and that's what got her talking out of her head, speaking the truth."

"Yeah. She was sick."

Sadie smiled cunningly. "What if we gave our moms a little medicine to help them be a bit more honest?"

Bellissima couldn't believe her ears. "Are you suggesting we drug our mothers? Are you insane!"

Dria stood. "Is it insane or is it genius?" she asked, holding up the empty yogurt container.

Bellissima gasped. "You're not suggesting that Sadie's come up with a logical plan, are you?"

"Sadie rarely has good ideas. I mean, she talked you into piercing your perfect nose; but if that nit-wit co-nurse of yours can drug someone, we can definitely pull it off without getting caught. Drugs will surely loosen their vault lips."

"I can't believe what I'm hearing!" said Bellissima. "Who are you people?"

Sadie grabbed Bellissima's shoulders. "We're Beaumonte' women, the only ones who don't know who they are. You said so yourself. We're all missing parts within us. It's time we all start feeling whole. It's not like we're gon' date rape them, it's just a little drugs for a good cause. You're a nurse, you know all about medicine, and correct dosage and stuff. What's the worst that could happen?"

"Even if I did entertain this ridiculous plot, what would we slip to them? I don't have enough high-grade prescription cough medicine to go around. That wasn't some over the counter mixture that's mostly water. It was a top-quality pharmaceutical. I can't just walk up to the first doctor I see and ask him for drugs without a good reason. It's not like I can tell him what we really need it for."

"We know where to find drugs already," replied Sadie.

"We do? Sadie, please don't tell me you have a few grams tucked in your vagina," said Dria.

"No, Mama's backpack," answered Sadie.

"Oh yeah, that's right," said Dria remembering their discovery in the shed.

"Auntie Minx has a backpack with drugs in it?" asked Bellissima, confused.

"Yeah, like nine or ten pills- more than likely some of that old flower child, free your mind shit. We found it in the shed. We forgot to tell you."

"You two have lost your minds! We have no idea what those pills are mixed with and how long they've been there! Not all narcotics lose potency the longer they sit, some of them become lethal! Not all drugs are created equally!" lectured Bellissima, turning to walking out.

"I know you still have questions about Cheniere," said Dria.

Bellissima faltered and stepped back into the room, battling her growingly persuasive conscience. Dria and Sadie stood quietly, nodding with their eyebrows raised. "Okay. How do we do it?"

"Order that Beijing beef you bought home our first night in town. Auntie Lou just couldn't stop raving about how tasty it was," said Sadie.

•

"Bellissima! You're home early! You bought dinner?" Asked Kay, genuinely excited to see her child- as she always was.

Bellissima entered the den where Kay and Lou Anna sat. "Yes, Mama. I thought I'd come home early today since Granny's birthday dinner is the day after tomorrow. There's still a lot to do, you know? We have to polish the silver. We must make sure the bathroom is spotless; can't have our quests relieving themselves in an unclean bathroom. The napkins, we still need to press those. No one likes a wrinkly dinner napkin!" stuttered Bellissima- laughing timorously.

"How thoughtful! You girls are finally taking this dinner seriously. I'm so proud of you. I'll take the food to the kitchen and fix us all a big plate," said Lou Anna- attempting to take the bags from her niece's grasp.

Dria rushed downstairs and into the den. "No! You rest yourself, Mama. "Let us handle that. We'll serve you."

"Knock me over with a feather! First the air conditioner and now you're catering to us? Have aliens abducted our daughters and replaced them with angels?"

"You think we're angels?" asked Bellissima- appearance clearly guilty, obviously having second thoughts about their manipulative plan.

Dria sensed Bellissima's wavering. "Yeah, you heard them, Lissima. We're angels, that's us," she hissed with her teeth clenched. "We'll be right back," she said, dragging Bellissima into the kitchen where Sadie stood mixing carbonated water and powdered fruit punch flavoring. "It's been years since I drugged someone! I forgot how exhilarating it is! I feel such a rush!" she said- stirring faster.

"You've done this before?" whispered Bellissima. "That fact alone is enough reason for us to abort this mission!"

Dria grabbed Bellissima's face, forcing her to focus. "You're spazzing out. We're not aborting. I've been reading up on somniloquy all afternoon. We follow the plan just like we talked about. Auntie Minxy's upstairs getting washed up for supper. You and I are going to go back out there to the den and keep Mama and Auntie Kay occupied while Sadie sneaks out to the shed and gets the pills. She'll sneak it in the beef before they sit down. The peppers pack a punch, they won't be able to taste the pills."

"Are you sure about this?" asked Bellissima- chewing her nails.

"No, I'm not sure! Now let's go, we have to keep them in the den for now," said Dria- shoving.

"-But you just said you weren't sure!"

"I know what I said and trust me, I meant it! I'm really not sure! Now, let's go!"

Sadie slipped out the back door and into the shed where she riffled through the backpack until she found the Quaaludes. She laid out an old comic book scrap and then looked around for something to crush them with. She decided on an old boot. Once the pills were nothing but dust, she scooped the bits in a gum wrapper. Sadie ran back to the kitchen and let herself in, only to find her mother already piling food on plates. Sadie quickly hid the drugs behind her back. "Mama! What are you doing?"

"I'm fixing plates, what does it look like silly? I guess we're having Asian cuisine again tonight. I found it just sitting here on the table still bagged up. I guess everyone's too tired to set the table. I don't mind, I slept in today. Last night was eventful, for lack of a better term."

"I heard," replied Sadie.

Minxy walked away from the food and moved closer to Sadie which made her anxious, saying as how she was hiding homemade truth dust behind her back. "I wanted to talk to you about that," said Minxy-twiddling her thumbs.

"About what, Mama?"

"- Last night."

"What's there to talk about?" asked Sadie- circling the table, looking down at the perfectly proportioned plates. She'd secretly panicked. There was no way she'd be able to dose the beef without them noticing that the food had been tampered with.

Minxy followed Sadie closely, mistaking her fidgety behavior for resentment. "I know your Aunts told you that they had to drag me out of a bar, but I didn't drink. I wanted to. I almost did, but I didn't."

Sadie used one hand to pick up the container of beef, to see if there was any left to mix with, but it was empty. "You didn't drink? So, then how'd you hurt your hand? It looks like you got wasted and fell off another stool."

Minxy looked down at her hand and removed the bandage. "This? No, there was just a little fight, is all."

"Another drunken club brawl?"

"No! I wasn't drunk when I hit her because I wasn't drinking," explained Minxy.

"Sure. Whatever you say, Mama." Sadie looked over at the kitchen counter where she'd left the pitcher of punch. She walked over and considered a plan B; a plan she hadn't discussed with her cousins. Minxy followed.

"Please Sadie, I need you to believe me," she pleaded. Sadie turned her back to the pitcher and inconspicuously unfolded the gum wrapper. "I don't want you to think I'm some backslider or…"

"-A hypocrite?" finished Sadie- quickly spinning around to stir the punch before Minxy noticed the dissolving bits.

Minxy sighed. "Sadie, I care what you think about me and I never thought twice about a person's opinion of me my whole life. You're my daughter and I got clean for you so I could be the kind of mother you deserve. It'll surprise you- the things you do for your child. You'll learn all about that one day when you become a mother."

Sadie stopped stirring. "Yeah. Maybe one day," she said- heading for the Den. "Plates are ready! Time to eat!" she yelled. Sadie waited for Lou Anna and Kay to disappear behind the kitchen door, then she pulled Dria and Bellissima into a huddle. "There's been a change of plans," she mumbled.

"Change? What change? We didn't discuss any changes. You can't go rogue on the mission!"

"While I was in the shed, Mama came down and fixed the plates. I couldn't slip the drugs into the food without her seeing me, so I slipped it in the punch instead."

"The punch? Why would you put it in the punch? The Beijing beef has red Savina habanero peppers in it, you moron!" said Bellissima. "They'll be taking a sip after every bite to keep their tongues from shriveling!"

"I had no choice!"

"It's a 2-quart pitcher. One or two pills in a pitcher *that* big won't hurt them," said Dria.

Sadie's face went pale. "One or two? I was supposed to only use one or two?"

Dria and Bellissima paused. "…Sadie…. how many pills did you crush and dump into the punch?"

"All of them," she answered slowly.

"Oh…My…God. We're going to go to jail for matricide, aren't we? We can plead insanity. They'll take one look at this family's history and believe us," said Dria- breathing heavy.

"Please don't have an asthma attack right now," begged Bellissima. "Only one of us can freak out at a time and I've been halfway there since you two came up with this dim-wit plan. I'm starting to sweat in strange places."

"When we get in there; I'll accidentally, on purpose, spill the punch and make more. We'll just have to come up with another plan," said Sadie.

The Beaumonte' grandchildren returned to the kitchen where they found an empty pitcher on the table. "Sadie! This punch is downright delicious! What did you put in it to give it that extra kick?" asked Kay- toasting Minxy with a half-empty glass.

Sadie felt weak. "-Pineapple juice," she stuttered.

Lou Anna downed a full glass and sighed, satisfied. "Well, it tastes like heaven! We've been downright famished in this heat, we couldn't help ourselves! Hurry up and mix a little more before you sit down."

"We're not really thirsty," said Bellissima- fanning her sweaty armpits.

"Wait until you get some of these peppers, you're going to need something to cool you down. Hurry up baby, Mix some! Then come and sit so we can bless the food," said Minxy.

"Yes, prayer. We should definitely pray," said Dria.

•

"Lissima, you haven't touched your plate. Are you feeling alright?" asked Lou Anna. Dria and Sadie turned their attention to Bellissima, whose forehead was damp. "You gon' let all this good food go to waste?"

"You think we're angels?" asked Bellissima again with a repentant expression.

"Yes. Angels. Now eat," muttered Dria out of the corner of her mouth.

"Are you not hungry for Asian food? You could have brought home anything, we're not picky. I think I saw some tofu in the fridge, you can have that," said Kay.

"No!" shouted Lou Anna- causing everyone to stare. "It's just that… it's probably expired by now. You should have some of this beef. It's got the right amount of spice," she said- chasing her fork full of beef with a big gulp of punch. Lou Anna lowered her glass and paused. Her face was suddenly glazed and her head tilted to the side, eyes squinted as if trying to read something from far away.

"You okay, Mama?" asked Dria.

Lou Anna surveyed her daughter's face before answering. "Yes. I believe so."

Kay dabbed her lips with a paper napkin and slurred after yet another big gulp, "You believe so? You don't know if you're okay or not?" she asked. Kay returned her drinking glass to the coaster and stared down at her plate. "I cannot get over how tasty this beef is! I have half a mind to import some of these peppers and use them at the restaurant." Her pronunciation garbled, and her tongue seemed heavier. "You ever notice how pretty food can be? Look at all the colors in my food, it's like they're going to leap right off the plate and start dancing," she said- buzzing off the potion. Kay put a whole fortune cookie in her mouth before removing the paper fortune hidden inside.

The girls turned their attention to Minxy who'd started the meal using chopsticks but was now scooping food into her mouth with her hands like a barbarian. "Yeah, I do notice that, Kay. This food tastes pretty."

"I don't think things can taste pretty," stammered Lou Anna. "- Can they?" she seriously pondered in a stupor.

Bellissima leaned over to Dria, "We fried their brains! We handicapped our own mothers! We're going to the slammer for sure! And then straight to hell after that!"

Minxy reached for her glass and Sadie slapped her hand. "No, I think you've had enough...punch. Have some of my water."

The Beaumonte' grandchildren watched as their mothers played imaginary instruments, talked with their mouths full and entertain themselves with cutlery. Eventually, their eyes got heavy and they passed out in their chairs.

"Do you think they're all the way out?" Whispered Sadie.

"They haven't moved in ten minutes. I'm pretty sure they're out cold. Let's take a minute to thank the good Lord they still have a pulse," Dria replied.

"Now what?" asked Sadie.

Bellissima stood. "We get them upstairs and wait until the pills start to wear off. When they're in between sleep phases, we'll get our chance to get them talking in their sleep."

"- Answering questions in their sleep," Dria corrected- grinning. "How are we going to get all three of them upstairs?" she asked, grin fading.

"I'm not carrying them!" said Sadie.

"Well it's not like they're going to walk up there themselves!" yelled Bellissima.

CHAPTERE TWENTY-SIX

"I cannot believe you dropped my Mama, Sadie!" yelled Bellissima- placing a pillow underneath Kay's head.

"For the thousandth time! I'm sorry! It's not my fault she puts on enough lotion to grease a train track! Her wrist just slipped right out of my hand!" said Sadie.

"She likes to moisturize! She has sensitive skin!"

"Stop bickering, you two! Just straighten them up in bed, take their shoes off, undress them and put their muumuus on so they'll think they walked themselves up here and got into bed," demanded Dria, tying up her hair.

"We have to strip our mothers? Minxy Beaumonte' hasn't worn underwear since she was 18. She's rumored to have a piercing down there. What if it matches mine! We already have matching tramp stamps! I don't want to find out!" complained Sadie.

"Next time think a plan all the way through," mumbled Bellissima.

Each Beaumonte' daughter tended to their own mother and when they finished, they collapsed on the bedroom floor- out of breath.

Bellissima took out her cell phone and pressed play on a playlist labeled: REST. Dria and Sadie listened. "What is that?" they asked.

"It's a playlist I made for when I can't get to sleep after working split shifts. I downloaded sounds of nature. The night Mama started talking, it was storming. Maybe if she hears the rain, it'll trigger the same effect as last time." Bellissima set the phone at the foot of the bed where their mothers slept. "Now we wait," she whispered ominously.

"How long?" asked Sadie.

"I don't know, I never gave anyone a Quaalude before," sassed Bellissima.

"Well, how long did it take Auntie Kay to start hallucinating and talking in her sleep when you dosed her with the cough medicine?"

"- two, maybe three hours."

"Well then we have to find something to occupy our time until then," said Dria- looking around the room. "We could do a puzzle or play a board game," she suggested.

Sadie discovered the basket of markers, confiscated by Lou Anna. She sneered, sneakily. "I don't know about you guys, but I'm feeling awfully artistic."

"You want us to draw on their faces? They'd kill us," said Bellissima.

"They were the firsts to fall asleep. Beaumonte' sleepover rules apply to them too. Besides, they're too tanked to know we're up here. They'll wake up and blame each other. Serves them right for being party poopers. We've got nothing but time to waste. You guys in?" she asked holding up three permanent markers.

Dria looked at Bellissima and Bellissima looked back at her. "They_did fall asleep before us," said Dria.

Sadie went to work on her mother, giving Minxy giant freckles and glasses. Dria made Lou Anna look like a mouse and Bellissima decided on a panda sketch for Kay. They'd gotten so carried away with their vandalism that they'd forgotten what they were waiting for. They were reminded when Minxy began to mumble in her sleep. "Hey, you guys- Mama's starting to talk," said Sadie- capping her marker.

All three girls knelt at the bedside and listened. "-No. No thank you. I'm not using anymore," she mumbled- barely audible.

"What should I do?" asked Sadie- turning to Bellissima and Dria.

Dria pulled out her notes on somniloquy and parasomnia. 'Calmly and slowly start asking her questions. Keep your voice low so she thinks she's just dreaming. Just keep her talking. If she starts tossing and turning too much, we have to stop. It means they're coming out of it."

Sadie leaned close to Minxy's ear. "Why did you leave me, Mama? You were right there with me when I was falling apart. Hell, you helped me fall apart; so why did you leave me when it was time to put myself back together? I only got the two hands God gave me, there were too many pieces for me to gather on my own. I didn't have my drugs and I didn't have you. Being sober and alone is a whole different kind of lonesome, one that hurts more than you could ever imagine. For the first time in my life, I didn't have a substance protecting me from my emotions. Those emotions didn't take turns, they hit me all at once and they refused to be ignored. You created a monster and then left to find your way out. I was left alone to fix the damage you cheered and condoned for years. No one was there to help me find my way out. Why Mama?"

At first, Minxy said nothing and the girls felt defeated, as if they'd failed. Then, Minxy's eyelids flickered. "I <u>had</u> to leave you. I was no good for you, Sadie. The things I allowed to go on, they weren't things a mother should let or help her child do. Lighter's life and death, it's a cautionary tale. That could have been my Sadie, dead. You were headed down the exact same path and I'm the one who led you out that far to begin with."

"Are you using when no one's looking?"

"No," answered Minxy. "I gave it all up for you."

"When you were pregnant with me, did you drink? Did you use drugs?"

"I loved you the second I found out you were growing. What kind of mother would do such a thing? I drank and used the day before I found out I was pregnant and I sure as hell drank and used the day after you were born. But not one single day in between. I promise."

Dria noticed Lou Anna's fingertips twitching. "Mama, It's me. I just need a minute of your time, that's all. I know you hate it when I take up too much of your precious, billable time."

"Dria. You're here?" asked Lou Anna- her voice a bit hoarse.

"Did it ever cross your mind, that he might touch me? When he first kissed you, did he swear it was a special and secret kind love that you had to keep to yourself? When he first kissed you did it confuse you like it confused me? Did you hate me because you got too old for him to prey on? Why did I lose you after he did that to me? Why couldn't you stand to look at me? What did I do wrong to make my father to touch me like a husband instead of loving me like a daughter?" Sadie's face turned pale and Bellissima quickly wiped away her tears before either of her cousins could see.

Lou Anna's hand turned palm up in bed and Dria put her hand in her mother's hand. "I thought he would adore you, the way my daddy adored me; in a pure way that made you feel safe and special. Sometimes you must step back to see the details in the big picture. By the time I stepped back to see, it was too late. Don't think it was your fault. The blame is on him for what he did. The blame is on me for not protecting you."

"I came to see you last year. I was falling apart. I had things I needed to say. As my mother, you're genetically designed to comfort me. I thought surely, you'd be able to feel my cry for help. You turned me away. You didn't even ask me inside. Why?" Bellissima's posture tensed, afraid that Lou Anna would tell Dria that she'd been in the city with her wrists bleeding.

"I *did* feel your distress. I didn't feel your need for me, though. I never have. When I reach out to hug you, do you not recoil? Every time, you pull away. I stopped trying. And she needed me."

"She needed you? Who?"

"I can't tell you," slurred Lou Anna. Bellissima exhaled, relieved

"Am I a disappointment, Mama?" asked Dria, in tears.

"No. Never could be, not even if you tried your hardest." Dria pulled her hand back turned away.

Bellissima stroked Kay's hair. "I know you're in there somewhere, Mama. I need you to come to the surface and talk to me for a minute."

Kay's nose wiggled, and she sighed. "-My Lissima." She mumbled.

"Does it hurt when you look at me, Mama? Do you sometimes wish I had a different face so that you don't have to think about Cheniere? Do you wish I'd gone with her that night and died with her so that you didn't have to separate the pieces of your heart- half here on earth and the other half in heaven? Do you think Cheniere hates me?"

"I hurt a little inside every time I see your face, every time I hear your voice; but it's the sweetest pain, Lissima. It's a pain I'd die without, because when I look at you I still see both my daughters. When people ask me if I have children, I tell them I have two perfect daughters with the same face. Cheniere's happy you didn't go with her to the bridge, she told me so in a dream once. Cheniere said that you were there with her in spirit and she sent your spirit home to go back to sleep. It wasn't your time. She felt no pain Lissima. God was with Cheniere and she'd left her worldly vessel long before it succumbed. God swooped her up and turned her away from the world before she could see herself take her last breath. He carried her into the clouds himself, the way he carries all his children home. My heart is just fine, Lissima. Don't you worry about me stretching it to heaven. How can you think she hates you? Cheniere doesn't love anyone the way she loves you. Not even me. She told me so."

"You once told me that Grandma Cat was to blame for Grandpa Jeremiah and Cheniere's death. What did you mean?"

"There was a bordello near the bridge, off to the side- built on a small islet. It was a house of ill repute that you could only reach by boat. A place where loose women worked. They made their money by laying on their back- letting married men sweat and hump on top of them for a few pennies. I'd been following daddy around town for weeks, to see if there was any truth to what Mama suspected."

"There was a whorehouse out where Burn Out bridge used to be?"

"Yes, a dirty little shack with a jukebox and piano with missing keys," mumbled Minxy. Her joining the conversation startled the girls. They weren't aware that she was still listening.

"Did you find Grandpa Jeremiah there, cheating on Grandma?" Asked Dria.

"Daddy was there, but he wasn't cheating. The bridge joined Texas' and Louisiana's most rural areas. The whole purpose of the bridge was to make travel easier for workers, to create a less crowded path for bartering; bring more blue-collar jobs and make the land more attractive to moguls so that they'd want to modernize the county. The state promised us more businesses and tourists which meant more jobs, but nobody ever said bootleggers couldn't use the bridge too," said Lou Anna.

"Bootleggers? Grandpa Jeremiah was a bootlegger?" asked Sadie.

Kay grinned in her daze. "Yes, he was and I'm still proud to call him my Papa. You heard Catherine talk about all our financial misfortunes- over and over again. That bridge brought workers over from Texas who needed work. Some folks in town say that's why it was torched. Longtime Louisiana natives were getting their jobs stolen right out from under them by Texans and that made them mad- mad enough to burn it down. Just a theory, though. A lot of good men had to find alternative ways to make money until those promising business opportunities came through. Daddy sure was in a whore house but he wasn't cheating on Catherine. He told me so himself when I went to the whorehouse." Dria couldn't believe what she was hearing. Sadie's jaw dropped. Kay continued. "Mama and those bored housewives had been gossiping about how daddy must have had another woman, another family. I couldn't believe it. I was determined to get to the bottom of those accusations. I'd been on daddy's scent for weeks, following him, asking questions. Finally, all my stalking paid off. Whatever daddy was doing, he was doing it in that brothel. There were men who made a living rowing people from both banks to that brothel on pirogues. I hid in the brush near the bank and watched Daddy walk into that club every other evening. The day he died, Mama picked a huge fight with daddy. They said thing's they'd never said before. When daddy sped off, I sneaked out the back door, hopped on my bike and followed him again. I'd started to cry, watching him stroll into that filthy place. I decided it was time to confront him. The pirogue man asked me how old I was when I told him to take me to the whore house, but I flashed a dollar and he rowed me right on over without any more questions. I marched right in and all the drunk grownups stared. I scanned the room and I didn't see daddy. *'Little lady, you ain't old enough to get a job here yet. Come back when you got a little hair on your kitten,'* said one of the prostitutes- trying to escort me out.

'Get your hands off me! I ain't one of you! I came here to speak to my daddy! I ain't leaving here until I see him!' I was huffing and puffing so hard my little cheeks had turned red.

'They're all daddy to me but who might your daddy be?'

'I am a Beaumonte'! My daddy is Jeremiah. You ain't fit to speak my surname so just point me in his direction- that's all you can do for me!' I yelled with my chest poked out- so grown up.

The whore puffed from her Bakelite cigar holder and blew the smoke right in my face. *'You're an angry child. Why you come in here on fire like this? You followed your daddy cause you think he's a bad man?'* I didn't answer her. She took a deep breath and held out her hand. *'I'll take you right to him darling.'*

'Cayenne, she ain't old enough to be back there!' yelled the owner.

'Hush now! Can't you see this child is scared and confused? She needs her papa. I got her, she won't get into anything.' That strumpet led me all the way to the back of the club, past rooms with dirty curtains instead of doors. I could see naked men getting serviced by lost women and it smelled like rotting salmon. *'You just keep looking straight forward, you hear?'* I tried but it was hard not to look to the left or right with all the strange noises of either pleasure or pain. We came to a room with a black door. She

239

knocked three times and said *'Contraband days'* like it was some sort of password. The door opened. I braced myself, thinking I'd find daddy on top of some harlot but all I saw was daddy stacking crates full of label-less jugs. His face when he saw me standing there, he may as well have been caught with his pants down. Daddy was ashamed. Having me find him there broke his heart. I could tell. He made the whore take me outside and she waited with me. *'What did you think, child? That you'd catch your daddy dishonoring your mother? Do you know your daddy at all? He's not that kind of man. Won't lie and say I didn't try him though. Not for the money, just for fun. You want a puff?'* she asked.

'No. Daddy caught me trying to smoke before. Made me eat tobacco.'

Cayenne laughed. *'Serves you right. Smoking's no good for you."*

"Then why do you do it?"

'Because it feels good. You're young. When you get older you'll discover lots of things that feel good but are very bad for you, like love.'

'Love feels bad?"

'-Sometimes."

While we were sitting out in front of the club waiting for daddy to come out, a woman stepped out of a boat and walked right up to that whore they called Cayenne. *'You messing around with my husband?'*

'Messing around? Your husband? You know how many husbands I see, lady? You gon' have to be more specific if you want me to give you an honest answer. Give me a name and I'll be kind enough to go into detail for you. I'll tell you every which way he throws my back when he comes here to see me; to get me to do all the foul things you're too much of a lady to do.'

'The tall one with the nice black car- Earl! You messing around with him or not?'

'Well, I guess that depends on what you mean by messing around. I perform a service for your husband and in exchange, he keeps me in all my finery. He's running a little late for our meeting today. When you get back home, you tell him to hurry up. I have appointments to keep. Without a schedule, I'm just a whore. With a schedule, I'm a working girl.'

'I hear they call you Cayenne. Hot pepper- how appropriate. Adulterers burn in hell. Since you like hot stuff, you'll be comfortable spending eternity with the devil. Adulterers all burn! They burn! You hear me!'

Cayenne pulled me close. *'Look here now, there's a child right here. You got a problem with your husband spending his hard-earned money on me, you can take it up with me some other time. You get your ass back in that boat and leave before I tell you to your face- all the reasons your husband don't love you no more.'*

'Burn in hell!'

Cayenne looked down at me, *'Price of doing good business.'* she said with a wink. She clutched my cheek. "*You remind me of my little girl. She's about your age.*"

Daddy finally came out and Cayenne left us alone. *'This isn't the place for a child, Kay.'*

"*Please don't slap my lips for saying, but this ain't no place for a married man either.*'

'-Only reason I ain't slapping your lips for talking back is cause you're right. Married men don't belong in places like this.'

'Then why you here daddy?'

'Desperation led me here, to a place where's there's money. It's dirty money, but it's money. I need money to take care of my family.'

"We don't have money?"

"If we were anywhere but here, I'd tell you not to worry about that. I'd tell you that money burdens are for parents only and that all you need to worry about is being a kid. Following me here makes me believe you're brave enough to handle the truth. Truth is, we're not doing so well. Plant owners hire you straight out of high school. They reel you in by promising you a few dollars more than minimum wage. When we start getting old and our health starts failing from breathing in their toxins, they let us go. The mill is steady work until your body gets worn out. When we start moving slower from all the back-breaking labor, they cut our hours. All we're left with are years of dedicated work, no education to fall back on. They don't tell you that, that we're expendable- nothing but a herd of cattle with strong black backs to carry loads to line some other man's pocket. When your back is finally broken, you don't have enough in the bank to still feel like a decent provider. Our crops aren't doing so well. The soil has turned its back on us. There are kids half my age, dropping out of school just to come over here and work from Texas. They don't know they're being set up, doomed to end up poor. You may be a child, *but you have ears. I know you've heard about the lack of jobs since this bridge came up. A lot of folks are mad about it."*

'Are you mad about it, Daddy?'

'No. I can't be angry at a man for wanting to survive. We're all just trying to survive. I hear them saying awful things about what they're willing to do to make things right. I want no part of it. We all have a right to make a living. I love you little Kay Beaumonte'. I love your mother and your sisters just the same, and your new baby niece. This money ain't clean but neither are the bill collectors coming for me. It's my job to take care of the women in my life.'

'If it makes things easier for you, I won't open a restaurant when I get older. I'll just dream of something cheaper.'

'Absolutely not, Kay. You're going to keep dreaming your same dream. I'm going to keep busting my hump until you achieve it.'

'You don't have another family?'

"Of course not. Catherine may be acting a little crazy lately but she's my wife. She's the only woman in the world for me. The only women I've seen even close to matching her beauty is the little women she gave birth to as a gift to me. I want you to go on home now. When I get back, I'm going to put this ring back on your mother's hand where it belongs and tell her how much I love her. Then I'm going to tell her that we've raised one hell of a little girl.'

My daddy put me in the boat and when I reached the Louisiana bank, I hopped on my bike and rode home full speed. There was a shadow chasing me. It was so long ago, and I was so young. Maybe I just imagined it; but back then I believed it was the shadow of something evil flying high in the sky. It could have been the Mothman sent to warn us all. It could have been just an eagle. I was almost home when I saw the smoke in the air. I stopped pedaling and looked behind me It was like I could feel daddy telling me to keep going, not to turn back. I made it back home and crept back upstairs. I couldn't understand what was taking daddy so long to make it back. It had been hours. Then I heard Mama scream. Minxy and I ran downstairs, and I tried to step out onto the porch where Mama had collapsed at the sheriffs' feet, but she yelled at me. *'Get back in the house!'* Daddy was dead. The bridge took him and then it took my other baby- Cheniere."

CHAPTER TWENTY-SEVEN

When the Beaumonte' grandchildren returned to the den to sleep, no one spoke; as if haunted into shameful, addled silences. Once the lights were off, they all cried and even though they could hear one another's whimpering- they did nothing to comfort one another. The whimpering went on all night and into the early morning. Once Sadie and Dria were finally asleep, Bellissima left for Pennycress to sit with her grandmother.

Bellissima sat near Catherine's bedside, watching her sleep. At last, Catherine stirred. "Hey there sweet pea," said Catherine as she woke- stretching.

Bellissima kissed Catherine's cheek. "Morning Granny."

"Your shifts starting earlier now?"

"No, Mam. I couldn't sleep so I decided to come here instead."

"You telling me you've been here since before daybreak?"

"Yes, Mam. You were out cold. I even changed your adult diaper a couple of times, you didn't even know I was here. Those must have been some sweet dreams you were having."

"If I did dream, I wouldn't be able to tell you what about. Does that nurse think she can pull a fast one on me and get away with it? She's got another thing coming."

"The weather channel says there might be some bad weather heading our way. I hope it holds off until your dinner is over."

"If it was going to rain tomorrow, I'd be able to smell it by now. It ain't gon' rain, I'm sure of it. Sometimes the firmament changes just to remind us that we should be grateful for every single day that the sky doesn't fall. It could fall at any time; you know? Thank God for his mercy and leniency. The sky must change so we remember how to be thankful. If we're lucky, the sky will just be changing. Sometimes it really will rain, though." She looked at the closet and noticed a covered hanger. "What's that hanging over there?"

"That's what you'll be wearing for your birthday dinner. Mama asked me to bring it over today. Your daughters are going to come and get you dressed before your dinner tomorrow and that's what you'll be wearing."

"Is it white? I bet it's white. That damn Lou Anna always puts me in white. Doesn't she know it's hard for an old lady like me to keep my hands from trembling? Putting a drink in my hand is like asking for a stain. What if I sit in something sticky or my old bladder starts leaking?"

"I think Mama and Auntie Minx picked it out. It's definitely not white."

"Good, Kays knows what looks good on me. Help me sit upright in this rock pit they call a bed."

Bellissima repositioned her grandmother, got a face towel and held it under the facet. "I got a warm towel here. Let me wake your face up," offered Bellissima- wiping the crust from Catherine's eyes. When she'd finished, she gave Catherine her glasses.

"Much better, my dear," said Catherine as she studied her granddaughter's chagrin propensity. "I know that look, Lissima. Something heavy is on you. Come, talk to me about it." As soon as Catherine wrapped Bellissima in her arms, Bellissima burst into tears. "Let it out, baby. Cry it on out of you and find a way to replace this pain with some kind of joy. Pull a little happiness from anywhere you can. Don't feel bad if it takes you a while. I've been trying now for years and I still haven't filled myself up on joy. There's not enough to fill a hole as deep as the one in me, or maybe I don't have any more joy stored down deep to borrow from. Your Grandma is right here and I've got you. It's okay to cry sometimes, Lissima."

"I don't know what I'm searching for or why I'm still searching. Why can't I stop digging when I know it'll only hurt more?"

"Being emotionally tortured in the dark is painful. Knowing in the light is painful too, just the lesser of the two pains. You've got be careful what you wish for dear."

"All this time, we've been so angry at our mothers for keeping things away from us. I never stopped to think about why they chose to do so. I just wanted things out in the open so that I didn't turn in to one of those people who keep their loved ones at a distance and can't explain to them why. I don't want to have to protect the ones I love from myself as broken people do. It's already started with me and my cousins, you know; us being dishonest and secretive and withdrawn. I don't think I've ever heard Dria and Auntie Lou say *I love you* to one another. Sadie's so harrowed that she spaces out for hours at a time. It's like an illness, the reticence and the lies."

"-And you?"

Bellissima released an exhale that escaped her body with an involuntary, self-pitied chuckle. "I almost checked myself into an Asylum for the mentally insane last October and I couldn't even tell my own mother."

Catherine's face soured. "Mentally insane? What on earth for? Beaumonte' women aren't crazy. We're high spirited- that's all."

"I saw Cheniere in my head. Maybe she was outside my head too. There were wet footprints in the cottage, all over; muddy swamp footprints. Mud prints from Burn Out bridge. She took my hearing, tied my tongue and then slit my wrists."

"Slit wrists? What's this you talking?"

"…Or maybe I cut them. I don't know Grandma Cat. I just don't know what happened!"

"Sweetheart, seeing someone you love from time to time in a dream is perfectly normal. Hell, seeing them outside a dream can be normal too. I once chased a man at the hardware store from the register clear out to the parking lot. I'd seen him from afar and I was certain he was my presumed-dead husband. He looked at me like I'd lost my mind when I asked him if he was sure his name wasn't Jeremiah. It's not in your head, it's in your heart. Seeing your sister does not make you crazy."

"She took my hearing away. She took my voice away. She wanted me to be mute just like her. Cheniere wanted me to know what it felt like."

Catherine paused. "I must really be getting old because I'm not understanding you, child."

"I don't understand it either, Grandma Cat." Bellissima wiped her tears with the damp towel. "I haven't been able to celebrate New Year's ever since it happened, since Cheniere passed. We used to look forward to the fireworks, all the lights in the sky. Cheniere woke me the night she died. She was still feeling guilty about all of us getting in trouble for cutting her hair. She thought it was her fault. She asked me if I hated her for it. *'Of course not. We're twins. We're supposed to get in trouble together.'*

Every year, the resolution was the same: Make our mothers tell us about our fathers. Cheniere confessed with her fast hands, signing, she had a different resolution. *'I want to talk. I want to hear'*

I told her. *'I don't think that's possible. We can pray for it some more, but I don't want you to lose hope waiting for something that was never in God's plan to give you.'*

Cheniere wouldn't let it go. *'God will make me right if I break the curse. Then maybe I'll hear and speak for the first time in my whole life when midnight gets here. Then, we'll really be twins. We'll finally be exactly the same.'*

I never felt sorry for Cheniere until then. She didn't like it when people expressed pity. I never knew she felt so incomplete. No one in this family ever made her feel different but I could see in her eyes that she knew she wasn't just like me. To me, we were already the same, we always had been. *'We are the same. There's nothing wrong with you. You're perfectly special. Mama said not to talk about the curse anymore. She said it's not a real thing. Go back to bed before we get into more trouble. Mama said if we don't behave ourselves we won't get to pop fireworks at midnight.'*

I thought Cheniere went back to bed. I didn't know she'd left for the bridge. Fireworks woke me. It was midnight. I wondered why Mama hadn't come upstairs to wake us. We hadn't made a peep all night. We'd been good little girls. When I got downstairs I saw all of you scrambling. Aunt Lou Anna was on the phone yelling at the sheriff; describing Cheniere's pajamas. Auntie Minxy was running around, looking for a flashlight. *'I'll check the graveyard.'* Mama was sobbing. And Grandma, you…"

"I was praying," finished Catherine. "I'd been there before, under the weight of the wait. I knew it was bad, what was coming."

"Yes. You were praying. Dria and Sadie came downstairs and Mama ran to us. *'Did she tell you where she went? Tell me! You won't get in trouble, I swear it! Just tell me where she is!'* Dria and Sadie told the truth, they didn't know. Mama looked at me and begged. *"Lissima, where's the other half of you?"* The way she worded the question, it unlocked something inside of me, like a door I believed led to nothing before that moment."

'I told her not to go there.' I mumbled.

'Where, Lissima?' Mama asked. Her face went white. She knew exactly where before I answered, but hoped I'd say otherwise. *'-Burn Out.'*

Catherine searched the depth of her darkest memory. "You couldn't see your hand in front of your face out there at Burn Out bridge that night. Everyone in town came out with either a flashlight or a candle. The Sheriff refused to let anyone in the water to look for her until the sun came up. He said he couldn't risk another life. When the sun came up, we found Cheniere. They pulled her out and placed Cheniere in Kay's arms. Kay rocked her child like she was just sleeping, but your sister's face was purple. She was still beautiful, though- like a lilac little doll that was just sleeping. The sky wasn't bluffing anymore. The dark clouds came rolling in and they did bring rain," said Catherine.

"She'd been asking too many questions about the bridge and the curse. I should have known she'd try something. Why didn't I do something? Why didn't I tell someone? Why didn't she let me come with her? Even though I didn't believe she could be fixed by diving for a stupid ring, I would have jumped in with her Grandma, I swear I would've!" Bellissima shouted.

"I know," said Catherine, teary-eyed.

•

The Beaumonte' daughters sat on the front porch without speaking. Lou Anna was reading, turning the pages of her book so hard that they sounded like they'd rip right of the spine. Kay played solitaire, scowling at her sisters every ten seconds. Minxy chewed sunflower seeds, mumbling profanity under her breath as she spat the shells into an old rusty tin. Bellissima returned from pennycress and stepped onto the porch. "I could cut the tension with a knife. What's going on now?" she asked.

"-Woke up this morning with a little more eyeliner than I'm used to. I thought we'd called a truce, but it seems your Mama and Aunt are in cahoots. Working together!" accused Minxy.

"-Keep pretending like it wasn't you, Minxy! You have been dying to play these reindeer games! You and Lou waited for me to fall asleep, so you make me look like a damn cartoon!" shouted Kay.

"I'm the one who made the girls quit this nonsense, only to have the two of you undermine me! You two did it! Just admit it already!" Lou Anna screamed.

"For the thousandth time Lou! It wasn't me! If it was me, I wouldn't have drawn on my own face too! The only one of us crazy enough to do a kamikaze mission like that is Minxy!" shouted Kay- pointing her finger.

Bellissima laughed, shaking her head.

"What is so funny?" asked Kay.

"I'll tell you what's funny. You three sound as immature as us, your daughters."

The Beaumonte' sisters looked at each other and then laughed at themselves. "I guess we do sound silly, don't we?" said Minxy.

"What's in the bag?" asked Lou Anna.

Bellissima looked down at her satchel. "I'm glad you asked, Auntie Lou. I have some vitamins here for you, a little protein powder and some spearmint muscle cream," Bellissima replied- handing each of them a bottle.

"What's the point of all this?"

"Well, my cousins and I talked it over and decided we'd all be running the obstacle course at the fair this year. All of us- that means you ladies too. I'm not sure if you gals remember how strenuous it was all those years ago, but I distinctly remember you all fighting over who was sorer and got to use the heating pad first. You want us sweating in the kitchen? We want you sweating on the course," said Bellissima with a wink.

"I know you were hoping we'd fight you on this, but you're out of luck. We think that's a great idea," said Kay.

"We do?" asked Lou Anna with her face bitter.

"Yes, we do and don't let these few grey hairs fool you. We'll pull our half of the victory."

"-Dria and Sadie up yet?" asked Bellissima.

"They've been awake for hours. They beat us out of bed this morning. We all woke up with the same headache. Dria said breathing in the fumes from the permanent marker must've made us sick. Doesn't seem right but it ain't like I can make enough sense of it to prove her wrong," answered Minxy.

"-All of you, woozy? Really? That's so weird," she said, fidgeting nervously again. "They're really up already? I should probably get in there and see what they're up to."

Bellissima entered the kitchen where she found Dria wearing an apron, dicing vegetables. Sadie sat, polishing silver and wrapping cutlery in faultlessly wrinkle-free napkins. Dria looked up from the cutting board. "Lissima, good morning! I didn't hear you take off. You must have left early."

"I had a hard time staying asleep after…everything."

"After what?" Asked Dria, turning her attention back to the veggies.

Bellissima looked around, making sure it was safe to talk. "-After we dosed our mothers," she mumbled.

"I don't know what you're talking about," said Dria. "Sadie, you have any idea what Lissima's talking about?"

"Nope, not a clue," answered Sadie.

"Seriously, we could have killed them. You two could at least act like you have a conscious."

"<u>Your</u> conscious is big enough for all three of us. Relax, they think they inhaled too much soluble ink. We're not going to get caught. No harm, no foul."

"Yes, the fumes. That's the best you could come up with? Permanent marker fumes? What about permanent brain damage? Their hangover symptoms could be masking some serious health problems."

Sadie chuckled. "I'm the only one in this room with actual huffing experience. Trust me, they'll be fine. I've had my share of brown paper bag highs. Minxy Beaumonte' hasn't suffered a rough hangover since she was 21. She's partied so hard she became immune. She got a good night's sleep at best."

"-And Lou Anna's a psychoanalyst who raised a morose, emotionally bruised daughter harboring an unhealthy quantity of resentment. She hasn't gone one night without a valium in ten years. She may have not been an addict like Auntie Minxy, but she's no stranger to sedatives."

"-And what about <u>*My*</u> Mama?" asked Bellissima.

"I tossed Auntie Kay an orange earlier to see if her reflexes were glitchy. She caught it. I challenged her to a backwards alphabet contest just for fun, she beat my time and I've had lots of practice because I get pulled over all the time. She's alright," said Sadie. "Where'd you run off to so early?"

"I went to see how Granny was. I dropped off her grand birthday ensemble. What are ya'll up to?"

"What's it look like? We're prepping for the dinner tomorrow. It's customary to get some of the side dishes cooked the night before. That's what Auntie Kay always used to say," answered Sadie. "I just hung the ivory tablecloth out to dry on the clothesline. Mama helped me dig the old candelabras out of the attic and I washed the plates by hand twice," she bragged.

"You washed them by hand because Grandma Cat doesn't have a dishwasher and you had to do them twice because you did such a crappy job the first go around. While she was preoccupied with the easy stuff, I was busy with the important stuff," said Dria- smiling at Bellissima haughtily. "I cleaned the oven and took the venison out of the freezer. I juiced all the limes by hand, no seeds and I'm almost done dicing all the garnish. I even peeled all the potatoes with that tiny paring knife that makes my fingers cramp." Bellissima just stood there looking at all their hard work, stunned. "-Catherine got your tongue?" Joked Dria.

"No, I'm just so surprised to see you two so dedicated," answered Bellissima.

"We heard what you said about doing things together. when we were walking to the other night. You're right. It does feel good being here. This really could be her last birthday," said Sadie. "Dria's even wearing an ugly apron. You might wanna get a quick picture."

"You better! You may not ever see it again," said Dria wiping her hands. She grabbed another apron and handed it to Bellissima. "You gon' just stand there or help us?"

Bellissima smiled and tied the apron around her waist. "Move aside, you're cutting those onions way too thick. Auntie Lou sees an onion, she'll try to eat around it. You gotta dice them thin so she doesn't know she's eating them. If ya'll want to learn, I'll teach you everything Mama taught me."

"We're ready to learn," said Sadie- joining them near the cutting board.

"When cooking a big feast, you're going to need at least two clean measuring cups. Get one and fill it with water."

"For what?" asked Dria.

"When you're cooking a big meal, you're going to have a lot of burners going at once. It's easy to get inattentive and let one of your dishes start burning. A little water keeps the bottom of a pot from charring while you're tending to other pots. When that happens, your whole dish tastes scorched, and it's only fit for a trash can. When something starts sizzling too hot, pour in a little water and the pot will calm down, that'll buy you some time until you figure out what you need to do- stir, add an ingredient or turn the fire down."

"-Two measuring cups, one full of water. Got it!" said Dria.

"I'm so happy we're doing this. Sadie, put some music on. Dancing makes the food taste better," said Bellissima.

"Did you see the sky on your way home? It's a little gloomy. It's supposed to be like that tomorrow too. Should we move some furniture around and move the party indoors? It might…"

"Bite your tongue and Knock on wood! It is not going to rain! This dinner will not be ruined!" huffed Bellissima.

Kay smiled. "You smell that? It smells like the good Lord guiding our daughter's hands in that kitchen."

"You hear that music? Sounds like they're having fun, too," Said Minxy.

"He sure answers prayers, doesn't he?" said Lou Anna- dabbing her eyes.

CHAPTER TWENTY-EIGHT

It was finally Catherine's birthday. It was finally dawn, but the Beaumonte' grandchildren had been up long before the sun preparing the banquet. Dria was supposed to be mashing bananas into a custard for the banana pudding but was nodding off while stirring. Bellissima had fallen asleep on a stool with her head on the counter, her face planted in a smear of gravy. Sadie, momentarily unsupervised, lifted the plastic lid off the cake and stuck her finger in the icing.

Lou Anna burst into the kitchen causing all three of them to flinch. "-Morning girls! It sure does smell good in here. I can smell the grub from the road. You three look beat," she said laughing at their pain.

"You find our exhaustion amusing?" asked Dria.

"Hell yes, I do," answered Lou Anna.

"- Cruel," grumbled Bellissima. "Where have you been all morning?"

"I went out to get you girls a little gift."

"Yay! Gifts!" shouted Sadie- leaping from her seat. She rushed over, grabbing at the bags.

Lou Anna slapped her hands. "No meddling! You'll get these later. Besides, no one should get gifts before the party starts. If Catherine found out, I'd be hearing about it until her next birthday- God spare. I'll go wrap these and lay something out for me to wear. We did a little cleaning upstairs in our old bedrooms last night so you'll all have a little space to get ready for the party. Don't expect it to be spotless, they're still full of junk; but we cleared a little primping room. That way you don't have to fight over the same mirror. You two better keep an eye on Sadie," said Lou Anna to Bellissima and Dria. "She has icing under her nails. Put Mama's cake where she can't reach it. You remember what happened to your graduation cake, Dria? There was no icing left by the time we lit the candles."

Dria and Bellissima slowly walked over to Catherine's birthday cake. They noticed the track marks. They turned their attention to Sadie, who was looking rather guilty. "I'm sorry! I'm hungry!"

"Then eat anything except the food we've been busting our assess to prepare and our Granny's cake!" yelled Bellissima.

Dria shook her head, disappointed. "Did you at least wash your booger-diggers?"

Sadie thought. "Just don't eat a slice from the left side of the cake," she replied.

"There's plenty of healthy fruit in the fridge," said Bellissima, sternly.

"-But we're almost out of salt," said Sadie.

"Salted fruit? That's defeating the purpose, Sadie. Salt makes it unhealthy. If you don't want the fruit, nibble on some of that tofu junk Auntie Lou bought. God knows no one else is going to eat it."

•

Minxy tapped on the door of her old bedroom. She poked her head inside and found Sadie sorting through necklaces; trying to find one worthy of the occasion. "You have a minute?" she asked. "I won't linger. I know how you like your privacy, lately."

"It's okay. You can come on in," Sadie replied- admiring her Mother's gown. "You know, you never needed much to look fantastic, but seeing you all dolled up this past Sunday and again today- It's nice. You must be immortal, Mama. Or at least aging backwards," she jeered.

"It's the genes, black don't crack." Minxy brought with her a small fold of fabric. "I know you have your own clothes, your own sense of style; but I wanted to bring you this dress." Minxy stepped behind her daughter and dangled the dress in front of Sadie's body. "It's a Kitenge maxi. We have beautiful things here in America too, but the love put into this sundress makes it one of a kind. I saw it the first week I was in Africa and thought of you."

"You were thinking about me?" asked Sadie.

"Who else would I have been thinking of?" she asked staring at Sadie adoringly. "You don't have to wear it if you don't want to. You can take it back to school with you and wear it some other time. I just thought you might like to wear it today. They call this color Tuscan sun. Such a fitting name for this shade, it complements the temperature outside. It's so hot out, it's nice and flowy and breathable. I bet the fabric will flow behind you like wings on an angel. The split rides up a little high, that way you don't feel like an old lady. Most importantly, it's loose-fitting, you know."

Sadie turned to her mother and stared into her telling eyes. "Thank you for this. I'd love to wear it today, Mama."

"Well. I'll leave so you can put it on," she replied- Kissing Sadie's cheek before leaving her alone.

Dria wiggled. Dria tugged. She shimmied, hopped up and down; but struggled to slide her dress up past her rear. Lou Anna stood at the opened bedroom door, giggling while shaking her head. Dria turned and discovered her mother standing there. "You're just full of laughter today, aren't you?"

"The women in this family have plump thighs and supple asses. It's a blessing until you have to wear something formfitting. Then it's just another curse. You girls lucked out; not an inch of belly fat or an ounce of cellulite. There are women out there paying surgeons to get the backside you got, you should be proud. Why didn't you just slide the dress over your head?"

"-Tried that, almost ruined my hair," Dria replied- still struggling. "That's a two-man job."

"You're one, I'm two- if you don't mind the help," offered Lou Anna; certain Dria would decline in her usual withdrawn manner.

To Lou Anna's surprise, Dria thought for a second and accepted. "-Well, if you don't mind…"

"You're my daughter, of course I don't mind," Lou Anna replied- so pleased to be needed by her child for the first time in a long time.

Lou Anna helped Dria get unstuck and then pulled up a small step stool. She covered Dria's head with a silk chiffon and Dria held her arms straight up over her head. Lou Anna slowly maneuvered the pencil dress over Dria's torso. The silk chiffon slid off Dria's hair without disrupting its bravura. Lou Anna then stepped down and zipped the back. "See now? It fits just right."

Dria noticed her mother's eyes were moist. "-Are you crying, Mama?"

"No," lied Lou Anna.

"Well, clearly you are. What for?"

"No reason at all. You look phenomenal, My child."

Bellissima, still wrapped up in her robe, sat on the floor with a chest of her Mother's jewelry on her lap. Kay waltzed in without knocking or asking if she could, she didn't need to. Kay's relationship with her daughter was different from the ones her sisters had with their daughters or at least she thought so. Kay clutched, in her right hand, the prescription script she'd found. She planned to passively confront Bellissima about it. Then she'd rapaciously confront Lou Anna about it; but tucked it away when she found Bellissima sitting, holding an old newspaper clipping that she never meant for Bellissima to find. Kay's intrusion startled Bellissima. Immediately, Bellissima tried to explain- stuttering. "-Mama, I was just looking for something to accent my dress and I found…"

"It's alright, Lissima," said Kay tenderly.

Bellissima looked back down at the clipping. "*-When it rains it pours: Bridge Strikes Beaumonte's Twice.*" she read. "Mama, who would print such an awful thing?"

Kay found a rag and laid it down over the dusty floor before sitting down next to her child. "Nobody in this town would ever be so audacious. No, this little piece of evil was printed in a paper out of Beauregard parish. The reporter meant no harm, really. The caption was purposely grim to get people's attention. Her name was Odette Monet', Cajun bred just like us. She'd read about the bridge and challenged the state; swore she'd expose what she believed to be government conspiracy if they didn't start answering some questions. Odette's research led her to me at the restaurant. She let one of my waitresses take a full order, sat there and ate it all before asking to see the owner. I was pretty sure she was ready to complain about the spices, but she asked me to sit. *Complain? I'll do no such thing. That may have been the best meal I've ever eaten. I'm here on business that's a little personal for us both.*" Odette had so many questions, but the most memorable question was the one she asked me about the spirit of the bridge. I thought maybe she meant to ask me about daddy's spirit or Cheniere's spirit, but she meant it just the way she asked it." *I'm talking about the ruins. The spirit of the bridge, does it haunt you?*"

"What did you tell her?" asked Bellissima.

"I told her the truth. Yes. It haunts us all. Odette didn't know there were two of you. She nearly jumped out of the booth when I showed her a picture of you and Cheniere together. She begged to meet you, said it would be like seeing the dead. I forbid it. Odette was terminated shortly after this article was published. I went to see her months later when she was packing up to leave town. I felt so bad for her. I felt like she lost her job trying to get answers for our family. She told me not to feel so bad. You see, that poor reporter grew up without a Mama. She'd spent all her life looking for the mother who walked out on her when she was barely crawling. There was an old whore house down by the bridge. It came and went long before you were even thought about. Somehow, Odette's research led to that whore house and then the trail went cold. You see when the fire started, posts from the bridge fell and crumpled the top of the club causing a second blaze. Folks climbed in the boats to make it back to land. Some of them were crushed by the burning pieces of debris plunging into the river. The ones who could swim got tired and sank before they reached land or bled to death after being ripped apart by the gators. Others were drowned by non-swimmers who'd panicked. I hear there were some people hiding in the club when the fire was put out. Rumor has it, cops canoed out to the club, lined up the hiding survivors and executed them all before adding more gasoline to keep folks from finding out there was a whore house operating right under their noses. Some say the cops were Dougie's best customers. The fire would have unveiled all their sin. Odette believed her mother died the day the bridge burned down. Odette looked me in the eye and told me that she believed her mother meant to come back for her when she had the means to take care of them both. I guess it was easier than believing that her mother never intended to come back for her at all. The investigation was handled so poorly, there was never even an official death toll, let alone death certificates."

"This article says that Cheniere wouldn't have died if the ruins hadn't been left there. Is that true Mama?"

"Maybe. Cheniere was a strong swimmer, both of you swam real good. I'd like to think that Cheniere was strong enough to swim back to land after she fell in or jumped in- whichever happened. Only God knows. I didn't get a lot of answers, but I did hear people talking down at the coroner's office. They think Cheniere's clothes got caught on something or she was held down. She wiggled free but just ran out of breath before she could reach the surface again. There were bites on my baby from the fish and the gators. They say she was long gone before they sank their teeth in her. They promised me she didn't feel a thing. It didn't make me feel no better though. The reporter, Odette, said the ruins were a hazard and contributed to Cheniere's death and if the bridge had never been burned in the first place, there would be no ruins. People with enough power never gave an explanation. They failed to protect Cheniere from the ruins. It's everyone's fault except the people who died there. I only think about it every single day that passes. Thinking about why bad things happen- that's dangerous. Thoughts like that, they keep the door to hell wide open. I won't feed those demons my precious tears. Nobody ever said we couldn't ask God a question, but you have to be careful about how you talk to him about those things. He might get the feeling you don't trust him. Asking God a question is something you do in prayer with your heart ready and willing to accept that you just may never know why. Saying to God, what you've done here is not fair and I demand you give my loved ones back- that's where we get to sounding ungrateful and unwilling to accept that his ways are not like ours. If we had it our way, we'd never lose the ones we love and in return miss out on all the lessons he means for us to discover and we won't become the proof he needs us to become to provoke the change he needs others to witness." Bellissima said nothing as she buried the article back beneath her Mother's jewelry where she'd found it. Kay reached in the box. "Look at these earrings. They're Cheniere's birthstone. They match your shoes, what do you say?"

Bellissima smiled, faintly. "I'd love to wear them, Mama."

"Now, let's get you dressed," said Kay- taking Bellissima's dress off the hanger. After she fastened the clasp on Bellissima's heels, she stood and spritzed daughter's face with cucumber water.

"How do I look, Mama?"

"-Like me, a thousand years ago," laughed Kay- taking both of Bellissima's hands in hers. "Little girl, do you know how much I love you and your sister?"

"-To the moon and back," Bellissima replied.

"That's right! You know Lissima. When you lost your twin, my biggest fear was that you'd feel like you didn't have a counterpart in this world anymore. I feared you'd feel like you had no one to talk to, confide in…"

Bellissima's eyebrows sank. "Don't be silly, Mama. I have you."

Kay paused and thought of the prescription again but didn't bring it up. "Yes. You have me, and you always will."

•

Lincoln arrived at the big house, early on purpose. He tapped on the door and waited. Kay opened the door and grinned. "Good evening Ms. Kay Beaumonte'. I'm not sure if Lissima asked your permission yet, but she invited me here this evening to celebrate this special occasion. I hope that's alright."

"Mr. Breaux, you've shared a meal with this family, in this home. You're always welcome here now, special occasion or not."

Lincoln looked up at the sky, "You still want to set up outdoors. The sun's still out, but it might not be for long. It could rain," he observed.

"Whatever you do, don't say that in front of Lissima. Bite your tongue, Child. She'll shit a sideways brick if one drop falls and ruins all her hard work. That determined child of mine," she laughed- shaking her head. Kay noticed three bouquets in Lincoln's arms. "Not one, not two- but three bouquets of flowers? My little Lissima must've made quite the impression," said Kay with a smirk.

"Only one's for Lissima. There's one here for you and the birthday girl, as well," Lincoln replied; handing Kay a cluster of lavender peonies.

"When you first came here I said to myself, this one's a gentleman. You have no idea how much I love being right."

Lincoln held out a bent elbow and Kay slid her arm in. They waltzed inside together arm-in-arm. "Something smells delicious," he said.

"Those are Lissima's hands at work in the Beaumonte' kitchen. Delicious is the only way she knows how to cook."

Lou Anna nudged Minxy as Kay and Lincoln entered the den. "Well, what do we have here?" she gushed.

"Lincoln decided to join us on this special day. Isn't that nice?" said Kay- smelling her flowers.

"Welcome," said Minxy.

"I'm a bit early, I know. I just thought I'd help with getting the serving table where it needs to be. You ladies shouldn't be doing any heavy lifting."

"The table? Is that the only reason you came?" asked Lou Anna- mischievously.

Lincoln blushed. "No Mam," he answered.

"Of course not. One of those bouquets better be for my niece."

"Yes, Mam. These lilies are for her Grandmother, but these magnolias; I picked by hand. I figured I'd give the magnolias to Lissima. I had to work a little harder for them. She strikes me as the kind of woman that would appreciate that kind of thing."

"-I declare," said Minxy- clutching her heart, affectionately moved by his thoughtfulness.

Lou Anna stood, walked over to Lincoln and straightened his tie. "Lissima! Come on down here for a minute, Cher."

Bellissima rushed to the den, clasping her earring- the final touch. Her elegance caused everyone, Lincoln included, to gasp and stare. Sadie washed Bellissima's hair with an aloe and tea tree oil then slicked her scalp with homemade honey pomade. She took her time on Bellissima's curls, making sure they had volume. With every step Bellissima took, the curls bounced, releasing the sweetest au natural aroma. Minxy had convinced Bellissima to wear something backless to show off her slender posterior. Lou Anna loaned Bellissima a tortoise clasp barrette to keep the coils from her eyes.

Bellissima fixed her eyes on Lincoln and paused as she reached the stair landing. "Lincoln, how long have you been here? Did they do anything to you?" she asked- scowling at her mom and aunts.

Lincoln laughed. "No, they've been quite gracious and inviting." Lincoln gave Bellissima the magnolias. "These are for you. The lilies are for Mrs. Catherine."

Minxy stood. "Speaking of evil, we should get going. We still need to make it to pennycress and dress her. I'll take the flowers with me; they'll make for a nice distraction. Maybe we can slip the clothes on her without her even noticing."

•

The Beaumonte' daughters stood in the hallway outside Catherine's room, staring at her closed door. Lou Anna used her handkerchief to wipe a smudge near the door decal. "Eventually one of us is going to have to pull the door handle. Folks are probably arriving at the house by now. We can't have them waiting to eat," said Minxy.

"It's easy for you to be in a rush. Mama didn't verbally assault <u>you</u> the last time we were here," said Lou Anna.

"Lou, those were the pills talking. I'm sure she's less combative today. You're a doctor, you of all people should understand how strong drugs can affect a person. You'd think doctors would exercise more caution when prescribing such powerful substances; consider how their actions may affect their relationships with their loved ones. I wonder if certain pills cause secrecy. When will you people learn?" mumbled Kay- through a tight-teeth smile.

"I can't help but think you have something to say to me, Kay," Lou Anna replied.

"Me? Something to say? No. Just eager to get back to my perfect daughter who has a perfectly functioning mind, with no quirks that need adjusting," hissed Kay.

Minxy opened the door and walked in. Her sisters followed. Catherine looked up from her sudoku and beamed. "My babies! My wonderful lil' darlings! What are ya'll doing here?"

"Well, it's the 25th Mama," answered Minxy- slowly.

Catherine thought for a minute. "The 25th? That can't be right. Are you sure?"

"It's true Mama. We're positive," said Kay.

"That means it's my birthday!"

Lou Anna looked at both her sisters, confused. "Yes. Why do you think we're all dressed up? Your dinner is today."

Catherine adjusted her glasses and sat up higher in bed. "Oh yes! You look so nice, all three of you! Come; stand out in front, one a time so I can see you twirl- like we used to for daddy before we left the house. Remember that? He always had to make sure we looked like ladies, wasn't showing off too much skin."

"We haven't done that since we were little children," said Kay, feeling a bit awkward her mother's nostalgic request.

"I know that. It'll still be fun. Come on, twirl for your Mama. Why are ya'll acting all scared?"

"We're scared you'll bite again today like you did the last time we came," Lou Anna mumbled.

Catherine scrambled to remember. "Last time? What did I do, babies? What did I say? I'm sorry, loves. I'm so sorry," said Catherine- tearing up- genuinely having no recollection of her brutality.

Minxy sighed and handed Kay her purse and the flowers. She stepped out, held her arms out and spun around slowly. "I decided on purple today, Mama. This shade reminds me of that ribbon I was wearing our last family picture before daddy died. You tried all my life to get me in a pair of opened-toed heels. It's your day so I thought I'd bother to polish my toes."

Catherine smiled, pleased. "-Beautiful Minx."

Minxy stepped back and took her purse back from Kay. Kay stepped up and twirled. "You can never go wrong with a little black dress- that's what you always told me. That and to never be afraid to wear black outside a funeral. Lissima gave me this fancy clutch, it matches the pearls. I've been looking for an excuse to wear them. Are the pearls too much?"

"No baby, they're just enough. You know, that scarf…"

"…Can double as a shawl if I get chilly," finished Kay.

"I taught you well, daughter," said Catherine. Kay stepped back. Lou Anna removed her cardigan and stepped up. She didn't say a word. "…White," said Catherine.

Lou Anna folded her arms. "Predictable right, Mama?" she said- looking at the floor, prepared for an insulting critique.

"No one wears white the way you do, Lou. They should retire the color and name it Lou Anna," said Catherine. Her kindness shocked all three of her children.

"Thank you, Mama."

"You're welcome, child?" Catherine wiped her eyes and collected her emotions. "Well, what ya'll waiting for? Come on, put that suit on me. I want all eyes on me when I get home."

•

Lincoln's hand accidentally touched Bellissima's hand as they positioned the table in the shade of the tree. She looked up at him with rosy cheeks. "I think this spot is perfect," she stuttered.

"I agree," said Lincoln. "What's next?"

"We should go ahead and lay the placemats down. Then we need to haul out the chairs from the shed; I'll get them."

"You most certainly will not. I came early to help, and I intend to do just that."

Bellissima grinned, smitten. "I appreciate this a lot. It's a hard habit to break- taking care of everything on my own. I'm not used to help."

"Maybe it's time to change that," said Lincoln- heading to the shed for the chairs.

Bellissima hadn't heard Sadie and Dria approaching with the plates. "I can smell the repressed sexual tension from all the way from in the house," said Sadie- jeering.

"It's rude to spy on people," said Bellissima.

"You've known me long enough to know that I operate under my own set of morals," said Sadie- carefully setting the plates down.

"I wish you'd pay closer attention so you could see the way he looks at you," said Dria.

"At the risk of sounding like a sperm bucket, I'll admit- I've had a lot of men in and out of my life. They came and stayed long enough to fulfill their purpose, no more than a few hours. It's safe to say I know what a part-time lover looks like. He doesn't look like a part-time lover," Sadie added.

"You've only seen him twice now. You really think you've seen enough of him to know what kind of lover he is?" asked Bellissima.

"Seeing him more than once without a selfish motive is enough to tell the difference. I knew he was different the minute I read that card you dropped out of your pocket. It was more than just a poem. You always hear about how people fell in love, but I've never seen it happen right before my very eyes."

"You read my card? We're going to have to have a talk about boundaries in this family!"

"Relax, we didn't show it to Auntie Kay. She'd be planning your wedding right now if we had. I was nice enough to slip it back in your pocket after Mama and Auntie Minxy read it," said Dria.

"You people are unbelievable," Bellissima mumbled.

"He's the kind of guy who sticks around to fix tables, lifts things for you, creates perfect moments to snap perfect pictures so you won't forget them and brings you flowers. Me, no. I'm the girl you rent by the hour. You're worth investing in," said Sadie. "He's a good man Lissima. You know you deserve that, right?"

"Deserve what?" asked Bellissima.

"Goodness. Good things," Sadie replied. She stared at Bellissima before hugging her tight. Sadie let go and wiped her eyes. "I'm sorry. I've been extra sensitive lately."

"Don't apologize for hugging me. I can never have too many of those from you," said Bellissima, pulling her back into another embrace.

Sadie looked over Bellissima's shoulder and her happiness faded. "Oh hell no!" she yelled.

"What?" asked Bellissima- turning back to find Emily and Colin approaching.

Dria took a deep breath and clenched her fist. "Lord give me patience and not strength. With more strength I just might strangle her," She grumbled.

"You don't look happy to see us," said Emily with a fake smile.

"- And here I was thinking we were doing a good job at hiding our true feelings. We're so bad at being plastic. We feel how we feel and tend to let it show proudly," said Sadie.

"Hello, Colin. I'm glad you could make it," said Bellissima; sincerely chivalrous.

Emily glared at Colin who was busy ogling Dria and then back at the Beaumonte' granddaughters. "Well aren't you happy to see me too?" she asked.

"You poor little oblivious thing. I believe it was the great Oscar Wilde who said: *'Some cause happiness wherever they go. Some cause happiness whenever they go.'* She better be housebroken, Colin," said Sadie.

Emily sighed, "Okay, I get it. The last time we were all together, things were a bit tense; but don't you think we should put all our petty differences aside; so we can celebrate in harmony?"

"Don't pretend like you came here with good intentions. If you think our mothers are going to sell you this land, you're crazier than you look. And if you think they're going to discuss that kind of business with you today, you're a lot dumber than you look. If you truly cared about this event, you would've stayed home," said Dria.

"I care," said Colin. "I did ask Emily to stay home for the sake of peace..."

"-But then we decided against that, as husband and wife. Where one of us goes, the other should be welcomed. If there's such a place or occasion where we're not both welcomed, neither of us should be at that place or occasion," interrupted Emily.

"Is that what you were going to say, Colin?" asked Sadie.

"No," he replied- looking down. "I'd be more than happy to leave Mrs. Catherine's gift and take Emily home."

Bellissima sighed. "No, that won't be necessary. We're still happy to have you, Colin and if you staying means Emily has to stay then we will have to adjust our expectation of comfort. You're like family and you'll be seated and served as such just as your family would sit and feed one of us."

"Is there anything we can do to help set up?" asked Emily.

"A good friend of mine, Lincoln, is in the shed getting chairs. Colin, would you mind helping him?" asked Bellissima.

"I'm on it. Thank you for your candor." Colin kissed Bellissima's cheek and headed for the shed, rolling up his sleeves.

"-And me, Lissima?" asked Emily. "What can I do to help? I'm at your disposal."

"I wish I could shove her down the disposal," whispered Sadie.

"You can stay out here with Sadie and do whatever she tells you to do," Bellissima replied. Bellissima turned to Dria. "Dria, let's go check on the main course."

The two of them turned, headed for the kitchen. Emily cleared her throat, "Actually, I'd like a minute alone with Alexandria. Do you mind if you and I swop duties, Bellissima?"

Bellissima's face turned red and she slowly stepped into Emily's personal space. "Her. Name. Is. Dria. That's the last time one of us is going to remind you nicely. Your bullshit will not be tolerated today. Do you hear me? I may be quiet when you see me strolling around town but make no mistake- I become the worst Beaumonte' that ever lived when you mess with my family." Bellissima's heavy breathing startled Emily a bit and she swallowed her discomfort.

Dria grabbed Bellissima's shoulder as if to calm her. "It's alright, Lissima. You stay out here with Sadie and finish up the fancy stuff. Emily can come inside with me," she said coolly.

"You sure about that?" asked Sadie.

"Oh yes," Dria replied.

Colin tapped on the opened shed door. "You must be Lincoln. Lissima said you could use some help with these chairs."

"I never turn down a helping hand," Lincoln replied.

Colin held his hand out for Lincoln to shake. "The name's Colin, nice to meet you."

Lincoln loaded Colin's arms with a stack of chairs. "You a friend of Lissima's too?" he asked.

Colin laughed. "No man. I'm a friend of the whole family." Colin hung his head. "I *used* to be real good friends with Dria. The tall one."

Lincoln could tell by the look on Colin's face that there was more to their story than just friendship. He looked around before asking, "It used to be love wasn't it?" asked Lincoln- feeling sorry for a man he barely knew.

"Is it that obvious?" asked Colin. Lincoln nodded. "Yeah, it was love for sure. Make sure you don't let things turn past tense with Lissima. Learn from my mistake. There's something special about these Beaumonte' women."

CHAPTER TWENTY-NINE

"Whatever ya'll cooking sure smells scrumptious! Forgive me if I start drooling," said Emily- following closely behind Dria; trying not to touch any kitchen surfaces, as if they were germ-ridden. Emily pulled a napkin from her purse and wiped her seat before sitting.

"-Bitches drool," mumbled Dria- sliding on the oven mitts.

"I beg your pardon," Emily replied.

"-Dogs, female ones- they're bitches. And you know, dogs drool," snapped Dria, bending over to check the venison.

Dria's bosom sat up high in her dress and her heels made her at least 4 inches taller, drawing even more attention to her perfect calves. Emily, involuntarily, examined Dria's ample backside. "I was the cheerleader back in high school. You were-"

"-Geeky?" finished Dria.

"Geeky- that's such a juvenile slur."

"Yes, I know. That's why I used it. If anyone can relate to juvenile things- It's you. Juvenile, immature...callow."

"A scholar- that's what you were. How you managed to keep your ass tighter than mine, a natural athlete, I'll never know," said Emily tilting her head to the side for a better look.

Dria straightened her posture, closed the oven hatch and removed the mitts. "Don't think you're fooling anyone, Emily. We all know why you're here."

"I'm here for Cat," replied Emily- unconvincingly sincere.

"Have you no respect for your elders? You will call her Mrs. Catherine Beaumonte' or Mrs. Beaumonte' – that will suffice. Only her loved ones call her Cat. You want to help me check on the food, huh? Such bullshit! Why don't you just tell truth? You wanted to see what the kitchen looks

266

like, maybe snap a few pictures, so you can dream up some remodel plans for a property you ain't never gon' get your pedicured claws on. Let me guess, you need to pee now? That way you'll have a reason to go to the bathroom, maybe linger upstairs- snoop around? I bet you're hiding a mini tape measure in your bag."

"I'm insulted, honestly," gasped Emily.

"Save it! You've been a bad actor since drama club, nothing's changed."

Emily clutched her heart, "Would it kill you to be nice?"

"I'd rather kill you than be nice."

"I didn't come to scope out any prospects!"

"I'm wrong? Then maybe you came to keep an eye on Colin, make sure he keeps his eyes off of me?" asked Dria with a sneer.

It was as if Dria had spat in Emily's face. Emily stood and slowly approached Dria. "I know you and Colin used to have a thing for each other a long time ago. I know you'd like to believe that it meant something. When you're young and in love, you see what you want to see," she said insultingly sympathetic. "I hate to be the one to tell you, but Colin and I had chemistry even way back then. Our attraction, it was like the pull of an invisible thread. You think he's stealing glances at you after all these years? He stole plenty glances behind your back when we were younger, always checking me out. Cheerleaders end up with guys like Colin. You think I'm suddenly worried about my marriage just because one of Colin's old groupies waltzed back in town? I won't deny it, I want this house. I want this land, but not just to add it to my long list of conquests. Once it's all mine, you won't have a reason to ever come back here again and try to stir up feelings that no longer exist." Dria could see the worry whelming in her eyes behind her hale disposition.

Dria laughed, throwing her head back. "Be careful Emily. Your insecurities are showing." She stepped into Emily's face. "You better cover that up before some see's just how bothered you really are."

Sadie and Bellissima entered the kitchen, both of them studied Dria's militant stance. Bellissima took off her earrings, mumbling vulgarities.

"Everything okay in here?" asked Sadie.

Dria and Emily never broke eye contact. "Everything in here is just fine, meat's looking good. You can put your earrings back on, Lissima.

Emily was just about to go to the bathroom to do some measuring and conceal some things while she's up there."

Dria's explanation confused her cousins. "...You mean put on some more concealer, like makeup?" asked Bellissima.

"If I had her face, I'd want to cover it as much as possible too," jeered Sadie.

"No makeup. She has other things to cover up. Come now, help me gather the rest of these candles and champagne flutes. We must finish setting up. Colin and Lincoln might need a hand. I feel the sudden urge to park my perfect ass in a chair. I bet there's a gentleman out there still willing to pull out a girl's chair for her. Good southern manners- you know how I like that?" said Dria strutting.

Once Sadie and Dria were gone, Bellissima looked at Emily from head to toe and laughed. "Something funny?" asked Emily.

"It's just something my granny said," answered Bellissima.

"What's that, your granny said,' asked Emily annoyed.

"It takes more than a painted face and a slim waist..."

•

Bellissima took a step back and looked at the outside venue she and her cousins put together. "Oh wow," she whispered. "Dria! Sadie! Come look!" she beckoned.

Dria and Sadie stood beside Bellissima. "Did <u>we</u> do all this? It looks like something out of one of those garden magazines!" exclaimed Sadie.

"Get closer, I'll take a picture," said Lincoln.

The Beaumonte' grandchildren pressed their faces together and smiled big. "Cheese!"

"That's a perfect picture if I ever saw one," said the Pastor; who'd arrived with a fistful of mauve balloons.

"Preacher! You came!" said Bellissima- rushing over into his waiting embrace.

"The devil swelled my old knee up the size of a ripe honeydew melon last night, but I prayed and asked the Good Lord to shrink it back down and look! Ain't I walking just fine! Even if I had to wobble down here with a cane, I wouldn't have missed this blessed occasion! Thank God for that blessed oil your Mama brought down to the church this past Sunday."

Sadie's eyes got big as she recalled the bacon grease fiasco. "We're so glad you could make it!" she said nervously snatching the balloons from his grasp. "I'll tie these to Grandma Cat's chair."

"Am I late?" yelled Otis.

"No! you're right on time!" said Dria.

Otis took a long hard look at Dria. "Boy, I tell you, If I wasn't scared your Grandfather's ghost would haunt me dead and I wasn't twice your age…"

"-Twice her age? Who are you kidding, you old buzzard? More like three times her age!" said Ora- causing everyone to laugh. She shuffled in with her faithful daughter by her side, carrying an oversized bear with a huge ribbon. She kissed everyone's cheek, even Lincoln's. He pulled out Ora's chair for her. "I thought all the gentleman died off. I'm so pleased there's still a few left."

"Please everyone, come and sit. Make yourselves comfortable. They'll be back with Grandma Cat real soon! I'll get you all something cool to drink!" said Bellissima who'd paused for a minute to watch everyone mingling. Lincoln and Bellissima's eyes met and he smiled at her gently.

More locals arrived, bearing festive gifts. There wasn't one empty chair at the table. While they waited; everyone laughed- telling stories about who Catherine used to be.

"I've had some unruly hellions under my wing, but none more boisterous than Catherine Beaumonte'. She sure caused her fair share of chaos, but I challenge you to find a more caring individual. The good book says that love covers a multitude of sin. Behind every outrageous act, there was deep seeded love to blame for her actions," said Pastor.

Ora's daughter held a drinking glass to her mother's lips to moisten her voice. "I first met Catherine in the grocery store. I must have looked so pathetic to her, standing in the soup aisle- crying. Have mercy on me, she stopped to see if I was alright. My husband, rest his soul, told me as nicely as he could- '*a wife should be able to nourish her husband.*' I married young, most all of us did. Back then women thought sharing last names and wearing a ring meant we'd won. I thought my work was done, that

I'd done enough to make him love me for life. No, marriage is a blessing that requires maintenance just like every other good thing in life that you want to keep working. I couldn't boil a pot of water if my life depended on it. Catherine told me to follow her back here, to the big house. She took me in that kitchen and made two big pots of red beans with pork sausage. Every time I close my eyes and think if Cat, I remember how sweet the Caribbean rice smelled. Her baby girl, Kay helped. When the food was done, she walked it out to my car and we strapped it down in the back seat. Catherine told me to rush home before my husband got off from the mill, add a cup of water and put the pot on the stove with the fire low. *'This is one of my favorite pots, you make sure you bring it back tomorrow- you hear?'* My husband was so pleased. She'd saved my marriage, kept my family together. I came back the next day to return the pot. When I got here, Catherine was waiting at the screen door with an apron. *'I'm afraid I lied to you. I don't really care for that pot as much as I led on. You could have kept it, but I had to get you back here somehow. Strap this apron on. The Lord will forgive us for pulling the wool over your husband's eyes that one time; but we're not going to make a habit of it. Everything he eats from now on will be made by you. I'm going to teach you how.'* A friendship formed between us over time. I went from emptying a can of cold corned beef in a bowl for my husband to nourishing the man I loved with my heart and soul. I wonder if she really understands what that meant to me?"

"I don't mean to brag, but I had a lot of floozies in my day. It was nice throughout my twenties, but it got old fast, you know? Hopping from one bed to the next. I didn't start thinking about the future until I met Jeremiah. I thought love was all about the flesh until I saw the way he kissed Catherine. They had the real thing. He always said that loving Catherine was easy because of who she was."

Bellissima looked down at her phone and read Lou Anna's text. She quickly stood. "They're 3 minutes away! Everybody on your feet!"

The party guests stood, and they waited anxiously. Lou Anna, Kay and Minxy hopped out of the car first and then Kay helped a blindfolded Catherine out of the backseat. "Watch your step, Mama," she ushered.

"Oh hell, child! I already know there's a party here waiting for me! Take this damn rag off my face so I can act surprised!" Catherine grunted. Lou Anna rolled her eyes and snatched the blindfold.

"Surprise!" yelled everyone- cheering and clapping.

Catherine looked at her daughters and grinned. "Is all this fuss for little old me?"

Dria, Bellissima, and Sadie all hugged Catherine at once and they helped her to her chair where her guests took turns kissing her forehead.

Dria cleared her throat. "Now that our lovely grandmother is here, we'd like to start serving. Pastor, before we start, would you be so kind as to say a prayer?"

The Preacher stood. "Young lady, I'd be honored. I'm going to ask that everyone bow their head and join hands with your neighbor." Everyone joined hands, everyone except for Colin and Emily. "Living to be hundred years old; it's an accomplishment Christians read about in the old testament. If it ain't illness, its unnecessary violence or senseless evil snatching away God's people. It's a miracle to live past 18 years old these days. It's truly an honor to celebrate the many years of our sister in Christ, Catherine Beaumonte'. God has made your life a living testament by increasing your number over and over again. Happy Birthday and Amen!"

Sadie entered the big house and returned with a tray. "Your appetizer this evening is a hot ramekin of gouda and provolone macaroni and cheese topped with pancetta and almond slivers." Bellissima surveyed her mother's face; pleased to see that Kay was impressed.

Lou Anna was the first to take a bite. "Well..." she lingered.

"Well, what?" questioned Dria- nervous.

"It's absolutely piquant," Lou Anna replied.

"It's unlike anything I've ever tasted," complimented Colin.

Emily rolled her eyes," It's simple mac and cheese. I make it for you all the time at home," she snapped.

"But this mac and cheese is actually edible," replied Colin.

Without looking up from her dish, Kay interpolated. "Little girl, you're barely welcome here. Mind your manners. You should eat. You're less inclined to partake in conversation if your mouth is full."

Emily took a bit of her pasta. It was, in fact, delicious; but she refused to admit it. "It's okay, I guess. What else is on the menu?"

"Next, we'll be having an escarole salad with scallops, for your palette cleanser this evening- frozen blackberries in a fresh strawberry puree;

leading up to the main course- 16 hour marinated broiled venison served with a variety of Southern side dishes. Cake, pie and hand churned sorbet follow." The dinner guests began to applaud.

"You have any other questions, dear?" asked Catherine- giving Emily a heart-stopping glare.

"No," mumbled Emily.

"It's no mam, Emily," snapped Colin- clearly tired of having to remind Emily to show respect.

"You all eat up, now," said Kay smiling.

Emily heaved and turned to Minxy. "Could you pass the champagne please?" she asked. Everyone at the dinner table stopped and stared at Minxy, which caused her to stare back at them. Then Minxy turned to Emily. "What?" questioned Emily.

Minxy calmly put down her spoon and wiped her mouth with Emily's napkin instead of her own. "I used to have a little problem with alcohol. That's what. Thank you for creating this very uncomfortable scene." Minxy grabbed the champagne bottle gave it to Sadie. "Sweetheart, will you please pour everyone a glass?" she asked, reaching for her own glass. Sadie watched as Minxy turned her own champagne flute upside down and grabbed her spoon again. "None for me though. I gave that up for something more important. I'll wet my throat when the lemonade makes its way around the table," said Minxy pinching Sadie's cheek.

"I'd be happy to Mama," Sadie replied- cutting her eyes at Emily.

The birthday dinner was in full swing. People were laughing. The food was phenomenal, even Kay said so. Most importantly, Catherine was happy.

After the main course, the Beaumonte' grandchildren gathered in the kitchen to ready the cake. "We better hurry, the wind is picking up. The sun's hiding again," said Sadie.

"It's not going to storm! It's not going to rain!" yelled Bellissima- again.

"Yes, we heard you; but the wind *is* picking up rather you acknowledge it or not. These cheap candles aren't going to work," said Dria.

"I think I saw some sparklers in the shed," said Sadie.

"-Sparklers?" replied Dria and Sadie simultaneously.

"Yeah, they've probably been in there since that New Years when we lost Cheniere; but I'm sure they'll still spark a bit."

"You want to put fireworks on our Grandmother's cake?"

"You got a better idea?" asked Sadie with her hands on her hips.

Dria looked at Bellissima and Bellissima looked down at the cheap wax candles.

CHAPTER THIRTY

"Happy birthday to you! Happy birthday to you! Happy birthday dear Catherine!" sang the Beaumonte' grandchildren, emerging from the big house with sparklers flaming. Everyone stood again. Colin and Lincoln helped Catherine to her feet and Pastor helped Colin keep Catherine on her feet while Lincoln snapped pictures. They placed the cake down in front of Catherine. She blew once. She blew twice. She blew three times but couldn't extinguish the sparklers. Sadie snatched the sparkler stems from the icing and put them out in a pitcher of tea. Everyone clapped and Bellissima cut a corner piece for her Grandmother. She turned to Dria. "Lemon?"

"Yeah. Lemon pudding cake with French Vanilla icing," confirmed Dria.

"I was sure you'd get marble with chocolate icing- that's your favorite."

"Yeah but you and Grandma love lemon," said Dria- nudging Bellissima playfully.

"I'm not watching my weight, Lissima! It's my day! Cut me a piece bigger than that!" demanded Catherine.

"I think now's a good time," whispered Minxy to Lou Anna.

Lou Anna reached under the table and took out a stack of flat boxes. "Attention all! We'd first like to thank you all for coming today. We don't get together much, these days. Life gets in the way. We get in our own way. Having you all come out to celebrate with us, it means the world to us." Lou Anna looked over at Kay and then back at Minxy. "Mama, you gave me two of the best sisters a girl could ask for. We might not always act like it, but we're blessed to have come from your belly. We have a gift for you, but first we have a little something for our daughters." Kay gave a

274

box to each of them. "Yesterday our children challenged us to compete in the Cal-Cam fair obstacle course."

"Did you accept?" asked Ora.

"Girls, open your gifts so your grandmother can see," said Kay.

Dria was the first to completely rip her box open. Inside she found a yellow tank top. Her face lit up. "-Yellow shirts!"

Bellissima opened her box and held her shirt up over her own torso. "-Just like the ones Cheniere picked out the year we won," she said- touched by the sentiment.

"Challenge accepted!" yelled Minxy, prompting more applause.

Kay reached into her purse and pulled out a large yellow envelope. "There's also this," she said- handing the envelope over to Dria. She kissed Dria's forehead. "Open it and read it, dear," she whispered.

Dria did just that and she clutched her heart. "You're giving us the big house and the land?" she asked- eyes wide.

"What?" asked Bellissima- grabbing the paperwork as if to make sure Dria had read it correctly.

"What?" questioned Sadie, again.

"Are you kidding me?" mumbled Emily to herself- chugging more champagne.

Catherine reached for the papers and adjusted her glasses. She looked over at her daughters, who were smiling at their daughters. Then, she fixed her heated glare on the documents. "Those original papers were fixed so that you and your sisters would get all me and your father worked for. You went and had papers drawn up to forfeit your birthright after I pass? You don't want all this?"

Lou Anna looked at her sisters and then back at her mother. "Of course, we want it; but we talked it over and we think it's better this way. Consider it a shortcut, we ain't as young as we feel. It's bound to end up theirs more sooner than later."

Catherine then stared at Kay. "I made you power of attorney because I trusted you more than my oldest. You go link arms with Lou Anna and do this without talking to me. Your father and I worked hard- tending to the crops. We fought every racist realtor that knocked on our door. We rode out every storm came our way. We took on every termite that threatened

275

this houses' structure. And you just pass on it? I'll die knowing I will have left our children nothing."

"Nothing? How can you think that Mama?" asked Minxy. "You left us more than you could ever imagine. You sacrificed so much for us and you raised us right. We're taking our cue from you, we're giving more to our daughters than we'd dare take for ourselves."

Catherine didn't respond. Her breathing was heavier, and her hands were shaking even more than before now. Lou Anna slid a smaller box in front of Catherine. "It's your turn now, Mama. Go on! Open it!" she urged.

Catherine's hands trembled as she reached for the box and slowly ripped it open. Inside there was a ring- chrysoberyl and corundum stones on a rose gold band. Everyone expected joy but instead, Catherine frowned. "What is this? What have you done?"

"What do you mean? Mama, it's a ring. It's your birthday gift from us, your daughters."

"A ring, yes! I can see that! Why are you giving it to me?"

Lou Anna was confused. "Mama, this ring has been designed just for you. These yellow stones are rare, from other countries- like the ones Minxy's been traveling to, changing the world. It cannot be replicated. There will never be another one just like it. You can't run the race with us, we thought it'd be nice for you to have something to match our shirts. You can sport the same colors as your family."

"-Sport the same colors!" yelled Catherine- grabbing the shirt out of Bellissima's hands and ripping it down the middle. Bellissima gasped and her bottom lip quivered as she fought to hold back tears. The familiar lost look was back. "I know what this is," mumbled Catherine. "You want to replace the wedding ring Jeremiah gave me. You think if I put this on, it will break the curse!"

Trying to salvage the mood, Pastor interjected. "I don't think that's what they meant by giving you this lovely, thoughtful gift."

Catherine picked up the ring and threw it across the table. "You get that away from me! It's upsetting them! Don't you hear it?" she shrieked.

Lincoln stepped back and allowed Lou Anna to near Catherine's side. "Hear what Mama?"

"Your father! And Cheniere! And that devil you dumped there! A burning bridge. A drowning. A murder."

"Mama, that's enough. You're embarrassing yourself in front of all these good people," whispered Lou Anna.

Catherine struck Lou Anna across the face. "Stop pretending like you don't hear them crying! You gave them false hope! You let them think that they'd be freed if I put on that imitation!"

Minxy rushed over and stood between her mother and her sister. "Do not hit her again!" she warned.

"She is my child! I will hit her as much as I please!"

"Well, she's my sister and I say no more!" countered Minxy. Lou Anna wasn't used to either of her sisters standing up for her. She stood in awe, astonished by Minxy's bravery, holding her throbbing cheek.

"You been traveling the world so long, you forget yourself? I brought you into this world and I'll take you out! You think you don't have to show me the proper respect anymore?" asked Catherine.

"I don't think that's what Minxy meant by asking you to stop the violence," said Pastor- again, trying to defuse the situation.

"You just know what everyone means, don't you?" yelled Catherine.

"No Catherine. I'd never claim to know every reason behind what a man or woman does. Only God knows that. I'm just an old friend, a teacher appointed by Him to protect his people from further damning themselves and hurting the people that love them," answered Pastor.

"Lies! No one here loves me! I have no friends! I have no family either! The bridge took some and the rest are right here at this table deceiving me! Everything and Everyone- nothing but salty lies! Only the truth will save us!" she rambled- in a confused state. "We should all be telling the truth."

"I've been living a lie! I'm an unhappy man in an unhappy marriage! There's no love in this union because I've never stopped loving Dria Beaumonte'," declared Colin.

Everyone at the dinner table gasped. "I knew it," mumbled Lou Anna- grinning. "Written in the stars."

The Pastor pulled his abridged bible from his coat pocket, "Oh my good Lord," he mumbled. "Young man, some confessions are better verbalized to God in prayer or to our loved ones in private, behind closed doors. I'm not sure Mrs. Catherine meant for us to all air our dirty laundry..." The

Pastor, realizing his own repetitive method, turned back to Catherine. "…
Is that what you meant?" second-guessing her intentions.

Emily slammed her napkin on the table and stood. "What the hell did
you just say, Colin?"

Colin apologized to Emily but never took his eyes off Dria. "I'm sorry.
It's hard for you to hear, I know, but it's been even harder to endure."
Colin looked down at the ring the Beaumonte' daughters had intend for
Catherine. He fished it out of the potato salad and looked to Dria's mother,
Lou Anna. "Is it alright?" he asked.

"Yes," she replied.

Emily's faced turned tens shades of red as she watched Colin leave her
side, walk over to Dria and kneel at her feet. "I'm sure it's not religiously
binding and all; saying as how I haven't made my leaving Emily official;
but will you look at the stars with me for the rest of our lives?"

"I wouldn't look at them with anyone else but you," Dria replied.

Colin placed the ring on Dria's finger, and she fell to her knees where
she and Colin's lips met with a belated fervor. Everyone clapped.

"Get your God-damned lips off my husband!"

The Reverend started sweating. "Please don't bring the Lord into this
mess," he prayed; but Emily's rage grew more ferocious.

She pulled at Colin's shirt collar. "Get your black ass up! Now! I
own you!"

Her poor choice of words offended everyone in attendance. "-Own
him? Like he's your slave?" asked Ora's daughter.

Emily, suddenly realizing everyone around her was of color or
mixed with more than one ethnicity, stuttered. "No. No. I meant like
marriage-ownership."

"Sure, you did," replied Colin- incredulously.

Emily threw a tantrum- stomping her feet and yelling. "We are leaving!
Right now! You're my husband! Do you understand me? Alexandria ain't
nothing but her daddy's leftovers!" Before anyone could rebuke Emily,
Bellissima swung her fist and struck Emily to the ground. She got up
slowly, wiping the blood from her nose and lip. "My lawyer takes assault
cases too! Best lawyer good green money can buy."

Bellissima turned to Dria who was smiling back at her. "Your lawyer
ain't better than mine. She takes my cases for free and she always wins," she

replied. Lincoln, both impressed and turned on by Bellissima's gallantry, casually wrapped a few ice cubes in a napkin and gave it to Bellissima to pad her knuckles.

Colin cleared his throat and grabbed his jacket. "Speaking of lawyers, you know any good divorce attorneys in the city?"

"Good? No. I know some great ones dying to do me a favor," said Dria.

"Good, we'll be sending them all wedding invites before the ink is dry on these divorce papers," replied Colin. "Emily, let's go! I want your things out of my Mama's house! The sooner you're gone, the sooner I can change the locks! It'll be me and Dria's summer home from now on! She'll be wanting to visit the family more often now that she owns Southern dirt."

"That took some heart," said Catherine, pointing at Colin's truck as they drove away. "This family lacks that. I see that now."

Kay shook her head in disbelief. "How can you be so ungrateful? Look around Mama! You're surrounded by nothing but love at a party your family worked their asses off to pull together!"

"Ain't no party 'gon break the curse!" shouted Catherine.

"Again, with this curse nonsense? Grandma this has to stop! Can't you see what it's doing to us! All this bitterness, all this secrecy- we've turned into ruins ourselves! Just like those burnt pieces of the bridge left over down there in the river! Weren't their deaths enough? Now we're ruining ourselves! We don't even know how to love each other anymore or how to tell the truth!" yelled Sadie. "Well, I'm not going to let tragedy and fear turn me into a deceitful, bitter person. I have something to say. I'm…"

"-She's leaving school," finished Bellissima- grabbing Sadie's hand tight, trying to be supportive.

Dria's face twisted, confused. "-Leaving school? That's not her secret. She's pregnant!"

"What?" gasped Bellissima and Lou Anna.

"That's not *really* a secret. Anybody with a nose can smell that bun baking," said Minxy- nonchalant.

Kay and Sadie turned to Minxy. "You knew?"

"You insult my intelligence by thinking I couldn't figure that one out on my own. I knew long before I found this pregnancy test all the way at the bottom of the wastebasket. Why are you still peeing on sticks? You're at least three or four months along! What, were you just making sure the baby was still in there hanging out? Where do think it's going to go?" Minxy replied, tossing the pregnancy test onto the table.

"I don't think we're going to be taking any leftovers home, not with a dirty pee stick on the table with the food," mumbled Ora's daughter.

"If you already knew Sadie was pregnant, why did you make me feel so bad for keeping it from you?" asked Kay.

"Because you're my sister and Sadie is *my* child. It's not right for you to keep something that big from me. It's just like Lou Anna and Lissima keeping things from you. It's not right."

Bellissima glared at Lou Anna. "You told Auntie Minx about the city?"

Before Lou Anna could answer, Kay, pulled out the prescription and laid it on the table. "You're right Minxy. With that being said, I think I'm owed an explanation."

"Where did you find that, Mama? Were you snooping through my things?" asked Bellissima- mortified.

"Never mind how I got a hold of it! One of you, please explain to me why I had to find out about my daughter's mental health problems like this?"

Dria picked up the paper and read it. Her eyes widened. "Mama, what were you thinking? This drug is too strong for Lissima. This is what you would give a person who's on suicide watch, not someone suffering from night terrors! I'd like to think Lissima and I are equally messed up in the head. The low dose prescription I was prescribed by my therapist knocks me on my ass and its candy compared to this!"

"You're seeing a therapist! Behind my back! I understand us not doing brunch or getting pedicures together, but this is your health we're talking about! Not only am I your mother but I'm a trained, licensed professional! How can you keep a secret like that from me?" yelled Lou Anna.

"Don't jump on Dria! And neither of you have a right to look down your noses at us. We're good at secrets because we learned from the best. Any of you care to finally drop the names of our fathers? And while we're pointing fingers, will the dying Beaumonte' daughter please step forward!" yelled Sadie.

Everyone got quiet. "That's right! I got hungry and tired of stealing icing, so I thought I'd help myself to some tofu. I figured I'd smother it in hot sauce, hot sauce makes just about anything taste good. That's when I found these!" Sadie tossed the medications onto the table next to Bellissima's prescription and the pregnancy test. "So, which one of you has cancer?"

The Beaumonte' grandchildren stared at their mothers. Minxy and Kay seemed frankly shocked and saddened by Sadie's discovery. Sadie and Bellissima noticed Lou Anna's shame then they both looked at Dria. She started to cry. "You're the one aren't you, Mama? You're dying?" she asked.

"Everyone's dying Dria. I'm just getting there a little faster than most, now. I was going to tell you about all of this, Dria. Really I was…" Lou Anna tried to explain.

"-Glass houses, Lou Anna. The pot calling the kettle black- all that jazz. How could you not tell me this?" asked Dria before running into the big house.

"Do you see what the curse has done to us all?" said Catherine.

"Shut up!" Kay screamed. "There is no curse, Mama! There's only you. You're the plague- the reason everything is what it is now."

Bellissima grabbed her mother's shoulder. "You're upset Mama. You have to mind your blood pressure. Have a seat. I'll pour you a glass of water."

"No Lissima. It's been a long time coming. She needs to hear what I have to say," continued Kay. "It's called guilt, Catherine. This thing you've been using to avoid the truth. You can't take it, can you? You can't even say it out loud, can you? Daddy died trying to please his ungrateful wife. If he had kissed you goodbye before he left, there'd be no need for all your folklore. Your husband took his last breath holding the ring that should have been on your finger- the symbol of your everlasting devotion, gratitude, and trust. Trust- you sure spit that back in daddy's face. Can't you see what you sewed, Catherine? Your superstition, your drinking, your inability to own your faults! You're a fine mess yourself! It was easier to fabricate some make-believe justification for everything bad that ever happened to us, wasn't it? You're so quick to condemn us, make us feel bad for not having daddies around for our babies. Did you ever stop to think that we became incapable of love because of you? Even after it took my baby, you wouldn't let go. You're an insecure woman, Catherine Beaumonte'. Daddy was never stepping out on you."

"It's true," said Otis- hanging his head. "Jeremiah and me- we ran illegal hooch from state to state for a little extra money. He wasn't even supposed to be making drops that evening. I was laid up with one of the whores from Dougie's club. Dougie found out she was making house calls, making money on the side and said he'd shoot me dead next time he saw me. I asked Jeremiah to run my load for me, just until Dougie calmed down and I could square things away with him. Jeremiah agreed."

"That man would have done anything for us. He didn't want us to be another black family living in poverty; only he had a man-hating, impressionable, distrustful raging alcoholic for a wife. Instead of you having faith in the man you married- you made him feel like a common whoremonger. Then you planted that evil seed in us and our children. You made up some wild curse in your head and it rotted us all to the core; making us believe that some curse would make sure we were never happy. You planted that in my daughter's head. She's dead because of it. Do you know the worst part of it all? I tricked myself into believing there was a curse for a few years. I had to, just to get by, because I couldn't understand why all the pain? I stopped praying because of you."

Catherine didn't blink. She stood staring at Kay as if her daughter's defiance had broken her heart. "I want to lay down now," said Catherine.

Bellissima grabbed her grandmother's arm. "Come, Granny, I'll take you in the big house to rest."

Catherine pulled away hard. "No! I want to go home! Take me back to pennycress. This here ain't home no more. You were right, my children. This house, this land, this family- it's just another heap of ruins; just like you said. Pastor; help me to your truck and take me home please."

"Granny, I can drive you back," offered Bellissima.

"No!" yelled Catherine- pushing Bellissima away.

The whole family just stood there with opened wounds, saying nothing as the party guests climbed into their vehicles and drove away- mumbling. Bellissima looked at Lincoln. "Thank you for coming," she mumbled- before grabbing a bottle of merlot from the table and dashing through the fields with it.

"Lissima! Wait!" yelled Kay. It was too late, she was gone.

CHAPTER THIRTY-ONE

Bellissima walked the dark dirt road, all alone, using her cell phone for light. A vehicle approached from behind and slowed. "You know you left a perfectly good car back there," said Lincoln.

"I thought about taking it, but I had a lot of champagne. The last thing I need right now is a DUI," Bellissima replied. "Walking under the influence, is that a crime?"

"I don't think so, but even if it was- I wouldn't tell on you. Your secret's safe with me." Bellissima stopped walking and hung her head. "Things got a little rough back there," said Lincoln, empathetically.

"-Understatement of the decade," Bellissima mumbled- kicking a rock. "I wouldn't blame you if you decided to not know me. It was a pretty bad first date."

Lincoln grinned. "Are you kidding me? I had good food. I witnessed a proposal and I got to sit next to the prettiest southern bell in the whole wide world, your mother." Bellissima laughed. "And then there was you..." Bellissima blushed. "...I'm just happy you're calling it date," he said. "The bankers are really dragging their feet. Every time I call to see when someone's going to come out to let me in the house, I get put on hold until I finally hang up. I keep on calling, but it's the same thing. I'm beginning to think they're giving me the run around on purpose."

"Most bankers are crooks. They're probably just trying to wait you out; see if you get tired of asking for help and give up. That way, they can ransack all or your Grandfather's stuff and throw an estate sale- make money on the house and everything in it too."

"My thoughts exactly. That's why I was just going to break in there tonight," said Lincoln- holding up a crowbar. "You feel like breaking the law? I know the timing is bad, but is there ever a good time to commit a felony?"

"-Bad time? Actually, it's the perfect thing to get my mind off what's probably going to go down as the worst dinner party in history."

•

Minxy searched every room of the big house but couldn't find Sadie anywhere inside. She wasn't out back under the shade tree either. Minxy looked around out back and noticed the gate to the Beaumonte' place of resting had been unlocked.

Minxy ventured through the woods and wandered into the family plot, whispering greetings to her dead ancestors as she strolled by. *"-Excuse me, Aunt Pearl. Don't mind me Uncle Robert- just passing through. I lived past 30 Aunt Emogene- guess you're not always right."* She found Sadie sitting in the grass between Cheniere's grave and the stone Catherine had made over a corpse-less grave, marking the spot where Jeremiah Beaumonte' would have been buried if they'd found his body. She was holding her old fishbowl. Sadie looked up at her mother. "What kind of dummy can't keep a fish alive?" she asked- sullen.

Minxy sad down in the grass beside her daughter. She looked down in the bowl and discovered the fish had gone belly-up. "Don't be so hard on yourself. Goldfish aren't supposed to live forever."

"Can you imagine me with a baby? Probably wouldn't be able to keep it alive any longer than I kept this fish alive. What was God thinking, making me a mother?"

"You know just as well as any Christian- God don't make no mistakes," said Minxy.

"He has too much faith in me; thinking someone like me could be responsible for another human being- especially one so small and innocent and fragile."

"God don't *think* nothing! He only *knows* things."

"I <u>know</u> I have no idea what to do. I <u>know</u> I can't do this. I <u>know</u> I'm scared that this baby just might have an addict for a mother."

Minxy cupped Sadie's chin. "Do you <u>know</u> you're not alone?" she asked. "Any mother who tells you she wasn't scared shitless to become a mother is a damn liar. Even the women who appear to have it all together-education, money, faith, dedicated and a faithful husband. Being held accountable for the path of another little person is scary. Then, you give birth to your baby, meet them and then you feel a whole new fear- scared by how much you love them. You suddenly realize you'll do anything for them- even kill if you have to. Mother's aren't magical creatures- immune to mistakes. We're allowed to mess up too, long as you make it right with your kid and make it right with God."

"Is that why you got clean?"

"Yes. I saw myself for the disease I'd become. My behavior would have eventually killed you and I can't lose you, Sadie. You're my child and I love you."

"I love you too, Mama." Said Sadie- hugging her Mother.

"So, who's the father?" asked Minxy.

Sadie's face twisted. "Are you serious?" she asked- appalled. "Do you really expect me to answer you when you've never answered a single question about my daddy?'

Minxy huffed. "You're right. Well, I guess now is as good a time as any. Ask what you need to ask."

"Who was he? Did he see me at all after I was born? Is he still alive? Do you think he'll want to meet his grandchild? Was it love, between you and him?" rambled Sadie.

"He was an older friend of Lou Anna's who liked to party. I remember thinking, how on earth are you and Lou friends? She was a prude, even back then. He was smart like her, but he liked to party and mingle on the count of him being so…flamboyant," answered Minxy.

"Flamboyant?"

"That's the world they used back in the day. They had other words for his lifestyle, but none I care to repeat. They're all so ugly and disrespectful." Sadie still looked confused. "You need me to spell it out for you girl? He was gay!"

"My daddy was gay? Is that why he didn't stay around, because he was living a lie when he was with you?"

"Who said he was living a lie?" Sadie looked even more confused. Minxy clarified. "Your father never lied about who he was. For that reason, his family fed him with a long-handled spoon. They tolerated him, but they did not love him or treat him well. He came here, to the big house, as often as he could. He spent many-o-nights sleeping on the floor, here. Catherine didn't mind, she always had love for anyone who needed it. When he got a little older, he wanted kids. These were different times. Gay men were denied a lot of the rights these young folks take for granted. There was no domestic partnerships or same-sex couple adoptions. We got drunk, got to talking and humped for about two full minutes- just long enough for me get pregnant with you."

"So, what happened after you gave birth to me?"

"Nothing, which is exactly what we planned. I had a beautiful daughter who inherited his amazing DNA and he was free to galivant knowing no matter who he ended up with, his legacy would live on."

"All those laws are different now, did he adopt or surrogate, or make any other kids the old fashion way?"

"No. You're an only child on his end too."

"Did you love him like a woman loves a man- like romantically?"

"Hell no! I loved him like a buddy loves a buddy. And don't go feeling sorry for him, he was an attractive man who never hurt for attention from either sex. He broke a lot of hearts before me and I'm sure he broke a lot more after me. He was one of those people who loved to love people. I don't think he wasted a single day being sad about anything. His family disowned him when they saw he had a little twist in his walk, so he walked right out of their lives and never looked back. His friends were his family. He and I had an understanding. He wanted a piece of him to be on this earth long after he was dead and gone. He trusted me enough to give that to him."

"And what did you want, Mama?"

"I lived wildly, my dear. The rate I was going, I knew for sure I'd die young. I had an opportunity to make something beautiful to leave behind just like your father wanted."

"Is he dead?"

"Nope," answered Minxy, smiling.

"Do you still talk to him at all?"

"Every now and then? Before you ask, the answer is yes. He does want to be in your life."

"Then why isn't he?"

"That's on me. I told him I wouldn't allow it until I had a chance to change and tell you about all this myself. I didn't want you finding out like Dria did, have some stranger waltz up on you and demand your love. No. Those are how the real wounds get cut. I told him you'd hear it from me or not at all."

"Is he somewhere far from here?"

"Not far at all. He practices law right here in town. Lissima's car is parked up front. You up for a drive in all this wind?" asked Minxy.

"I sure am, Mama or should I say Grandma?" answered Sadie- smiling at her mother.

•

Dria sat on her Grandmother's bed wrapped up in the family quilt, with her back turned to the door. Lou Anna tapped and let herself in. "I'd like to be alone! Thank you!" shouted Dria, without turning around.

"I figured as much, but it's better to address sudden emotional strain while it's still fresh, confront it head-on before the emotional strain becomes a mental and emotional roadblock. Once those roadblocks are formed it's harder to get to the root of our issues because we bury them deep..."

"-You can cut than phyco-babble bullshit, Lou Anna. I'm not one of your loony patients," snapped Dria.

"Yes, I heard. You have a doctor and it ain't me. Your doctor; is he or she one of those shrinks who always blames the mother?" joked Lou Anna. Dria didn't laugh. Lou Anna sat down next to her daughter. "I don't know what to say, Dria. I never know what to say to you."

"How could you not tell me about this. I know you and I have built comfortable lives by keeping one another at a distance but this is just cruel, Lou Anna."

"I wanted to tell you, but Mama's condition worsened. On top of that, you were just starting to love me. We could finally be in the same room with one another. I didn't want to mess that up."

Dria turned to face her mother. "*I was just starting to love you?* I've always loved you, Mama," said Dria.

"You really mean that? It's so hard to tell sometimes. I know I don't make it easy for you to love me."

"You're my mother. You're extraordinarily flawed, Lou Anna Beaumonte'; but when you truly love someone, you're allowed to dislike things about them. That don't make you love them no less." Dria grabbed hold of her mother's hand. "How bad is this cancer?"

Lou Anna took a deep breath. "Not so bad that I need to go buy me a wig yet. Bad enough for me to tell my patients in the city to find someone healthier to lay their burdens on."

"You're going to retire, Mama?" asked Dria- worried.

"Don't look so sad, Cher. It'll give me more time to help my only daughter plan her wedding," said Lou Anna holding Dria's left hand up closer to her face. "You're going to be a beautiful bride. Finally! I don't know what took you two so long to reunite but thank the heavens and the stars!"

"The courthouse will do just fine," said Dria.

"It most certainly will not! Not for my child! Not for a Beaumonte'! It's customary for the bride's family to pay for the ceremony and I will do just that! I've had money stashed away for your wedding since you were 16 years old!"

"Really? I didn't know that!"

"Well, initially it was your college fund, but your grades were so good that people were throwing money at you left and right. I just had to wait for Colin to man up and claim the brightest star in the galaxy."

"You couldn't have known Colin and I would end up together," said Dria in disbelief.

"We've all known that," replied Lou Anna.

"All?" questioned Dria. "You, Auntie Kay and Auntie Minx?"

"-And Catherine. Hell, I even think Emily knew it- deep down."

Dria laughed; but then her smile faded. "I wish Grandpa Jeremiah was here to walk me down the aisle."

"Me too. But Don, your Godfather, has been waiting for this opportunity his whole life," said Lou Anna squeezing her daughter's hand, tight. "I heard what that devil, Emily, said down at the table- right before Bellissima socked her." Dria hung her head. Lou Anna lifted her chin. "*Leftovers?* If Lissima hadn't hit her, I would have wrapped my hands around her neck and I wouldn't have let go until her soul wasn't here on earth no more. I hope you never thought that of yourself. *Leftovers.* I know you have questions about your father. I wish I could say I never told you about him because I didn't want you to start hurting all over again, but that's not entirely true. I felt so guilty for not protecting you. I never spoke his name to you because *I* didn't want to start hurting even more than I already do." Lou Anna took another deep breath and looked Dria in the eye. "Your father was a man who had an unhealthy, malevolent attraction to little children. Your Grandmother opened my eyes to it and at first, I did not want to believe it. When I accepted it, I cut him out of our life. I did, you have to believe me. He came back again and took advantage of your need to know who he was. I left you vulnerable to his wicked will. He knew I'd left too many blanks and he wanted you to believe he'd come back to fill in those blanks but no. He came to prey on you. What happened, it wasn't your fault. Your father did not soil you, he did not ruin you. You are not his leftovers. When we found out what he'd done to you, we searched for him. We wanted him to pay."

"Did you find him?" asked Dria.

"Oh yes," answered Lou Anna eerily.

"Is he in jail? Is that why he never bothered us again after that?"

"No, but justice was served, Dria. I want you to know that."

"How was it served if he's out there in the world somewhere free? He could be hurting other children."

"Your father is not free, Dria. He's not hurting any other children and he's not just somewhere in the world."

"You know exactly where he is, don't you Mama?"

"Yes. It was the perfect place to leave him. A place with so many sunken bones, that no one would ever be able to sort his."

Dria's heart started beating faster. "He's dead?"

"Yes, child."

Dria swallowed hard. "Did you kill him?"

"You're my lawyer, Dria. Sometimes it's best for clients to keep their counsel in the dark about things that may challenge their ethical ability to represent, if representation in a court of law were ever necessary," answered Lou Anna.

"I see," said Dria nodding. "What if I asked you again, but this time as your daughter and not your lawyer?"

"I'd say I failed you many times, but Mama took care of that boogeyman who stole your childhood away. He ain't under your bed. He ain't in your closet. He's under the river now."

Dria wrapped her arms around her mother and hugged her tight.

•

Lincoln and Bellissima parked outside the old rusty gate separating Breaux's land from the county road. The two of them hopped out and Lincoln popped the lock with the crowbar. Bellissima swallowed a big gulp of wine, removed the chain and pushed the gate open. Lincoln looked up at the sky and noticed the tree branches swaying ferociously. "The wind is really picking up!" he yelled- stretching his voice over the howling.

"Quick! Break the door lock!" yelled Bellissima.

Bellissima ran behind Lincoln as he dashed for the house. After a few bangs, Lincoln was able to free the second lock from the front door. He swept Bellissima up in his lithe arms just before a big branch fell from the sky, nearly crushing her spine. Lincoln slammed the door shut behind them. "That was close," he said- out of breath. He gave Bellissima a compact flashlight from his back pocket.

Bellissima switched the light on and shined it all around. Even with the flashlight, the house was dark and bleak. "There's a cold fog trapped in here, like it's been just waiting for Breaux to come back."

"Let's look around for some candles or a lantern?" said Lincoln- holding his hand out. Bellissima placed her hand in his and together they roamed the manor.

"Look at all these discolored squares on the wallpaper. Looks like there used to be a lot more pictures hanging in here."

"I guess he got rid of everything that reminded him he had a family. That's what Mama did with his pictures to help her forget all about him. I'll try and find the kitchen and see if I can find something to help light the place up. Wait here," said Lincoln. While waiting, Bellissima pushed open a door with a silver crucifix hanging on it. She crept inside. It appeared to be Breaux's bedroom. Everything inside was covered in a thick layer of dust. In Breaux's private bathroom, Bellissima noticed the toilet was still running. In the past Breaux complained about never getting to fix it before he was forced out of his home. Bellissima assumed he was just an old man looking for things to worry about. On the bedside table, she discovered a box of returned letters. "Lissima!" yelled Lincoln.

Bellissima scooped up the box and followed the sound of Lincoln's voice. They regrouped down the hall in a room with crackerjack posters lining the walls. Bellissima tripped over a medium sized box. "Ouch! Shit!" she yelped.

"-Your foot okay?" asked Lincoln- rushing over to clear the box from her path.

"Yeah, I'm still alive," Bellissima replied. "Any luck with the search for light?"

Lincoln held up a kerosene lamp. "-Just this, not a lot of fuel left in it; but we'll make good use of it," he said- wiping a large mirror. He set the lamp in front of the mirror and the light reflected, illuminating the room.

"Wow, that's impressive in a geeky way. I've always found resourceful men, very sexy."

"Thank you," Lincoln replied.

"Do you think this was your mother's room?"

"That's a safe bet. The door was hidden behind a bookshelf."

"Breaux sealed his daughter's room off from the rest of the house?"

"I guess so. It wasn't until I had to push that shelf aside to reach the knob that I finally understand how painful all this must have been for them both. Hate has its casualties- that's what my daddy used to always say. She lost a father. He lost a daughter..."

"-And you lost a grandfather," finished Bellissima.

"Yeah, I did." Lincoln sat down on the bed and it crinkled.

"Is that a plastic mattress pad I hear?" asked Bellissima- laughing.

"Yeah, I guess it is. How retro-classy," he joked- looking out the boarded window. "Not even sunlight was welcome here in this room. That wind sounds even angrier. Should we be worried?"

"It's not going to rain," said Bellissima- sitting down next to Lincoln. "I found these in Breaux's bedroom."

Lincoln took the box, picked a letter and held it up to his face. "Look how worn the ink is. The envelope is tattered."

"If it was returned here and not to the PO box, it's definitely old. I hope it provides some comfort, knowing he really did try and reach you. He wanted to know you, Lincoln."

"I'm curious, did Breaux have the same genetic disease my mother has? Did he die slowly, painfully?"

"Breaux's liver was shutting down on him. All his other organs crashed along with it. When Breaux checked in, his health was so bad he could barely wheel himself around. By the time he passed, he couldn't hold his own glass to drink. I can't say if it was painful or not. I mean, we gave him pain pills every now and then for the arthritis, but I'm not fit to say what he felt or didn't feel. He was a complainer, but never about pain."

"I worry for my mother. Tell me truly, is Pennycress a good place?"

Bellissima nodded. "Yeah. Don't get me wrong, people are still dying but everyone dies. They're old. Death just paces itself. They live a little longer at Pennycress because there are a few of us that are actually decent. Is dying slower such a bad thing? I mean, it is when you're suffering or unhappy. It being good or bad, it's all how the dying person sees it, I suppose."

"Which is more painful, do you think? Going out fast- leaving your loved ones behind abruptly or having them watch you decline slowly- if it means you get more time here on earth with them? Is it selfish to want to stay and make them watch you be less yourself every day?"

"Believe it or not, I struggle with that question all the time. Some patients at Pennycress are happy people. They have visitors, family members, and lifelong friends, that come to see them often. They sit. You can always tell when people don't want to be there, they never sit. They always stand like they're afraid to catch old age. They're squirmy. Happy patients get guest that are happy to be there. Then, there's the other kind of patient. The kind that waits by the phone because the loved ones that dropped them there promised they'd check in regularly. The kinds that don't leave their rooms on the holidays to avoid being taunted by the seasonal decorations. What's sad is seeing them put on their most expensive threads every day only to hang them back up every night thinking, maybe they'll come tomorrow or drive down next weekend. Maybe next time, someone will see me, look at me. Can anyone still see me, alive here- still breathing? I ain't old yet. I'm not young either, but if the Lord says the same- I've got a lot of years left. I got a million more miles to travel. I've suffered some hard times, some tragedies and heartbreaks. I thought I knew enough about pain to complain. Watching people get old- it's by far the most painful thing I've ever had to watch. Maybe those who die young, like Cheniere, are the lucky ones. That way you don't have to see everyone who cares for you wrestle with all the mental stuff, trying to figure out how life is supposed to go on without you. Loved ones leaving abruptly?- I have experience with that. She was my twin. She left abruptly."

"I heard your family speak her name. Cheniere."

"Yes. There was a horrible accident. Maybe it wasn't an accident at all, not like we can ask her to clear that part up. Sometimes I wish I could have said goodbye. Then, there are days when I'm glad it was over quickly for her. It's funny, I contemplate silence all the time because of Cheniere. When I was little, all I wanted to do was hear what she heard or couldn't hear, for that matter. There was always so much crying and yelling in my family. I can't believe she wanted to be just like me. I was the one who wanted to be just like her. Sometimes I daydream I'm caring for her. I picture us old and grey, and I'm still a nurse at pennycress looking after Cheniere. She'd have me there to tend to her every day and Dria and Sadie would visit. She'd be one of those happy patients. Silly isn't it?"

Lincoln moved even closer. "I don't think that's silly at all," he said- grabbing Bellissima's hand. "What kind of patient was Breaux, truly?"

"He was a fighter. That's the way he made me promise to keep his memory."

"Do me now?" said Lincoln.

"Excuse me?" asked Bellissima- appalled; thinking he was asking was for sex in a not-so-subtle manner.

"Do me. Seems like you have a good eye when it comes to pegging people."

"Oh," replied Bellissima- relaxing again. "It doesn't work like that. You have to be around someone for a while before you can figure them out."

"You'll have time to figure me out," said Lincoln.

"I will?" asked Bellissima- trying hard not to let her enthusiasm show.

"Yeah. You're the kind of patient that makes people want to stick around."

"-And here I was thinking *I* was the nurse. I didn't know I was a patient too."

"You are. You don't need a doctor or medicine, though. You just need a little love is all. I'm not a pro at figuring people out like you are but I get the sense it's hard to love yourself as much as you're supposed to when you're surrounded by so much tragedy. I bet you give all your love away, even your own portion? You give love to your mother. You give love to your cousins and aunts. You give love to everyone at Pennycress who needs a shoulder to lean on or someone to just sit with them until it's all over. Someone has to replenish that love if you insist on giving away so much of it, Lissima."

Staring into Lincoln's captivating eyes, Bellissima involuntarily leaned in- enthralled. At first, she was unsure if Lincoln would lean in too; but he reached out to caress Bellissima's cheek and his lips grazed hers. He ran his thumb along her bottom lip and she kissed his fingertip. "Do you feel that?" she asked- her forehead creased.

"I do feel it," answered Lincoln. "What is it?"

"I don't know, but I don't think I've ever felt it before right now. *Thus mellowed to that tender light...*" Bellissima replied.

"*...Which heaven to gaudy day denies...*" finished Lincoln- moving even closer. His lips gently devoured Bellissima's and he quaked- feeling her reciprocate his burning desire.

Bellissima moved in even closer, causing the plastic to crinkle atop the mattress. Its squeak almost deadened the moment, but Lincoln smiled at her blushing shyness. They both laughed and fell back into their passionate kiss as if it had never been interrupted. The wind outside whistled mightier and mightier as Lincoln laid Bellissima's trembling body down and slowly climbed on top of her. He lowered his pelvis against hers and felt Bellissima's warm palms clutching his torso, pulling tighter. Lincoln buried his face in Bellissima's neck, caressing and gently biting. Her pulse raced, and a fever settled between her thighs and Lincoln stiffened. Bellissima helped Lincoln out of his shirt and he helped Bellissima out of her dress. Lincoln unbuckled his belt and slid down his slacks. He paused for a minute, staring into Bellissima's eyes, his girth throbbing between her legs. Lincoln held his position for her to feel as he kissed her forehead, her nose and then her lips again.

"Yes. Now," she whispered- her eyes closed.

"Yes?" asked Lincoln.

"Yes," she nodded.

Lincoln sank inside of Bellissima and the pressure of ecstasy fulfilled anticipation immersed them both. With every stroke, Lincoln's phallus burrowed deeper and Bellissima cried sweet ravishment. It bellowed alongside the whistling wind and to Lincoln, it sounded like soft music. When it was over, Lincoln wrapped Bellissima up in his arms and kept her warm as she slept. Even though they were breaking and entering, they were in no rush to leave.

CHAPTER THIRTY-TWO

After all the leftovers were packed away in plastic containers, the tablecloth was washed, pressed and folded, and the kitchen was spotless; kay stayed on the porch waiting for Bellissima to return to the big house. Per Kay's request, Dria drove out to the cottage; but regretted to report: "She wasn't there Auntie Kay. She'll come back once she's had some time to process everything."

"Come inside, Kay. These mosquitos are going to eat you alive," begged Minxy.

"Won't you come inside and wait for her, Auntie Kay? Help me eat some of this left-over cake," begged Sadie.

Kay refused. "No. I'm not leaving this spot until my baby comes home."

Lou Anna believed in Kay's defiance. She didn't bother trying to persuade her. "At least wrap yourself up in this blanket," said Lou Anna, wrapping Kay in a cashmere throw.

Lou Anna turned to go back inside. Kay grabbed her wrist. "I know you would never do anything to hurt Lissima. You're my sister and Bellissima's Aunt but you're also a doctor. If you prescribed her something, I trust that you did so because it's what you felt she really needed it. I'm sorry if I made you feel like a bad doctor. I'm even sorrier if I made you feel like you weren't being a good sister and auntie."

"It's alright, Kay. Lissima and I owe you a few apologies too…"

"Shhh…" said Kay. "Later. Go back inside and get some rest. I didn't get a chance to tell Dria, congrats. You tell her for me? And tell her I love her?"

The Vast Uncertainty of a Raindrop

"Of course, I will."

•

Bellissima slept soundly in Lincoln's arms with her head rested comfortably on his bare chest. Lincoln had been awake for hours, fixated on a fluorescent yellow rain slicker hanging on a rusty nail in the corner of the room. He'd woke in the middle of the night and it had startled him momentarily, thinking the hollow silhouette was a person in the room watching them sleep. Once he realized no one was there, he pulled Lissima closer and went back to sleep. The sun was up now and Lincoln laid awake comparing the rain coat's brightness to all the other things that had been entombed in Breaux's house. The walls were corroded with muck. The dresser of drawers was covered in cobwebs. The paint on the bedroom door was chipped but the raincoat appeared oddly clean and radiant against the grimy backdrop. Lincoln thought hard, *"Was that hanging in here when I first walked in?"* Bellissima stirred. Lincoln tightened his grip and kissed the top of her head. She opened her eyes and smiled. "We have to be the dumbest criminals that ever lived; breaking and entering and staying the night."

"It was worth it. I don't think I've ever slept so good," Lincoln replied.

"In a bed covered in plastic, without a pillow or a blanket? This clear cover can only do so much, I'll be surprised if we don't get a bed bug rash or scabies from all this old upholstered furniture," said Bellissima.

"It was what I had that made it the best night of my life; something so amazing that I barely noticed what I didn't have," said Lincoln; staring at Bellissima's immaculate physique as she stood to slide her undergarment on. "You better hurry if you're going to make it to the fair in time to sign your family up for that obstacle event. I'll treat you to a corn dog after you win."

Bellissima snarked. "After what happened yesterday, I'm not even sure if we're all still family."

Lincoln stood and ran his fingertips down Bellissima's naked back and helped her pull her dress up. "Nonsense. I may not know much about you ladies, but I know love when I see it. Love only works if there's passion. That's why loved ones fight so much, the love is seeded deep because you want the best for the ones you love, you worry for them, you dream for them and sometimes your love twists intentions and bends them so that they look a lot worse than they really are. Anger's bound to flare up from time to time. But even when anger veers its ugly head, it's still love."

Bellissima's eyes swelled with tears. "So many awful things were said and revealed. I don't know if we can look each other in the eye, let alone compete together. What, do we just all show up and pretend nothing happened?"

"Yes, that's exactly what you should do- for now. The resolutions and explanations and apologies you all need and owe- pay up and collect later. Today, stand together and win. I'm willing to bet everyone from the dinner party has already found something else to talk about. This is the South. I'm willing to be they're going to go hoarse cheering you on."

"Grandma Cat ripped my yellow shirt. Even if I wanted to compete, I have nothing to wear to match my team." Lincoln grinned and looked to the rusty nail in the corner again.

Bellissima followed his line of sight and noticed the raincoat. "You can't be serious? I'll look ridiculous!" she asked laughing at the very thought.

"It's yellow. -And if it happens to rain, you'll be the only one prepared," said Lincoln with an affectionate, amused smirk. "I'll be waiting at the finish line with my camera, that way I get an action shot when you ladies win."

"How do you know we're going to win?"

"Call it a hunch," said Lincoln, kissing her nose. Bellissima grabbed the slicker and took off running. "Wait! Your shoes!" yelled Lincoln.

"I'll never make it in time if I wear those heels! Mama said I spent half my childhood barefoot anyway!"

"At least let me give you a ride!"

"No! I need the warm up! Me and Cheniere, we're the runners! The runners bring home the win!"

•

Bellissima blazed full speed down the dirt road to the big house leaving a trail of disrupted dust behind her quickly beating feet. Kay, who hadn't left the porch all night, saw Bellissima from the porch and stood. "Dria!

Sadie! Lou! Minxy! - Get out here!" The Beaumonte' women gathered on the front porch.

"Why is she running?" asked Dria, panicked. She stepped down from the porch. "Lissima! What's wrong?" she yelled.

Kay shuffled down the steps and out into the yard. Bellissima ran straight into Dria, crashing into her arms. "You're getting married!" she yelled, out of breath; hugging Dria tight.

"Who's after you baby? Minxy, get the gun!" yelled Kay- spinning Bellissima around as if to check for wounds.

"Nothing's wrong. I just woke up with passion, that's all."

Sadie sucked her teeth and grinned, "-Passion? Yeah, I bet. She's still wearing the same clothes she had on yesterday. *Walk of shame*- now that I've heard of, but the *run of shame?* Where's Lincoln at? I bet he's running shamefully too," whispered Sadie- nudging her mother with a giggle.

Bellissima caught her breath. "No one's after me, please don't get the gun! I'm just warming up!" she explained. Bellissima grabbed her mother's shoulders. "Mama, about a year ago I had a little breakdown. I might have taken something sharp to my wrists. Maybe Cheniere did it or the devil. Maybe one of them made me it. It doesn't matter, I think I'm okay now. Seeing how hurt you are, that I kept something like that from you, I know now that I should have told you. As a concerned mother, I know you're ready to hear all about it; but I'm not ready to talk about it. I'm not sure if I ever will be and you have to accept that. If I ever feel strong enough to talk to you about it, I won't leave out a single terrifying detail but today is not that day. Today we have more important things to do. We'll pay up and collect our resolutions and apologies later."

They all exchange glances, hoping that the other half understood what Bellissima was talking about. Neither of them followed. "How much champagne did you have at dinner yesterday, honey? You're a lightweight, it's nothing to be ashamed of," said Minxy.

"I had just enough champagne and wine, not too much nor too little," answered Bellissima- tossing the raincoat to Sadie. "You still remember everything Grandma Cat taught you on the old sewing machine?"

Sadie caught the coat. "Yeah. Why?" she asked- still confused.

"-Because I need you to take a few inches off the bottom. It ain't pretty but it is yellow and rain resistant. Make it work."

A smile curled on Kay's face. "You mean it? You still want to compete?"

"Yeah. I want to win, too. What do you say?"

"Beaumonte' family! We must ready ourselves for combat at once!" declared Minxy in her best warlord impression. "Everyone! Get on your yellow!"

CHAPTER THIRTY-THREE

"It's almost game time folks! We need all teams to report to the obstacle field at this time!"

The Beaumonte' family shoved through the crowd. "Hurry up!" rushed Bellissima.

"We missed sign up, we're too late!" said Sadie.

"No! We're doing this! We can make it before they start!" encouraged Bellissima. They reached the field where teams stretched, wearing assorted colors making the land look like one giant rainbow. Bellissima found Oscar and ran to him, pulling on his sleeve. "Hey, I need another favor!"

"Well if it isn't the best nurse in all Louisiana! I meant what I said to you; anything you ever want or need you just ask and it's done!" said Oscar.

"I know we missed the signup but me and my family would really like to compete this year. We <u>need</u> to compete this year, Mr. Oscar. Is there any way you could scribble us in on the bottom of the roster?"

Before Oscar could reply, Katina stepped forward. "What's this I hear? You trying to slink your way in? They missed signup! This year's grand prize is a slightly used camper! I plan on winning that camper! Letting them compete after we were all here on time is unfair! You snooze you lose!"

"Nice black eye. I told you you'd get hit in the face. And they say your family has the gift of sight? Maybe we're the ones who can really see the future," said Sadie- high fiving Minxy.

Katina rolled her eyes. "You're not going to let them compete, are you?" she asked with attitude.

"This is the Beaumonte' clan. They're loved. Letting them compete would ruffle your feathers a bit. Not letting them compete would piss of the whole county." Oscar stood on the old soapbox and spoke into his megaphone. *"Attention Cal-Cam! We have a late entry on our hands! All of you know the Beaumonte' women! Does anyone, besides this very loud young lady here to my left, have a problem with them joining the festivities?"*

"Let 'em in!" yelled Colin from the back of the crowd, causing everyone at the fair to clap and cheer in agreement.

Oscar looked down at Katina and Bellissima, smiling. "The people have spoken!" Oscar stepped off the box. "Alright! Now we've got ourselves a competition going on! Everyone get with your team and nominate your first two competitors! First, we have the rope climb!"

Bellissima huddled with her aunts and cousins. "Okay! Dria, Auntie Lou? Ya'll think you can still handle the ropes?"

Lou Anna turned to her daughter and grinned. "That new rock on Dria's finger might slow her down, but I'm certain I can still handle a little old rope! You think you can handle it, Dria?"

Dria turned back and looked at Colin, who smiled back at her and blew her a kiss. "You know I love to show off Mama!" she replied.

"Competitors! Take your mark!" Two members from all seven teams stepped up. "You know the rules! At the top of one rope, you'll find the mallet. At the top of the other rope, you see the bell! Both team players have to make it to the top; place the mallet in your partner's hand so your partner can ring the bell! The ropes are a test of speed! All you have to do to advance, is avoid being last. The last team to ring their bell will not advance. Fail to make it up the ropes, you will not advance. Ready! Set! Climb!"

"Go Dria!"

"You can do it, Lou!"

Team members grabbed hold of their ropes and pulled themselves up like coiling snakes. Some lost their grip and fell down into the foam pit. Some never got off the ground. Some made it halfway up, looked down and panicked; causing the safety volunteers to set up ladders and coax them back down safely. The stronger members made it to the top and with the help of their partners, rang the bell; like Dria and Lou Anna. Bellissima cheered! "They did it! We're on to the next round!"

Dria rubbed ointment on her mother's calloused hands while Colin massaged the rope burn on Dria's inner thigh with menthol balm.

"Next up! The test of balance! It's time to face the high wire over the giant mud pit! Select your team members with the best balance and have them step forward- a member at each end of the wire! That's two members for those of you bad with numbers! Before the challenge begins! You will be given a colored flag that matches the flag pole on the other end of the rope, behind your team member! You must walk the wire without falling, grab hold of your teammate at the middle, rotate without causing your teammate to fall and make your way across to reunite your colored flag with the proper pole color! Once both flags are attached, the challenge is complete! Again, you are not required to complete the challenge before your competitors, just don't be last! Last place means disqualification! Completion will guarantee your spot in the next challenge; but the team that finishes first will get to pick the order of the next challenge- the talent round! That's just a little incentive to put some fire under your rear ends."

Sadie held out her hand. "You ready Grandma Minxy?" she quipped? "Granny Minx sounds better. It makes me sound younger and you know you're as young as you feel." Sadie and Minxy took their positions. "Ready! Set! Walk!" Most of the opposing competitors tumbled into the mud almost immediately, but not Sadie and Minxy. They never broke eye contact and paced slowly, in-tune with one another's steps.

Kay held her breath when they reached the middle. "This is the hard part!" she said hiding her face. "I can't watch!"

Sadie and Minxy paused, putting their hands on each other's shoulders as they crisscrossed their feet. "They did it!" yelled Lou Anna. All of a sudden, Sadie started to wobble, as if losing her poise. "Oh no!" yelled Lou Anna- squeezing Kay's arm.

Sadie looked down, panicked. "It's alright," Whispered Minxy, still steady. "Don't take your hand off my shoulder. Steady yourself, that's my grandbaby you got in there. I'm not going to let either of you fall and risk getting hurt." Sadie's waist wiggled back and forth as she struggled to regain her balance. She looked at her mother in the eye and smiled. "See, you go it. I got you," Minxy whispered with a wink.

Slowly, both Sadie and Minxy made it to the end of the wire and then back on the ground where they successfully tethered their flags. Only two other teams succeeded. Katina's team, the orange team, was one of them.

"Looks like team Beaumonte' will be choosing the order on the talent roster! Who's going first?" asked Oscar with his clipboard ready.

Sadie surveyed the faces of her teammates, who were all shouting different colors in numerical order. "The pink team goes first and after them, the red team." Sadie noticed Katina's team plotting their next move. "We're going last."

"The best for last!" yelled Lincoln approaching from afar.

"Sho ya right!" yelled Don in agreement, who'd already reserved the shadiest spot on the bleachers to sit and watch. He took out his cockade fan and waved to Minxy and Sadie.

"The performance order is set in stone! Pink, then red, and then yellow! *At this time, we'll break for 45 minutes! Not 46 minutes! Not 44 minutes, either! Feel free to stretch your legs while we finish setting up the stage, but you will need to report back here in time or face disqualification!*"

Bellissima and Lincoln strolled the fairgrounds, sharing a blooming onion. "How long have you been here?"

"I arrived just in time to hear the whole town vote you and your family in. These people really love you."

"Yeah, I guess they do. You do a little good here and there and people don't forget it. That's how things work in a small town," said Bellissima.

"There are a lot of people out here on your side. You must have done more than just a little good. Look at all these people with their hands in the air," said Lincoln, scrolling through the pictures in his camera for Bellissima to see.

"You're really good at your job," she complimented.

"Capturing a beautiful moment around you ain't hard at all, but thank you," Lincoln replied- leaning in to kiss Bellissima. Just as their lips touched, little Gabby Withers ran between the two of them. "Ms. Lissima! Come and ride the carousel with me!" she begged, propitiously.

Bellissima smiled down at Gabby and fluffed her frizzy pigtails. "I'm sorry, I can't sweetie."

Gabby hung her head. "Is it because you hate my mommy? Do you hate me too now?"

Bellissima picked Gabby up and Gabby wrapped her legs around Bellissima's waist. "Hate? Gabby no. Hate is a bad thing. I don't hate anyone. Sometimes your mother says means things, is all. I may have said some mean things back, but that doesn't mean I hate her and you're too cute for anyone to hate."

"She such a bitch," said Gabby- cursing without blinking, like it was second nature. Lincoln nearly choked on his onion, laughing.

Bellissima gasped. "Gabby Lynn Withers! That's a very bad word!"

"That's what my mommy's boyfriend calls her sometimes. My great Grandmother says she's stupid for answering to it cause that ain't her name."

"I'm sorry you heard that Gabby. That's an awful thing to call a woman, especially a mother. Your mother's boyfriends shouldn't be saying that; but just because you hear it doesn't mean you can repeat it."

"Can I tell you a secret?"

"Of course, you can."

"Mommy says if we win the camper we can pack up like a thief in the night and leave him behind to degrade someone else. *A thief in the night?* - I don't know what that means but we ain't leaving, I'm sure of it. There's no way mommy can beat you in the race."

Bellissima glanced over at Lincoln, who looked back at her with the same disquietude. Bellissima kissed Gabby's nose. "Don't worry, you and your mommy are going to get that camper."

"We are!" exclaimed Gabby.

"Shhh…. Yes, you are, but it's a secret for now. So, you have to keep quiet. We got about twenty more minutes before the talent round starts. Me and Mr. Lincoln here are going to watch my mother out-talent the hell out of those preteens with their caked-on make-up. Take this money and go buy some tickets. I'll ride the carousel with you before the show starts, but you have to hurry. And no talking to strangers!"

Gabby rushed off to get the tickets. Lincoln leaned in. "You're going to lose the race on purpose, so they can win the mobile home?"

"Lose? Hell no! We're still going to kick their asses, but when we win- We'll give the prize to Katina so her and her little girl can start a new life," Bellissima replied.

Lincoln moved in to claim the kiss that had been interrupted. "You're one hell of a woman Bellissima Beaumonte'; a hell of a woman with the heart of an angel."

"Sho ya right!" said Bellissima running off to the carousel.

As predicted, Kay Beaumonte' outshined the other contestants, advancing the Beaumonte' team to the final event.

"Attention runners! It's time for the toughest of all obstacle events! The long ride, the mile-long stretch! The oval track loops through the woods! Stay on the track and the finish line will circle right back here where we're starting! The team representative who finishes first wins the grand prize for his or her team! With two of you per team on track, you have a 50/50 chance at the grand prize!"

Lincoln rubbed Bellissima's shoulders and Sadie double knotted Bellissima's sneakers. Lou Anna gave Bellissima a sip from her water bottle while Kay tied her daughter's hair back. "This is it Lissima! It's time for you to shine! I don't want you to feel like you have to win. I don't want you to push your body. If you need to walk for a while, you walk- okay?" said Kay- worried.

"- *Feel like I have to win?* What a silly thing to say. Of course, I have to win! You've all done your part. It's time for me to finish what we came here to do," replied Bellissima- determined.

"They'll start off sprinting, silly fools- they'll burn all their energy before they're midway. Hang back and jog. Just when they think there's no way you'll catch up- bring home the win. We'd love you just the same if you lose," said Minxy.

"Ya'll worry too much. I've got this," said Bellissima stretching.

"Take your mark!"

Bellissima hugged Lincoln, then her mother and aunts. She stepped up to the line and stood beside her opponents, who had a member of their own team racing beside them. Oscar patted Bellissima's shoulder, "You running alone this year," he asked.

Bellissima looked to her left and then to her right. She expected it to feel odd, not having her sister next to her; but she didn't expect it to make her feel so sad. "-No Beaumonte' twins this year. Just me. Mama had to do the talent round alone this year, without Grandma Cat. If she can go solo, I can too," she mumbled- sullen.

Dria and Sadie moved closer together, contemplating the same thought. "It just doesn't seem right, her running alone," said Dria.

Sadie nodded, "I know. It's not her fault Cheniere's not here."

Bellissima, putting on a brave face, turned around and gave her loved ones two thumbs up. Oscar held his pistol in the air. *"On your mark! Get set!" Pow!* The crowd went wild, cheering encouragements as they sped off.

"You thinking what I'm thinking?" asked Sadie.

"I think so," Dria replied.

"Then what are you girls waiting for?" asked Lou Anna.

Sadie and Dria took off behind Bellissima. Naturally, Katina's teammates complained. "The mile is ran in pairs! All three of them can't compete, that's not fair!"

"No one cares! Let them have this!" said Oscar- smiling as they rounded the corner. "Are they really asking for much, after what the bridge took from them?"

CHAPTER THIRTY-FOUR

Jan waltzed into Catherine's room with a glass of water and a fistful of medication. Just beyond the doorway, a small puddle of orange juice formed, causing Jan to slip and fall flat on her back. She hit the floor with a loud thump. "Ouch! What the hell?" she screamed- scrambling to her feet. Jan discovered Catherine's breakfast on the floor. "Mrs. Beaumonte', why is your food on the floor?"

"I told you I wasn't hungry; but still- you insisted on leaving that bland heap of dog shit in here to stink up my room," answered Catherine without looking up from her bible.

"So, you decided to throw your tray on the floor?"

"Yes," answered Catherine plainly. "Before you start a useless debate that you won't win, I'd like to say one thing."

"What's that?"

Catherine closed her Bible and turned to Jan. "I know you drugged me, you little devious bitch."

Jan squirmed and looked away. "...drugged you?" she stammered.

"Denying it will only further piss me off, child. It'll make me feel like you take me for a fool. You don't want to do that, piss me off more. Now, I'm not eating a damn thing you bring in here. I don't want any doctors in this room today. I don't want any nurses in here. I will not be bothered; my solitude will not be disturbed. You understand? You best be on your way now."

Jan swallowed hard before responding. "Yes, mam."

"Smells like rain today. You smell it" asked Catherine- wheeling her chair closer to the window.

Jan was confused. "I didn't know rain had a scent."

"It sure does. You weren't raised in the South, were you?"

"No mam, I wasn't. My family moved here right before I graduated."

"Figures. <u>We</u> can smell it, 100% Louisiana purebreds. I suggest you find yourself an umbrella. You'll be needing it for later. Go on now," said Catherine shooing Jan away.

Once Jan left the room, Catherine wheeled herself to the closet, grabbed the bottle of blessed oil, placed it on her lap and wheeled herself to the door. She poked her head out into the hall and saw the preoccupied staff busy with other patients and documentation. No one noticed Catherine as she slowly wheeled her way to the back door that led out to the courtyard.

Slowly, Catherine inched down the paved walkway between the gardens. She stopped where the pavement ended. Thunder cracked the sky, causing the pennycress patients to head inside. One of the patients, an older man, stopped and placed his hand on Catherine's shoulder. "-Bad weather coming. I knew it this morning. My old war joints started aching. I still got enough energy to push you back inside before the rain gets here. What do you say, Cat?"

"-*Cat?*" mumbled Catherine. His voice sounded familiar, so familiar the hairs on the back of Catherine's neck stood. "Jeremiah?" she asked, looking up.

"Jeremiah? No, Mrs. Beaumonte'. It's me, Barron. We met at the movie night when they screened *Dirty Dancing*."

Catherine was disappointed. "Oh yes. I remember. I was just hoping you were someone else."

"Well, I'm sorry to let you down. What do you say? You want me to wheel you in before the sky falls?"

"No thank you. I'm going to sit out here for a while," answered Catherine.

"-Suit yourself. You want me to come back out here and check on you later?"

"No. Please don't. I don't want you to do anything but go away. I want to sit, alone." Once Catherine was all alone outside, she uncorked the blessed oil and lifted it above her head. She emptied it all over her hair, down her face and back. Once the bottle was empty, Catherine stood, without help, for the first time in months. She unbuttoned her gown, exposing her ripened naked flesh and an adult diaper. The wind picked up and it carried her gown away. Her feeble knees wobbled as she stepped off the pavement and into the grass.

•

Bellissima leveled her breathing. "In through the nose, out through the mouth," She mumbled focusing on the tempo of her opponents stampeding. She hadn't heard Dria and Sadie approaching from behind. They caught up and steadied their pace alongside Bellissima; Dria on the left side and Sadie on her right. After a quick double-take, Bellissima gasped. "What are you doing?"

"What does it look like? We're running the mile with you," answered Sadie.

"You don't have to do this," said Bellissima- secretly touched by their ardor.

"We know," said Dria. "Mind your speed! Let these rookies get tired and fall back! <u>We</u> got this!"

The sky flashed up above. All three Beaumonte' grandchildren looked up, without slowing down. The storm's natural light irradiated their uniqueness and their beauty imprinted the wind. "Rain or no rain, we're finishing- even if we all have to crawl under what's left of that raincoat," said Sadie.

Catherine inched further and further away from the facility. The dark clouds rolled in and Catherine felt a single raindrop fall down on her cheek. She held her hands high and began to pray aloud. When her prayer was finished, Catherine collapsed.

•

Two opponents gave up. One wheezing competitor sat on the route, panting. Dria tossed him her spare inhaler as they passed. The rest went from running to walking to barely putting one foot in front of the other. "So that's what quitting looks like?" she mumbled.

Bellissima spotted a neon pennon in the woods. "There's the halfway marker! We're making good time!"

Sadie turned to see the marker and her pace slowed. "You gotta be shitting me!" she yelled.

"What?" asked Dria.

"It's the damn bunny! It's alive! It's been alive this whole time!" shouted Sadie in disbelief.

Bellissima and Dria surveyed the woods. "Bunny? Where? I don't see anything."

"It was right there! I'm sure of it!" said Sadie- leaving the course.

"What are you doing?" asked Dria- confused.

"Go! Keep running! Stay on route! I'll cut through and finish with you! I promise!" yelled Sadie- disappearing in the weald.

"Sadie no! The woods aren't the same as they used to be! You could get lost!" warned Bellissima.

"I'll be okay! I'm going to get that little runt's bunny back!"

"Her name is Gabby!" corrected Bellissima, pausing.

Dria grabbed her arm. "She'll be okay, Lissima! Let's go!"

Kay couldn't stand still. "The sky's getting darker. What if it starts pouring on our babies?"

"They're not babies, Kay. So, what if it does rain? It wouldn't be the first time our daughters played in the rain. Those children of ours won't stop. They're going to win, you know? It'll be another Beaumonte' war story," said Minxy- comforting her sister.

Back at Pennycress, nurse Jan was almost finished with her rounds. Every patient on her list had been checked off, all except Catherine Beaumonte'. Jan doubled back to see if Catherine's temper had decimated. Maybe then she'd be more cooperative. Jan tapped on the door. "Mrs. Catherine, it's me again- Jan. I realized I never said I was sorry for what I did. I really <u>am</u> sorry. I'm going to enter now. If you have something in your hand to throw at me, I'd like you to put it down. If there are any more liquids on the floor, please warn me. Mrs. Beaumonte'? I'm coming in." Jan stepped into Catherine's room and realized she was no longer inside."

Jan rushed to the nurses' station. "Lockdown the building. Contact each department representative and tell them to radio in when they've located Catherine Beaumonte'."

•

Sadie Beaumonte' ran through the woods, like a wolf after warm flesh, with her eyes locked on Gabby's fluffy white pet. The rabbit weaved effortlessly through the forest debris, causing Sadie to leap and hurdle hazardously. "Slow down damn it! I'm not the enemy! I'm trying to rescue you, you little shit!" She was hot on the rabbit's tail when she tripped over a downed log. Sadie fell forward and tried to brace herself with both palms out, but was unable to protect her womb from a large tree stump. Sadie screamed and began to cry immediately. "No! No! No!" she yelled-trembling. She rolled over onto her back, lifted her shirt and looked down at her belly. "Move! Kick! Do something please! Just let me know you're okay! Are you okay, baby?" she begged. Sadie paused, as if waiting to hear her unborn child answer. Her womb was still beneath the throbbing agony. As she lay there sobbing, an immaculate glowing light appeared in the distance as if lightening touched the ground. As it neared, it grew brighter and brighter. Out of the light, stepped the form of a woman who shared Bellissima's likeness. Sadie sat up against the stump and wiped her eyes. "Lissima?" she asked- confused. There was no answer. "Then…Cheniere?" asked Sadie- in complete shock.

The spirit of Cheniere kneeled, hovering its hand over Sadie's bruised abdomen. Her hands moved quickly, signing. "Why are you crying?"

"I think I hurt it," answered Sadie.

Cheniere put her ear to Sadie's abdomen and listened. When she picked her head up again she smiled at her little cousin. "Don't cry. She will live. She will be the strongest of us all," she signed.

"-A girl?" asked Sadie.

"Yes," nodded Cheniere. "Get up now. I hear the rain coming."

"You can hear the rain?" asked Sadie- sobbing again.

"Yes," nodded Cheniere. "I always could," she signed.

"We miss you," said Sadie, eyes streaming harder as her hands moved-releasing all her bottled grief at once.

"I miss you all too," said Cheniere- with a voice this time.

Sadie clutched her own heart. "You have a voice in heaven? Your voice, it's so beautiful," she sobbed.

The spirit of Cheniere said nothing more. She simply kissed Sadie's face and gradually faded. "Wait! Don't go!" Sadie pleaded. Just as quickly as Cheniere appeared, she was gone again.

Sadie stood and dusted her clothes. When she looked up again, the little rabbit was right in front of her, nibbling on a root. Sadie scooped it up and rushed through the woods to finish the race.

Katina, who'd gone from sprinting to jogging to walking fast, turned back to find Dria and Bellissima right on her heels. "Damn it!" she mumbled- disgusted. Katina sped up, looking back every few steps to scowl menacingly. Dria and Bellissima stared back, determined. Katina should have been more focused on her own footing. If only she had kept looking forward, she would have noticed the stone in her path. Katina stepped on the stone and her ankle twisted. "Ouch!" she yelped, tumbling. Dria and Bellissima saw the fall, but kept on running right past her, ignoring her distress, leaving her collapsed in a cloud of dust. "You think it's fractured," asked Dria.

"Nope, probably just Achilles tendinitis or a sprain," answered Bellissima- casually.

"Are we just going to leave her there?"

"Of course not. I'm a nurse ain't I? I took an oath to care for the diseased, impaired, in need and injured. I'm turning back. Just wanted her to get a good look at my ass first," said Bellissima with a sneer.

The two of them turned back to check on Katina's injury. They found her crawling. She looked up at Dria and Bellissima. "No! You go! I don't need your pity!"

"Good, because we don't have any for you," Dria replied.

"Let me have a look at your ankle," said Bellissima.

"What?" questioned Katina- not sure if she should trust Bellissima's intentions.

"Did I stutter? Your ankle, the one that's swelling up like a pumpkin, let me see it."

"Why you want to see about me? Don't you want to win?" asked Katina.

"Oh, we're still going to win; no doubt about it. We counted our adversaries and we've passed them all. It's just you and us. We got enough time to leave the track, get lunch and come back; we'd still win," teased Dria.

Katina hung her head. "You have no idea how bad I needed to win this. I was going to kick old the spoon and needle. I was going to get better for my kid."

Bellissima kneeled and removed Katina's shoe. "We know. I talked to Gabby." Katina's eyes widened. "We're not going to let you keep the medal and the bragging rights will be all ours, but the camper is yours. We'll see to it," vowed Bellissima.

Katina stopped crying and wiped her nose. "What? I don't understand."

"After you eat our dust, we're going to give you the camper," said Dria as she helped Bellissima lift Katina off the ground.

"-But what about all those horrible things I said to you. The things I said about your family and Cheniere. I never even apologized. Why would you all help me, still?"

"It's the Beaumonte' way," Said Sadie- emerging from the woods with Captain Crisp tucked in her arms. She walked over to her cousins and they bumped fists. "She okay?" Sadie asked turning to Bellissima. "What's the prognosis?"

"She'll live. Ya'll ready to cross the finish line?" Bellissima asked.

"Hell yeah!" exclaimed Sadie.

"Wait! Lincoln's waiting with the camera. How's my hair?" asked Bellissima- turning to Sadie for her expert opinion.

Before Sadie could answer, the clouds burst. "It doesn't matter now. Either way, you're finishing soaking wet and smelling like a wet dog," laughed Dria.

The Beaumonte' grandchildren ran side by side, spanning the width of the track, their footsteps pounding in unison.

"There they are!" yelled Lou Anna, causing everyone to turn their attention and cheer. Thunder shook the earth as they ripped through the tape. The flash on Lincoln's camera caught lighting touching the earth again in the background.

"We have winners!"

Dria hugged her mother and then jumped in Colin's arms. Minxy kissed Sadie's cheek, then the rabbit and then Sadie's belly. Kay grabbed hold of Bellissima and squeezed tight.

Katina wobbled across the finish line, clapping. Her teammates rushed to her side. Once everyone was done hugging, Oscar placed the medal around Bellissima's neck and handed her the keys to the compact motor home. The whole town watched as the Beaumonte' grandchildren approached Katina's team. "-Like we said, the camper is yours."

"I don't deserve it," said Katina- pushing the key away.

"We know, but the runt deserves a fresh start; far away from here. Get her away from the ruins," said Sadie.

"It's Gabby, Sadie," corrected Bellissima.

"Gabby! Right! I'm not so good with names or kids."

"You better get better at both real fast," said Kay- rubbing her niece's stomach. "God! I'm so glad the cat's out of the bag. I've been dying to touch this belly!"

"Speaking of Gabby, where is she? I'm sure she wants to see old long lost Crispy here," said Sadie- dangling the bunny.

"I'm right here!" answered a small voice from the back of the mob.

Katina's joy melted into panic immediately. There was Gabby, waving, mounted high on Robbie's shoulders. Katina limped as she pushed through the crowd. "Gabby, you get down here!"

"What's the rush?" asked Robbie, ominously.

"I already told you, Mr. Robbie. Mommy said we're going to leave and live the life of a lamb," answered Gabby.

"I think you mean, live life on the lam. It's something folks say when they plan on disappearing," said Robbie.

"Gabby stop talking!" yelled Katina.

Katina's abusive lover grinned. "You planning on leaving? -And without saying goodbye?" Katina froze. "Why don't you let these good people celebrate their victory? Come on, let's go home where we can talk about this in private," suggested Robbie- his eyes ferociously locked on Katina.

"No. I want you to put Gabby down," said Katina.

"I said let's go!" he shouted.

"She's not going anywhere with you," said Dria.

"No one's talking to you, bitch!"

Colin removed his watch and stepped forward. "Call her out of her name again, I dare you," he challenged.

"I don't think he's that crazy," said Bellissima.

"-Ain't I though?" huffed Robbie.

Bellissima marched right up to Robbie and held her hands out. "In order to scare someone, you have to be scary. I ain't scared of you. Give her to me, now!"

Robbie's breathing quickened as he realized he was no longer in control of the situation. Otis approached Bellissima's side and loosened his cuff button. He rolled up his sleeves. "You best be putting that child in Ms. Lissima's arms like she asked," he threatened.

"-Nice and slow," said Lincoln- staring Robbie down.

Robbie jerked Gabby down from his shoulders and dropped her in Bellissima's arms. "Good dog," Bellissima mumbled. She turned her back to Robbie. "I thought I told you to tell your Mama to keep a better eye on you. I told you to tell her you ain't molester bait," she whispered to Gabby.

"I forgot," Gabby replied, innocently.

Katina grabbed her daughter and wept. "God bless you Beaumonte' women."

"It's got a full tank. You go now and take God with you for the ride," said Oscar.

Jan frantically pushed her way through the pack with a hoodie on to shelter her head from the drizzle. "Lissima! Lissima!" she screamed.

Bellissima followed the sound of her name and spotted Jan. "Hey! We won! I told you we would!" she gloated; but then Bellissima noticed what appeared to be despair riddled across Jan's face.

"I need you to gather your family and come with me," said Jan.

Dria and Sadie stopped celebrating and the joy ceased as they observed Jan's regret.

"Don't you work with Lissima down at Pennycress? What's the matter? Is Mama giving ya'll a hard time down there?" asked Lou Anna.

"Yes Mam, I work there. No, she's not giving us trouble. It's not that," answered Jan.

"Then what?" asked Sadie.

"John sent me, Lissima. I'm so sorry," answered Jan, her eye contact remorseful and then broken.

"John? Who's that?" questioned Minxy.

Bellissima's face sank. "He's the closer."

CHAPTER THIRTY-FIVE

The Beaumonte' daughters shared a black umbrella as they rushed the walkway to Pennycress. The Beaumonte' granddaughters weren't far behind, but their steps were much slower. No one uttered a single solitary word. Lincoln and Colin held the doors open and everyone in Pennycress stood as they entered. Nurses stopped working. Patients stopped complaining. Phones stopped ringing. The Beaumonte' family pushed through the lobby, passed the front station and marched out the back to the courtyard. Men in suits were there, prepared to move Catherine's corpse. "Wait! No please! Don't take her yet! She's our mother," begged Minxy.

Lou Anna wailed, and it echoed just as loud as the thunder. "Mama! No!" Kay fell to her knees and towered over Catherine's still body. Lincoln removed his jacket and held it over Kay's head to keep her from getting any wetter.

The storm got worse, much worse. It was unexpected and uncertain- the severity of the weather. It was unexpected and uncertain- the severity of the loss. It was an unexpected, gravitating change in the weather and warning of inevitable calamity.

Back at the big house; Bellissima sat on the porch alone, shining the medal to pass the time. The screen door slammed behind her and Kay walked out. "Did that nice Lincoln fellow leave?" she asked- sitting down beside her daughter.

"Yes, Mam. He didn't want to, but I made him. It's not easy being a bystander to all this Beaumonte' drama. He should rest, see his mother."

"-Or at least change his clothes," said Kay grinning. "Why <u>was</u> he wearing the same clothes from yesterday?"

Bellissima grinned back but didn't answer. "How you are holding up, Mama?"

"I'd be lying if I said I was okay. Your Auntie Minx is upstairs collecting all of your Grandmother's favorite things. She swears it's all going to fit in the casket with your Grandmother. That's what Catherine wanted. Every time we told her, *'you can't take it all with you when you die'*, Mama would just laugh. *'Watch me'* - she'd say. Lou Anna's been on the phone for hours, trying to buy the best of everything. She knows it won't matter to Mama, but Lou just needs to preoccupy herself or else she'll just breakdown. Me? I think I'm somewhere in between denial and relief," said Kay.

"Relief?" asked Bellissima- appalled.

"Yes, Child. Your Grandmother's been gone for a long time. She left in the flesh today, but she's been long gone. Her vessel was here for our sake. Loved ones, we get selfish in the end; wanting them to stay even when they're suffering. Catherine missed Cheniere and daddy. She wanted to be with them. She made her mind up long ago and put one foot out the door."

"You think she's up there with them in heaven?"

"Oh yes. There was probably a gathering at the pearly gates just for Catherine," said Kay- wrapping her arms around her daughter. "You know, your father wanted to name you that- Pearl."

Bellissima's eye widened. "What?"

"Your father had that name picked out back when we didn't know if we were going to have a boy or a girl. Little did we know, we had two to name. Pearl was what he wanted to call his baby daughter, if it was a girl. It was his Mother's middle name. When we found out I was carrying twins, we decided against any kind of tradition. It was an untraditional pregnancy. You girls needed your own names, unique ones. People would be named after you, not you after them. We put so much thought into your names, we weren't sure what we'd call you until the day we got to take you home. Finally, your daddy got tired of people calling you girls *baby A* and *baby B*. He took the clipboard and scribbled down two random names without asking me if I liked them. I was furious until I read the names aloud. I wanted to be angry with him, but the names fit. *'They're not just letters of the alphabet! They're little people!'* He ranted. He was so passionate about the things that really mattered; especially the little things, they mattered to him the most."

"You've never talked to me about him, Mama."

"I know. Minx and Lou told me they had talks with their daughters. Don't seem fair for me to give you nothing."

"Grandma Cat said he left us all alone. She said that you planned to marry my daddy and that he broke your heart. Was it another woman?"

"Hell no! Look at me! You think any man would have me and leave me? He'd have to be blind! I'm a knockout!" laughed kay.

"Then what happened?"

"When you and Cheniere came, things got tense. Two babies are a lot to handle. He noticed something was different about Cheniere. He tried to make me see it, accept it; but it was hard for me. He and I found out about Cheniere's disability long before I told the family. I felt we needed to prepare ourselves for their reactions and questions, but your father started to change on me. I noticed he stopped holding Cheniere. He'd only hold you. Cheniere would be screaming to the top of her lungs with a wet diaper and he would not tend to her. After a while, your little baby brain started noticing the pattern in Cheniere's crying. She'd squeal whenever you were picked up and she was left in the crib. After a while, you refused to let your daddy hold you; as if to say- you either love us both or keep your love."

"He stopped loving Cheniere because she had special needs?"

Kay nodded. "I don't think he meant to. I think he just didn't know how to. Instead of praying we blamed ourselves and then we blamed each other. The afternoon before he abandoned us, he came in and tried to pick you up. You pulled away and grabbed hold of your twin. You wouldn't let go. I woke up the next morning, found some money in a crinkled envelope. That was all. I didn't see him again until we buried Cheniere."

"I wouldn't have known him if he was right in front me; but did I see him? Did he see me?"

"He saw you. Minxy had you wrapped up in her arms and you were crying. The look your aunties gave him, he didn't dare come near you or me. I hope he didn't think that old brown trench coat was much of a disguise. He kept his distance, but at least he came."

"Why didn't he console us?"

"My guess? He didn't think he had the right to after the way he left things. He'd been gone so long, Lissima. Maybe he felt like he didn't have the right to be sad or pretend to miss her now that she was gone."

"I can't believe I waited so long to get answers that only further confuse me. I don't know how I feel about all of it," said Bellissima.

"That's alright. Don't be so hard on your heart. Don't rush to decide on one specific emotion. Give it time. Let the weather change."

CHAPTER THIRTY-SIX

Cloaked in all back with their arms linked at the elbow, the Beaumonte' grandchildren strolled the moss draped footpath nearest the bayou. After a steady lull and multiple lachrymose heaves, Dria severed the silence. "I know this is going to sound strange, but the universe felt different today when I woke up. I could feel that Granny was no longer a part of this world."

"I thought I was the only one," Sadie added.

"I can't believe Catherine Beaumonte' no longer exists."

Bellissima pulled back her black veil, exposing her puffy eyes- raw from weeping. She used her mother's white handkerchief to wipe her nose. "She'll still exist, in other forms beyond simple flesh and bone. I'm sure one day we'll see a bird and swear we've seen it before or smell a familiar scent dancing with a passing breeze that blew in from out of nowhere. We'll think of Granny Cat immediately and we'll smile."

"I never thought in a million years that she'd die. Isn't that silly? I'm an adult. I know all about how our days here on earth are numbered. She was old. She was sick, but I never imagined her dying, not once," said Dria.

"I bet they're showing up by the boatload back at the big house for the funeral. Granny is probably tickled pink in heaven, just loving all the attention," said Sadie- laughing a bit for the first time since they learned of Catherine's passing.

"Sho ya' right!" said a voice from the porch of a run-down shack, nearly overrun with cattails and spider webs.

The Beaumonte' grandchildren froze in their tracks and their heads spun. There, on a puny porch swing, sat old Mrs. Creasie. She smiled at the granddaughters while swinging back and forth, wearing wrinkled memorial attire. She chuckled and looked up at the sky as if looking for Catherine. "That woman sure knew how to work a room; demanded attention without asking for it. Knowing Cat, she probably approached the great gold gates half expecting Jesus Christ himself to bow down to her."

Bellissima smiled back at the sweet old lady. "Mrs. Creasie," she Whispered- relieved to see her face after such a long time.

It took Dria and Sadie a moment to recognize her." "My goodness. It is you!" said Sadie, running up the steps with her arms stretched out.

Mrs. Creasie embraced Sadie and squeezed tight. "Look at you, all grown up! My little Neapolitan girls!"

"Neapolitan girls?" Dria questioned.

"Yes, just a little nickname I called you girls behind your backs. You all used to pick your Grandmother's pocketbook clean and come running up on my porch. You always craved the same thing. Sadie wanted Vanilla. Lissima and Cheniere wanted the strawberry. Dria…"

Dria smiled, remembering the gaiety of their childhood. "…chocolate. I had to have the chocolate on a sugar cone," she finished.

"That's right! - a Neapolitan mix," said Mrs. Creasie as she welcomed Dria's hug, then Bellissima's. "I'm so sorry to hear about Cat. Believe me when I say, she will be missed. Why aren't you girls back at the big house? Aren't your mothers getting ready for the service?"

"Yes Mam, they're making the necessary preparations back home. We just…" Dria had paused, letting the weight of Catherine's death levitate in midsentence.

"Oh I see…things got a bit overwhelming?" Finished Mrs. Creasie.

Bellissima exhaled, relieve she'd said it for them. "Yes Mam. I know it's selfish and all, leaving our mamas to handle the bulk of it but…I don't think we're ready to see her in that pine box."

"You poor babies, come on sit for a spell. I got a fresh block of ice to shave. Sure is hot enough for a snow cone, ain't it? Seems only fair to whip you girls up a treat," said Mrs. Creasie, ushering the Beaumonte' grandchildren to the porch swing.

Sadie's eyebrow raised. "You still serving up those snow cones with a scoop of ice cream in the center? And what about some sour worms for topping?" she asked, mouth nearly watering.

Mrs. Creasie grinned, just happy feeling needed. "As luck would have it, I got a fresh pale of Neapolitan and a cabinet full of fixings."

The Grandchildren sat on the porch, indulging. No one asked her too, but Mrs. Creasie fetched her hair pomade and started braiding Dria's hair. Dria didn't seem to mind, preoccupied with her treat.

"How many people you think done made it to the big house?" asked Sadie, shoveling a mouthful of syrup covered ice in her mouth.

"By now? At least a hundred," Bellissima estimated.

Mrs. Creasie grunted and smiled. "Probably even more than that. Your grandparents influenced so many lives. Aside from the seats reserved for you and your mothers, there's probably only standing room. Have you little ladies thought of what you're going to get up there and say in front of all those people?"

Bellissima swallowed hard. "No Mam."

"I'm no good with speeches," confessed Sadie.

Dria scrunched her nose and raised a brow. "Really? But you and Auntie Minx sound so rehearsed in front of all those judges."

Bellissima cut her eyes at Dria but relaxed when both Dria and Sadie started laughing instead of bickering. "Don't worry, you won't be up there alone. Me and Lissima will be standing right beside you, just as stumped."

"Don't fret on it. When it's all said and done, you'll end up saying exactly what your heart intends. I'd be lying if I said I wasn't surprised, though." Said Mrs. Creasie.

"About what?" asked Sadie.

"The way Catherine went out. I would have bet my bottom dollar on that damn bridge, those damn burnt stumps out there, that river…" Bellissima hung her head and Dria rubbed her back as Mrs. Creasie continued. "Us folks around here, we all have our opinions on things, but one thing we all have in common is our hatred for old Burn Out. It's the kind of ghostly monument that just keeps on taking and taking. Some way, somehow; I believed the bridge would get her. We might not all be superstitious, but it was a unanimous fear we all shared. After the bridge went down, we blamed it for a lot of things; especially all the things that happened to your family. If the creamer turned at bingo, the bridge did it. If the melons weren't sweet, it was the bridge's fault. Whenever the rainfall got scary, it was the bridge. No one ever just assumed it was just a thunderstorm. No. The bridge brought on the wrath of the dark clouds. Silly ain't it, how impressionable Southerners can be? The bridge made me wonder things, many things; but it never had power over me concerning the loved ones that I lost. My Doca'lee, it was a stroke that called him home. My baby, it never saw the light of day. No, it just slipped right out my womb and onto the floor to form a bloody puddle before it could even be recognized as a person. There's a small bit of peace knowing how they went, even though we never know when and why we lose them. I can't imagine how difficult life has been for you good people. At least it wasn't the bridge that took her," Mrs. Creasie sighed. "You girls get going now. You mamas will beat you raw if you're late."

"Thank you so much for this," said Dria. They each kissed her cheek. "Hush now child. Don't mention it. In my heart, all you children round here mine just the same as you all belong to your birth mothers." Mrs. Creasie grabbed Sadie and pulled her in close. "I expect to see you back here as soon as the doctor says that baby can weather the outside air."

Sadie smiled sweetly. "Yes Mam. I will."

"It smells like a girl," said Mrs. Creasie with a wink.

"So I've heard," whispered Sadie, teary-eyed.

The Beaumonte' family lined the first row, hiding their red-rimmed eyes behind black tinted shades. "Who the hell are all these people?" hissed Sadie out of the corner of her slightly closed mouth.

"Bite your tongue before Catherine Beaumonte' jumps out of that coffin, grabs the horse strap and beats us all blue!" whispered Dria.

"I'm sorry. I'm just so damn hot and hungry!" explained Sadie.

"Here let me fan you," offered Don- massaging Sadie's belly.

"Give it a rest daddy! No matter how much you rub it! Ain't no genie gon' come shooting out of my ass!"

"Someone's grouchy! You need to eat. Just endure a little while longer, we got the crawfish purging. We'll boil 'em up so spicy your sinuses gon' start draining. A pregnant lady can't live on funeral finger foods alone," said Don- dabbing his daughter's forehead.

"-Crawfish? Thank God! Let's get the pot and burner ready."

"No crawfish until after we bury your Grandmother, you hear?" said Minxy, slapping Sadie's hand.

"I'm sorry, Mama. This baby's stretching all four limbs at once and I can't stand hearing all these long speeches. We should have asked everyone to keep their tributes under five minutes."

Before we close, Catherine's granddaughters would like to say a few words," announced Pastor.

"- Speaking of speeches, it's our turn," said Dria.

Bellissima cleared her throat. "Thank you all for coming. It's so good to see you all..."

"Considering the circumstances," interrupted Dria.

"Yes, right- the circumstances," continued Bellissima- looking back at the casket. "I've been dreading this moment since I first found out Granny was sick. There are things we should say right now, things we'll regret not saying. There are so many things I know you all expect us to say; but standing up here beside my Grandmother, all I can think about is what she would say if she could talk to us all. *At least the bridge didn't take me. I didn't give it the satisfaction*- That's what Catherine would say. Finally, a goodbye that discredits her greatest fear for us. There is no curse, only coincidental misfortune that plagued a decent enough family. It's okay for us to live our lives without looking over our shoulders- waiting on old ghosts to rise from the ruins and take back with it another one of our loved ones. Thank the Good Lord, no more shadows over our precious memories. We don't have to be afraid to make a life now." Bellissima kissed her fingertips and then touched the coffin. The Beaumonte' Grandchildren stepped down.

CHAPTER THIRTY-SEVEN

Two months later...

"I read in the listing that the floors are only three years old, what about the roof? We refuse to invest in a location with a poorly patched ceiling. This here is the South. We have hurricanes," said Don.

"The roof took a cave in about four years back. It was a tree from the property next door. They kindly took full responsibility and had a new roof up in a matter of weeks."

"-And the plumbing? There will be lots of hair washing and foot soaking. How are the pipes?" asked Dria.

"Water flows through so clear it looks like God sifted it himself. You can check the toilets if you want, no ring around the bowl like most old buildings round this way- no unsightly mineral or calcium staining."

"My daughter is very pregnant, and her staff will consist of mostly women. I'm concerned about their safety," said Don- turning his attention to the rusty deadbolt.

"As soon as we get a signature, the locks will be changed- shiny and brand new. Also, we have no problem allowing alarm installation- at the lease holders expense of course."

Don turned to Dria who stood next to an anxious Minxy and Sadie. "What do you think, Niece?" he asked.

"Change those CAM fees to quarterly instead of monthly and you've got yourself a deal," said Dria.

Sadie jumped up and down. "I can't believe it! My own salon! Thank you Dria! Thank you, Daddy!"

"Don't thank us! Lissima's the one who invested. We're just making sure you and that baby get the best running start," said Dria- hugging Sadie.

Minxy looked down at her watch, "Sadie! We have to get going! It's almost time for the baby's appointment! We can't be late to the appointment! If we're late for the appointment, we'll be late getting to the airport! Let's go! Scoot now!"

"Oh right! We have to go!"

"You want us to tag along?" asked Don.

"For the last time! We will not be revealing the sex of this baby, Don! You may not tag along! You'll wait just like everyone else in this family!" lectured Minxy.

"Yeah. Sorry daddy. Only the mother and Godmother will know if this piglet is a boy or girl," said Sadie- patting him on the shoulder.

"Godmother?" asked Dria smiling.

Sadie grabbed her mother's hand. "Yeah, Minxy Beaumonte' will have a dual role in this baby's life- Grandmother and Godmother."

"You're next in line if I die, Dria. Don't tell Lissima," said Minxy kissing Dria's cheek.

"Speaking of time, you still have to get over to Ora's for your final fitting," reminded Don.

Dria looked at her phone, referencing her task manager. "You're right! Please don't forget to make sure security has an updated picture of Emily. She is not allowed to be within 500 feet of my fiancé'," Said Dria.

"I'm on it, Dear. I've been so kind as to mail her a physical copy of the restraining order since she's actively dodging the sheriff. I'm hoping she decides to be a lady, and not try my patience. She'll be cuffed on sight. You just make sure you send a series of inappropriate photos to Colin's phone tonight during his bachelor party, so he knows what he has waiting on him at home. You need any pointers on that, you give your old Uncle Don a call. I've had practice child, but I doubt Colin would do anything lose you twice. You're just too outright priceless," said Don with a wink and snap.

"Thank you, again, for walking me down the aisle."

"Don't thank me dear. I made a promise to your Mama long ago. I promised her you wouldn't take that walk alone. I should be thanking you for letting me. I've always wanted to have a family," said Don. Dria wrapped her arms around Don. "Go on now! Before you make me cry in public, you know I hate to make a scene! We will regroup at the airport!"

•

Kay and Lou Anna stood among the intertwined olive vines. "Thank you for taking time out of your schedule to meet with us last minute like this, Pastor. You see, we're heading to the city for Dria and Colin's wedding and we just need a little prayer first. Lou's been feeling a little weak. We need her strong for the big day."

"The good book says where two or three gather, he will be God in the midst. I believe he is a healer in the midst. Bless us please." The harvesters stood beside Pastor as he soaked his hands in the oil and anointed Lou Anna's head. "A healer indeed. Let us say Amen! Bow your heads. Set your mind on him and all he's done for you in the past. Set your mind on what he's got planned for your future. Set your mind on his walk when he carried his own cross. On his suffering. On his resurrection. On his promise. There is a sickness in this woman's body. She frets. However, her faith has not been defeated. She comes to you with a hopeful heart, asking that she be made well. With the same breath, she prays- If it is meant for this sickness to stay, then may your will be done. If it be so, then let her namesake go down in history as a vessel for your work. Her spirit says Lord, either take it away or help me to maintain my walk and suffer with grace until your will has been done for my life. Amen."

•

Bellissima parked far back on purpose. It was a nice day out and she whistled as she eased down the walkway to Pennycress. She noticed an elderly woman sitting, just before the entrance, on a bench out by the bus stop. "Hello there, are you all alone?" asked Bellissima.

The elderly woman looked up. "I don't know," she answered- blamelessly. Bellissima sat down on the bench beside her. "How did you get here?"

"I believe they put me on the bus," she answered.

"*They?*" Bellissima questioned.

"Yes. *They. Them.* My children from my second life."

329

"Second life?" mumbled Bellissima- almost sure the poor woman was suffering from some form of dementia.

"Do you have a purse or fanny pack, any identification at all?" asked Bellissima, severely concerned.

The elderly woman held up a big brown envelope, that had been sealed with duct tape. "This is all *they* sent me with," she answered sadly.

"I see. May I have a look inside?" Inside the envelope, Bellissima found a stack of personal documentation; a state ID, expired license, a tattered birth certificate, and various insurance forms. At the bottom of the stack, Bellissima found a check made out to the Pennycress retirement facility. It was clear, this old woman's family had put her on a bus to fend for herself and had the driver drop her off."

"What's inside? Tell me, please. Am I who I think I am? Am I in the right place?" she asked- worried.

Bellissima grabbed a hold of her hand and held it tight. "Yes Alexina, you're in the right place."

"Alexina? Oh, thank goodness! I'm so glad I am who I think I am? And where is the right place? Where is this place that I am now?"

"You're at Pennycress."

"Pennycress! Yes! I know this place! I came here years ago to make sure he was taken care of by the best of people."

"He?"

"I can't remember his name, but I know we used to be married in my first life. I left him all alone and my child from my first life, I left her too. I abandoned them, but I never forgot about them. I thought of them every day. I cared for them from afar. The child I shit out, I watched her grow. The husband I left behind, I watched him go down. That's how I got into this mess here. My husband and my kids, they sat me down and asked me about the money I'd spent. I tried to lie; tell them I'd just stowed it away for a rainy day, but they found out about the life I had before I became the woman they knew and loved. I had to tell them the truth. I told them I'd taken the money and set my first husband up in a fancy place back home, the place I was raised. I had to tell them I spent it all. I had to make sure he didn't die alone, but I could tell by the looks on their faces- they didn't understand. I already broke his heart; wouldn't that be a horrible thing for me to just let happen- let him die alone? They couldn't believe their ears; hearing they had a sister. My husband looked at me like I was trash, you see; he thought he'd married a virgin. I broke more hearts trying to make things right. No good deed goes unpunished. My husband, right before he struck me down with his fist, called me a floozy and burned all my things. He asked me what my last name had been from before. I told him it was the last name of a white man. It started with a B. That's all I can remember. B. B. B."

Bellissima's heart began to beat faster. "It started with a B?"

"Yes. I can't remember the other letters though. I told my family where I had sent my first husband and they told me they hope I rot here with him, so here I am. Ready to rot. Do you think he'll know me when he sees me, sweet girl?"

"No one forgets the love of their life, no matter how much he or she hurt them," answered Bellissima. She took a second look at the driver's license. "You're almost ten decades old, just like granny and Breaux…"

The sweet old lady's face switched, and she pondered as if remembering. "Breaux. Breaux. Breaux. Breaux…," she said repeatedly like parrot. "What did you say my name was again?"

"It's Alexina, but how about we just call you Mrs. B? Would that be alright? It's sure easier for you to remember," said Bellissima.

"Yes. I suppose that'd be alright. Can't remember what my last name is now anyhow. Hell, what's it matter? I may as well forget the last name of the family who tossed me out."

"Come, let's go inside and get you settled in. They're serving peach cobbler today. It's my absolute favorite. The recipe they use here, it's my Mama's. She owns restaurants; best damn food this side of the Mississippi. You know you have a unique name. You know what it means to have that name?"

"Don't it mean house nigger?" asked Mrs. B bluntly.

"No, I don't mean house nigger! You're named after a very brave light skinned freedom seeker. I hope one day you'll see all this as just another way to be free. You've made your peace with your wrongs. That's freedom."

"You think God's going to bless me for righting my wrongs? If he does, I hope he's been listening to all my prayers. I really only want one thing."

"What's that?" asked Bellissima- holding the door open for Mrs. B to enter.

"I want to meet my little girl face to face again. For her, it'll be like the very first time."

Bellissima smiled, "I think that's doable for God."

Bellissima stood out in the courtyard looking up at the sky. She thought of her Grandfather. She thought of Cheniere. Then she thought of Catherine. "There you are, I've been looking all over for you," said Jan.

"I just came out for some fresh air. I haven't been out here since she passed," said Bellissima.

"How are you holding up these days?"

"It's a struggle. Some days are harder than the others and I miss her a lot. There are so many things that remind me of her, like when I smell collard greens cooking or I see a disobedient child making a scene at the grocery store, just begging for a beating."

"You're a strong woman, Lissima."

"I believe you. When I sit down and calculate my woes, I'm surprised by how much I can take," said Bellissima- fishing a folded piece of paper from her pocket. "I was going to come and find you later to give this to you; but since you're here."

"What's this?" asked Jan.

"It's a copy of my resignation. I made it official this morning. We've been working side by side for years, didn't seem right- you having to hear about it from upper management."

"You're leaving Pennycress?" asked Jan- confused.

"There's no curse, Jan. It's time for me stop using it as an excuse to keep from living. Don't worry, I already have someone to cover the New Years' shift for you. I hope you all have fun at the bash. I have a much better place to be," said Bellissima hugging Jan, then turning to leave.

"-And where's that?"

"-A wedding. My cousin Dria has decided to tie the knot on New Years'. She said it's high time I enjoy fireworks again and she's right. You know it's snowing in the city. I've always wanted to see the snow."

"-But…"

"Don't try to convince me to stay. You'd be wasting your breath, besides my wedding date is also my wedding gift- the photographer. When I get back to Louisiana, I'm going to help Sadie around her new shop and help Mama manage the business so she can keep on expanding. The world needs good food like it needs love. You take care now, you hear? -And Jan. I need a favor. In a few months, there's going to be a lady checking in. She's Lincoln's mother. Make sure her room is close to the little old lady I just brought in here. They have some catching up to do. It's fate. Crazy damned but fair fate."

•

Everyone took their turn showering the bride with attention. Minxy caught the bouquet while Sadie stole licks of icing off the back of the wedding cake. Dria's dress, embellished with hand beaded constellations, sparkled as she and Colin danced in the spotlight. "It was a beautiful ceremony wasn't it?" said Kay.

"It sure was Mama," answered Bellissima.

"I can't wait for the day I see you walking down that aisle. I can't believe my little Lissima is going steady with a good man!" said Kay- pulling at her daughter's cheeks.

Going steady- thought Bellissima. What an erstwhile thing to say. Bellissima pulled her face away, embarrassed. "Mama! People are looking! You'll mess up my blush! Sadie worked hard to make me look good today."

"She barely had to do a thing, you're perfect."

"-And don't go making any plans in that head of yours! Just cause Lincoln and I are going steady doesn't mean I'm destined to be married soon."

Kay and Bellissima spotted Lincoln in the far corner of the ballroom. He beckoned for Bellissima to come over. "I'd never claim to know the future, my child; but a mother knows things," said Kay- disappearing into the crowd of wedding partiers.

Lincoln walked Bellissima out to the rooftop where snowflakes were still falling. He wrapped his jacket around her shoulders. "How does it feel to finally see the snow?"

Bellissima lifted her hands, catching tiny snowflakes in her palms. "There are no words," she replied. "Everything about today was magical."

"I agree. Did I ever thank you for bringing me along for the ride?"

"Did I ever thank you for coming into my life? You know, you really do have perfect timing."

"I think so too," agreed Lincoln. "I got some amazing ceremony shots of your family. You want a sneak peek?"

"Yeah!" answered Bellissima, anxiously. Lincoln gave Bellissima his camera and stepped back as she flipped through. She held the camera close to her face. "Wow, these are phenomenal. Dria will be so pleased." Bellissima scanned until she came to a group photo of the wedding party. Lincoln was at the center, on bended knee. She lowered the camera and saw Lincoln in that very position, right before her very eyes.

"I brought my tripod. I set it up and asked everyone you love to pose with me. I also asked them for your hand in marriage." Bellissima turned to find her family huddled, staring from the grand ballroom glass. "I don't want a *yes* unless you're ready to spend the rest of your life with a man who cherishes you."

"Only if you promise to take lots of pictures so that when we're old, we don't forget a single memory," she whispered. Tears of joy sprang from Bellissima's eyes as Lincoln slid the ring on her finger.

"You've got yourself a deal," whispered Lincoln.

Back inside the venue, Dria stood to make a toast. "Sadie, Lissima! - Please join me!"

Her cousins ran to her side. "Thank you all for coming! A lot of you traveled a long way! I just want to say thank you. It's no secret, this family has had its fair share of misery. I'm so happy to start this new chapter with the man I love, surrounded by the people I love. No more secrets to hide behind. Cheers!"

Everyone clapped, instead of Bellissima. "What is it?" asked Sadie.

Bellissima began to squirm. "Don't you dare, Bellissima," warned Dria.

"Dria and Sadie made me drug the punch!"

The Beaumonte' daughters gasped. "I knew it!" yelled Minxy.

"-And the drawing on our faces?" asked Lou Anna.

"Yes! That was us too!"

Dria cut her eyes at Bellissima. "Lissima, you are such a tattle tell!"

"Snitch," coughed Sadie.

Made in the USA
Coppell, TX
23 August 2021